A Textbook of

I0642547

BIOPHARMACEUTICS

For
B. Pharm and M. Pharm Students

Ms. Priya Patel
M. Pharm.
Assistant Professor,
Department of Pharmaceutical Sciences,
Saurashtra University, Rajkot.

Ms. Aashka Jani
M. Pharm.
Assistant Professor,
Department of Pharmaceutical Sciences,
Saurashtra University, Rajkot.

Ms. Hina Bagada
M. Pharm.
Assistant Professor,
Department of Pharmaceutical Sciences,
Saurashtra University, Rajkot.

NIRALI PRAKASHAN
ADVANCEMENT OF KNOWLEDGE

N1615

BIOPHARMACEUTICS

ISBN 978-93-5164-624-2

First Edition : February 2016

© : Authors

Published By :   Polyplate

NIRALI PRAKASHAN

Abhyudaya Pragati, 1312, Shivaji Nagar,
Off J.M. Road, PUNE – 411005
Tel - (020) 25512336/37/39, Fax - (020) 25511379
Email : niralipune@pragationline.com

☞ DISTRIBUTION CENTRES

PUNE

Nirali Prakashan : 119, Budhwar Peth, Jogeshwari Mandir Lane, Pune 411002, Maharashtra
Tel : (020) 2445 2044, 66022708, Fax : (020) 2445 1538
Email : bookorder@pragationline.com, niralilocal@pragationline.com

Nirali Prakashan : S. No. 28/27, Dhyari, Near Pari Company, Pune 411041
Tel : (020) 24690204 Fax : (020) 24690316
Email : dhyari@pragationline.com, bookorder@pragationline.com

MUMBAI

Nirali Prakashan : 385, S.V.P. Road, Rasdhara Co-op. Hsg. Society Ltd.,
Girgaum, Mumbai 400004, Maharashtra
Tel : (022) 2385 6339 / 2386 9976, Fax : (022) 2386 9976
Email : niralimumbai@pragationline.com

☞ DISTRIBUTION BRANCHES

JALGAON

Nirali Prakashan : 34, V. V. Golani Market, Navi Peth, Jalgaon 425001,
Maharashtra, Tel : (0257) 222 0395, Mob : 94234 91860

KOLHAPUR

Nirali Prakashan : New Mahadvar Road, Kedar Plaza, 1st Floor Opp. IDBI Bank
Kolhapur 416 012, Maharashtra. Mob : 9850046155

NAGPUR

Pratibha Book Distributors : Above Maratha Mandir, Shop No. 3, First Floor,
Rani Jhanshi Square, Sitabuldi, Nagpur 440012, Maharashtra
Tel : (0712) 254 7129

DELHI

Nirali Prakashan : 4593/21, Basement, Aggarwal Lane 15, Ansari Road, Daryaganj
Near Times of India Building, New Delhi 110002
Mob : 08505972553

BENGALURU

Pragati Book House : House No. 1, Sanjeevappa Lane, Avenue Road Cross,
Opp. Rice Church, Bengaluru – 560002.
Tel : (080) 64513344, 64513355,Mob : 9880582331, 9845021552
Email:bharatsavla@yahoo.com

CHENNAI

Pragati Books : 9/1, Montieth Road, Behind Taas Mahal, Egmore,
Chennai 600008 Tamil Nadu, Tel : (044) 6518 3535,
Mob : 94440 01782 / 98450 21552 / 98805 82331,
Email : bharatsavla@yahoo.com

niralipune@pragationline.com | www.pragationline.com
Also find us on ⨍ www.facebook.com/niralibooks

PREFACE

We have immense pleasure to present the book **'Biopharamaceutics'** for the pharmacy students.

Drug performance is a vital aspect of new drug development as it draws on interdisciplinary expertise from both pharmaceutics and pharmacokinetics disciplines. It is at the key interface that the discipline of biopharmaceutics has emerged. The past two decades have witnessed considerable advances in biopharmaceutics, particularly with regard to bioavailability / bioequivalence, product quality and regulatory standards of approval. In the world of drug development, the meaning of the term "biopharmaceutics" often evokes confusion, even among scientists and professionals who work in the field. It is often humbling for the drug discovery group to bring out a novel molecule with remarkable potential only to be shot down by the formulation group as a worthless exercise in taking it to a deliverable form. Preformulation is a science that serves as a big umbrella for the fingerprinting of a drug substance or product both at the early and latter stage of development in pharmaceutical manufacturing. Also explain about theory in formulation development with global stability requirements. Pharmacokinetic parameters will help in design of drug delivery system and development of pharmaceutical formulations.

This book is concered with several aspects related to the fate of drug in the body. It also involves the quantification of drug in different processes like adsorption, distribution and excetion. This book is broadly divided into biopharmaceutics part, Pharmacokinetic part and stability concept. Each chapter contains remarkably improved illustrations and more tables and examples that make concepts easily understandable and memorable.

It is composed of carefully crafted sections introducing key concepts and advances in the areas of dissolution, BA/BE, BCS, IVIC, and product quality, with specific focus on integration of regulatory considerations and highlighting the biopharmaceutics strategies adopted in development of successful drugs.

In this book, we introduce about preformulation studies, emphasis on Different factors affecting on formulations, Solid state characteristization along with techniques, Drug Excipients compatibility study along with highlight on preformulation studies of Biotechnological derived products.

This book also explains theoritical aspects of solubilization system and technique for improvement of drug solubilization for development of various dosage forms.

Along with importance about BCS classification it also give knowledge about selection of dissolution media for different dosage form.

It gives concise information about basic concept of stability study, factor affecting on stability of the formulation along with regulatory requirements related to stability testing.

The book depict about basic concept and importance of biological half-life, volume of distribution, renal clearance, total body clearance, plasma protein binding, absorption rate constant, and elimination rate constant along with compartment modeling with concerns related to IVIVC.

We take the opportunity to express our deep sense of gratitude to Publisher Mr. Dinesh Furia and Mr. Jignesh Furia and staff of Nirali Prakashan and Dr. S. B. Gokhale for his constant encouragement.

Suggestions for improvement in the book are welcome and will be taken care of in the next editions.

February 2016   **Authors**

CONTENTS

Chapter 1

PRE FORMULATION

1.1 INTRODUCTION

Definition:

Preformulation is described as a phase of the research and development process where the researchers characterizes about the physical, chemical and mechanical properties of a new drug substance, in order to develop stable, safe and effective dosage form. Prior to the development of major dosage forms, it is essential that the physical and chemical properties of the drug molecule and other divided properties of the drug powder are determined. This information decides many of the subsequent events and approaches in formulation development. This first learning phase is known as *preformulation*. Preformulation involves the application of biopharmaceutical principles to the physicochemical parameters of a drug with the goal of designing an optimum drug delivery system.

Preformulation is a link between drug discovery and drug development. It is the fundamental step in the rational development of dosage form.

Objectives:

The preformulation investigations confirm that there are no significant barriers to the development of a compound as a marketed drug.

Preformulation is a multidisciplinary development of a drug candidate. (Table 1.1) In Preformulation, the applications of biopharmaceutical principles to the physicochemical parameters of drug substance are characterized with the goal of designing optimum drug delivery system.

1.1.1 Goals of Preformulation Study
- To determine its kinetic rate profile.
- To establish necessary physicochemical parameters of new drug substance.
- To establish its compatibility with excipients.

1.1.2 Importance of Preformulation Study
- To develop desired quality dosage forms.
- To achieve high degree of uniformity, physiological availability and therapeutic qualities.
- To develop an optimum dosage form.
- For targeted drug delivery systems.

- To improve patient compliance.
- To minimize cost of finished product.
- To minimize errors in formulation of dosage form.

1.1.3 Stages at Which Preformulation Study is Required

- It starts immediately after the synthesis and initial toxicity screening of a new drug.
- When a newly synthesized drug shows pharmacological evidence that requires further evaluation in human.
- At the time of finalizing new formulation.
- If any changes are required in formulation and dosage form.
- After approval of NDA, production can start.

1.2 PRINCIPAL AREAS OF PREFORMULATION

1. Bulk Characterization
   - (i)   Crystallinity and polymorphism
   - (ii)   Hygroscopicity
   - (iii) Fine particle characterization
   - (iv)   Powder flow

2. Solubility Analysis
   - (i)   Aqueous solubility
   - (ii)   Equilibrium solubility
   - (iii) PKa Determination
   - (iv)   Thermal effects
   - (v)   Solubilization
   - (vi)   Partition coefficient
   - (vii) Common Ion effect
   - (viii) Dissolution

3. Stability Analysis
   - (i)   Stability in toxicology formulation
   - (ii)   Solution stability
   - (iii) Solid state stability

4. Chemical Characteristics
   - (i)   Hydrolysis
   - (ii)   Oxidation
   - (iii) Photolysis

(iv) Racemization

(v) Dehydration

(vi) Polymerization

(vii) Isomerization

(viii) Decarboxylation

(ix) Enzyme Decomposition

(x) Elimination

1.3 BULK CHARACTERIZATION

When a drug molecule is discovered, all the solid-forms are hardly identified. So during bulk characterization the following characteristics are studied.

1.3.1 Crystallinity and Polymorphism

Crystal habit and internal structure of drug can affect the physicochemical property which ranges from flow ability to chemical stability. Habit means the description of outer appearance of a crystal. While internal structure describes the molecular arrangement within the solid, changes in internal structure usually alter crystal habit.

Example : Conversion of sodium salt to its free acid formed by change in internal structure and crystal habit.

Evaluation of crystal structure, polymorphism and solvate form is an important preformulation activity. The changes in crystal characteristics can influence bioavailability, chemical and physical stability.

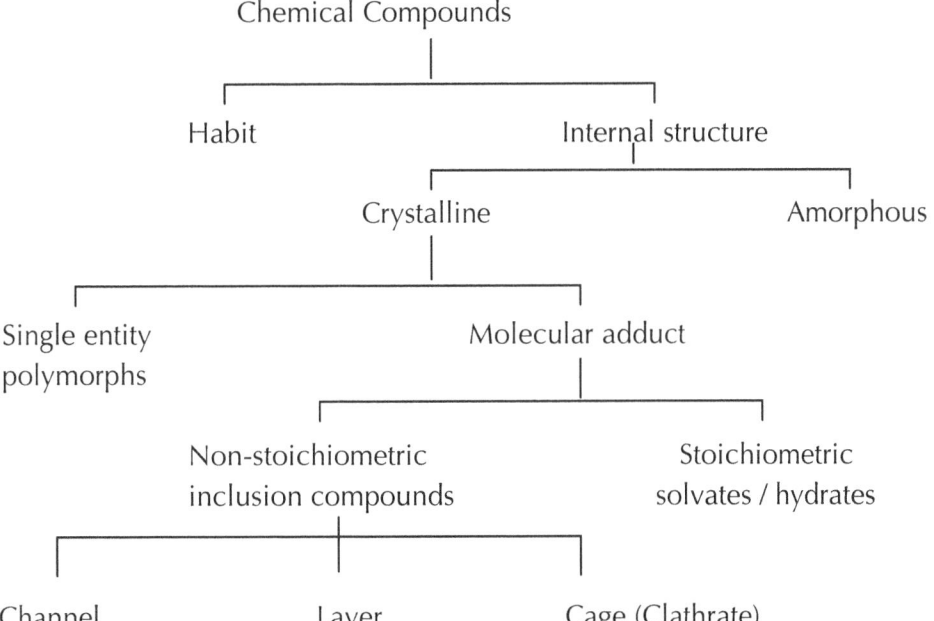

Table 1.1 : Preformulation Flow Chart

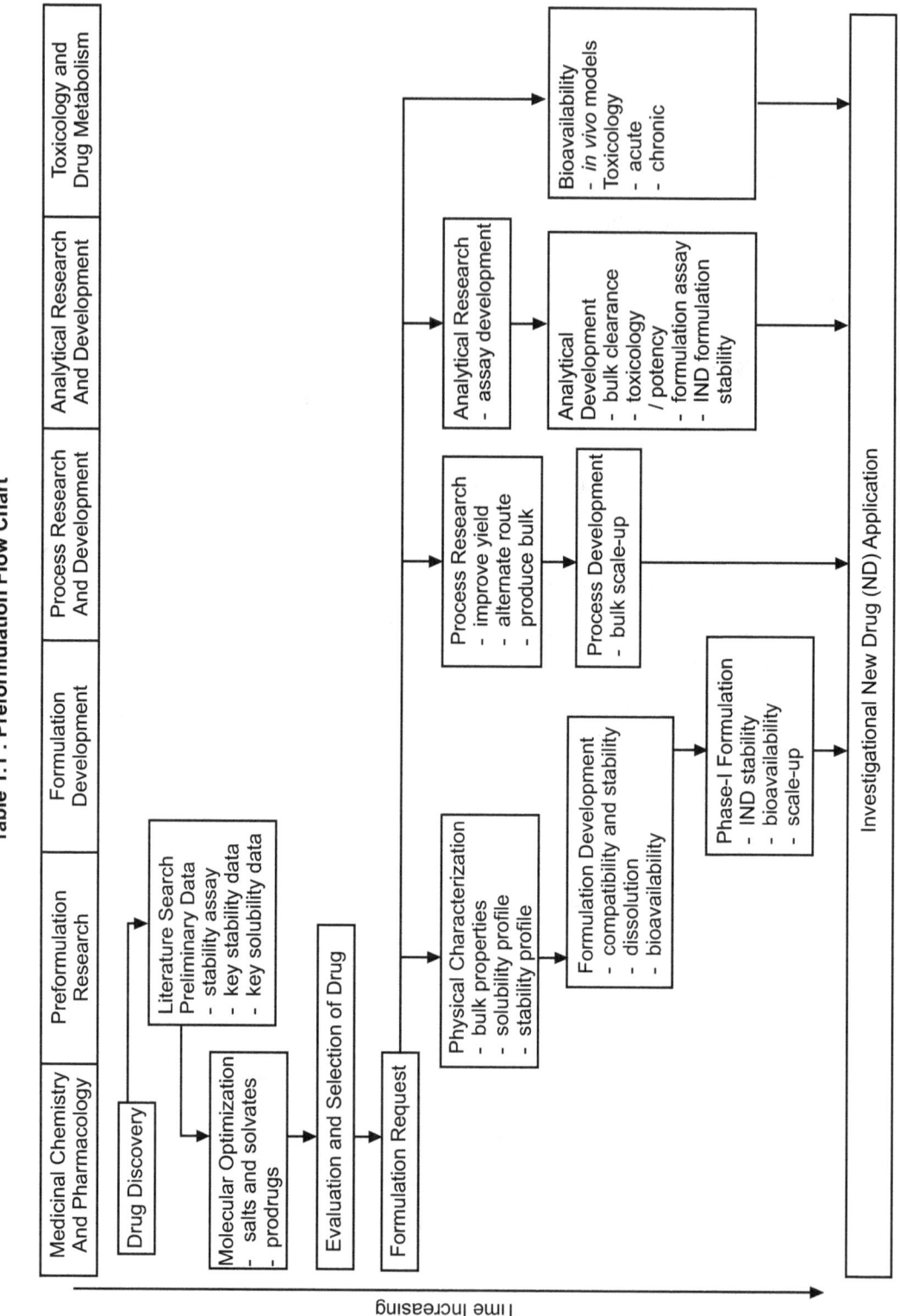

Medicinal Chemistry And Pharmacology	Preformulation Research	Formulation Development	Process Research And Development	Analytical Research And Development	Toxicology and Drug Metabolism

Drug Discovery

Literature Search Preliminary Data
- stability assay
- key stability data
- key solubility data

Molecular Optimization
- salts and solvates
- prodrugs

Evaluation and Selection of Drug

Formulation Request

Physical Characterization
- bulk properties
- solubility profile
- stability profile

Formulation Development
- compatibility and stability
- dissolution
- bioavailability

Phase-I Formulation
- IND stability
- bioavailability
- scale-up

Process Research
- improve yield
- alternate route
- produce bulk

Process Development
- bulk scale-up

Analytical Research
- assay development

Analytical Development
- bulk clearance
- toxicology / potency
- formulation assay
- IND formulation stability

Bioavailability
- *in vivo* models
Toxicology
- acute
- chronic

Investigational New Drug (ND) Application

Time Increasing

In case of an amorphous atoms, molecules are randomly placed as liquid. While polymeric form may contain stiochiometric or non-stiochiometric solvents. If the solvent is water, the complex is called a *hydrate*. The term hemihydrates, monohydrate, dihydrate etc. describe hydrate forms with molar equivalence of water. A compound not containing any water molecule within its crystal structure is termed as anhydrous. Anhydrous forms are more soluble. Non-stoichiometric adducts such as inclusions or clatharates involve entrapped solvent molecules within crystal lattice.

[A] Habit:

Habit is the description of the outer appearance of a crystal. A single internal-structure for a compound can have several different habits, depending on the environment for growing crystals. Different habits of crystals are given in Fig. 1.1.

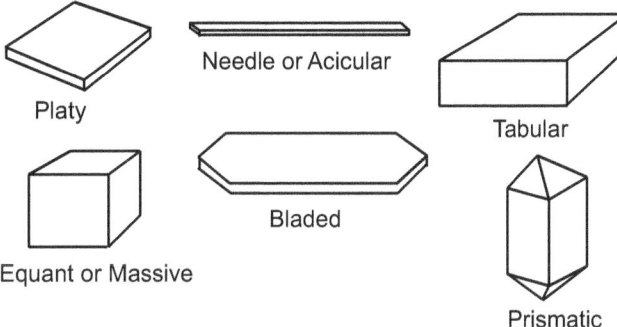

Fig. 1.1 : Crystal habit of drug

Condition also plays a key role during crystallization process depicted in below Table 1.2.

Example: Ammonium nitrate undergoing 4 transitions depending on temperature.

$$\text{Tetragonal} \underset{-17^\circ C}{\rightleftharpoons} \text{Rhombic 1} \underset{32.1^\circ C}{\rightleftharpoons} \text{Rhombic 2} \underset{84.2^\circ C}{\rightleftharpoons} \text{Rhombohedral} \underset{125.2^\circ C}{\rightleftharpoons} \text{Cubic}$$

Table 1.2: Different Conditions during Crystallization Process

Conditions during crystallization	Change in habit	Example
Supersaturation	Prism or granular to needle	Sucrose
Cooling rate and agitation	Platy to prism	Naphthalene
Crystallizing solvent From benzene From butyl acetate	Platy to Needles Squat prism	Resorcinol
Addition of cosolvents	Prism to Cubic Prism to Octahedral	NaCl Urea

[B] Internal Structure

[I] Crystalline State:

Atoms or molecules are arranged in highly ordered form and is associated with three-dimensional periodicity.

Polymorphs

When a substance exists in more than one crystalline form, the various forms are called Polymorphs and this phenomenon is called polymorphism. E.g. Chloramphenicol palmitate has three polymorphs A, B and C.

Various polymorphs can be prepared by crystallizing the drug under diverse conditions. Depending on their relative stability, one of the several polymorphic forms will be physically more stable than the others. Such a stable polymorph represents the lowest energy state, has highest melting point and least solubility. The representing polymorphs are called metastable forms which represents higher energy state, and have a thermodynamic tendency of conversion to the stable form. A metastable form cannot be called unstable because if it is kept in dry place, it will remain stable for years.

Molecular Adducts

During the process of crystallization, some compounds have a tendency to trap the solvent molecules.

1. Non-stoichiometric inclusion compounds (or adducts):

In these crystals, solvent molecules are entrapped within the crystal lattice but the number of solvent molecules are not included in stoichiometric number.

Depending on the shape, these are classified in three types :

(1) Channel: Crystals formed, like continuous channels with the solvent molecule.

(2) Layers: Solvent molecules are entrapped inbetween layers of crystals.

(3) Clathrates (Cage): Solvent molecules are entrapped within the cavity of the crystal from all sides.

2. Stoichiometric inclusion compounds (or stoichiometric adducts):

This molecular complex has incorporated the crystallizing solvent molecules into the specific sites within the crystal lattice.

When the incorporated solvent is water, the complex is called hydrates and when the solvent is other than water, the complex is called solvate. Depending on the ratio of water molecules within a complex, the nomenclature is give as below.

(i) Anhydrous : 1 mole compound + 0 mole water

(ii) Hemihydrate: 1 mole compound + ½ mole water

(iii) Monohydrate: 1 mole compound + 1 mole water

(iv) Dihydrate : 1 mole compound + 2 moles water

Properties of Solvates / Hydrates :

1. Generally, the anhydrous form of a drug has greater aqueous solubility than its hydrates. This is because the hydrates are already in equilibrium with water and therefore have less demand for water. For example, anhydrous forms of theophyline and ampicillin have higher aqueous solubility than the hydrates form.

2. Non-aqueous solvates have greater aqueous solubility than the non-solvates. For example, chloroform solvates of griseofulvin are more water soluble than their non-solvate forms.

[II] Amorphous Forms:

In these forms, atoms or molecules are randomly placed as in a liquid, and do not have any fixed internal strucutre.

e.g. Amorphous Novobiocin.

In general, the amorphous state has a higher dissolution rate and higher solubility than the crystalline state. Amorphous materials are usually more prone to chemical degradation.

At particular temperature, an amorphous solid shows the major changes in the properties. This temperature is called as glass transition temperature (T_g).

Methods commonly used to produce amorphous materials are melt quenching, lyophilization, spray drying, desolvation and re-crystallization from different solvents.

Basic Properties of an Amorphous Material:

*   Can exist in either the "glassy" or "rubbery" state.
*   Above the glass transition temperature (T_g), the material is in the rubbery state and mobility is high.
*   Below the glass transition temperature, the material is in the glassy state, and mobility is significantly reduced.
* T_g can be changed based upon moisture content. T_g of amorphous material can be lowered by adding small molecules called plasticizers, that fits between the glassy molecules, giving them greater mobility. Water is a good plasticizer for many materials, and so T_g will usually reduce in presence of water vapour.

Difference between Crystalline and Amorphous Form:

Crystalline forms	Amorphous forms
(i) Crystalline forms have fixed internal structure.	(i) Amorphous forms do not have any fixed internal structure.
(ii) Crystalline form has lower thermodynamic energy than its amorphous form.	(ii) Amorphous form has higher thermodynamic energy than its crystalline form.

(iii) Crystalline forms are more stable than its amorphous forms.	(iii) Amorphous forms are less stable than its crystalline forms.
(iv) Crystalline form has low solubility than its amorphous form.	(iv) Amorphous form has high solubility than its crystalline form.
(v) Crystalline form has lesser tendency to change its form during storage.	(v) Amorphous forms tend to revert to more stable forms during storage.

1.3.1.1 Analytical Methods for Characterization of Solid Forms

Table 1.3: Methods of Studying Solid Forms

Method	Material required per sample
Microscopy	1 mg
Hot stage microscopy	1 mg
Differential Thermal Analysis (DTA)	2 - 5 mg
Differential Scanning Calorimetry (DSC)	2 - 5 mg
Thermogravimetric Analysis (TGA)	10 mg
X-ray Powder Diffraction	500 mg
Infrared Spectroscopy	2 - 20 mg
Dilatometry	2 mg

1. Microscopy

In this technique, material was analyzed by using optical microscopy.

In this type of microscope light passes through cross-polarizing filters.

Amorphous substances (For example, super-cooled glass and non-crystalline organic compounds or substances with cubic crystal lattices e.g. NaCl) have single refractive index, so the amorphous substances do not transmit light, and they appear black. They are called *isotropic* substances. This technique can be used to distinguish rapidly between the crystalline and amorhous form of materials.

2. Hot-stage Microscopy

In this microscopy, the polarizing microscope is fitted with a hot stage to investigate polymorphism, melting points, transition temperatures and rates of transition at controlled rates.

It facilitates in explaining the thermal behaviour of a substance from the DSC and TGA curves.

Main disadvantage of hot stage microscopy is that organic molecules can degrade during the melting process, and recrystallization of the melt may not occur, because of the presence of contaminant degradation products.

3. Thermal Analysis

(i) Differential Thermal Analysis (DTA)

In DTA instrument a record is produced by *temperature difference (ΔT)* between the sample and reference material is plotted against temperature (T) when two specimens are subjected to an identically controlled temperature regime. Typical DTA graph is shown in Fig. 1.2.

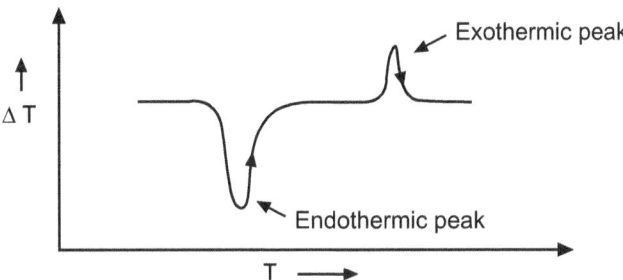

Fig. 1.2 : Typical DTA graph

Alumina, keiselguhr are commonly used as a reference materials.

The heat capacity of the sample remains relatively constant throughout the analysis unless the material undergoes a form change. In case of amorphous material at the glass transition temperature, heat is produced by sample (exothermic) when the material recrystallize, and heat is absorbed by the sample (endothermic) when it metls.

(ii) Differential Scanning Calorimetry (DSC)

In DSC method, the difference in *energy inputs (ΔH)* into a sample and reference material is measured as a function of identically controlled temperature programme. Typical DSC curve is shown in Fig. 1.3.

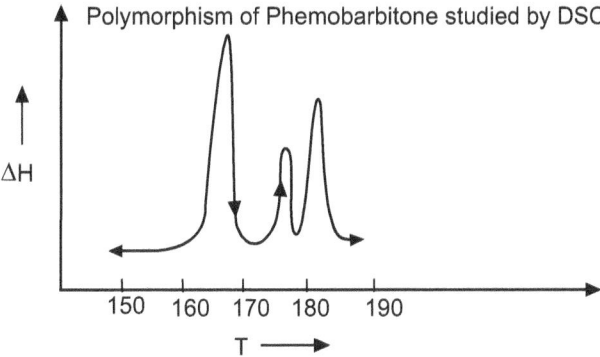

Fig. 1.3 : Typical DSC Curve

Samples like powders, fibres, single crystals, polymer films, semi-solids and liquids are commonly studied by DSC and DTA.

Applications of DTA / DSC in Preformulation Studies:

1. To determine the purity of a sample.

2. To determine the number of polymorphs along with the ratio of each polymorph.

3. To determine the heat of solvation.

4. To determine the thermal degradation of a drug or excipients.

5. To determine the glass-transition temperature (t_g) of a polymer.

(iii) Thermogravimetric Analysis (TGA)

TGA measures the changes in sample weight as a function of time (isothermal changes) or temperature (Fig. 1.4). This technique is primarily used to monitor loss of solvent or decomposition reactions. It is used in conjugation with DSC to compare the enthalpy of transitions with the resulting weight gain or loss.

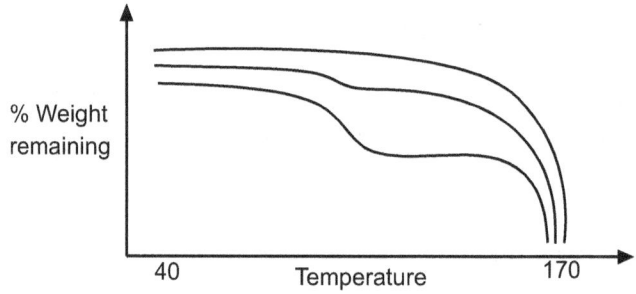

Fig. 1.4 : Thermogravimetric effect

Applications of TGA in Preformulation Study:

1. Desolvation and decomposition processes are monitored.

2. Comparing TGA and DSC data recorded under identical conditions can greatly help in the explanation of the thermal process.

For e.g. TGA and DSC analysis of an acetate salt of an organic amine that has two crystalline forms, anhydrous and dihydrate. Anhydrous / dihydrate (10:1) mixture was prepared by dry blending. Heating rate was 5°C/min.

From TGA curve (Fig. 1.5), it is evident that at 70 – 90°C weight-loss was due to the loss of two molecules of water and the weight loss at 155°C was due to vapourization of acetic acid and decomposition.

From DSC curve, it is evident that the dihydrate form loses two molecules of water via an endothermic transition between 70°C and 90°C. The second endotherm at 155°C corresponds to melting process.

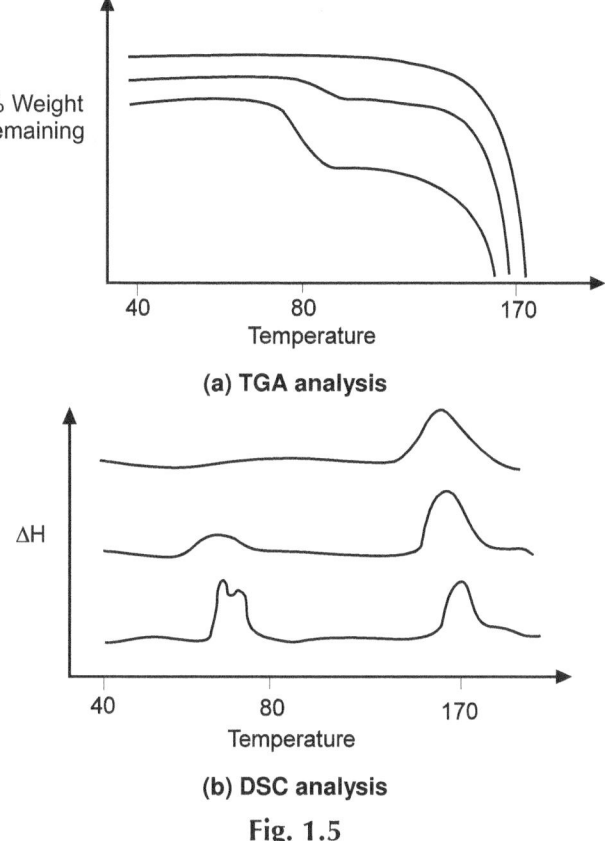

(a) TGA analysis

(b) DSC analysis

Fig. 1.5

4. X-ray Diffraction

X-ray diffraction is a common technique for the analysis of polymorphism in crystalline solids.

When a X-ray beam falls on a powder, the beam is diffracted. This diffraction is found only in case of crystalline powder. Amorphous forms do not show X-ray diffraction.

Uses:

(i) Each diffraction pattern is characteristic of a specific crystalline lattice for a given compound. So in a mixture, different crystalline forms can be analyzed using normalized intensities at specific angles.

(ii) Identification of crystalline materials by using their diffraction pattern as a 'finger print'.

First, the powder diffraction photograph or diffractometer trace are taken and matched with a standard photograph. All the lines and peaks must match in position and relative intensity.

(i) Single crystal X-ray diffraction technique:

It provides the detail information about the identification and description of solid state. This method is based on the scattering of X-ray by crystal. It is tedious, time consuming method, hence it is not used for routine purpose.

(ii) Powder X-ray diffraction technique :

Important technique for establishing the batch to batch reproducibility of crystalline form. Random orientation of crystal lattice in a powder sample causes X-ray to scatter in a reproducible pattern of peak intensities. An amorphous form does not produce a pattern.

5. I.R. Spectroscopy

Infrared spectroscopy works on the principle that, a sample is irradiated with a broad spectrum of Infrared light, in which fraction of light will be absorbed by sample.

Different packing arrangements will affect energy of the molecular bond thus altering the I.R. spectra.

6. Dilatometry

In this method, the change in volume caused by thermal or chemical effects depend upon the difference between the density of solid and liquid. This technique is extremely accurate, however it is extremely tedious and time consuming.

7. Other Methods

Other methods such as PMR - Proton Magnetic Resonance, NMR – Nuclear Magnetic Resonance, SEM - Scanning Electron Microscopy are also used for characterization.

1.3.1.2 Importance of Crystallinity in Preformulation Studies

Effect on Solubility and Bioavailability

- It can be commonly used for improved solubility and bioavailability. For e.g., The antibiotic, novobiocin is essentially inactive when administerd in crystalline form, but in amorphous form, absorption from G.I.T (gastro intestinal tract) proceeds rapidly with good therapeutic response. Thus, due to difference in solubility amorphous novobiocin is 10 times more bioavailable.

- The more soluble form of chloramphenicol palmitate, form B shows greater bioavailability after oral administration as compared to form A.

- Similarly in chlortetracyclin hydrochloride β form is more soluble and bioavailable than corresponding α form.

Chemical Stability

- In other instances, crystalline forms of drugs have greater stability than corresponding amorphous forms.

  e.g. crystalline forms of penicillin G as potassium or sodium salt are more stable.

Suspension Syringeability

- It mostly affect the mechnical property i.e. suspension of plate shaped crystals may be injected through a needle with a greater ease than the needle shaped crystals of same dimensions.

Effect on Granulation

- Sulphathiazole can exist in different crystalline forms, out of which form III has water adsorption of 0.046 mg/m^2 while form I has water adsorption of 0.031mg/m^2. So form III shows better wetting property and hence easy granulation.

- Use of amorphous form of calcium pentothenate in multi-vitamin tablets prepared by wet granulation process, is not desirable because polymorphic transformation makes the granulation mass sticky.

Hardness of Tablet

- Sulphamerazine is available in two different crystalline forms SMZ-I and SMZ-II. SMZ-II tablets show faster dissolution rate than SMZ-I due to difference in compressibility of both the forms. SMZ-I forms harder tablets than SMZ-II at same compression pressure and so it shows delayed release effect.

- Both these forms can be used in single tablet by compression coating, in which the core is formed of SMZ-I and coat is made up of SMZ-II to get repeat action.

Effect on Consolidation

- Substances possessing the cubic lattice arrangement were tabletted more satisfactorily than those with rhombohedral lattice. The isotropic nature of former group contribute to better tabletting because no alignment of particular lattice plane is required. In addition, three equal planes for stress relief at right angles to each other are provided.

Directly Compressible Excipients

- The DC grade excipients are microgranulations, since they consist of masses of small crystallites randomly embedded in a matrix of glue-like (often amorphous) material. Such a combination imparts the desired overall qualities which results in strong tablet by providing a matrix to relieve internal stresses and strongly bonding surfaces (the faces of crystallites) to enhance consolidation.

Polymorphic Transformation

- Many drugs undergo polymorphic transformation during various processes. For example; during grinding drugs like digoxin, estradiol, spironolactone, phenylbutazone undergo transformation.

- By granulation of theophylline with water, it converts into monohydrate form from anhydrous form.

- Similarly by drying and compression drugs shows polymorphic transformation.

1.3.1.3 Latest Technique Developments in Crystallization

1. Spherical Crystallization :

It is a solvent exchange crystallization method in which crystal agglomeration is induced through the addition of third solvent termed as "Bridging liquid" which act as granulating agent.

It is a novel technique to improve compressibility, good flowability and bioavailability of pharmaceuticals. In addition to this, the tablets manufactured by this technique have greater mechanical strength and lower friability.

Various drugs have been successfully undergone this process to acquire improved micromeritic properties like salicylic acid, mefenemic acid, aminophylline, tolbutamide and thus have shown increased dissolution rate.

Methods of Spherical Crystallization:
  1. Simple Spherical Crystallization
  2. Quasi-Emulsion-Solvent-Diffusion Method
  3. Ammonia Diffusion Method
  4. Neutralization Method

2. Controlled Crystallization :

By this method get microcrystals in very narrow size range for hydrophobic drugs. It is more effective than micronisation method because it gives greater bioavailability due to uniform sized particles. For example; anti-inflammatory drug β-methasone dipropionate, triamcinolone acetonide, beclomethasone.

3. Amorphous Form Stabilization :

Amorphous forms have highest solubility but it is very unstable and during storage may get convert to crystalline form. Additives with high glass transition temperature or with the stabilizing additives prevent the conversion of amorphous form to crystalline form.

4. Super-Critical Fluid Crystallization :

In this technique, precipitation of small organic molecules from aqueous solution was studided using a mixture of supercritical carbon-di-oxide and ethanol as drying medium and as anti-solvent. This method is used for production of polymorphs and pseudopolymorphs.

1.3.2 Hygroscopicity

Many pharmaceutical materials have a tendency to adsorb atmospheric moisture (especially, water-soluble salt forms). They are called hygroscopic materials and this phenomenon is known as *hygroscopicity*.

Equilibrium moisture content depends upon:
  1. Atmospheric humidity.
  2. Temperature.
  3. Surface area.
  4. Exposure time.
  5. Mechanism of moisture uptake.

The following classification was proposed, based on the water uptake after storage for one week at different conditions:

- Class I, non-hygroscopic (no water sorption below 90% RH, and < 20% and 90% RH);
- Class II, slightly hygroscopic (no water sorption below 80% RH, and < 40% at 80% RH);
- Class III, moderately hygroscopic (< 5% below 60% RH, and < 50% at 80% RH);
- Class IV, very hygroscopic (> 5% below 60% RH).

Several mechanisms of solid-water interactions have been proposed like surface adsorption, capillary condensation, hydrate formation, deliquescence and absorption into amorphous materials.

Tests of Hygroscopicity

Procedure :

Bulk drug samples are placed in open containers with thin powder bed to assure maximum atmospheric exposure. These samples are then exposed to a range of controlled relative humidity (RH) environments prepared with saturated aqueous salt solutions.

Fig. 1.6 shows the assembly for test of hygroscopicity.

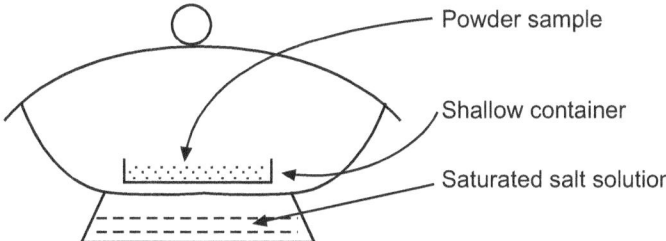

Powder sample

Shallow container

Saturated salt solution

Fig. 1.6: Desiccator

The amount of moisture adsorbed can be determined by the following methods:

(i) Gravimetry

(ii) Thermogravimetric analysis (TGA)

(iii) Karl-Fischer titration (KF-titration)

(iv) Gas chromatography (GC)

Significance of Hygroscopicity Test

(a) To decide special handling procedure (with respect to time).

(b) To decide

    (i) the storage condition i.e. at low humidity environment.

    (ii) special packaging – e.g. with desiccant.

(c) Moisture level in a powder sample may affect the flowability and compactibility, which are important factors during tableting and capsule filling.

(d) After adsorption of moisture, if hydrates are formed then solubility of that powder may affect the dissolution characteristics of the material.

(e) Moisture may degrade some materials. So humidity of a material must be controlled.

1.3.3 Fine Particle Characterization

Particle size is quoted as the diameter of the sphere equivalent to the particle in the weight, volume, surface area or sedimentation velocity. Shape and surface area are most important properties of individual particle. Particle size distribution has to be uniform and optimum.

Most important parameters measured are given below:

(i) Particle size and size-distribution

(ii) Shape of the particle

(iii) Surface morphology of the particles

Type of Powder According to Particle Size:

1. Monodisperse powder: All particles are of same size.

2. Polydisperse powder: Particles of different size.

1.3.3.1 Significance of Particle Size

Drugs are formulated in various dosage forms and may contain finely divided material as essential components.

Particle size has importance in following areas:

- **Particle size distribution:** In SDFs, to maintain content uniformity it is necessary. Any interference with uniformity of fill volume may alter mass of drug incorporated into tablets or capsules and hence reduce content uniformity of formulations.

- **Sedimentation and flocculation rates:** Degree of suspendibility is affected by particle. Mostly affected in suspensions. In concentrated deflocculated suspension, large particles exhibit hindered settling and smaller particles settle more rapidly. In flocculated suspensions, particles are linked together into flocs which settle according to size of floc and porosity of aggregated mass. Flocculated suspensions are preferred having fewer tendencies to cake and are more rapidly dispersible. Therefore, it is apparent that ultimate H_u of sediment depends on H_u/H_o, that is degree of suspendibility to prepare satisfactory dosage forms.

- **Rate of dissolution:** Dissolution rate is faster for small particles because it depends upon specific surface area in contact with dissolution medium.

It is described by Modified Noyes-Whitney equation :

$$\frac{dA}{dt} = KS\,(\,C_s - C\,)$$

A = Amount of drug in solution.

K = Intrinsic dissolution rate constant.

S = Surface area.

C_s = Concentration of saturated solution of drug.

C = Drug concentration at time t.

For exmaple; Griseofulvin. Micronized form rapidly dissolves and 50% dose is reduced in this form.

- **Flow properties:** Powder with different particle sizes have different flow and packing properties which alters volume of powder during compression event.

- **Particle size reduction:** Particle size reduction to extremely small size (< 10 μm) may be inadvisable as it acts as dissolution rate-limiting steps. Entrapped air adsorbed on surface of particles and/or surface electrical charges impart undesirable properties of drugs. Entrapped air prevents drug wetting while electrically induced agglomeration decreases exposure of drug surface to surrounding dissolution medium. Milling or other methods lead to degradation and polymorphic transformation.

1.3.3.2 Different Instrumental Methods

[I] Instrumental Methods of Particle Size Characterization

(1) Light Microscope

First, the small number of particles are spread over a glass slide and placed on the stage of the microscope. Particles are focussed and the particle diameters are measured. Several hundred particles are measured and reported as a histogram.

Two types of microscope methods are commonly used such as :

(i) Scanning electron microscope:

- It is a type of electron microscope that produce image of a sample by scanning with beam of electron.

- First, fix sample to aluminum stubs before sputter coating with film of gold.

- Near the bottom, a set of scanning coils moves the focussed beam back and forth across the specimen, row by row.

- As the electron beam hits each spot on the sample, secondary electrons are knocked loose from its surface. A detector counts these electrons and sends the signals to an amplifier.

- The final image is built-up from the number of electrons emitted from each spot on the sample.

(ii) Transmission electron microscope:

• It is a microscopy technique in which a beam of electrons is transmitted through an ultrathin specimen.

• Sample is set in resin, sectioned by microtome and supported on metal grid before metallic coating.

Advantages:

    (i) Relatively inexpensive.

    (ii) Each particle individually examined - detect aggregates, shape etc.

    (iii) Permanent record i.e. photograph is available.

    (iv) Small sample sizes are required.

Disadvantages:

    (i) The procedure is time consuming.

    (ii) Very low throughput.

    (iii) No information on 3D shape.

(2) Sieve Analysis

A powder sample is passed through a standard sieve set. The particle size is plotted against % weight retained on each sieve.

Sieve analysis is performed using a nest or stack of sieves where each lower sieve has a smaller aperture size than that of the sieve above it.

Sieves can be referred to either by their aperture size, mesh size or sieve number (BP, PhEur).

US: The mesh size is the number of wires per linear inch.

250 µm = No. 60

125 µm = No. 120

Advantages:

    (i) Easy to perform.

    (ii) Wide size range.

    (iii) Inexpensive.

Disadvantages:

    (i) Wear/damage in use or cleaning.

    (ii) Irregular/agglomerated particles.

    (iii) Rod-like particles: overestimate of under-size.

    (iv) Labour intensive.

(3) Stream Counting Devices

    Examples:

    (a) Coulter counter - Electrical sensing zone method.

    (b) Malvern particle and droplet sizer – Laser diffraction method.

(a) Electronic scanning zone (Coulter counter):

In this method, particles are suspended in electrically conductive fluid. The suspension flows through suitable aperture with an immersed electrode on either side and particle concentration is arranged so that one particle travels at a time. When particle passes, some resistance is seen, that change is measured.

Principle:

Particle suspension is drawn through aperture accurately through sapphire crystal set into wall of hollow glass tube. Electrodes situated on either side of aperture and surrounded by electrolyte solution, monitor change in electrical signal that occurs when a particle momentarily occupies orifice and displaces its own volume of electrolytes. Volume of suspension drawn through orifice is determined by suction potential created by mercury thread rebalancing in convoluted U-tube. Volume of electrolyte fluid which is displaced in orifice by presence of particle causes change in electrical resistance between electrodes proportional to volume of particle. Change in resistance is converted into voltage pulse which is amplified and processed electronically. Pulse falls in pre-calibrated limits or thresholds are used to split particles size distribution into many size ranges. (Fig. 1.7).

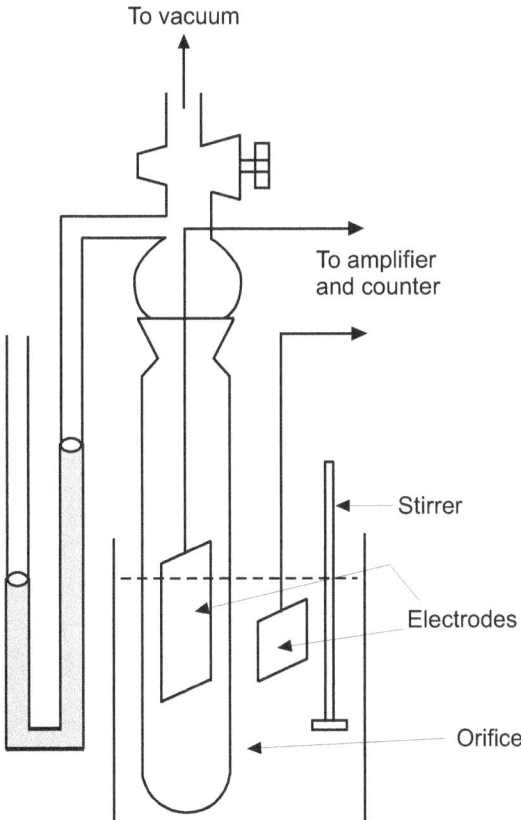

Fig. 1.7: Coulter counter

Procedure:

- Samples prepared for analysis are dispersed in a conducting medium (e.g. saline) along with a few drops of surfactant (to disperse the particles uniformly).
- A known volume (0.5 to 2 ml) of this suspension is then drawn into a tube through a small aperture (0.4 to 800 μm diameter) across which a voltage is applied.
- As each particle passes through the hole, it is counted and sized according to the resistance generated by displacing that particle's volume of conducting medium. Size distribution is reported as histogram.

Advantages :

(i) Fastest counting (1000 particle count at one second).

(ii) More reliable since large number of particles are counted.

(iii) True volume distribution.

(iv) High resolution.

(v) Wide range of measurement: Particle diameter from approx. (0.5 - 400 μm).

Disadvantage :

(i) Coarser particle leads to block small orifice, while finer particles in larger orifice will cause too small relative change in volume. So necessary to change orifice diameter to carry out wide size range analysis.

(b) Laser light scattering method:

This method is classified in two ways:

(i) Laser Diffraction Particle Size Analysis (Particle size range 0.02 - 2000 μm/ 0.013500 μm).

(ii) Photon Correlation Spectroscopy (Particle size range : 1nm to 5 μm).

(i) Laser diffraction :

- In laser diffraction, the particles pass through an expanded and collimated laser beam in front of a lens, in which focal plane is positioned as a photosensitive detector consisting of a series of concentric rings (Fig. 1.8).

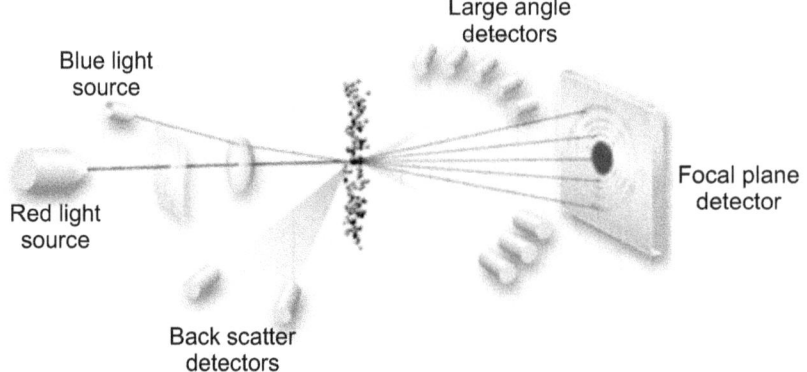

Fig. 1.8: Laser diffraction pathway

Distribution of scattered intensity is analysed by computer to yield the particle size distribution.

The angle of diffraction is inversely related to the particle size.

Advantages:

(i) Non-intrusive: Uses a low power laser beam.

(ii) Fast: Typically < 3 minutes to take a measurement and analyse.

(iii) Precise and wide range upto 64 size bands can be displayed covering a range of upto 100,000:1 in size.

(iv) Absolute measurement: No calibration is required; the instrument is based on fundamental physical properties.

(v) Simple to use.

(vi) Highly versatile.

Disadvantages:

(i) Expensive.

(ii) In volume measurement, all other outputs are numerical transformations of this basic output form, assuming spherical particles.

(iii) Must be a difference in refractive index between particles and suspending medium.

(ii) Photon corelation spectroscopy :

• Large particles move more slowly than small particles, so that the rate of fluctuation of the light scattered from them is also slower.

• In photon correlation spectroscopy, the Brownian motion of sub-micron particles is measured as a function of time. The technique is based on the principle that smaller particles move with higher velocity than large particles.

• A laser beam is diffracted by sub-micron particles in suspensions (Fig. 1.9).

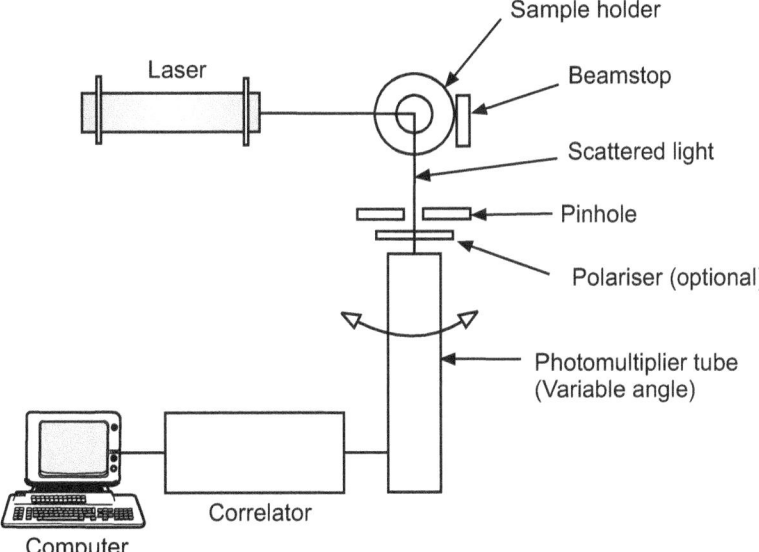

Fig. 1.9 (a) : Typical layout of photon co-relation spectroscopy

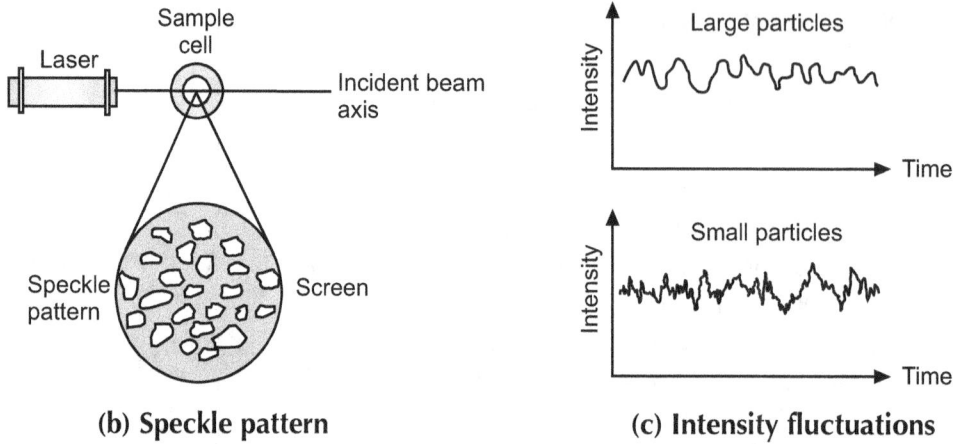

(b) Speckle pattern   (c) Intensity fluctuations

Fig. 1.9: Process layout of photon correlation spectroscopy

- Comparison of a "snap-shot" of each speckle pattern with another, is taken at a very short time (microseconds) (Fig. 1.9 (b)).

- Fig. 1.9 (c) illustrates typical intensity fluctuations arising from a dispersion of large particles and small particles.

- The time dependent change in position of the speckles relates to the change of position of the particles and hence particle size.

- The dynamic light signal is sampled and correlated with itself at different time intervals using a digital correlator and associated computer software.

- The relationship of the auto-correlation function obtained to time intervals is processed to provide estimates of the particle size distribution.

Advantages:

(i) Non-intrusive.

(ii) Fast.

(iii) Nanometre size range.

Disadvantages:

(i) Sample preparation is critical.

(ii) Vibration, temperature fluctuations can interfere with analysis.

(iii) Restricted to solid in liquid or liquid in liquid samples.

(iv) Expensive.

(4) Sedimentation (>1μm)

These methods depend on the fact that the terminal velocity of a particle in a fluid increases with size. The particle size distribution of fine powder can be determined by examining a sedimenting suspension of the powder.

Principle:

In this method, particle size can be determined by examining the powder as it sediments out.

(a) In cases where the powder is not uniformly dispersed in a fluid it can be introduced as a thin layer on the sufrace of the liquid.

(b) If the powder is lyophobic, it may be necessary to add dispersing agent to aid wetting of the powder.

(c) In case where the powder is soluble in water it will be necessay to use non-aqueous liquids or carry out the analysis in a gas.

Particle size analysis by sedimentation method can be divided into two main categories accroding to the method of measurement used.

1. One of the type is based on measurement of particle in a retention zone.

2. Another type is based on measurement of particle in a non-retention zone.

An example of a non-retention zone measurement is known as the **pipette method**.

In this method, known volumes of suspension are drawn off and the concentration differences are measured with respect to time.

One of the most pupular pipette methods was developed by Andreasen and Lundberg and commonly called the Andreasen pipette.

The Andreasen fixed-position pipette consists of a 200 mm graduate cylinder which can hold about 500 ml of suspension fluid. A pipette is located centrally in the cylinder and is held in position by a ground glass stopper so that its tip coincides with the zero level. A three way tap allows fluid to be drawn into a 10 ml reservoir which can then be emptied into a beaker or centrifuge tube. The amount of powder can be determined by weight following drying or centrifuging.

The weight of each sample residue is known as the weight of undersize and the sum of the successive weight is known as the cumulative weight of undersize. It can be expressed directly in weight units or per cent of the total weight of the final sediment.

The data of cumulative weight of undersize is used for the determination of particle weight distribution, number distribution.

The largest particle diameter in each sample is then calcualted from Strokes's Law.

The particle size may be obtained by gravity sedimentation as expressed in Strokes' law.

$$d_{st} = \left[\frac{18\,\eta_0\mu}{(P_s - P_0)\,g} \right]^{1/2}$$

Where,

μ = Rate of settling

h = Distance of the fall, in time t

d_{st} = The mean diameter of the particles based on the velocity of sedimentation.

ρ_s = Density of the particles

ρ_o = Density of the dispersion medium

g = Acceleration due to gravity

η_o = Viscosity of the medium

(5) Elutriation

Elutriation is a procedure in which the fluid moves in opposite direction to sedimentation movement, so that in the gravitational force. Example, the particle will move vertically downwards and fluid moves vertically upwards.

If velocity of fluid is higher than the particle, then particles are carried upwards and vice versa.

Size of particles that will separate depends on their position in tube i.e. largest in the center, smallest towards outside.

(6) X-ray Diffraction Method

Principle :

An X-ray irradiation produce a highly specific diffraction pattern passed from a crystal of material.

An X-ray diffraction pattern from the crystal, forms a series of dots of varying intensity with fixed angles and recorded on photographic film (Fig. 1.10).

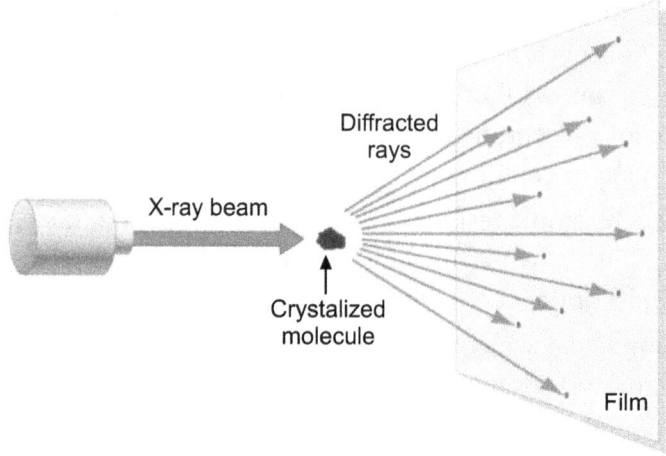

Fig. 1.10: X-ray diffraction pattern

Advantages:

(i) Very sensitive.

(ii) Use in identification of polymorphs.

Disadvantage:

(i) Very expensive.

(7) Cascade Impaction (0.1 - 80 microns)

It can be used to obtain the size distribution of an aerosol formulation.

Cascade impactor consist of several stages on which particles are deposited on impaction plate.

Particles will impact on certain stage depending on their size.

A series of scanning microscopy may be identified and related to a size range in which elevated counts were noted with a particle counter.

This device can be used in combination with scanning microscopy to identify small particles present in the air.

Schematic presentation of cascade impactor is shown in Fig. 1.11.

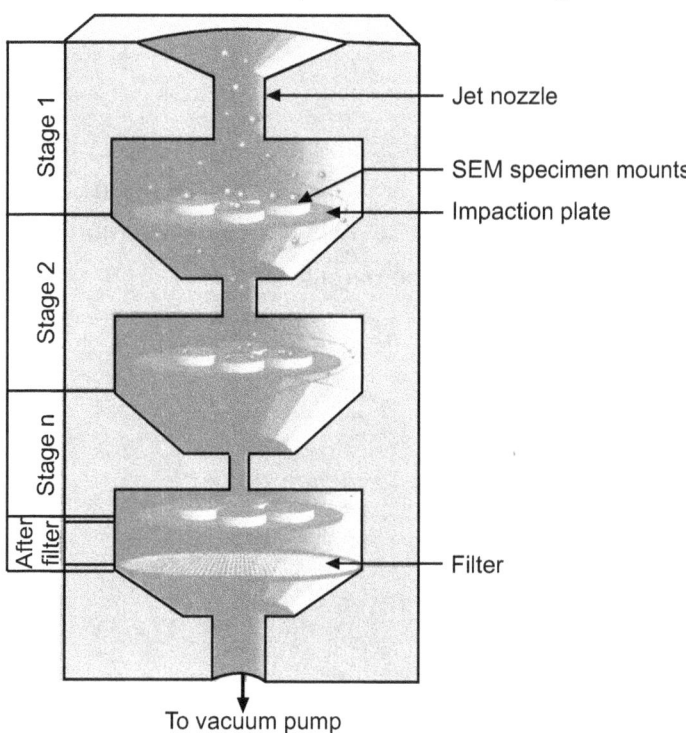

Fig. 1.11: Cascade impactor

Advantage :

(i) Multistage give wide range of data.

Disadvantages:

(i) Particles bouncing off.

(ii) Over loading.

(iii) Fluctuation occur.

(8) Rotating Drum Method

This method is suitable to determine the distribution of particle of respirable or inhalable size. It can be commonly used for dry powders, granules friable products.

1.3.3.3 Properties of Drug that are Affected by Particle size and Particle Size Distribution

1. Surface area
2. Density, Porosity and Compressibility
3. Angle of repose and Flow property
4. Bulkiness and Packaging criteria
5. Hygroscopicity
6. Electrostatic charge

1. Surface Area

Surface area is important for drug absorption, dissolution, solubility and bioavailability. As particle size decreases, the surface area of particle increases. The particle size and surface area of drug exposed to medium can affect the actual solubility.

Below equation is used to estimate the particle size.

$$\text{Log}\left(\frac{S}{S_0}\right) = \left(\frac{2\gamma V}{2.303 + RTr}\right)$$

Where,

S = Solubility of small particle

S_0 = Solubility of large particle

γ = Surface tension

V = Molar volume

R = Gas volume

T = Absolute temperature

r = Radius of small particle

According to Noyes-Whitney equation, increase in the total surface area of drug in contact with GIF will cause increase in dissolution rate, because of particles initially wetted by GIF. The effective surface area exhibited by drug is directly proportional to particle size.

Hence smaller the particle size, greater will be effective surface area, higher dissolution rate and it will result in higher bioavailability.

Therefore, in some drugs bioavailability increases with reduction in particle size, For example: Sulphadiazine.

$$\frac{dC}{dT} = KS(C_S - C_F)$$

where, $\frac{dC}{dT}$ = Rate of dissolution

     K   = Dissolution rate constant

     S   = Surface area

     C_S = Concentration of drug in immediate proximity of dissolving particle that is solubility of drug

     C_F = Concentration of drug in bulk fluid

(2) Density, Porosity and Compressibility

Apparent Bulk Density (g/cm³):

Bulk drug powder is sieved through 40 mesh screen. Weight is taken and poured into a graduated cylinder via a large funnel. The volume is called *bulk volume.*

$$\text{Apparent bulk density} = \frac{\text{Weight of the powder}}{\text{Bulk volume}}$$

Tapped Density (g/cm³):

Bulk powder is sieved through 40 mesh screen. Weight is taken and poured into a graduated cylinder. The cylinder is tapped 100 times on a mechanical tapper apparatus. The volume reached a minimum – called *tapped volume.*

$$\text{Tapped density} = \frac{\text{Weight of the powder}}{\text{Tapped volume}}$$

True Density (g/cm³):

Solvents of varying densities are selected, in which, the powder sample is insoluble. Small quantity of surfactant may be mixed with the solvent mixture to enhance wetting and pore penetration. After vigorous agitation, the samples are centrifuged briefly and then left to stand undisturbed until floatation or settling has reached equilibrium.

The sample that remain suspended (i.e. neither suspended not floated) is taken. Density of the powder is then determined accurately with a pycnometer.

Significance:

(i) **Bulk density:**

Bulk density is required during the selection of capsule size for a high dose drug.

In case of low dose drug mixing with excipients is a problem if the bulk densities of the drug and excipients have large difference.

(ii) **Tapped density:**

To get the idea about the dose and tapped density of the formulation, the capsule size can be determined.

(iii) True density:

From bulk density and true density of powder, the void volume or porosity can be measured by using below equation.

$$\text{Void volume} = \left(\frac{m}{\rho_{bulk}} - \frac{m}{\rho_{true}} \right) = m \left(\frac{1}{\rho_{bulk}} - \frac{m}{\rho_{true}} \right)$$

$$\text{Porosity} = \frac{\text{Voild volume}}{\text{Bulk volume}} = \frac{m \left(\dfrac{1}{\rho_{bulk}} - \dfrac{1}{\rho_{true}} \right)}{\dfrac{m}{\rho_{bulk}}} = 1 - \frac{\rho_{bulk}}{\rho_{true}}$$

(3) Angle of Repose and Flow Property

It is most important property of drug that is affected by particle size (PS) and particle surface density (PSD).

Cohesion and adhesion force are occurred at surface of particle that will affect flowability of powder. Fine particles with very high surface to mass ratio are more cohesive than coarse particles. Particles greater than 250 micron are free flowing. As particle size decreases below 100 micron, particle becomes more cohesive.

Angle of Repose:

It is most important tool for estimation of flow property of powder. It can be determined by "fixed height funnel method".

$$\text{Tan } \theta = \frac{h}{r}$$

Where, h = Height of the pile

r = Radius of base of pile

Importance:

When particle size decreases, angle of repose decreases due to cohesive forces and flow property increases.

Powder flow properties depend on :

(i)   particle size

(ii) density

(iii) shape

(iv) electrostatic charge and adsorbed moisture, that may arise from processing or formulation.

A free-flowing powder may become cohesive during development. This problem may be solved by any of the following ways.

(i)   by granulation

(ii) by filling special auger feed equipment (in case of powder)

(iii) by changing the formulation.

Flow Property of Powder:

A simple flow rate apparatus consisting of a grounded metal tube from which drug flows through an orifice onto an electronic balance, which is connected to a strip chart recorder. Several flow rate (g/sec) determinations at various orifice sizes (1/8 to 1/2 inch) should be carried out.

The greater the standard deviation between multiple flow rate measurements, the greater will be the weight variation of the product (tablets or capsules). It will affect the compressibility. Particle size decreases with decrease in the bulk density of powder hence more air is absorbed on to the surface porosity.

Compressibility :

$$\% \text{ Compressiblity} = \frac{\rho_t - \rho_o}{\rho_t} \times 100$$

ρ_t = tapped bulk density

ρ_o = Initial bulk density

There must be suitable balance between particle size, density, porosity and compressibility.

(4) Bulkiness and Packaging

As particle size increases, bulkiness decreases. It is a reciprocal of bulk density.

Bulk property is also important for packaging criteria of powder.

(5) Hygroscopycity

Hygroscopycity is an important property from various physical properties of drug.

Decrease in particle size give larger surface area that will give high susceptibility for moisture absorption.

(6) Electrostatic Charges

Electrostatic charge mostly affects dispersed system like suspension, emulsion.

Particle size, particle size distribution, cohesion, adhesion and electrical double layer property are mostly affected by it.

1.3.3.4 Importance of Particle Size and Particle Size Distribution

1. Particle size affects many physical properties of drug like surface area, density, porosity, compressibility, moisture absorption, surface properties like solubility, absorption, dissolution and bioavailability.

2. **Tablet:** Particle size and particle size distribution is important for selecting granulation process. It also affect average tablet weight variation, granule properties like uniformity of colour, size uniformity, uniformity of dose, absorption, dissolution and bioavailability.

3. **Suspension:** Affect the sedimentation rate, suspendibility, redispersibility, coalescence and agglomeration.

4. **Aerosol:** Aerosol affects site of absorption in the bronchopulmonary tract.

5. **Bioavailability:** Bioavailability is increased by particle size reduction. For example, Sulphadiazine, Phenothiazen, Tolbutamide, Spironolactone, Aspirin, Nitrofurantoin.

But in case of Nitrofurantoin, increase in bioavailability may resulted in increase in its side effects.

In case of Penicillin-G and Erythromycin, if particle size decreases, surface area increases.

Greseoflavin, if micronized, then increases rate of absorption and finally the dissolution.

In case of poorly soluble hydrophobic drug, if particle size decreases then chance of formation of agglomerates increases.

Particle size and particle size distribution also affects the porosity and bulkiness, so affects packing.

1.3.4 Powder Flow

Compaction: Compaction means, some level of mechanical force is applied over the powdered solids.

Compression: Compression is reduction in the bulk volume of the material due to the displacement of gaseous phase.

Consolidation: Consolidation is to increase in mechanical strength of material due to the particle–particle interactions.

1.3.4.1 Process of Compression

Steps Involved in Process of Compression :

1. Transitional repacking/particle rearrangement.
2. Deformation at point of contact.
3. Fragmentation.
4. Bonding.
5. Decompression and Ejection.

(1) Transitional Repacking

At initial stage of compression, the particles are subjected to the low pressure. During this, particles move with respect to each other.

Small particles enters in void space between the larger particles.

Thus, volume decreases and density increases. Spherical particle undergoes lesser rearrangement than irregular particles.

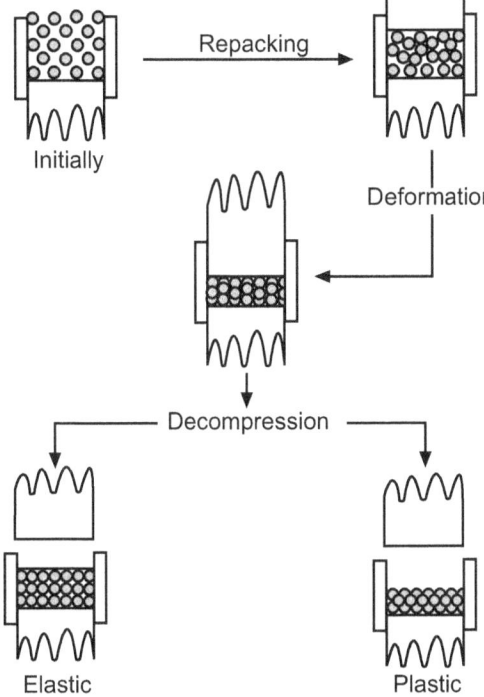

Fig. 1.12 : Effect of compression

(2) Deformation at Point of Contact

When the particles of granules are so closely packed, no further filling of voids can occur. Increase in the compressional force causes deformation at the point of contact.

If the deformation disappears completely upon release of the stress it is known as 'Elastic deformation'. A deformation that does not recover completely after release of stress it is known as 'Plastic deformation'. The force required to initiate plastic deformation is known as 'Yield stress'.

(3) Fragmentation

As the compressional force increases, the deformed particles starts undergoing fragmentation. Because of high load, the particles break into smaller fragments leading to formation of new bonding areas.

Some materials undergo structural breakdown called as 'Brittle fracture'.

(4) Bonding

When close particles are seperated out, at that time unsatisfied forces are present on their surfaces and they lead to formation of strong attractive force. This process is known as cold welding.

Fusion Bonding

In this phase, forces are applied to the powder mass and it must pass through this bed of particles.

Factors affecting the Bonding :

(i) Chemical nature of material.

(ii) Available surface.

(iii) Presence of surface contaminants.

(iv) The interface distance.

(5) Decompression and Ejection

The success or failure of powders depends upon the stress induced by elastic rebound and the associated deformation produced during decompression and ejection and if any dimensional change during the decompression, it must occur in the axial direction.

Various Forces Involved in Compaction

1. Frictional Forces
   (i) Interparticulate
   (ii) Die-wall
2. Distribution Forces
3. Radial Forces
4. Ejection Forces

Methods of Evaluating the Compaction Process

1. Compaction profiles (Force time, Displacement time)
2. Tablet expansion
3. Pressure-Volume relationships
4. Pressure transmission
5. Energy of compaction
6. Radial Vs. Axial force
7. Acoustics
8. Temperature

1.3.4.2 Evaluation of Compaction

1. Strain index (SI): Measures internal strain associated with a powder when compacted.
2. Bonding index (BI): Measure ability of material to bonds.
3. Brittle fracture index (BFI): Measures brittleness of material.
   - Higher is the BI index, stronger is the tablet.
   - Higher is the SI index, softer is the tablet.

1.3.5 Polymorphism

Ability of compound or element to crystallize in more than one crystal form is called polymorphism.

There is also potentially large difference in their physical properties so that they behave as distinct chemical entities.

Solubility, melting point, density, crystal shape, optical and electrical properties and vapour pressure are often very different for each polymorph.

Polymorphism is common within certain structural groups. For example, 63% of barbiturates, 67% of steroids and 40% of sulphonamides exhibit polymorphism.

Number to polymorphs is given in order of stability. Form-I usually have the highest melting point and the lowest solubility. In suspension formulation it is essential to use the least soluble polymorph because of Ostwald ripening.

1.3.5.1 Method to Identify Polymorphic Forms

- **Hot-stage microscopic method:**

Polarizing microscope is fitted with a hot or cold stage to determine stability, transition temperature, melting point and rate of transition. The heating rate is constant. Phase transitions can be recorded as melting proceeds. By using this method one can get more accurate values.

- **X-Ray powder diffractions:**

Powered crystal material give characteristic diffraction pattern made up of peaks in certain position and varying intensities. In this method, very small sample size is needed and it is non-destructive method.

- **Dilatometry:**

Analytical technique that measures volume change as a function of temperature or chemical effect is called 'dilatometry'. It is extremely accurate but very tedious and time consuming so not widely used. Change in weight due to temperature can be measured by *thermal gravimetric analysis* (TGA).

- **Differential Scanning Colorimetric (DSC):**

It measures enthalpy of transition.

- **Differential Thermal Analysis (DTA):**

It gives information such as melting and freezing points.

- **Other**:

PMR, NMR, Electronic microscopy.

1.3.6 Drug Excipeients Compatibility Study (DECS)

In the formulations, there are two or more active ingredients and/or excipients with each other, if they are antagonist and do not show any adversely changes in appearance, elegance and therapeutic efficacy then they are said to be incompatible with each other.

Importance of Drug Excipient Compatibility Study

1. It helps to improve stability of the dosage form. Any physical or chemical interaction between drug and excipient can affect bioavailability and stability of drug.

2. It helps to avoid the surprise problems. By performing DECS, we can know the possible reaction before formulating final dosage form.

3. It bridges the drug discovery and drug development. Drug discovery can emerge only new chemical entity. It becomes drug product after formulation and processing with excipients. By using DECS data, we can select the suitable type of the excipient with the chemical entities emerging in drug discovery programs.

4. DECS data is essential for IND (investigational new drug) submission. Now, USFDA has made it compulsory to submit DECS data for any new coming formulation before its approval.

1.3.6.1 Types of Incompatibility

(A) Physical incompatibility: It involves the change in the physical form of the formulation like colour changes, liquefaction, phase separation or immiscibility.

(B) Chemical incompatibility: It involves undesirable change in formulation which is due to formation of new chemical compatibility due to the hydrolysis, oxidation, reduction, precipitation, decarboxylation, racemization.

(C) Therapeutic incompatibility: It involves change in therapeutic response of the formulation which is undesirable to patient as well as physician.

1.3.6.2 Compatibility Tests

General view regarding solid and liquid dosage forms.

(A) Solid state reactions :

Solid state reactions are much **slower** and more **difficult to interpret** than solution state reactions, due to a reduced number of molecular contacts between drug and excipient molecules, and also occurrence of multiple phase reactions.

(B) Liquid state reactions :

It is easier to detect liquid state reactions as compared to solid state reactions.

For detection of unknown liquid incompatibilities, the program set up is same as solid dosage forms according to "Stability guidelines" stated by FDA.

Following conditions can be evaluated in studies on solutions or suspensions of bulk drug substances:

1) Acidic or alkaline pH.
2) Presence of added substances like - chelating agents, stabilizers etc.
3) High Oxygen and Nitrogen atmospheres.
4) Effect of stress testing condition.

1.3.6.3 Methods Used to Detect Drug Excipient Compatibility

1) FT-IR Spectroscopy
2) DSC- Differential Scanning Calorimetry
3) Accelerated Stability Study

4) DRS-Diffuse Reflectance Spectroscopy

5) Chromatography

6) Miscellaneous

   I. Radiolabelled Techniques

   II. Vapour Pressure Osmometry

   III. Flourescence Spectroscopy

Table 1.5: Examples of Some Known Incompatibilities

Functional group	Incompatibility	Type of reaction
Alcohol	Oxygen	Oxidation to Aldehyde and Ketones
Sulfhydryl	Oxygen	Dimerization
Phenol	Metal	Complexation
Gelatin- Capsule Shell	Cationic Surfactant	Denaturation
PEK	Phenol, Tannic acid and Salicylic acid	Softening and Liquifaction
	Sulphonamide and Dithranol	Discolouration
Primary amine	Mono and Di-saccharides	Amine-Aldehyde and Amine-Acetal

1.3.6.4 Compatibility Studies in Different Dosage Forms

(A) Drug-Excipient Compatibility Studies in Solid Dosage Forms

Example :

Millard reaction: It is a non-enzymatic bimolecular browning reaction between reducing sugar and amines.

Mechanism:

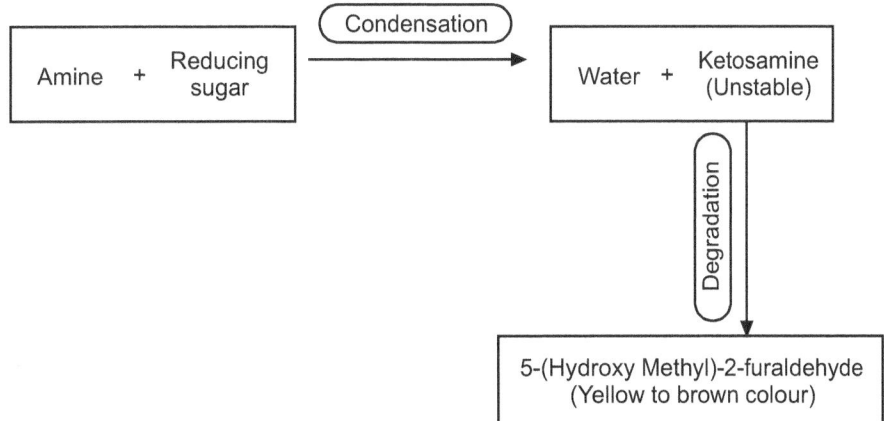

(B) Drug Excipient Compatibility Studies in Aerosols

Example 1: Interaction of propellent-11 with aqueous drug products.

- Propellent -11 is trichloromonofluoromethane.
- Interaction of above with the aqueous drug is as follows:

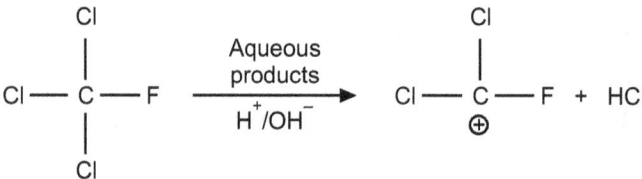

- HCl corrodes the Al-container.
- Therefore, Propellent -11 is incompatible with aqueous products.

Example 2: Beclomethasone - Hydroflouroalkane interactions.

- BDP is a Steroidal drug used in Asthma. It react with hydroflouro alkene, gets aggregated due to charges and hence aerosolisation properties are diminished. It should be prevented by coating with anphiphilic excipients.

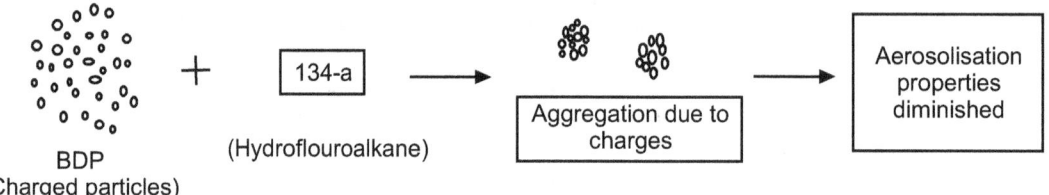

(C) Drug Excipient Compatibility Studies in Parenteral Products

Excipients are important in parenteral formulations to assure safety, minimize pain, irritation upon injection, and control or prolong drug delivery. Examples of positive or synergistic interaction between excipient and drugs are discussed below:

(I) Anti-oxidants:

(A) **Ascorbic acid:** It is incompatible with drugs like Penicillin-G, Phenylephrine HCl, Pyrilamine meleate, Salicylamide, Theobromine.

(B) **Sodium bisulfite:** It is a strong Nucleophilic anti-oxidant. It can interect with drug as below:

- Epinephrine + Sodium bisulfite ⟶ Sulphonic acid derivatives.
  - It can be prevented by addition of Na-borate which produces complex with Epinephrine and prevent its interaction with Na-bisulfite.
- It is incompatible in Opthalmic solution containing phenyl mercuric acetate especially when autoclaved.

(C) **Edetate salts:** Used in stabilization of drugs sensitive to metal catalyzed oxidation and / or photolysis.

- Edetate salts are incompatible with Zn Insulin, Thiomerosal, Amphotericin and Hydralazine HCl.

(II) Preservatives:

(A) Phenolic preservatives:

- Phenolic preservative is used with formulation containing lente insulin. It breaks the Bi-sulphide linkage in Insulin structure. But when used with Protamine-Insulin at that time, phenol plays important role.

  It forms tetragonal oblong crystals which are responsible for prolong action of insulin.

(III) Surface active agents:

(A) Polysorbate 80 used as a solubilizing agent, wetting agent and emulsifying agent.

- PS 80 $\longrightarrow$ Polyoxyethylene sorbitan ester of Oleic acid (Unsaturated fatty acid).

- PS 20 $\longrightarrow$ Polyoxyethylene sorbitan ester of lauric acid (Saturated fatty acid).

- So PS 20 is less prone to oxidation than PS 80.

(IV) Cosolvents:

(A) Sorbitol: Increase the degradation rate of penicillin in neutral and aqueous solutions.

(B) Glycerol: Increase the mobility of freeze-dried formulation leading to peptide deamidation.

1.4 SOLUBILITY ANALYSIS

1.4.1 Aqueous Solubility

For therapeutic efficacy, drug must require aqueous solubility in pH range 1 to 8 at 37°C. Poor solubility (<10 mg/ml) affect the problems into bioabsorption. If solubility of drug is less than 1 mg/ml it indicates the need for a salt form for solubility, particularly if the drug will be formulated as a tablet or capsule.

There are **2 fundamental properties** mandatory for a new compound.

(A) Intrinsic Solubility (C_0).

(B) Ionization Constant (pKa).

(A) Intrinsic Solubility (C_0):

The solubility of weakly acidic and weakly basic drug as a function of pH can be predicted with the help of below equation.

$$S = S_0 \{1 + (K_1 / [H^+])\} \qquad \text{-------- for weak acids.}$$

$$S = S_0 \{1 + ([H^+] / K_2)\} \qquad \text{-------- for weak bases.}$$

Where, S = Solubility at given pH.

S_0 = Intrinsic solubility of the neutral form.

K_1 = Dissociation constant of weak acid.

K_2 = Dissociation constant of weak base.

Methods to Determine Solubility :

   (1) Equilibrium solubility method.

   (2) Turbidometric solubility method.

   (3) Ultra-filtration LC/MS solubility method.

   (4) Direct solubility method.

(B) Ionization Constant (pKa):

The unionized forms are more lipid soluble and more rapidly absorbed from gastro intestinal tract. 75% of all drugs are weak bases, 25% are weak acids, and only 5% are non-ionic amphoteric.

When a weakly acidic or basic drug partially ionizes in gastro intenstinal fluid, generally, the unionized molecules are absorbed quickly.

Handerson-Hasselbach equation provides an estimate of the ionized and unionized drug concentration at a particular pH.

$$HA + H_2O \rightleftharpoons H_3O^+ + A^-$$

$$\underset{\text{acid}}{\text{Weak}} \qquad\qquad\qquad \underset{\text{base}}{\text{Strong}}$$

For acidic drug:

For example, $\quad pH = pKa + \log \dfrac{[\text{ionized}]}{[\text{unionized}]} = pKa + \log \dfrac{[A^-]}{[HA]} = pKa + \log \dfrac{[\text{base}]}{[\text{acid}]}$

For basic compounds:

For example,

$$B + H_3O^+ \rightleftharpoons BH^+ + H_2O$$

$$\underset{\text{base}}{\text{Weak}} \qquad\qquad\qquad \underset{\text{acid}}{\text{Strong}}$$

$$pH = pKb + \log \frac{[\text{ionized}]}{[\text{unionized}]} = pKa + \log \frac{[B]}{[BH^+]} = pKa + \log \frac{[\text{base}]}{[\text{acid}]}$$

Methods to Determine pKa of a Drug :

   (1) Spectrophotometric method.

   (2) Dissolution rate method.

   (3) Potentiometric method.

   (4) Conductivity method.

   (5) Liquid-Liquid partition method.

1.4.2 Equilibrium Solubility

To determine equlibrium solubility, the drug is dispersed in a solvent. The suspension is agitated at a constant temperature. Samples of the suspension are withdrawn as a function of time, clarified by centrifugation, and assayed to establish a plateau concentration (Fig. 1.13).

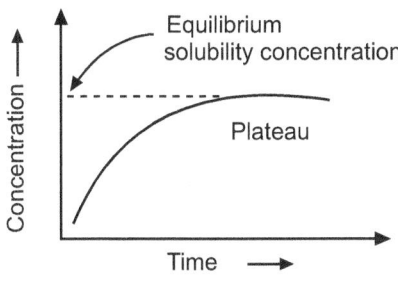

Fig. 1.13

Drug concentration is determined by the following analytical methods:

    (i) HPLC

    (ii) UV –Spectroscopy

    (iii) Fluorescence Spectroscopy

    (iv) Gas Chromatography

Solubility depends on:

    (i) pH

    (ii) Temperature

    (iii) Ionic strength

    (iv) Buffer concentration

Significance:

    (i) A drug for oral administration should be examined for solubility in an isotonic saline solution and acidic pH. This solubility data may provide the information regarding *in vivo* dissolution profile.

    (ii) Solubility studies identify those drugs having a bioavailability problems. For example, Drug having limited solubility (7%) in the fluids of GIT often exhibit poor absorption.

1.4.3 Effect of Temperature on Solubility

Effect of temperature on the solubility of drug can be determined by measuring heat of solution (ΔH_s) by using following equation.

$$\ln S = \frac{-\Delta H_S}{R \times T} + C$$

Where, S = Molar solubility at temperature T (K).

       R = Gas constant.

Heat of solution, ΔH_S represents the heat released or absorbed when a mole of solute is dissolved in a large quantity of solvent.

Importance:

Determination of temperature effect on solubility helps in predicting storage condition and dosage form designing.

Most commonly, the solubility process is endothermic. For example, non-electrolytes, unionized forms of weak acids and bases $\Rightarrow$ ΔH is positive $\Rightarrow$ Solubility increases if temperature increases.

Solutes that are ionized when dissolved releases heat $\Rightarrow$ The process is exothermic $\Rightarrow$ ΔH_S is negative $\Rightarrow$ Solubility increases at lower temperature.

1.4.4 Solubilization

The process of solubilization involves the breaking of intermolecular or inter-ionic bonds in the solute, the separation of the solvent molecules provide space in the solvent for the solute interaction between the solvent and the solute molecule. Solubilization process occurs into three steps. (Fig. 1.14).

Step 1: Holes opens in the solvent

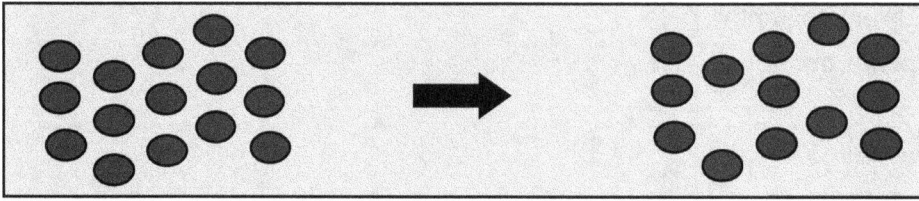

Step 2: Molecules of the solid breaks away from the bulk

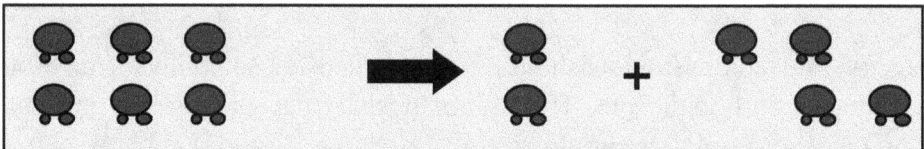

Step 3: The freed solid molecule is integrated into the hole in the solvent

Fig. 1.14: Solubilization process

Many different approaches have been developed to improve drug solubility.

Micronization: It is very common approach for reduction of particle size and it leads to increase effective surface area.

E.g. Griseofulvin shows increased solubility by reducing particle size.

pH Adjustment:

In this approach, solubilization can be defined as, 'the spontaneous dissolving of a substance by reversible interaction with the micells of a surfactant in water to form a stable isotropic solution.

At the surfactant concentration above the cmc, the solubility increases with the concentration of surfactant indicating that solubilization is related to micellization.

Drug should be dissolved in an aqueous media. The ionized form of the drug is responsilble for solubility of drug.

For weak acidic drug, higher pH $\longrightarrow$ more soluble drug

For weak basic drug, lower pH $\longrightarrow$ more soluble drug

Miceller Solublization

Examples are antidiabetic drugs such as gliclazide, glyburide, glimepiride, glipizide, repaglinide, pioglitazone and rosiglitazone.

Cosolvency

Addition of a water miscible solvent can often improve the solubility of a weak electrolyte or non-polar compound in water by altering the polarity of the solvent.

These co-solvents disrupt the hydrophobic interactions of water at the non-polar solute / water interfaces.

The choice of suitable cosolvent is limited for pharmaceutical use because of possible toxicity and irritancy.

Ideally suitable blends should possess values of dielectric constant between 25 - 80.

Commonly used cosolvents are ethanol, sorbitol, glycerin, propylene glycol, dimethylacetamide (DMA), DMSO etc.

Solubilization by Surfactant

Surface active excipient that can solubilize poorly soluble drugs, For e.g. SLS.

Complexation

The solubility of poorly soluble drug can be improved by using complexing agent. For example, The complexation of iodine with 10 - 15% polyvinylpyrolidone (PVP) can improve aqueous solubility of active agent.

Formation of Inclusion Compound

Solubility increases by forming inclusion complex with various guest molecules with suitable polarity and dimension.

For example, The aqueous solubility and chemical stability of Quercetin can be improved via complexation with β-cyclodextrin.

Chemical Modification

Many poorly soluble drugs can be modified into salt form (water soluble).

Use of Metastable Polymorphs

For example, B form of Chloramphenicol palmitate is more water soluble than A and C forms.

Solid Dispersion

In solid dispersion active ingredient is dispered in an inert hydrophilic matrix.

The solubility of various poorly soluble drugs like celecoxib, halofantrine1, ritonavir can be improved by solid dispersion using suitable hydrophilic carriers.

Solubilizing Agent

Solubility can be increased by addition of solubilizing agent.

The aqueous solubility of the antimalarial agent halofantrine is increased by the addition of caffeine and nicotinamide.

Other techniques like complexation, nanotechnology approach and crystallization methods are also used to improve solubility.

1.4.5 Partition Coefficient

Partition coefficient is defined as, "the ratio of un-ionized drug concentrations between the organic and aqueous phases, at equilibrium".

$$K_{O/W} = \left[\frac{C_{oil}}{C_{water}} \right] \text{ at equilibrium}$$

Generally, octanol and chloroform are taken as a oil phase.

Various organic solvents are used in determination of partition coefficient like chloroform, ether, amyl acetate etc.

Solubility parameter of **n-octanol** ($\delta = 10.24$) lies midway in the range for major drugs ($\delta = 8 - 12$). Thus, in formulation development, the n-octanol-water partition coefficient is commonly used.

$$P = \frac{(\text{Concentration of drug in octanol})}{(\text{Concentraion of drug in water})} \quad \text{--- For unionizable drugs.}$$

$$P = \frac{(\text{Concentration of drug in octanol})}{(1 - \alpha) \times (\text{Concentraion of drug in water})} \quad \text{--- For ionizable drugs.}$$

Where α = degree of ionization.

$P > 1 \rightarrow$ Lipophilic drug

$P < 1 \rightarrow$ Hydrophilic drug

The value of P at which maximum activity of controlled release dosage forms is observed is approximately 1000:1 in octanol/water.

Methods to determine partition coefficient
  (a) Shake Flask Method
  (b) Chromatographic Method (TLC, HPLC)
  (c) Counter Current and Filter Probe method

Significance:
  (1) Drug molecules having higher $K_{O/W}$ will cross the lipid cell membrane.
  (2) Measurement of Lipophilic character of molecules.
  (3) Recovery of antibiotics from fermentation broth.
  (4) Study of distribution of oil between oil and water in emulsion.

1.4.6 Common Ion Effect

Common ion effect is responsible for the reduction in the solubility of an ionic precipitate when a soluble compund combining one of the ions of the precipitate is added to the solution in equilibrium with the precipitate.

Addition of a common ion decrease solubility, as the reaction will shift towards the reactant and cause precipitation.

1.4.7 Dissolution

Dissolution is to be considered of 2 types:

Intrinsic Dissolution

Intrinsic dissolution is defined as "the dissolution rate of pure substances under the condition of constant surface area".

The dissolution rate of solid in its own solution is adequately described by **Noyes-Whitney Equation.**

$$\frac{dc}{dt} = \frac{DA}{hV} (C_S - C)$$

Where, D = Diffusion coefficient of the drug in the dissolution medium.
  h = Thickness of the diffusion layer at the solid/liquid interface.
  A = Surface area of drug exposed to dissolution medium.
  V = Volume of the medium.
  C_S = Concentration of saturated solution of the solute in the dissolution medium at the experimental temperature.
  C = Concentration of drug in solution at time t.

When A = constant and if $C_S \gg C$ the equation can be rearranged as

$$\frac{dC}{dt} = \frac{DA}{hV} C_S \quad \text{or,} \quad \frac{V\,dC}{dt} = \frac{DA}{h} C_S \quad \text{or, } W = k\,At$$

Where, $k = \dfrac{D}{h}$

Where, W = Weight (mg) of drug dissolved at time t.

$$k = \text{Intrinsic dissolution rate constant} \left(\frac{mg}{min\ cm^2} \right)$$

This equation helps in predicting about absorption would be dissolution rate limited or not.

Methods to Determine Intrinsic Dissolution:

(1) Rotating disk method or Wood's apparatus:

This method allows for the determination of dissolution from constant surface area, obtained by compressing powder into a disc of known area with a die-punch apparatus.

(2) Particulate dissolution:

This method determines the dissolution of solids at different surface area.

A weighed amount of powder sample from a particular sieve fraction is introduced in the dissolution medium. Agitation is usually provided by a constant speed propeller.

It is used to study the influence on dissolution of particle size and surface area.

IDR is used for

(1) Evaluation of drug solubility in accordance to BCS.

(2) Developments of dissolution methods.

(3) Comparison of different forms/salt of the same compound.

1.5 STABILITY ANALYSIS

Preformulation stability studies are the first quantitative assessment of chemical stability of a new drug. This may involve:

(1) Stability study in toxicology formulation

(2) Stability study in solution state

(3) Stability study in solid state.

1.5.1 Stability Study in Toxicology Formulation

A new drug is administered to animals through oral route either by:

(i) Mixing the drug in the feed.

(ii) In the form of solution.

(iii) In the form of suspension in aqueous vehicle.

Feed may contain water, vitamin, minerals (metal ions), enzymes and different functional groups that may severely reduce the stability of the new drug. So stability study should be carried out in the feed and at laboratory temperature.

For solution and suspension, the chemical stability at different temperature and pH should be checked.

For suspension-state the drug suspension is occasionally shaken to check dispersibility.

1.5.2 Stability Study in Solution State

Objective: Identification of conditions necessary to form a stable solution.

Stability of a new drug may depend on:

(1) pH　　　　　　　(2) Ionic strength　　　　　　　(3) Co-solvent

(4) Light　　　　　　　(5) Temperature　　　　　　　(6) Common degradation route

(1) pH Stability Study

(i) It confirms the decay at the extremes of pH and temperature. Three stability studies are carried out at the following conditions:

(a) 0.1N HCl solution at 90°C.

(b) Solution in water at 90°C.

(c) 0.1 N NaOH solution at 90°C.

All these studies are intentionally done to confirm the assay specificity and for maximum rates of degradation.

(ii) Aqueous buffers are used to produce solutions with wide range of pH values but with constant levels of drug concentration, co-solvent and ionic strength.

All the rate constants (k) at a single temperature are then plotted as a function of pH (Fig. 1.15).

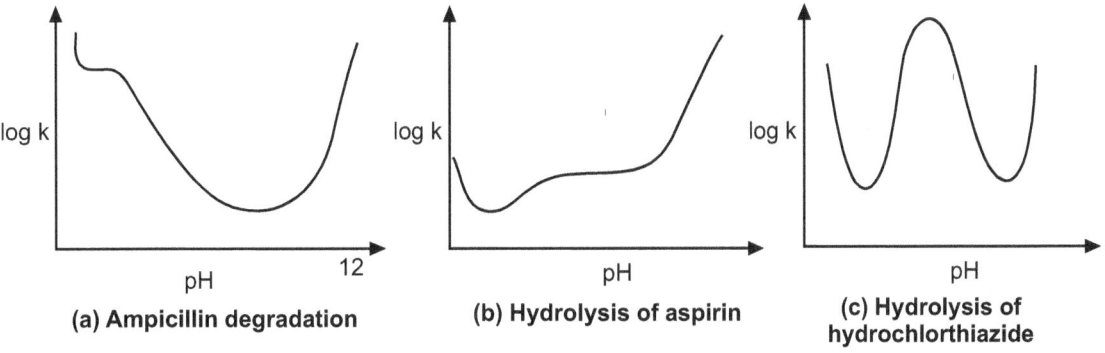

(a) Ampicillin degradation　　　(b) Hydrolysis of aspirin　　　(c) Hydrolysis of hydrochlorthiazide

Fig. 1.15: Rate constants as a function of pH

(2) Ionic Strength

Since most pharmaceutical solutions are intended for parenteral routes of administration, the pH-stability studies should be carried out at a constant ionic strength that is compatible with body fluids. The ionic strength (μ) of an isotonic 0.9% w/v sodium chloride solution is 0.15.

Ionic strength for any buffer solution can be calculated by following equation:

$$\mu = \frac{1}{2} \sum m_i Z_i^2$$

Where, m_i = Molar concentration of the ion

Z_i = Valency of that ion

(3) Co-solvents

Some drugs are not sufficiently soluble to give concentrations of analytical sensitivity. In those cases, co-solvents may be used. However, presence of co-solvents will influence the rate constant. Hence, k values at different co-solvent concentrations are determined and plotted against % of co-solvent. Finally, the line is extrapolated to 0% co-solvent to produce the actual k value (i.e. in pure solvent).

(4) Light

Stability study is carried out in different containers given below.

Drug solutions are kept in -

(a) Clear glass ampoules.

(b) Amber colour glass container.

(c) Yellow-green colour glass container.

(d) Container stored in card-board package or wrapped in aluminium foil – this one acts as the control.

(5) Temperature

The rate constant (k) of drug degradation reaction varies with temperature according to Arrhenius equation.

$$k = A.e^{-E_a/R_T}$$

where, e = Exponential constant

       k = Rate constant

       A = Frequency factor

       E_a = Energy of activation

       R = Gas constant

       T = Absolute temperature

Procedure :

Buffer solutions were prepared and kept at different temperatures. Rate constants are determined at each temperature and the ln k value is plotted against (1/T).

Uses :

Shelf life of the drug may be calculated.

For example;

Time	Concentration of drug remaining
0	100%
$t_{10\%}$	90%

Therefore, $\ln C = \ln C_0 - k_1 t$

$$\ln \frac{C}{C_0} = - k_1 t$$

or, $\ln \dfrac{90}{100} = -k_1 t_{10\%}$ or, $t_{10\%} = \dfrac{\ln 0.90}{-k_1} = \dfrac{0.105}{k_1}$

Where, $t_{10\%}$ = time required for 10% decay to occur if the reaction follows 1st order kinetics

1.5.3 Solid State Stability

Objectives :

Identification of stable storage conditions for drug in the solid state and identification of drug excipients for compatibility.

Characteristics :

Solid state reactions are much slower than solution state, so the rate of appearance of decay product is measured (not the amount of drug remaining unchanged).

- To determine the mechanism of degradation, thin layer chromatography (TLC), fluorescence or UV / Visible spectroscopy may be required.
- To study polymorphic changes, DSC or IR-spectroscopy is required.
- In case of surface discolouration due to oxidation or reaction with excipients, surface reflectance equipment may be used.

Techniques for Solid State Stability Studies

- Solid State NMR Spectroscopy (SSNMR).
- Powder X-ray diffraction (PXRD).
- Fourier Transform IR (FTIR).
- Raman Spectroscopy.
- Differential Scanning Calorimetry (DSC).
- Thermo Gravimetric Analysis (TGA).
- Dynamic Vapour Sorption (DSV).
- Neclear Magnetic Resonance (NMR).

1.5.4 Chemical Characteristics

- Normally, pharmaceutical products should have shelf-life of 3 years. The potency should not fall below 95% under recommended storage conditions.
- By investigation of the intrinsic stability of drug, it is possible to advise on formulation approaches and indicate types of excipients, specific protective additives and packaging which are likely to improve the integrity of drug and product.
- Drug degradation occurs by 4 main processes:
  - Hydrolysis
  - Oxidation

o Photolysis

o Chelation

- When stability problems are identified, it is important to define pathway of degradation and initiate studies to stabilize compound with appropriate additives.

1. Hydrolytic Degradation

Hydrolysis is one of the most common degradation chemical reactions over wide range of pH. Hydrolysis is a solvolytic process in which drug reacts with water to yield breakdown products of different chemical compositions. Water as a solvent or as moisture in the air comes in contact with pharmaceutical dosage forms is responsible for degradation of most of the drugs. Drugs with functional groups such as esters, amides, lactones or lactams may be susceptible to hydrolytic degradation. It is probably the most commonly encountered mode of drug degradation because of the prevalence of such groups in medicinal agents and the ubiquitous nature of water. Water can also act as a vehicle for interactions or facilitate microbial growth.

For example, aspirin combines with water and hydrolyzed to salicylic acid and acetic acid.

Number of conditions catalyze the breakdown are given below:

o Presence of OH^-

o Presence of H_3O^+

o Presence of divalent metal ions

o Ionic hydrolysis

o Heat

o Light

o Solution polarity and ionic strength

o High drug concentration

Types of Hydrolysis

(1) Ester hydrolysis

For example, Cocaine has two ester bonds that hydrolyze to produce benzoylecgonine or ecgonine methyl ester.

Lactones or cyclic esters; pilocarpine, dalvastatin and warfarin undergoes ester hydrolysis due to ring opening.

(2) Amide hydrolysis

Acetaminophen, chloramphenicol, lincomycin, indomethacin and sulfacetamide, all of which are known to produce an amine and an acid through hydrolysis of their amide bonds.

Instability due to hydrolysis can be overcome by:

- By preparing insoluble salt or by preparing solid dosage form:

  Insoluble chlorthiazide is stable in neutral aqueous suspensions, but solution of sodium salt at relatively high pH decomposes rapidly.

- Replacement of water by other solvent reduces the hydrolysis rate:

  Acetylsalicylic acid suspensions containing high concentration of sorbitol improve stability.

  Ampicillin was shown to be more stable when concentration of alcohol was increased.

- Formation of molecular complex:

  Complexes with aromatic esters reduces hydrolytic rate of degradation.

2. Oxidation

Oxidation mechanisms for drug substances depend on the chemical structure of the drug and the presence of reactive oxygen species or other oxidants. Catechols such as methyldopa and epinephrine are readily oxidized to quinones.

Oxidation reaction depends upon several factors:

- Temperature
- Oxygen concentration in liquids
- Impurities
- Concentration of oxidizable components.

Minimization of Oxidative Degradation

- pH should be maintained if pH is critical as H^+/OH^- concentration is involved in degradation.
- Light accelerates degradation; store the product in dark container to maintain it in stable form.
- Photochemical changes causes formation of reactive compound or free radicals which is function to propagate decomposition. To minimize this, free radical sequestering agents are used as additives.
- Auto-oxidation i.e. in absence of light when fats and oils stored in presence of air become degraded so special temperature maintanance and storage condition should be provided.
- Heavy metal ion e.g. Cupric and ferric, accelerates oxidation of ascorbic acid and phenothiazines.
- Ascorbic acid is more stable in 90% propylene glycol or Syrup USP than in water because of lower oxygen concentration in these vehicles.
- Preparations sensitive to oxygen are stabilized by effectively removing oxygen or by addition of suitable additives.
- For example; Nitrogen flushing is done to remove oxygen.

3. Photodegradation

Photodegradation is the process by which light-sensitive drugs or excipient molecules are chemically degraded by light, room light or sunlight. The variation of degradation depends on the wavelength of light, because shorter wavelengths cause more damage than longer wavelengths. Before a photodegradation reaction can occur, the energy from light radiation must be absorbed by the molecules. Photodegradation of the chloroquine and primaquine gives the various products through different pathways.

Two way in which photodegradation can occur are: the light energy absorbed must be sufficient to achieve the activation energy or the light energy absorbed by molecules is passed onto other molecules which allow degradation to take place.

Photodecomposition : Electronic configuration of drug overlaps with spectrum of sunlight or any artificial light, and thereby energy is absorbed by electron and it goes to the excited state.

They are unstable and release the acquired energy and come to the ground state and decompose the drug.

Photosensitization means molecules or excipients which absorbs energy, but do not participate themselves directly in the reaction and pass the energy to other that will cause cellular damage by inducing radical formation.

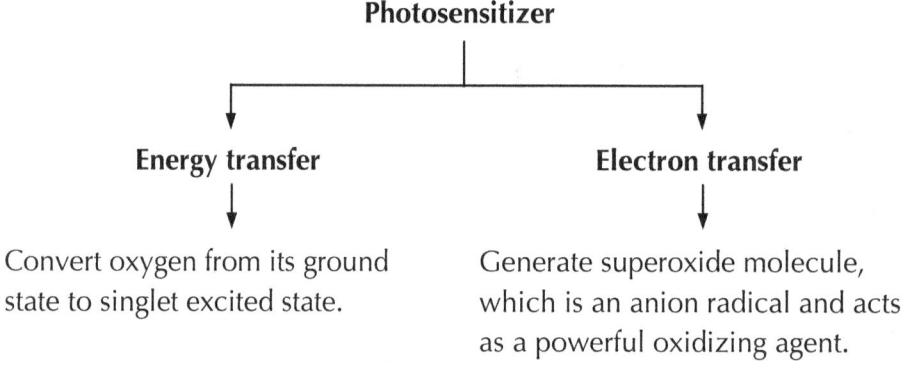

Prevention of Photodecomposition

    (1) Suitable packing.

    (2) Anti-oxidant.

    (3) Protection of drug from light.

    (4) Photostabilizer (light absorber).

    (5) Coating.

4. Racemization

Racemization refers to partial conversion of one enantiomer into another which can lead to different Pharmocokinetic properties (ADME) as well as different Pharmacological and toxicological effects.

Epinephrine is oxidized and undergoes racemization under strongly acidic conditions.

For example, L-epinephrine is 15 to 20 times more active than D-form, while activity of racemic mixture is just one half of the L-form.

5. Dehydration

Dehydration also affects the chemical properties. For example, Sugars such as glucose and lactose are known to undergo dehydration to form 5-(hydroxymethyl) furural.

6. Polymerization

It is a continuous reaction between molecules. More than one monomer reacts to form a polymer.

For example, Darkening of glucose solution is attributed to polymerization of breakdown product [5- (hydroxyl methyl) furfural].

7. Isomerization

Isomerisation is the process by which one molecule is transformed into another molecule which has exactly the same atoms, but the atoms are rearranged.

For example, A-B-C → B-A-C

Pilocarpine undergoes epimerization by base catalysis.

Tetracyclines such as rolitetracycline and ergotamine exhibit epimerization by acid catalysis.

Etoposide converts reversibly to picroetoposide, a cis-lactone, and then hydrolyzes to cis-hydroxy acid in the alkaline pH region.

Its occurrence is rare case.

8. Decarboxylation

Drug substances having a carboxylic acid group are sometimes susceptible to decarboxylation.

For example, 4-Aminosalicylic acid.

The reaction which follows 1st order kinetics is highly pH dependent and is catalysed by hydronium ions.

9. Enzyme Decomposition

'Chemical degradation due to enzymes induced by drug' is called enzyme decomposition. It can be prevented by using prodrug.

10. Elimination

In elimination reaction, some groups of the substance are eliminated.

For example, Trimelamol eliminates its hydroxymethyl group and forms formaldehyde. Levothyroxine eliminates iodine group.

1.6 GENERAL PRINCIPLES AND APPLICATIONS OF VARIOUS CHARACTERIZATION TECHNIQUES

Thermal method of analysis is group of techniques in which changes in physical or chemical properties of a substance are measured as a function of temperature. Thermal analysis and calorimetric methods have demonstrated a wide array of applications in the preformulation and formulation development. Thermal analytical methods can measure the weight loss on drying, enthalpy, glass transition temperature, gas evolution, electrical conductivity, optical characteristic, magnetic properties, changes in form; in dimension and viscoelastic properties of substance. Simultaneous Thermal Analysis (STA) generally refers to the simultaneous application of Thermogravimetric (TGA) and Differential scanning calorimetry (DSC). Various hyphenated techniques are utilized now-a-days: like, for better interpretations TG-DTA and TG-DSC while for identification of gas involved in thermal analysis TG-IR, TG-GC-MS and TG-MS are used. Apart from that, DSC-THERMOMICROSCOPY, DSC-FTIR, DSC-TEM and DSC-XRD were explored in this field.

1.6.1 General Principle Involved in Thermal Technique

(1) Thermogravimetry

TGA measures the amount and rate (velocity) of change in the mass of a sample as a function of temperature or time in a controlled atmosphere.

Thermogravimetric analysis (TGA) is an analytical technique used to determine a material's thermal stability and its fraction of volatile components by monitoring the weight change that occurs as a specimen is heated. The measurement is normally carried out in air or in an inert atmosphere, such as Helium or Argon, and the weight is recorded as a function of increasing temperature. Thermobalance Instrument is used for thermogravimetry having mainly three components like sample container, furnace assembly and balance (Fig. 1.16). Data should be recorded in thermogram.

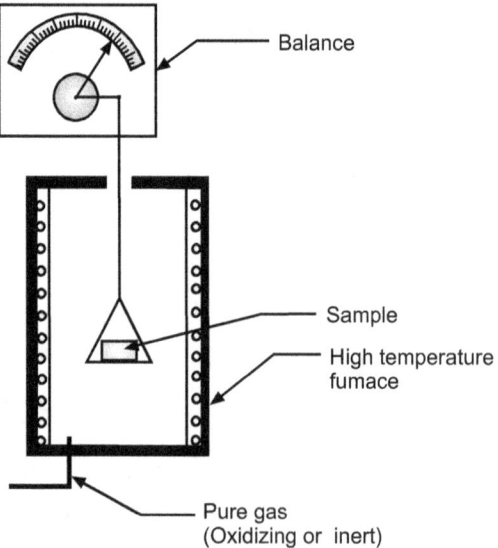

Fig. 1.16: Thermogravimetry instrument

2) Differential Thermal Analysis (DTA)

A technique in which the temperature difference between a substance and a reference material is measured as a function of temperature, while the substance and reference are subjected to a controlled temperature programme. The DTA uses a dynamic measuring principle. This instrument will measure endothermal and exothermal heat flow between the sample and reference material (enthalpy). In general, these heat flows are characteristic of chemical or physical changes of the sample. The test sample and an inert reference material are heated simultaneously in the same atmosphere. Endothermic sample reactions absorb heat and exhibit a lower sample temperature when compared to the reference material. Exothermic reactions produce heat and exhibit a higher sample temperature when compared to the reference material. (Temperature range is RT to 1600°C, the sensitivity range of the Delta T-signal is selectable between 50 - 1000 µV).

(3) Differential Scanning Calorimetry (DSC)

Differential scanning calorimetry is a thermoanalytical technique in which the difference in the amount of heat required to increase the temperature of a sample and reference are measured as a function of temperature. Both the sample and reference are maintained at very near or the same temperature throughout the experiment.

The basic principle underlying this technique is that, when the sample undergoes a physical transformation such as phase transitions, more (or less) heat will need to flow to it than the reference and to maintain both at the same temperature. Schematic diagram of DSC was depicted in below Fig. 1.17.

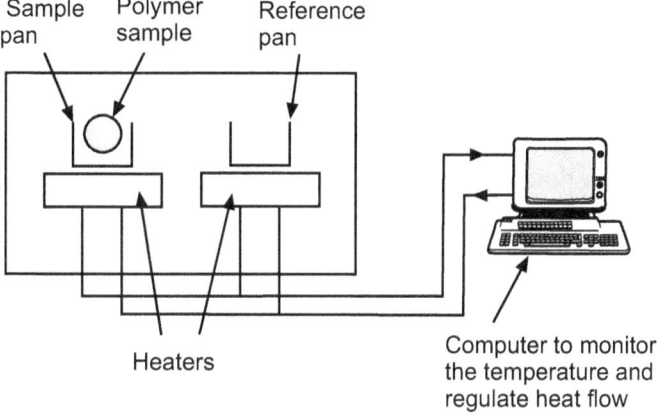

Fig. 1.17: Schematic diagram of DSC

(DSC) is widely used to characterise the *thermophysical properties* of polymers. DSC can measure important *thermoplastic properties* including:

- Melting temperature
- Heat of melting

- Per cent crystallinity
- Glass transition temperature
- Crystallization
- Plasticizers
- Polymer blends (presence, composition and compatibility)

(4) Thermo Mechanical Analysis (TMA)

A Technique in which changes in dimension of substance are measured as function of temperature. TMA is useful for the measurement of changes in shape (volume or dimension), penetration characteristic and viscoelastic properties of different material as a function of controlled temperature elevation.

(5) Thermomicroscopy

This technique essentially involves the observation of a sample through a microscope fitted with a stage that can be heated or cooled at a controlled rate.

By this method we can determine:

a) Investigation of the changes according to heat
b) Crystallization
c) Detection of melting point
d) Crystal transformation
e) Crystal pseudomorphs
f) Sublimation
g) Desolvation

(6) Microcalorimetry

Calorimetry is defined as "a measurement of the relationship of the change of temperature according to time during the process of program-controlled temperature".

Isothermal and adiabatic calorimetry are the different ways of measuring the heat of samples maintained at constant temperature. The output of the instrument is measured by the rate of heat exchange (dq / dt) as a function of time.

1.6.2 Innovation in Thermal Analysis

(1) Multielemental Scanning Thermal Analysis (MESTA)

Identification and characterization of solid samples has been relatively difficult due to the limited separation techniques available. MESTA is the method for the identification and characterization of solid substance, which is simple, rapid and sensitive alternative for routine examination of solid sample. Volatile components in the sample are carried to a high temperature combustion tube where the C, N, S are oxidized to their respective oxides and detected by the detector.

(2) Micro Thermal Analysis (MTA)

Micro thermal analysis is a relatively new technique that combines the resolution of an Atomic Force Microscope (AFM) with thermal conductivity measurement. MTA is useful for polymorph analysis. In this technique, thermal conductivity is measured as a function of temperature. MTA is used for identification of components in compressed tablet and analysis of tablet coats. It is also used for the characterization of drug-loaded polylactic acid microspheres, the analysis of tablet coats, and the identification of amorphous and crystalline regions in semicrystalline samples.

(3) Modulated DSC

It is also called as oscillating DSC. Advantage of modulated DSC over traditional DSC method includes increased sensitivity, increased resolution, separation of complex transitions and measurement of crystallinity.

(4) Dynamic Mechanical Analysis

Mechanical response (Dynamic Modulus and/or damping) of a sample is measured as it is deformed under oscillating load against temperature/time.

(5) Fast Scan DSC

Fast scan DSC distinguishes melting, melting degradation, sublimation and thermal stability of drug. It is useful for stability study where stability of drugs is based on a comparison of their thermal properties at various heating rates. It uses the characterization of polymorphs and polymorphic transitions, the solubility of drugs in polymers and characterization of dosage forms.

Advantages :

(i) Allows the separation of overlapping thermal events due to its sensititivity.

(ii) Reduce the drug degradation during scanning process.

(6) Optothermal Transient Emission Radiometry (OTTER)

In optothermal transient emission radiometry a sample material is irradiated (excited) with optical wavelength radiation in the form of short-duration pulses and the thermal emission transient is observed by means of a wide-band infrared detector. This technique is suitable for the *in situ* non-destructive study of surfaces, and has been used to measure the thermal diffusivity of polyester films and pigments. More recently OTTER has been extended to the *in vivo* study of water concentration gradients in the stratum corneum.

(7) Specific Heat Spectroscopy

Specific heat spectroscopy (SHS) is a non-adiabatic technique used to measure the frequency-dependent heat capacity of organic materials near the glass transition over a wide frequency range. Using the fact that molecular relaxation time increase rapidly as the glass transition is approached from $T > T_g$, the dynamics of the liquid phase can be studied.

(8) Thermally Stimulated Current (TSC)

Thermally stimulated current (TSC) spectroscopy is used to characterize the relaxation processes and structural transitions occurring in samples that have been polarized at a greater temperature.

(9) XRD

This technique allows measurement of both crystalline and non-crystalline materials. The analysis is non-destructive in nature and handle samples in the form of powders, solids and liquids. The X-ray diffraction of a single crystal is employed for the determination of the absolute chemical structure. Quantitative ratios of two polymorphs and their percentage of crystallinity may also be determined.

(10) Infrared Spectroscopy (IR)

IR spectroscopy is used for fingerprint identification of a drug molecule and the proof of its structure. IR absorption bands are characteristic of the functional group of a molecule as well as the structure configuration. The wavelength of the IR spectrum is 750 – 2500 μm. The sampling preparation techniques for IR determination are solution, drug dispersion in a KBr pellet, Nujol mulls, and direct determination by microscopic ATR preparation.

(11) Raman Spectroscopy

When a particle is irradiated at a certain frequency, radiation scattered by the molecule contains photons of the same frequency as the incident radiation and may contain photons (weak signal) with a changed or shifted frequency. Fourier Transform - Raman may be used for quantitative determination of polymorphs in a preformulation study.

(12) Mass Spectroscopy

Mass spectra are the result of detection of charged particles or ions separated according to their mass to charge (m/e) ratio after ionization and acceleration through magnetic field. Mass spectra gives information about molecular weight of substance and degraded or metabolic products.

Applications of Thermal Analysis in Preformulation :

1. Characterization of hydrates and solvates.
2. Study of various polymers.
3. Detection of impurity.
4. Study of various polymorphisms.
5. Prediction of stability of drug.
6. Degree of crystallinity.
7. Study of phase diagram.
8. Drug excipient compatibility study.
9. Study of complexation.

1.7 TRACES OF ORGANIC VOLATILE IMPURITIES (OVIs) AND THEIR REGULATORY LIMITS (RESIDUAL SOLVENTS)

Residual solvents in pharmaceuticals, commonly known as organic volatile impurities (OVIs), are chemicals that are either used or produced during the manufacture of active pharmaceutical ingredients (APIs), excipients and drug products.

Organic solvents play an essential role in drug-substance and excipient manufacture (e.g., reaction, separation and purification) and in drug-product formulation (e.g., granulation and coating). Some organic solvents are often used during the synthesis of active pharmaceutical ingredients and excipients or during the preparation of drug products to enhance the yield, increase solubility or aid crystallization.

These process solvents cannot be completely removed by manufacturing. Therefore, some residual solvents may remain in drug substance material.

Typically, the final purification step in many pharmaceutical drug-substance processes involves a crystallization step, and the crystals thus formed can entrap a finite amount of solvent from the mother liquor that may cause degradation of the drug, OVIs may also contaminate the products during packaging, storage in warehouses and/or during transportation.

1.7.1 Residual Solvents are Classified on the Basis of Risk Assessment

1. **Class 1 solvents (Solvents to be avoided):** Known human carcinogens, strongly suspected human carcinogens and environmental hazards. E.g. benzene and carbon tetra chloride.

2. **Class 2 solvents:** Most commonly used solvents e.g. methanol (3000 ppm), pyridine (200 ppm).

3. **Class 3 solvents:** These have permitted daily exposure of 50 mg or less, ICH guideline should be strictly followed for these solvents e.g. acetic acid butenol, etc.

1.7.2 Environmental Regulation of Organic Volatile Solvents

Several of the residual solvents frequently used in the production of pharmaceuticals are listed as toxic chemicals in Environmental Health Criteria (EHC) monographs and in the Integrated Risk Information System (IRIS). The objectives of such groups as the International Programme on Chemical Safety (IPCS), the U.S. Environmental Protection Agency (EPA), and the U.S. Food and Drug Administration (FDA) include the determination of acceptable exposure levels. The goal is protection of human health and maintenance of environmental integrity against the possible deleterious effects of chemicals resulting from long-term environmental exposure. The methods involved in the estimation of maximum safe exposure limits are usually based on long-term studies. When long-term study data are unavailable, shorter term study data can be used with modification of the approach such as use of larger safety factors. The approach described therein relates primarily to long-term or lifetime exposure of the general population in the ambient environment (i.e., ambient air, food, drinking water and other media).

1.7.3 Types of Impurity

There are two types of impurities :

(a) Impurities associated with APIs

- Organic impurities
- Inorganic impurities
- Residual solvents
- Other materials

(b) Impurities that are created during formulation and/or with aging or that are related to formulated forms.

Sources of Impurities :

- Starting materials
- Intermediates
- Final intermediates
- By-products
- Interaction products
- Related products
- Degradation products

1.7.4 Limit of Residual Solvents

Below Table 1.7 depicts examples of solvents with limit.

Table 1.7: Examples of residual solvents

Class 1		Class 2		Class 3	
Solvent	Limit (ppm)	Solvent	Limit (ppm)	Solvent	Limit (ppm)
Benzene	2	Acetonitrile	410	Acetic acid	0.5
Carbon tetrachloride	4	Chlorobenzene	360	Acetone	0.5
1,2-Dichloroethane	5	Chloroform	60	Anisole	0.5
1,1-Dichloroethene	8	Cyclohexane	3880	1-Butanol	0.5
1,1,1-Trichloroethane	1500	1,2-Dichloroethene	1870	2-Butanol	0.5

1.7.5 Regulations for Residual Solvents

The impurities in pharmaceuticals are regulated by Food and Drug Administration (FDA) and International Conference on Harmonization (ICH) guidelines.

Because many solvents produce a major risk to human health, national and international regulatory bodies such as the United States Food and Drug Administration (U.S. FDA), the United States Pharmacopoeia (USP), the European Pharmacopoeia (EP), and the International Conference on Harmonization (ICH) require analysis for residual solvents in pharmaceutical drug substances, excipients and final products. In herbals, residual solvents may results from their use as an extraction solvent in liquid extracts and tinctures or when added as a diluents to liquid pharmaceutical preparation.

A number of organic solvents such as methanol, ethanol, acetone, benzene, cyclohexane etc. are used for manufacturing herbal medicines, and can be detected as residues of such processing. These are known as residual solvents or organic volatile impurities. They should be controlled through good manufacturing practices (GMPs) and quality control. For the proper regulation, World Health Organization (WHO) has provided guidelines for accessing the quality of herbal medicines with respect to these residual solvents. The term "permitted daily exposure" (PDE) is proposed by WHO defining the maximum acceptable intake per day of residual solvent in pharmaceutical products.

Food and Drug Administration in 1997 published the ICH guidance for industry, Q3C "Impurities: Residual Solvents" (ICH Q3C) for the future control and regulation of residual solvents in herbals and other pharmaceuticals. These guidelines recommend the use of less toxic solvents, set criteria for analytical methods used to identify and quantify residual solvents as well as provide acceptable concentration limits for them. Exposure limits in guideline (ICH Q3C, 1997) are established by referring methodologies and toxicity data described in Environmental Health Criteria (EHC) and the Integrated Risk Information System (IRIS) monographs.

1.7.6 Pharmacopoeial Status

Different pharmacopoeias have different aspects in regards to residual solvents but most of the pharmacopoeia has adopted the ICH guidelines for their proper regulation. The following summarizes the status of different pharmacopoeia:

United States Pharmacopoeia (USP) :

In 1988, the United States Pharmacopoeia (USP) provided control limits and testing criteria for seven organic volatile impurities (OVIs) under official monograph no. 467 but before 1997, these guidelines were not fully implemented in the actual testing done in the pharmaceutical industry. In July 2007, USP has fully adopted ICH guidelines for residual solvents.

European Pharmacopoeia (EP) :

The European Pharmacopoeia (EP) has fully adopted ICH guidelines regarding residual solvents under title "Identification and control of residual solvents" in 1997. In EP two procedures (systems) A and B are presented. System A is preferred for identification while system B is employed for confirmation of identity.

Japanese Pharmacopoeia (JP) :

The JP volume XIV has adopted the ICH guidelines for residual solvent determination. JP defines residual solvents as 'those residual organic solvents in pharmaceuticals that should be tested using gas chromatography to comply with the limits specified in the ICH Guideline'.

Indian Pharmacopoeia (IP) :

Indian Pharmacopoeia is still lacking in control of residual solvents in herbals as well as other pharmaceuticals and does not give any information regarding their regulation, control or identification.

Analytical Techniques for Residual Solvent Determination :

Different analytical techniques are available for the estimation of residual solvents in herbals and pharmaceutical formulations including gravimetric analysis i.e. Loss on Drying (LOD), Thermo Gravimetric Analysis (TGA), Differential Thermal Analysis (DTA), Differential Scanning Calorimetry (DSC), Thermal Desorption (TD)-GC/MS, ChemSensor and some spectrometric and spectroscopic procedures. But Gas chromatography based test procedures are the most popular and are chemically specific for residual solvents.

1.7.7 Preformulation Studies of Biotechnological Derived Products and Reference Guidelines

Biotechnology means 'any technological application that uses biological systems, living organisms, or derivatives thereof, to make or modify products or processes for specific use'.

Establish the identity and physicochemical parameter of a new drug substance with its kinetic rate profile and compatibility with common excipients.

Proteins are typically primary, secondary, tertiary and quaternary and the order of stability is from primary to quaternary. Protein structure is determined by SDS-gel electrophoresis, HPLC, Amino acid analysis, N-terminal sequencing etc.

A protein's conformation describes its physical properties. It can be detected by X-ray diffraction, N-terminal sequencing, Spectroscopic techniques like UV, IR, Raman, Fluorescence. This technique provides a valuable idea about the protein's physical and chemical stability.

Examples of Biotechnological drugs: Hepatitis B virus, Human rabies vaccine (neural tissue), Diphtheria Tetanus vaccine, Live yellow fever, Oral polio virus, Plague, Small pox (freeze dried), Tetanus etc.

1.7.8 Chances of Impurities

Process Related and Product Related

- Process related impurities include cell-culture media, host cell proteins, DNA, chromatographic media, solvents and buffer components.

- Product related impurities are molecular variants which are different from the desired product. The methods used to detect impurities are HPLC, Mass spectrometry, Amino acid analysis, N-terminal sequencing etc.

1.7.9 Physical Characterization of Biotechnology Product

- **Crystallinity:** Many peptides exhibit in an amorphous state than crystalline. Crystallinity is detected by X-ray Diffraction pattern, Solid state NMR, Differential scanning calorimetry (DSC), Thermo gravimetric analysis (TGA).
- **Hygroscopicity:** Humid environment affect the stability of the hygroscopic products. The estimation of water content is done by the HPLC method.
- **Molecular weight:** The molecular size of peptides and proteins are 1 to 3 time larger than that of conventional drug molecules and it is a major factor limiting their diffusion across the biological membranes, Larger the size, lower the permeation across biological membranes. Molecular size also restricts diffusion of the biopharmaceutical across the polymeric barriers, used in the fabrication of proteins and peptides delivery systems.
- **Thermal denaturation:** Most proteins can be reversibly denatured with an increase in temperature and continued increase can result in irreversible denaturation to determine a particular limit of thermal denaturation temperature to set the acceptable storage criteria for biopharmaceuticals.

1.7.10 Physical Instability

- **Denaturation:** The loss of the globular structure of proteins is referred to as denaturation. Factors affecting are - Temperature, pH, Ionic strength, addition of organic solutes or organic solvents. It can be reversible or irreversible. Denaturation, results in, decreasing solubility, loss of biological activity, loss of crystallizing ability, changes in molecular shape and susceptible to enzymatic hydrolysis.
- **Surface adsorption:** Peptides and proteins are amphiphilic on adsorption, they form van der walls, hydrophobic and ion pair bonds which may result in further denaturation of the molecules. Biological activity is changed or lost due to adsorption. This also causes a reduction in the concentration of drug available.
- **Aggregation and precipitation:** Aggregation on a macroscopic scale resulting in precipitation. This phenomenon is due to interfacial adsorption. It is dependent on the relative hydrophilicity or hydrophobicity of the surfaces. Agitation increases aggregation and precipitation.

1.7.11 Chemical Instability

Hydrolysis

- **Deamidation:** In deamidation, the hydrolysis of side chain amide linkage of an amino acid residues occurs. Phosphate buffers increase the deamidation rates in protein. The rate of deamidation is favoured by extremes of pH and elevated temperature.

- **Proteolysis:** It is hydrolysis of one or more peptide bonds in the protein pH and high temperatures affect this process. Resistance to proteolysis seems to be dependent upon higher levels of protein structure. Denaturation renders protein susceptible to proteolytic degradation. Use of the specific protease inhibitor prevents proteolysis but such inhibitors are avoided due to their toxicity.

- **Oxidation:** The side-chain of amino acid residues in the proteins are susceptible to oxidation. pH, temperature, metal ions, and buffer content affect the rates of oxidation. Oxidation is minimized by replacing the air and addition of antioxidants.

- **Racemization:** It convert protein to non-metabolizable forms of amino acids and reduces the biological activity. The rate of racemization depends on particular amino acids and are influenced by temperature, pH, ionic strength and meta ion chelation Aspartic acid and serine residues are more prone to racemization.

1.7.12 Methods to Improve Stability

1. Chemical modification of protein like modification of molecules site.
2. Appropriate choice of conditions.
3. Addition of additives.
4. By using appropriate method.

1.7.13 Guidelines on the Stability of the Biotechnological Product

- ICH guidelines for biotechnological product were finalised in November 1995. This document augments the stability guideline and deals with the particular aspects of stability test procedures needed to take account of the special characteristics of products in which the active components are typically proteins and/or polypeptides.

- It is necessary to give specific guidance for biotechnological drug products i.e. for maintenance of biological activities dependent on non-covalent, covalent interactions and for products particularly sensitive to environmental factors such as temperature, oxidation, light, ionic content, shear, and most important stringent conditions for storage.

- ICH Q5C intends to give guidance to applicants regarding the type of stability studies to be provided in support of marketing authorization applications for biological medicinal products.

1.7.14 Stability Data for Drug Substance

There are at least 3 batches, representative of the manufacturing scale of production.

"Representative" data:

- Representative of the quality of batches used in pre-clinical and clinical studies.

- Representative of manufacturing process and storage conditions.
- Representative of containers.

Stability data for Drug Substance

If shelf life claimed:

- > 6 months: minimum 6 months data at the time of submission.
- < 6 months: submission data discussed on a case-by-case basis.

Stability data for Drug Product (DP)

At least 3 batches of the final container product, representative of manufacture scale.

Drug product batches should be derived from different batches of Drug substance.

If shelf life claimed:

- > 6 months: minimum 6 months data at the time of submission.
- < 6 months: submission data discussed on a case-by-case basis.

1.7.15 Storage Conditions

Temperature

Since most finished biotechnological/biological products need precisely defined storage temperatures, the storage conditions for the real-time/real-temperature stability studies may be confined to the proposed storage temperature.

Humidity

Biotechnological/biological products are generally distributed in containers protecting them against humidity. Therefore, where it can be demonstrated that the proposed containers (and conditions of storage) afford sufficient protection against high and low humidity, stability tests at different relative humidities can usually be omitted. Where humidity-protecting containers are not used, appropriate stability data should be provided.

Light

It should consult the appropriate regulatory authorities on a case-by-case basis to determine guidance for testing of light.

Container/Closure

Changes in the quality of the product may occur due to the interactions between the formulated biotechnological/biological product and container/closure. Stability studies should include samples maintained in the inverted or horizontal position (i.e., in contact with the closure), as well as in the upright position, to determine the effects of the closure on product quality. Data should be supplied for all different container/closure combinations that will be marketed. In addition to the standard data necessary for a conventional single-use vial, the applicant should demonstrate that the closure used with a multiple-dose vial is capable of withstanding the conditions of repeated insertions and withdrawals so that the product retains its full potency, purity and quality for the maximum period specified in the instructions-for-use on containers, packages, and/or package inserts. Such labelling should be in accordance with relevant national/regional requirements.

1.7.16 Labelling

For most biotechnological/biological drug substances and drug products, precisely defined storage temperatures are recommended. Specific recommendations should be stated, particularly for drug substances and drug products that cannot tolerate freezing. Wherever required, recommendations for protection against light and/or humidity, should appear on containers, packages, and/or package inserts. Such labelling should be in accordance with the relevant national and regional requirements.

Chapter 2

SOLUBILIZATION AND SOLUBILIZED SYSTEM

2.1 INTRODUCTION

Solubilization of poorly soluble drugs is a frequently encountered challenge in screening studies of new chemical entities as well as in formulation design and development. Solubility is defined as 'the number of millilitres of solvent in which 1 gm of solute will dissolve'.

Saturated solution is 'the solution in which the solvent is in equilibrium with the solid phase (solute)'.

Unsaturated solution is 'the solution containing the dissolved solute in a concentration below that necessary for complete saturation at a definite temperature'.

A supersaturated solution is 'the solution that contains more of the dissolved solute than it would normally contain at a definite temperature'.

2.2 AIM OF STUDYING SOLUBILITY

Currently in the market, only 8% of new drug candidates have both high solubility and permeability, so it is necessary to do proper study for improving solubility such as

1. The best solvent medium for a drug or combination of drugs.
2. Help in overcoming certain difficulties that arises in the preparation of pharmaceutical solution.
3. And furthermore, can serve as a standard test of purity.

2.3 TYPES OF SOLUBILITY

1. Solubility of gases in liquids
2. Solubility of liquids in liquids
3. Solubility of solids in liquids

2.3.1 Solubility of Gases in Liquids

The solubility of a gas in a liquid depends on temperature, the partial pressure of the gas over the liquid, the nature of the solvent and the nature of the gas. The most common solvent is water.

Carbonated beverages is an example based on Henry's law used in everyday life.

The dissolved carbon dioxide stays in solution in a closed bottle or where the partial pressure of carbon dioxide was set at a high value during bottling. When the bottle is opened, the partial pressure of CO_2 is much lower and the dissolved carbon dioxide will gradually escape from the bottle. When the new low partial pressure equilibrium is established, the soda will be "flat". This loss of dissolved carbon dioxide will happen faster for warm soda than for cold.

Gas solubility is always limited by the equilibrium between the gas and a saturated solution of the gas. The dissolved gas will always follow Henry's law.

The concentration of dissolved gas depends on the partial pressure of the gas. The partial pressure controls the number of gas molecule collisions with the surface of the solution. If the partial pressure is doubled, the number of collisions with the surface will double. The increased number of collisions produce more dissolved gas. Pharmaceutical solution of gases includes hydrochloric acid, ammonia water and effervescent preparation containing carbon dioxide (Aerosol) that are dissolved and maintained in solution under positive pressure.

The solubility of such system depends primarily on the pressure, temperature, presence of salts and chemical reaction (salting out).

- **Effect of pressure:** As the pressure increases, the solubility of gases also increases. So the effect of pressure is important while considering the solubility of dissolved gases in Aerosolized products.
- **Effect of temperature:** As the temperature increases, the solubility of most of the gases decreases.

2.3.2 Solubility of Liquids in Liquids

Frequently two or more liquids are mixed together in the preparation of pharmaceutical solutions.

For example, alcohol is added to water to form hydroalcohlic solutions of various concentrations. Liquid-liquid systems can be divided into two categories according to the solubility (a) Complete miscibility and (b) Partial miscibility.

(a) Complete miscibility : Polar and semipolar solvents such as water and alcohol are said to be completely miscible as they can be mixed in any proportion.

(b) Partial miscibility : Solubilities of partially miscible liquids are influenced by temperature. In a system such as phenol and water, mutual solubilities of the two phases increase with temperature until they can reach the critical solution temperature.

2.3.3 Solubility of Solids in Liquids

In interfacial reaction that results in liberation of solute molecule from the solid phase, the solution in contact with solid will become saturated (Cs).

The solute molecules migrate through the boundary layers surrounding the crystal to the bulk of solution, at which concentration is (C). Boundary layer is nearly static and surrounds all wetted surface of the solid. Mass transfer is slowly through the boundary layer to the bulk of solution.

The rate of dissolution obeys Fick's law

$$\frac{dC}{dt} = K \, \Delta C$$

Where, K is the dissolution rate constant.

ΔC is the difference in concentration of solution at the solid surface (Cs) and the bulk solution (C).

For e.g., phenol is weakly acidic and only slightly soluble in water, but is quite soluble in dilute NaOH solution.

$$C_6H_5OH + NaOH \rightarrow C_6H_5O^- + Na^+ + H_2O$$

Most of these weak electrolytes are not soluble in water but are soluble in dilute acids. Addition of an alkali to a salt solution of these compounds precipitates the free base from solution, if solubility of the base in water is low.

2.4 PROCESS OF SOLUBILIZATION

The process of solubilization involves the breaking of intermolecular or inter-ionic bonds in the solute, the separation of the molecules of the solvent to provide space in the solvent for the solute and interaction between the solvent and the solute molecule or ion. Solubilization process into three steps. (Fig. 2.1).

Step 1: Holes are formed in the solvent.

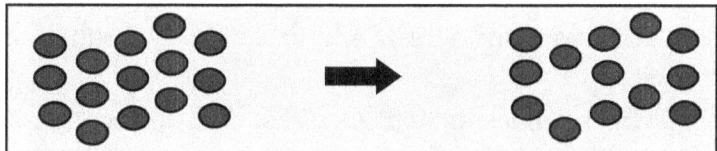

Step 2: Molecules of the solid breaks away from the bulk.

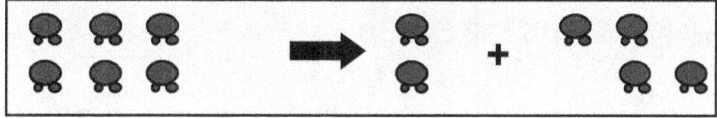

Step 3: The free solid molecules are integrated into the hole in the solvent.

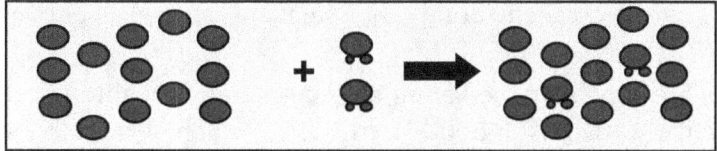

Fig. 2.1: Process of solubilization

For gases, solubility decreases as temperature increases. The physical reason for this is, when most of the gases dissolve in solution, the process is exothermic. This means that, heat is released as the gas dissolves. This is very similar to the reason that vapour pressure increases with temperature. Increased temperature causes an increase in kinetic energy. The higher kinetic energy causes more motion in the gas molecules which break intermolecular bonds and escape from solution. Below we discuss some case studies related to solubility.

CASE I: Decrease in solubility with temperature:

If the heat given in the dissolving process is greater than the heat required to break apart the solid, the net dissolving reaction is exothermic. The addition of more heat inhibits the dissolving reaction, since excess heat is already being produced by the reaction.

CASE II: Increase in solubility with temperature:

If the heat given in the dissolving process is less than the heat required to break apart the solid, the net dissolving reaction is endothermic. The addition of more heat facilitates the dissolving reaction by providing energy to break bonds in the solid. This is the most common situation where an increase in temperature produces an increase in solubility for solids.

The effect of temperature on solubility can be explained on the basis of **Le Chatelier's Principle**.

Le Chatelier's Principle states that, 'if a stress (for example, heat, pressure, concentration of one reactant) is applied to an equilibrium, the system will adjust, if possible, to minimize the effect of the stress'. This principle is of value in predicting how much a system will respond to a change in external conditions. Consider the case, where the solubility process is endothermic (heat added). An increase in temperature puts a stress on the equilibrium condition and stress is relieved because the dissolving process consumes some of the heat.

Therefore, the solubility (concentration) increases with an increase in temperature. If the process is exothermic (heat given off).

2.5 MECHANISM OF SOLUBILIZATION

Solubilization mainly depends on solvents.

Polar Solvents

1. Polar solvents reduce the force of attraction between oppositely charged ions in crystals due to their high dielectric constant.
2. Polar solvents break covalent bonds of potentially strong electrolytes by acid base reactions.
3. Polar solvents are capable of solvating molecules and ions through dipole interaction forces, particularly hydrogen-bond formation, which leads to the solubility of compound.

Non-polar Solvents

The non-polar solvents would not obey the above mechanism of solubilization, so they are unable to dissolve the ionic and polar solutes. Non-polar solvents can dissolve the non-polar solute with similar internal pressure through induced dipole interactions.

Solubilization takes place by consideration of,

1. Polarity,
2. Dielectric constant,
3. Association,
4. Salvation,
5. Internal pressure,
6. Acid-base reaction.

2.6 FACTORS AFFECTING SOLUBILITY

Solubility mainly depends on the nature and composition of solvent medium. Factors, which affects the solubility are :

1. Temperature
2. pH
3. Particle size
4. Crystal structure
5. Molecular structure
6. Pressure
7. Nature of solute and solvent
8. Molecular size
9. Polarity
10. Polymorphs
11. Rate of solution

1. Temperature

As the temperature increases, the solution process absorbs energy and the solubility increases. But if the solution process releases energy then the solubility will decrease with increasing temperature. Solubility of gas decreases as the temperature increases.

- Generally, as the temperature increases the solubility increases.
- For effect of temperature on solubility consider two criteria: endothermic reactions and exothermic reactions.

Endothermic reactions:

- During dissolution process, the energy (heat) is absorbed.
- Thus, rise in temperature will lead to increase in solubility of a solid in the solution, with a positive heat of solution.
- For e.g., solubility of potassium nitrate increases with increase in temperature.

Exothermic reactions:

- During dissolution process, the energy (heat) is evolved.
- Thus, rise in temperature will lead to decrease solubility of a solid in the solution with a negative heat of solution.
- For e.g., solubility of calcium oxide decreases with increase in temperature.

Non-polar compounds:

- The forces, holding the particles together are small, and any interaction between solute and solvent is small.
- Heat does not produce any effects on non-polar substances.

Polar compounds:

- In polar substances, it takes energy to separate the molecule from surrounding molecules if energy is supplied in the form of heat.
- Also there is the possibility of interaction between the solute and solvent with formation of a dipole-dipole type bond, this interaction will tend to give out heat.

2. pH

pH effect is considered for non-ionizable and ionizable substances.

Non-ionizable substances:

- There is little effect of pH on non-ionizable substances.
- Solubility can be increased by change of dipole moment.

Ionizable substances:

- pH of ionizable substances depends on HEDERSON-HESSELBALCH equation.

    For Acidic drug:

    $$pH = pKa + \log \frac{(S - S_0)}{S_0}$$

    For basic drug:

    $$pH = pKa + \log \frac{S_0}{(S - S_0)}$$

    Where,

    S = Overall solubility of substance

    S_0 = Solubility of unionized species

    $S - S_0$ = Solubility of ionized species

pH of a substance is related to its pKa and the concentration of the ionized and unionized forms of the substance.

3. Particle Size

The size of the solid particle influences the solubility because as a particle becomes smaller, the surface area to volume ratio of the particle increases. The larger surface area allows a greater interaction with the solvent.

As the particle size decreases, solubility increases due to increase in the surface area.

But very small particle size will decrease solubility due to formation of agglomerates. The effect of particle size on solubility can be described as,

$$\log\left(\frac{S}{S_0}\right) = \frac{2\gamma M}{2.303RT\rho r}$$

Where,

S = Solubility of small particle of radius r   M = Molecular weight

S_0 = Normal solubility   R = Gas constant

γ = Surface tension ρ = Density

4. Crystal Structure

Amorphous form of drugs is more soluble than crystalline form.

Solvates are more soluble than anhydrous and hydrate forms.

Crystal structure can have direct effect on the solubility of a solid, in particular solvent. Force of attraction between solute and solvent molecule must overcome the attractive force holding the solid intact and solvent aggregate. The solvation free energy released upon dissolution must exceed the lattice free energy.

5. Molecular Structure

Change in the molecular structure highly affects solubility of compound.

Non-polar liquids like benzene dissolve readily in any non-polar liquids but not readily in polar liquids. Same way polar liquid like $HO-CH_2-CH_2-OH$ dissolve readily in polar liquid rather than non-polar liquids.

For example;

1. Mixing of hydrophilic group: Hydrophilic substance may improve the solubility. If benzene is dissolved into phenol, there is increase in solubility of benzene.

2. Conversion into salt form also improve the solubility.

3. Esterification

   Chloramphenicol is converted into chloramphenicol palmitate for taste masking as well as to improve solubility.

6. Pressure

For solid and liquid solutes, changes in pressure have practically no effect on solubility but have strong effect for gaseous solutes. In gaseous solutes, an increase in pressure, increases solubility and a decreases in pressure, decreases the solubility.

7. Nature of the Solute and Solvent

Nature of the solute and solvent also affect on solubility. For example; In 100 ml water at room temperature, only 1 gram of lead chloride, while 200 gram of zinc chloride can be dissolved. The great difference in the solubility's of these two substances is due to the differences in their natures.

8. Molecular Size

The solubility of the substance is decreased when molecules have higher molecular weight and higher molecular size. Molecules are more difficult to surround with solvent molecules in order to solvate the substance. In the case of organic compounds, the amount of carbon branching will increase the solubility since more branching will reduce the size (or volume) of the molecule and make it easier to solvate the molecules with solvent.

9. Polarity

Polarity of the solute and solvent molecules will affect the solubility. Generally, 'like dissolves like' phenomena was followed. Means non-polar solute molecules will dissolve in non-polar solvents and polar solute molecules will dissolve in polar solvents. The polar solute molecules have a positive and a negative end to the molecule. If the solvent molecule is also polar then positive ends of solvent molecules will attract negative ends of solute molecules. It is a type of intermolecular force which is known as *dipole-dipole interaction*. The other forces called *london dispersion forces,* the positive nuclei of the atoms of solute molecule will attract to the negative electrons of the atoms of a solvent molecule.

10. Polymorphs

Polymorphs can vary in melting point. Since the melting point of the solid is related to solubility, so polymorphs will have different solubilities. Generally, the range of solubility differences between different polymorphs is only 2-3 folds due to relatively small differences in free energy.

11. Rate of Solution

The rate of solution is defined as how much amount of drug fast substances dissolve in solvents[1]. Various factors affecting rate of solution are discussed below:

   (a) **Size of the particles :** Breaking a solute into smaller pieces increases its surface area. When the total surface area of the solute particle is increased; the solute dissolves more rapidly because the action takes place only at the surface of each particle and hence increases its rate of solution.

   (b) **Temperature :** For liquid and solid solutes, increase in the temperature not only increase the solubility but also increase the rate of solubility. For the gases, reverse phenomenon occurs.

   (c) **Stirring :** With liquid and solid solutes, stirring brings fresh portions of the solvent in contact with the solute, thereby increasing the rate of solution.

2.7 SOLUBILIZATION TECHNIQUES

There are various techniques available to improve the solubility of poorly soluble drugs. Some of the approaches to improve the solubility are:

1. pH Adjustment

By applying a pH change poorly water soluble drugs with parts of the molecule that can be protonated (base) or deprotonated (acid) may potentially be dissolved in water. pH adjustment principle can be used for both oral and parenteral administration. Upon intravenous administration, the poorly soluble drug may be precipitated because blood is a strong buffer with pH between 7.2 - 7.4. To assess the suitability of the approach, the buffer capacity and tolerability of the selected pH are important to consider. In the stomach, the pH is around 1 to 2 and in the duodenum the pH is between 5 - 7.5, so upon oral administration the degree of solubility is also likely be influenced as the drug passes through the intestine. The ionized form of drug is favoured over unionized form to be solubilized in the aqueous solvent.

As per pH-partition hypothesis and Handerson-Hesselbatch equation, ionization of a compound is dependent on the pH of media and pKa of drug.

For weakly acidic drug : - High ph $\rightarrow$ Ionized form $\rightarrow$ More solubility

For weakly basic drug : - Low ph $\rightarrow$ Ionized form $\rightarrow$ More solubility.

Advantages of pH adjustment:

(i) Simple to formulate and analyze.

(ii) Simple to produce and fast track.

(iii) Uses small quantities of compound.

Disadvantages of pH adjustment:

(i) Risk of precipitation upon dilution with aqueous media having a pH at which the compound is less soluble. Intravenously this may lead thrombolitis, orally it may cause variability in dose.

(ii) As with all solubilized and dissolved systems, dissolved drug in an aqueous environment is frequently chemically less stable compared to formulation of crystalline solid.

2. Microemulsion

A microemulsion is an optically clear pre-concentrate, isotropic, thermodynamically stable transparent (or translucent) system, containing a mixture of oil, hydrophilic surfactant and hydrophilic solvent which dissolves a poorly water soluble drug. Upon contact with water, the formulations spontaneously disperse (or 'self emulsifies') to form a very clear emulsion of exceedingly small and uniform oil droplets containing the solubilized poorly soluble drug. Microemulsions have been employed to increase the solubility of many drugs that are practically insoluble in water, along with incorporation of proteins for oral, parenteral, as well as percutaneous/transdermal use. These homogeneous systems, which can be prepared over a wide range of surfactant concentration and oil to water ratio, are all fluids of low viscosity. Surfactants, surfactant mixtures and cosurfactants in microemulsions play an important role in improving the solubility of drugs formulated as microemulsions. An anhydrous system of microemulsions is that self microemulsifying drug delivery system (SMEDDS) or microemulsion pre-concentrate. It is composed of oil, surfactant and cosurfactant and has the ability to form o/w microemulsion when dispersed in aqueous phase under gentle agitation. The agitation required for the self-emulsification comes from stomach and intestinal motility. The surfactants like polyoxyethylene, Brij 35, sorbitan monooleate (Span 80), sodium dodecyl sulphate, lecithin (phosphatidylcholine) etc. are commonly used. Lecithin is very popular because it exhibits excellent biocompatibility. Due to the liquid nature of the product, most self-emulsifying systems are limited to administration in lipid-filled soft or hard-shelled gelatin capsules. Interaction between the capsule shell and the emulsion should be considered so as to prevent the hygroscopic contents from dehydrating or migrating into the capsule shell. Combinations of ionic and non-ionic surfactants are also found to be effective. Microemulsion preconcentrates remain optically clear after dilution and usually contain a higher amount of water soluble surfactant and a higher content of a hydrophilic solvent compared to macroemulsion pre-concentrates. Solubilization using microemulsion pre-concentrates is suited to poorly soluble lipophilic compounds that have high solubility in the oil and surfactant mixtures.

Advantages of microemulsion:

(i) Easy to manufacture.

Disadvantages of microemulsion:

The major disadvantages of microemulsions are :

(1) High concentration of surfactant/co-surfactant, making them unsuitable for IV administration. Dilution of microemulsions below the critical micelle concentration of the surfactants could cause precipitation of the drug; however, the fine particle size of the resulting precipitate would still enhance absorption.

(2) The precipitation tendency of the drug on dilution may be higher due to the dilution effect of the hydrophilic solvent.

(3) The tolerability of formulations with high levels of synthetic surfactants may be poor in cases where long term chronic administration is intended.

(4) Formulations containing several components become more challenging to validate.

3. Physicochemical Modification of Poorly Soluble Drug for Solubility Enhancement

(a) Effect of pH and Salt formation on solubilizing poorly soluble drugs:

Changing the pH of the system may be simplest and most effective means of increasing aqueous solubility of the ionizable solutes. A drug that can be efficiently solubilized by pH control should be either weak acid with a low pKa or a weak base with a high pKa. For non-ionizable solutes, solubility can be improved by changing the dielectric constant by the use of solvents rather than the pH of the solvent. Salt formation is the most common and effective method of increasing solubility and dissolution rates of acidic and basic drugs.

(b) Polymorphism

Polymorphism is the ability of an element or compound to crystallize in more than one crystalline form. Different polymorphs of drugs are chemically identical, but they exhibit different physicochemical properties including solubility, melting point, density, texture, stability etc. Generally, the anhydrous form of a drug has greater solubility than the hydrates. This is because the hydrates are already in interaction with water and therefore have less energy for crystal breakup in comparison to the anhydrates (i.e. thermodynamically higher energy state) for further interaction with water. On the other hand, the organic (non-aqueous) solvates have greater solubility than the non-solvates. Some drugs can exist in amorphous form (i.e. having no internal crystal structure). Such drugs represent the highest energy state and can be considered as supercooled liquids. They have greater aqueous solubility than the crystalline forms because they require a less energy to transfer a molecule into solvent. Thus, the order for dissolution of different solid forms of drug is,

Amorphous > Metastable polymorph > Stable polymorph.

(c) Micronization

Micronization increases the dissolution rate of drugs through increased surface area. Micronization of drugs is done by milling techniques using jet mill, rotor stator colloid mills etc. Micronization is not suitable for drugs having a high dose number because it does not change the saturation solubility of the drug.

4. Particle Size Reduction

The bioavailability of poorly soluble drugs is often intrinsically related to drug particle size. By reducing particle size, the increased surface area may improve the dissolution properties of the drug to allow a wider range of formulation approaches and delivery technologies.

The larger surface area allows a greater interaction with the solvent which cause increase in solubility.

Conventional methods of particle size reduction, such as comminution and spray drying, rely upon mechanical stress to disaggregate the active compound. The mechanical forces inherent to comminution, such as milling and grinding, often impart significant amounts of physical stress upon the drug product which may induce degradation. Due to the thermal stress, in spray drying the thermosensitive or unstable active compounds may be degrade. Also, this traditional method is often incapable of reducing the particle size of nearly insoluble drugs (<0.1 mg/ml).

Nowadays, particle size reduction can be achieved by micronization and nanosuspension. Each technique utilizes different equipments for reduction of the particle size. In micronization, the solubility of drug is often intrinsically related to drug particle size. By reducing the particle size, the increased surface area improves the dissolution properties of the drug. These processes were applied to griseofulvin, progesterone, spironolactone and diosmin, fenofibrate. For each drug, micronization improves their absorption, and consequently their bioavailability and clinical efficacy.

Nanosuspension:

Nanosuspension is another technique which is sub-micron colloidal dispersion of pure particles of drug, which are stabilised by surfactants. The nanosuspension approach has been employed for drugs including tarazepide, atovaquone, amphotericin B, paclitaxel and bupravaquon.

Advantages of Nanosuspension:

(i) Increased dissolution rate due to larger surface area exposed,

(ii) Absence of Ostwald ripening due to the uniform and narrow particle size range obtained, which eliminates the concentration gradient factor.

Liquid forms can be rapidly developed for early stage testing (pre-clinical) that can be converted into solids for later clinical development. Typically, low excipient to drug ratio is required. Formulations are generally well tolerated provided that strong surfactants are not required for stabilisation. Nanosuspensions are produced by homogenization and wet milling process.

Recrystallization of poorly soluble materials using liquid solvents and antisolvents has also been employed successfully to reduce particle size.

Disadvantages of Nanosuspension:

(1) Due to the high surface charge on discrete small particles, there is a strong tendency for particle agglomeration.

(2) Developing a solid dosage form with a high pay load without encouraging agglomeration may be technically challenging.

(3) Technically, development of sterile intravenous formulations is even more challenging.

Ball Milled Products:

This process is widely used in nonpharmaceutical applications particularly in cosmetics to obtain ultrafine particles for sun block. Examples of pharmaceutical products include rapamycin (Rapamune®, 1 mg and 2 mg tablets, Wyeth).

Homogenization:

Homogenization involves the forcing of the suspension under pressure through a valve having a narrow aperture. This causes bubbles of water to form which collapses as they come out of valves. This mechanism breaks the particles. The instrument can be operated at pressures varying from 100 to 1500 bars. In some instruments, a maximum pressure of 2000 bars can be reached. Drugs such as carbazepine, bupravaquone, aphidicolin, cyclosporin, nimodipine paclitaxil were also prepared by high pressure homoginizer.

Other Techniques for Reduction of the Particle size:

Other Techniques for Reduction of the Particle size:

(i) Sonocrystallization

(ii) Supercritical fluid process (SCF)

(i) Sonocrystallization:

It is the novel approach for particle size reduction on the basis of crystallization by using ultrasound. Sonocrystallization utilizes ultrasound power characterised by a frequency range of 20 - 100 kHz for inducing crystallization.

(ii) Supercritical fluid process (SCF):

Supercritical fluids are fluids whose temperature and pressure are greater than its critical temperature (T_c) and critical pressure (T_p). The most widely employed methods of SCF process are: Rapid Expansion of Supercritical Solutions (RESS), Gas Antisolvents Recrystallization (GAR) , Both are employed by the pharmaceutical industry using carbon dioxide as the SCF due to its favourable characteristics like, low critical temperature $(T_c = 31.1°C)$ and pressure $(P_c = 73.8 \text{ bar})$.

5. Drug Dispersion in Carriers for Solubility Enhancement

Solid solution: A solid solution is a binary system comprising of a solid solute molecularly dispersed in a solid solvent. Since the two compartments crystallize together in a homogeneous one phase system, solid solutions are also called as *molecular dispersion* or *mixed crystals*. Because of reduction in particle size of molecule solid solutions show greater aqueous solubility and faster dissolution. They are generally prepared by fusion method whereby physical mixture of solute and solvent are melted together followed by rapid solidification. Griseofulvin in solid solution form dissolves 6 to 7 times faster than pure griseofulvin.

Solid dispersion: Solid dispersion (SD) technique has been widely used to improve the dissolution rate, solubility and oral absorption of poorly water-soluble drugs. The term 'solid dispersions' is defined as the dispersion of one or more active ingredients in an inert carrier in a solid state, frequently prepared by the melting (fusion) method, solvent method, or fusion solvent-method".

6. Co-solvency

The solubility of a poorly water soluble drug can be increased frequently by the addition of a water miscible solvent in which the drug has good solubility known as cosolvents. Co-solvents are mixtures of water and one or more water miscible solvents used to create a solution with enhanced solubility for poorly soluble compounds. Cosolvency has been utilised in different formulations including solids and liquids.

Examples of solvents used in co-solvent mixtures are PEG 300, propylene glycol or ethanol. Various concentrations (5 - 40%) of the solid binary systems with polyethylene glycol 6000 were employed to increase solubility and dissolution of poorly soluble drug.

Co-solvent formulations of poorly soluble drugs can be administered orally and parenterally. Parenteral formulations may require the addition of water or a dilution step with an aqueous media to lower the solvent concentration prior to administration.

Cosolvency techniques have also found use in spray freezing of liquid like in danazol with polyvinyl alcohol, poloxamer 407, and polyvinylpyrrolidone K-15 in a micronized powder formulation. Poorly soluble compounds which are lipophilic or highly crystalline that have a high solubility in the solvent mixture may be suited to a co-solvent approach. Co-solvents can increase the solubility of poorly soluble compounds several thousand times compared to the aqueous solubility of the drug alone.

The most frequently used cosolvents for parenteral use are propylene glycol, ethanol, glycerin and polyethylene glycol.

Co-solvents may be combined with other solubilization techniques and pH adjustments, to further increase in solubility of poorly soluble compounds. Dimethylsulfoxide (DMSO) and dimethylacetoamide (DMA) have been widely used as cosolvents because of their large solubilization capacity for poorly soluble drugs and their relatively low toxicity.

Advantages:

(i) Simple and rapid to formulate and produce.

Disadvantages:

(i) Toxicity and tolerability of all excipilents and solvents has to be considered.

(ii) Uncontrolled precipitation occurs upon dilution with aqueous media. The precipitates may be amorphous or crystalline and can vary in size. Many of the insoluble compounds are unsuited with co-solvents alone, particularly for intravenous administration. This is because the drugs are extremely insoluble in water and do not readily redissolve after precipitation from the co-solvent mixture. In these situations, there is a potential risk for embolism and local adverse effects at the injection site.

Example of Marketed Products:

Nimodipine Intravenous Injection (Nimotop®, Bayer) and Digoxin Elixir Pediatric (Lanoxin®, GSK) are examples of co-solvent formulations.

7. Hydrotrophy

Hydrotrophy means the increase in solubility of water due to the presence of large amount of additives. It improves the solubility, is more closely related to complexation involving a weak interaction between the hydrotrophic agents (sodium benzoate, sodium acetate, sodium alginate, and urea) and the solute. Example: Solubilization of theophylline with sodium acetate and sodium alginate.

Hydrotropic agents are ionic organic salts. Additives or salts that increase solubility in given solvent are said to "salt in". If the solute and salts that decrease solubility are said to be "salt out".

Several salts with large anions or cations that are themselves very soluble in water result in "salting in" of non-electrolytes called "hydrotropic salts" and a phenomenon is known as "hydrotropism".

The classification of hydrotropes on the basis of molecular structure is difficult, since a wide variety of compounds have been reported to exhibit hydrotropic behaviour. Specific examples may include ethanol, aromatic alcohols like resorcinol, pyrogallol, catechol, α and β-naphthols and salicylates, alkaloids like caffeine and nicotine, ionic surfactants like diacids, SDS (sodium dodecyl sulphate) and dodecylated oxidibenzene.

The aromatic hydrotropes with anionic head groups are large in number because of isomerism and their effective hydrotrope action may be due to the availability of interactive p-orbitals. Hydrotropes with cationic hydrophilic group are rare, e.g. salts of aromatic amines, such as procaine hydrochloride. Besides enhancing the solubilization of compounds in water, they are known to exhibit influences on surfactant aggregation leading to micelle formation, phase manifestation of multicomponent systems with reference to nanodispersions and conductance percolation, clouding of surfactants and polymers etc. Other techniques that enhance the solubility of poorly water soluble drugs include salt formation, change in dielectric constant of solvent, chemical modification of the drug, use of hydrates or solvates, use of soluble prodrug, application of ultrasonic waves, spherical crystallization etc.

8. Nanosuspension

A pharmaceutical nanosuspension is biphasic system consisting of nano sized drug particles stabilized by surfactants for either oral, topical, parenteral and pulmonary administration.

This technology is applied to poorly soluble drugs that are insoluble in both, water and oils. The particle size distribution of the solid particles in nanosuspensions is usually less than one micron with an average particle size ranging between 200 - 600 nm.

There are various methods for preparation of nanosuspension. Among these, Media Milling (Nanocrystals), High Pressure Homogenization and combination of Precipitation and High-Pressure Homogenization methods are commonly used.

9. Cryogenic Techniques

Cryogenic techniques have been developed to create nanostructured amorphous drug particles with high degree of porosity at very low temperature conditions, to enhance the dissolution rate of drugs.

Cryogenic inventions can be defined by the type of injection device (capillary, rotary, pneumatic and ultrasonic nozzle), location of nozzle (above or under the liquid level) and the composition of cryogenic liquid (hydrofluoroalkanes, N_2, Ar, O_2 and organic solvents).

After cryogenic processing, dry powder can be obtained by various drying processes (spray freeze drying, atmospheric freeze drying, vacuum freeze drying and lyophilisation).

10. Nanocrystallization

The nanocrystallization is defined as 'a way of diminishing drug particles to the size range of 1-1000 nanometers'. There are two distinct methods used for producing nanocrystals; 'bottom-up' and 'top-down' development. The top-down methods (i.e. Milling and High pressure homogenization) start milling down from macroscopic level, e.g. from a powder that is micron sized. In bottom-up methods (i.e. Precipitation and Cryo-vacuum method), nanoscale materials are chemically composed from atomic and molecular components.

Methods of Preparation of Nanocrystals:

(i) Milling:

Nanoscale particles can be produced by wet milling process. In ball mills, particle size reduction is achieved by using both impact and attrition forces. The most common models are a tumbling ball mill and a stirred media mill.

(ii) High pressure homogenization:

In high pressure homogenization, an aqueous dispersion of the crystalline drug particles is passed with high pressure through a narrow homogenization gap with a very high velocity. Homogenization can be performed in water or alternatively in non-aqueous media or water-reduced media.

The particles are disintegrated by cavitations and shear forces. The static pressure exerted on the liquid causes the liquid to boil forming gas bubbles. When exiting from the gap, gas bubbles collapse under normal air pressure. This produces shock waves which make the crystals collide, leading to particle disintegration. A heat exchanger should be used when operating on heat sensitive materials.

The particle size obtained during the homogenization process depends primarily on the nature of the drug, the pressure applied and the number of homogenization cycles.

(iii) Precipitation :

In the precipitation method, a dilute solution is first produced by dissolving the substance in a solvent. The solution with the drug is then injected into water, which acts as a bad solvent. At the time of injection, the water has to be stirred efficiently so that the substance will precipitate as nanocrystals. Nanocrystals can be removed from the solution by filtering and then dried in air.

(iv) Cryo-vacuum method:

In the cryo-vacuum method, the active ingredient is first dissolved in water to attain a quasi-saturated solution. This method is based on cooling of a solvent by immersing the solution in liquid nitrogen (–196 °C) which causes a very fast rise in the degree of saturation based on the decrease of solubility and development of ice crystals when the temperature drops below 0 °C. 'This leads to a fast nucleation of the dissolved substance at the edges of the ice crystals. The solvent must be completely frozen before the vessel is removed from the liquid nitrogen. After that, the solvent is removed by sublimation in a lyophilization chamber where the temperature is kept at constant –22 °C and the pressure is lowered to 10 - 20 bar. Cryo-assisted sublimation makes it possible to remove the solvent without changing the size and habit of the produced particles, so they will remain crystalline.

11. Nanomorph

The Nanomorph technology is to convert drug substances with low water-solubility from a coarse crystalline state into amorphous nanoparticles. A suspension of drug substance in solvent is feed into the chamber, where it is rapidly mixed with another solvent. Immediately the drug substance suspension is converted into a true molecular solution. The admixture of an aqueous solution of a polymer induces precipitation of the drug substance. The polymer keeps the drug substance particles in their nanoparticulate state and prevents them from aggregation or growth. Water redispersable dry powders can be obtained from the nanosized dispersion by conventional methods, e.g. spray-drying. Using this technology, the coarse crystalline drug substances are transformed into a nanodispersed amorphous state, without any physical milling or grinding procedures. It is commonly used in the preparation of amorphous nanoparticles.

12. Co-crystallization

A co-crystal is defined as 'a crystalline material that consists of two or more molecular (and electrically neutral) species held together by non-covalent forces'. Co-crystals can be prepared by evaporation method or by grinding. Another technique for the preparation of co-crystals includes sublimation as well as crystal growth from the slurry preparation. The formation of co-crystals is important for salt formation, particularly for neutral compounds or those having weakly ionizable groups.

13. Solubilization By Inclusion Compound

(a) Clathrates:

In a special type of inclusion compound, the host molecules form a crystal lattice containing spaces, into which guest molecules can fit. The macrocyclic molecule is called the host. The small molecule is the guest. The inclusion process gives rise to host-guest chemistry.

In case of clathrates chemical bonds are not involved. It is only based on the molecular size of the encaged component.

Ideal requirement: Host molecule must be hydrophilic yet able to bind the lipophilic guest molecule by means of hydrophobic interactions. Stability of a clathrate is due to the strength of the structure.

(b) Cyclodextrin

The most commonly used inclusion complexing molecules in pharmaceutical application. Cyclodextrins are the monomolecular clathrates which involve the entrapment of a single guest molecule. Cyclodextrins are natural cyclic oligosaccharides that are formed through enzymatic degradation of starch. They are the cyclic oligosaccharides containing a minimum of six D-(+)-glucopyranose units attached by α-1→4 linkages.

The cavity size of the α, β and γ cyclodextrin is the principal factor in determining, which guest molecule is best suitable for complexation.

- Alkyl groups well fit into the cavity of α-cyclodextrin. The β-cyclodextrins are best suited for accepting single aromatic rings. The γ-cyclodextrins have large enough cavities to accommodate larger hydrocarbons such as pyrene.

- The degree to which solute molecule is solubilized by the cyclodextrin molecule depends upon the **several properties:**

  (i) The solute molecule must have a significant non-polar portion in order to be squeezed from the water and into the Cyclodextrin cavity.

  (ii) Since the interior dimensions of a given cyclodextrins are fixed, a significant part of the molecule must fit inside the cyclodextrin.

However, there are certain **dis-advantages of cyclodextrins:**

1. Strict co-relation is required between the structure of guest molecule which is to be embedded and also affect the diameter of the cavity of the cyclodextrin molecule.

2. Because of re-crystallization of the native cyclodextrin and its complexes, there is particle formation in solution after longer storage time which produce high nephrotoxicity by parenteral use (β-CD).

3. Only amorphous CD-derivatives (e.g. Hydroxy propyl β-CD) which are physiologically well-tolerated can be used in the parenteral applications. Generally, 1:1 or 1:2 complexes are formed so that higher excipient concentrations are required.

For this purpose, numerous derivatives have been prepared from the base cyclodextrins.

Two major derivatives are:

1. Hydroxy-propyl β-cyclodextrins (HP-β-CD)

2. Sulfobutyl-ether β-cyclodextrins (SBE-β-CD)

14. Solubilization of salt:

Salt formation improve solubility and dissolution characteristics in comparision to the original drug. It is generally accepted that, a minimum difference of 3 units between the pKa value of the group and that of its counter ion is required to form stable salts. For example, Alkali metal salts of acidic drugs and strong acid salts of basic drugs are more water-soluble than the parent drug. Factors that influence salt selection are physical and chemical properties of the salt, counter ion, therapeutic indications and route of administration.

The mathematical equations for solubility predictions of a weak acid and weak base are:

$$S_T = S_w (1 + 10^{(pH - pKa)}) \qquad \qquad ...(2.1)$$

$$S_T = S_w (1 + 10^{(pKa - pH)}) \qquad \qquad ...(2.2)$$

Equations (2.1) and (2.2) assure that ionized species of a solute has infinite solubility.

However, an ionized solute can form salts with appropriate counter ions. The formation of a solute is governed by the solubility product (K_{sp}) of the salt complex. For example, the thermodynamic equilibrium for a chloride salt, BH^+Cl^- is given by

$$BH^+Cl^-_{(solid)} \xrightarrow{K_{sp}} [BH^+] + [Cl^-]$$

Where, $BH^+Cl^-_{(solid)}$ represents the solid chloride salt, BH^+ is the ionized base and Cl^- is a chloride counter ion. As a result, the concentration of the ionized species will be limited by the solubility of the salt.

For example, solubility of β-methasone alcohol in water is enhanced 1500 times by forming its derivatvie disodium phosphate ester.

15. Inorganic salts

Inorganic salts also shows the systematic effect on the aqueous solubility. Salts were divided into kosmotropes (polar water-structure makers) or chaotropes (polar water-structure breakers). This distinction was based on the degree to which ions would interact with the adjacent water molecules.

A kosmotrope like a doubly charged ion (e.g. SO_4^{-2}) or an ion with a high charge density (e.g. F^-) was proposed to interact with the adjacent water molecules more strongly than bulk water.

A chaotrope like a large ion with a single charge (e.g. ClO^{4-} or SCN^-) was proposed to interact with adjacent water molecules less strongly than bulk water. Example: Caffeine solubility in different salt solutions is shown in Fig. 2.2.

Different salts have different effects on the solubility. Addition of $NaClO_4$ or NaSCN increase the caffeine solubility, whereas addition of Na_2SO_4 or NaCl decreases it, and addition of NaBr did not show any significant effect. It can be seen in below figure that, chaotropes increase xanthine solubility whereas kosmotropes decrease it. Because, all the investigated salts were sodium salts, and the differences in salt effects were attributed to their anions.

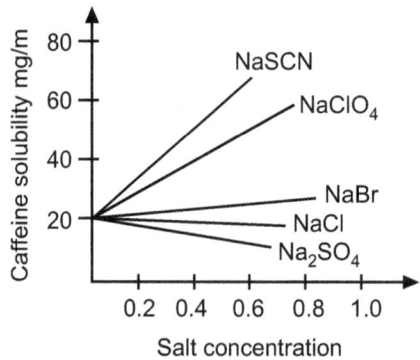

Fig. 2.2: Caffeine solubility in different salt concentrations at 25°C.

The solubility was also determined by using the empirical Setschenow equation:

$$\log \left(\frac{S^\circ}{S} \right) = k/C_s$$

Where,

S° = Non-electrolyte solubility in water

S = Solubility in salt solution

k = Setschenow constant

C_s = Salt concentration

The k values are positive for salts that decrease solubility and negative for salts that increase solubility.

Limitations :

(i) It is not feasible to form salts of neutral compounds.

(ii) It may be difficult to form salts of very weak bases or acids.

(iii) The salt may be hygroscopic, exhibit polymorphism or has poor processing characteristics.

(iv) Conversion of salt to free acid or base form of the drug on surface of solid dosage form prevents or retards drug release.

16. Solubilization by Surfactants

Surfactants are very useful to enhance dissolution rate as well as permeability of durg. Surfactants are molecules with distinct polar and nonpolar regions. Most surfactants consist of a hydrocarbon segment (usually in the form of a long aliphatic chain segment) connected to a polar group.

The polar group can be anionic (such as a carboxylate, sulfate or sulfonate), cationic (such as ammonium, tri-alkylammonium or pyridinium), zwitterionic (such as glycine or carnitine) or non-ionic such as polyethylene glycol, glycerol or sugar.

Non-classical surfactants like cholic acid, polysorbate, and poloxamer do not contain a single aliphatic chain and a simple polar head group but they contain distinct polar and non-polar regions.

Ideal Properties of Surfactants:

(i) It must be non-toxic.

(ii) It must be non-irritant according to its route of administration.

(iii) It must be compatible with other ingredients.

(iv) It must possess good solubilizing power and stability.

(v) It must be free from disagreeable odour and taste.

Due to differences in properties of the polar and non-polar regions, surfactants tend to accumulate and orient at interfaces so that each region of the surfactant interacts with a separate phase. The polar portion of the surfactant will associate with the more polar phase (especially if it is water) and the non-polar portion of the surfactant will remain in the more non-polar solvent.

In the water, as the concentration of surfactant increases above a critical value, its molecules self-associate into soluble structures called *micelles*. The concentration at which they begin to form is called the *critical micelle concentration* (or the CMC).

These micelles are normally spherical with the non-polar regions of the surfactant molecules gathered in the center (core) and surrounded by a mantle of the polar regions which are in contact with the water as shown in the Fig. 2.3.

Micelles are labile entities formed by the non-covalent aggregation of individual surfactant monomers. Therefore, they can be spherical, cylindrical, or planar (discs or bilayers). Micelle shape and size can be controlled by changing the surfactant chemical structure as well as by varying solution conditions such as temperature, overall surfactant concentration, surfactant composition (in the case of mixed surfactant systems), ionic strength and pH. Solubilizing capacity for surfactant with the hydrocarbon chain length increases in the order:

Anionic < Cationic < Non-ionic

A non-polar drug, which is squeezed out of water, can locate within the micelle core. A semi-polar drug can locate between or partially within the core and the mantle. Since the micelles are soluble in water any drug that is incorporated into the micelle will also be soluble in the aqueous system.

The general solubilization curve for surfactants is given in the Fig. 2.4. If the monomers of surfactant in solution do not affect the solubility of the solute, then the solute concentration will remain constant (at the intrinsic solubility, S_w) until the CMC. After the CMC, the solute concentration will increase linearly with increasing surfactant (micelle) concentration.

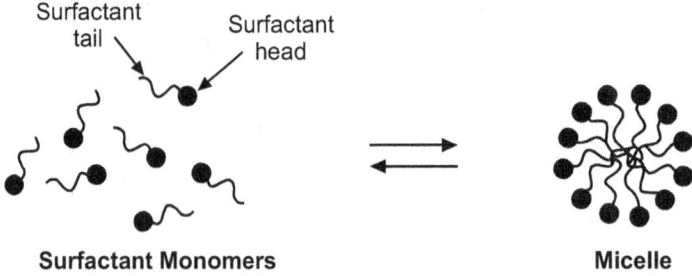

The *black circles* represent the surfactant heads (hydrophilic moieties)
and the *black curved lines* represent the surfactant tails (hydrophobic moieties)

Fig. 2.3: Schematic illustration of the reversible monomer-micelle thermodynamic equilibrium

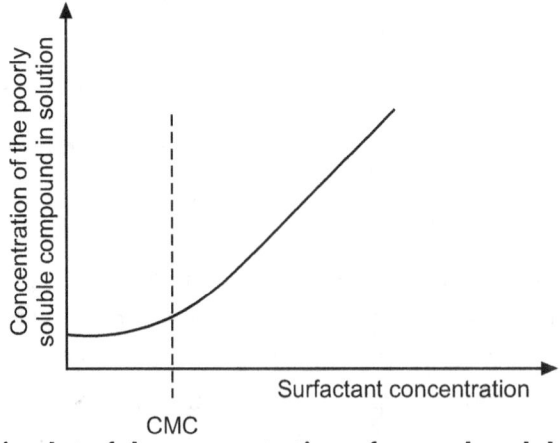

Fig. 2.4: Schematic plot of the concentration of a poorly soluble compound as a function of the surfactant concentration in aqueous solution

There are a number of possible ways of solubilization for a drug in a micelle, as represented in the Fig. 2.5.

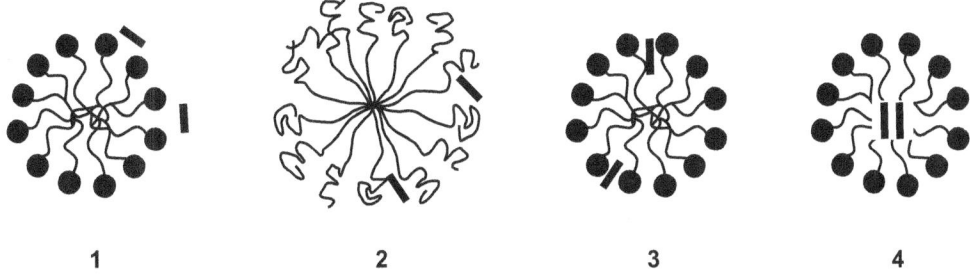

The *black bold lines* (▬) represent the drug at different sites in the micelle.

The *black circles* represent the surfactant heads.

The *light black curved lines* represent the surfactant tails.

Fig. 2.5 : Solubilization of drugs in surfactant micelles, depending on the drug hydrophobicity

Accordingly, hydrophilic drugs can be adsorbed on the surface of the micelle (1), drugs with intermediate solubility should be located in intermediate positions within the micelle such as between the hydrophilic head groups of PEO micelles (2) and in the layer between the hydrophilic groups and the first few carbon atoms of the hydrophobic group, that is the outer core (3), and completely insoluble hydrophobic drugs may be located in the inner core of the micelle (4).

A simple mathematical representation for a solute's total solubility, S_T, in a surfactant system is

$$S_T = S_W + K (C_{surf} - CMC) \qquad\qquad ....(2.3)$$

Where, C_{surf} is the total concentration of the surfactant and K is the solubilization capacity. The solubilization capacity reflects the number of the surfactant molecules that are required to solubilize a single drug molecule. Deviations from the above equation are the result of changes in micelle shape or size that occur as the concentration of the surfactant increases.

C_{surf} - *CMC* is approximately equal to the surfactant concentration in the micellar form and, therefore, K is equal to the ratio of drug concentration in the micelles to the surfactant concentration in the micellar form.

A micelle is a dynamic aggregation of any number of individual surfactant molecules, or monomers. Although the molecules are intertwined, they are in constant motion like those of a liquid. Thus, the interior of a micelle can be thought as a separate phase and a micellar solution can be thought of as a micro dispersion of that phase in water. If the micelle is considered to be a separate phase, it is then convenient to evaluate the solubilization capacity (K), in terms of the partition between the micelle and water. The micellar partition coefficient ,K_m, is defined as 'the ratio of the solute concentration in the micelle, C_m, to that of water, C_W'.

$$K_m = \frac{C_m}{C_W}$$

$$K_m = \frac{S_T - S_W}{C_W}$$

$$K_m = \frac{K\,(C_{surf} - CMC)}{C_W}$$

If $C_{surf} = 1M$ then molar micelle partition coefficient can be defined as

$$K_m = \frac{K\,(1 - CMC)}{C_W}$$

The lower is the CMC value of a given surfactant; the more stable are the micelles. This is especially important from the pharmacological point of view, since upon dilution with a large volume of the blood, considering intravenous administration, only micelles of surfactants with low CMC value still exist, while micelles from surfactants with high CMC value may dissociate into monomers and their content may precipitate in the blood.

The capacity of surfactants in solubilizing drugs depends on numerous factors, such as chemical structure of the surfactant, chemical structure of the drug, temperature, pH, ionic strength etc. Non-ionic surfactants usually are better solubilizing agents than ionic surfactants for hydrophobic drugs, because of their lower CMC values. In order to obtain solubilization in water, very hydrophilic surfactants with a HLB value above 16 must be used. Conversely, one can obtain solubilization in a lipophilic base by using surfactants with a HLB value of less than 8.

In the hydrophilic systems for pharmaceutical reasons of tolerance, non-ionic surfactants of PEG-ester and PEG-ether are used. The solubilizing effect of the micellar systems is not as molecule specific as with the complex formation. Any drug which is reasonably soluble in oil can be taken up by micelle.

Regarding the influence of structure of the drug, crystalline solids generally show less solubility in micelles than do liquids of similar structure. For polar drugs, the depth of penetration into the micelle varies with the structure of the drug. In general, the amount of drug solubilized in a micellar system increases with the increase in temperature.

The addition of small amount of salts decreases the repulsion between the similarly charged ionic surfactant head groups, thereby decreasing the CMC and increasing the aggregation number and volume of the micelles. The increase in aggregation number favours the solubilization of hydrophobic drugs in the inner core of the micelle. The addition of salts to solutions of PEO non-ionic surfactants may also increase the extent of solubilization of hydrophobic drugs because of the increase in aggregation number. The pH of micellar solutions can also show significant influence on the extent of solubilization of drugs, since it may change the equilibrium between ionized and molecular forms of some drugs.

Solutes that have surface-active physicochemical properties themselves (i.e., they have separate polar and non-polar regions) tend to be more soluble than expected because they can accumulate at the core interface. In essence, weekly amphiphilic solutes can act as co-surfactants and form mixed micelles with non-ionic surfactants as well as with ionic surfactants. This can alter both the CMC and the size of the micelle. In most cases, this leads to a higher degree of solubilization.

Applications of Surfactants:

- Solubilization may lead to enhanced absorption and an increased biological activity. It improves the intestinal absorption of vitamin A and the percutaneous absorption of oestrone.
- Alphadolone acetate and alphaxolone are together solubilized with polyoxyethylated castor oil to produce a solution suitable for intravenous administration as an anaesthetic.
- Solubilization of fat soluble vitamins such as phytomenadione using polysorbates enable their inclusion with water-soluble vitamins in the same formulation, thus improving the appearance and an unpleasant taste.
- Non-ionic surfactant like polyethylene glycol ether is used to disperse phytomenadione parenterally.
- Lysol contains 50% cresol (water solubility 2%) in an aqueous system by the use of the potassium soaps of oleic, linoleic and linolenic acids.
- Solubilization of iodine to produce iodophores is achieved by the use of macrogol ethers.
- Lanolin derivatives have been used for the solubilization of volatile and essential oils.

Problems with Surfactants :

1) Very high concentration of surfactent is necessary.
2) Poor stability of the solubilized systems due to the incompatibility between the surfactant and the drug.
3) Changes in the bio-availability due to micellar inclusion, as due to the thermodynamic stability of the associates, the drug release is delayed.
4) Inadequate physiological tolerability e.g. a strong bitter taste of many surfactants prevent application in nasal or oral formulations or the haemolytic effects makes the parenteral application impossible.

Although a large number of anionic, cationic and non-ionic surfactants are available for use as solubilizing agents, only polysorbate-80 and Cremophor EL (CrEL) have been used to any significant extent in parenteral products. CrEL has been used for solubilization of a wide variety of hydrophobic drugs such as anaesthetics, photosensitizers, sedatives, immunosuppressive agents and anticancer drugs.

Examples of some products that contain surfactants are given below:

Table 2.1: Example of Product Containing Surfactants

Drug (Product)	Manufacturer	Route of administration	Surfactant composition (% w/v)
Chlorodiazepoxide HCl (Librium)	Roche	IM/IV (diluent)	4% Polysorbate 80
Etoposide (VePesid)	Bristol	IV Infusion after dilution	8% Polysorbate 80
Multi-Vitamin (M.V.I.)	Armour	IV Infusion	1-1.7% Polysorbate 20

17. Solubilizing Agents:

The solubility of poorly soluble drug can also be improved by various solubilizing agents. EG: PEG 400 improvs the solubility of hydrochlorthiazide.

Modified gum karaya (MGK), a recently developed excipient was evaluated as carrier for dissolution enhancement of poorly soluble drug like nimodipine .

The aqueous solubility of the antimalarial agent halofantrine is increased by the addition of caffeine and nicotinamide.

2.8 DETERMINATION OF SOLUBILITY

There are commonly two methods for solubility determination:

1. Modified Shake Flask method, 2. Potentiometric Titration method.

1. Modified Shake Flask Method:

The drug is added to a standard buffer solution until the saturation occurs. The pH is measured and if necessary, readjusted with dilute acid or alkali. The flask is shaken for 24 hours. The amount of dissolved drug is determined by suitable assay of the solution after filtration. This method is time consuming.

2. Potentiometric Titration Method:

Titrations are performed using dilute acid or base titrants in 0.15 M KCl ionic strength buffered solution. Solubility of the salt is not determined with this technique. The solubility-pH profile is provided over the entire pH range excluding the onset of salt precipitate. The potentiometric method requires an accurately measured pKa.

2.9 APPLICATIONS OF SOLUBILITY

- Solubility have a fundamental importance in a large number of scientific disciplines and practical applications, to the use of medicines, and the transport of pollutants.

- Solubility represents a fundamental concept in fields of research such as chemistry, physics, food science, pharmaceutical and biological sciences.

- The solubility of a substance becomes specially important in the pharmaceutical field because it often represents a major factor that controls the bioavailability of a drug substance.

- Solubility is commonly used to describe the substance, to indicate a substance's polarity and it also helps to distinguish it from other substances.

- Moreover, solubility and solubility-related properties can also provide important information regarding the structure of drug substances, and in their range of possible intermolecular interactions.

- Solubility of drug is most important factor that controls the formulation of the drug as well as therapeutic efficacy of the drug, hence it is the most critical factor in the formulation development.

Chapter 3

DISSOLUTION STUDY

3.1 INTRODUCTION

Dissolution test is widely used in the pharmaceutical industry for optimization of formulation and quality control of different dosage forms.

Dissolution rate may be defined as "Amount of drug substance that goes in the solution per unit time under standard conditions of liquid/solid interface, temperature and solvent composition". It can be considered as a specific type of certain heterogeneous reaction in which a mass transfer results as a net effect between escape and deposition of solute molecules at a solid surface.

3.2 HISTORY OF DISSOLUTION

It all started in 1897 with the first reference to dissolution. Noyes and Whitney published a paper on "The Rate of Solution of Solid Substances in Their Own Solution". They suggested that the dissolution rate was controlled by a layer of saturated solution that forms instantly around a solid particle.

A few years later in 1900, **Brunner** and **Tolloczko** proved that 'dissolution rate depends on the chemical, physical structures of the solid, the surface area exposed to the medium, agitation speed, medium temperature and the overall design of the dissolution apparatus'.

In 1904, **Nernst** and **Brunner** modified the Noyes-Whitney equation by applying Fick's law of diffusion. A relationship between the dissolution rate and the diffusion coefficient was established.

3.2.1 Steps in Dissolution Process:

Dissolution Process Involves following:
- Initial mechanical lag
- Wetting of dosage form
- Penetration of dissolution medium into the dosage form
- Disintegration
- Deaggregation
- Dissolution
- Occlusion of some particles of the drug

Fig. 3.1 indicates the dissolution process of tablet dosage form.

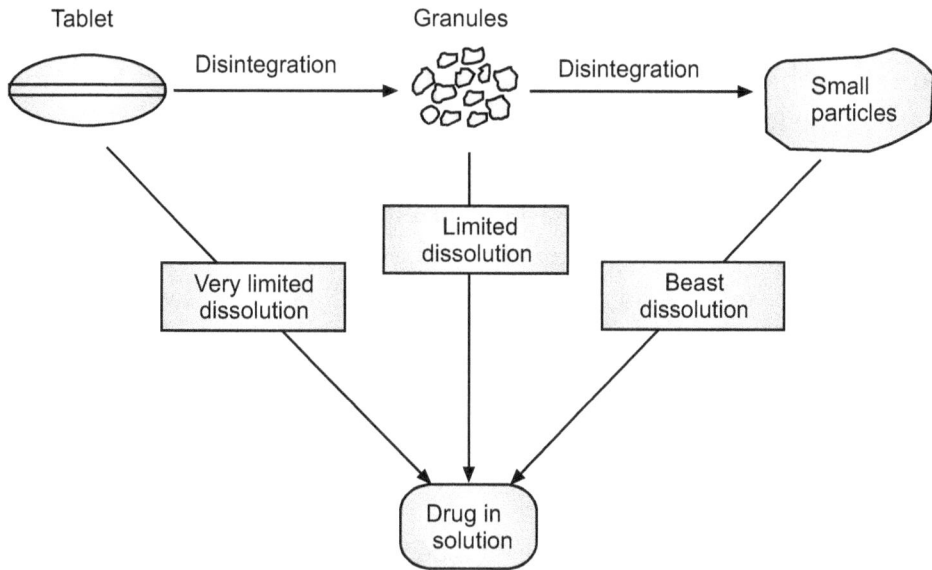

Fig. 3.1: Dissolution process

3.3 IMPORTANCE OF DISSOLUTION

1.   Results from *in vitro* dissolution rate experiments can be used to explain the observed differences in *in vivo* availability.

2.   Dissolution testing provides the means to evaluate critical parameters such as adequate bioavailability and provides information necessary to formulate or in development of more efficacious and therapeutically optimal dosage forms.

3.   Most sensitive and reliable predictors of *in vivo* availability.

4.   Dissolution analysis of pharmaceutical dosage forms have emerged as single most important test that will ensure quality of product.

5.   It can ensure bioavailability of product between batches that meets dissolution criteria.

6.   It ensures batch-to-batch quality equivalence both *in vitro* and *in vivo,* but also to screen formulations during product development to arrive at optimally effective products.

7.   Physicochemical properties of model needed to mimic *in vivo* environment can be understood.

8.   Such models can be used to screen potential drugs and their associated formulations for dissolution and absorption characteristics.

3.4 THEORIES OF DISSOLUTION

Physical models have been set up to account for the observed dissolution of dosage forms: there are three models which either alone or in combination, can be used to describe the dissolution mechanisms.

1. Film Theory/Diffusion Layer Model:

When solid particles are immersed in agitated liquid and allowed to dissolve, bulk liquid will be continuously exposed to the solid surface. So a stagnant layer or film surrounds the particle is called as *nernst bruner thickness layer*.

This model (Fig 3.2) assumes that a layer of liquid, h cm thick, adjacent to the solid surface remains stagnant as the bulk liquid passes over the surface with a certain velocity. The reaction at the solid/liquid interface is assumed to be instantaneous forming a saturated solution, C_S, of the solid, in the static liquid film. The rate of dissolution is governed entirely by the diffusion of the solid molecules from the static liquid film to the bulk liquid according to Fick's first law:

$$J = - D_f \frac{dc}{dx}$$

where J is the amount of substance passing perpendicularly through a unit surface area per time, D_f is the diffusion coefficient and $\frac{dc}{dx}$ is the concentration gradient.

After a time t, the concentration between the limit of the static liquid layer and the bulk liquid becomes C_t. Once the solid molecules pass into the bulk liquid, it is assumed that there is rapid mixing and the concentration gradient disappears.

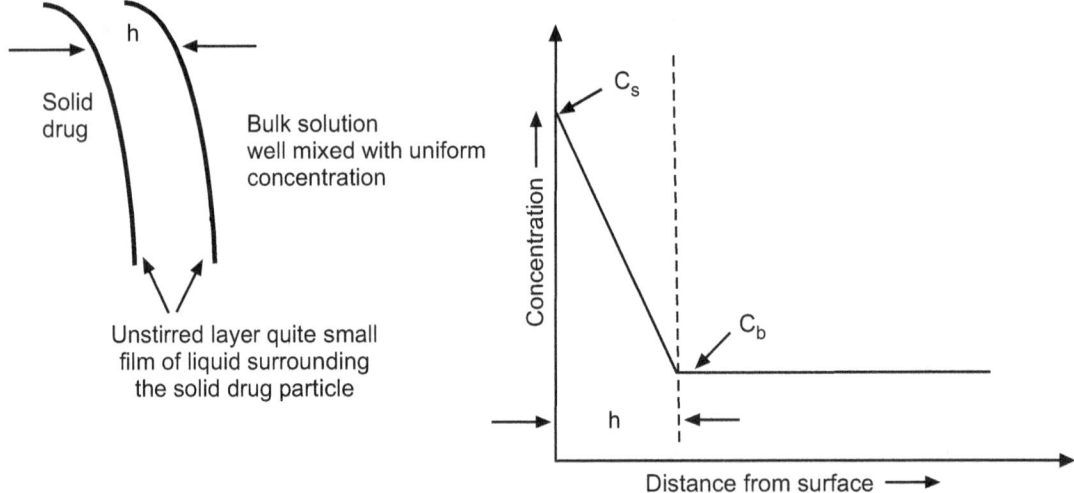

Note: h is the thickness of stagnant layer

Fig. 3.2: Diffusion layer model

It is assumed that this concentration gradient imparts a concentraion 'C' at the boundary between the film and bulk solution and that at the surface is saturation concentration C_s. (Fig. 3.3)

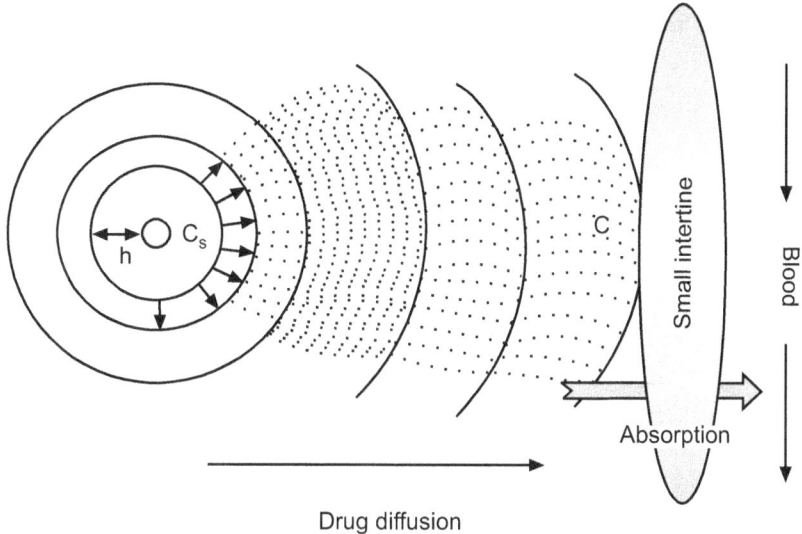

Fig. 3.3: Drug Diffusion process/Diffusion model

Assuming steady state, Fick's first law,

$$\text{Rate of Solution} = \frac{D \cdot A \cdot (C_s - C_b)}{h}$$

If C_b is much smaller than C_s then we have so-called "Sink Conditions" and the equation reduces to,

$$\text{Rate of Solution} = \frac{D \cdot A \cdot C_s}{h}$$

Here the surface area is assumed to remain constant and this assumption is not always true.

The change in the surface area during dissolution can be explained by employing Hixson Crowell rule.

The theory predicts that 'if the concentration gradient is always constant i.e. $C_s - C_t$ is constant because $C_s \gg C_t$ ("sink" conditions which usually mean $C_s > 10\ C_t$) then a uniform rate of dissolution is obtained'.

2. Surface Renewal Theory/Danckwert's Model:

Danckwert's Model opposed the existence of a stagnant layer by assuming the turbulance extended to the surface and there was no laminar boundary layer.

Danckwert takes into account macroscopic mass of eddies or packets.

It is supposed that surface is being continuously replaced by fresh pockets of solvent. (Shown in Fig. 3.4). During residence at the interface, the pockets adsorb solute by diffusion. Since the surface of the solid is exposed and is renewed; the theory is called as the *surface renewal theory*.

This model can be represented by the equation:

$$d_m = S^{1/2} \cdot D^{1/2} (C_s - C_g)$$

Where,   S   = Mean rate at which fresh surface is produced.

         D   = Diffusion coefficient of drug

         $C_s - C_g$ = Concentration gradient for diffusion of drug.

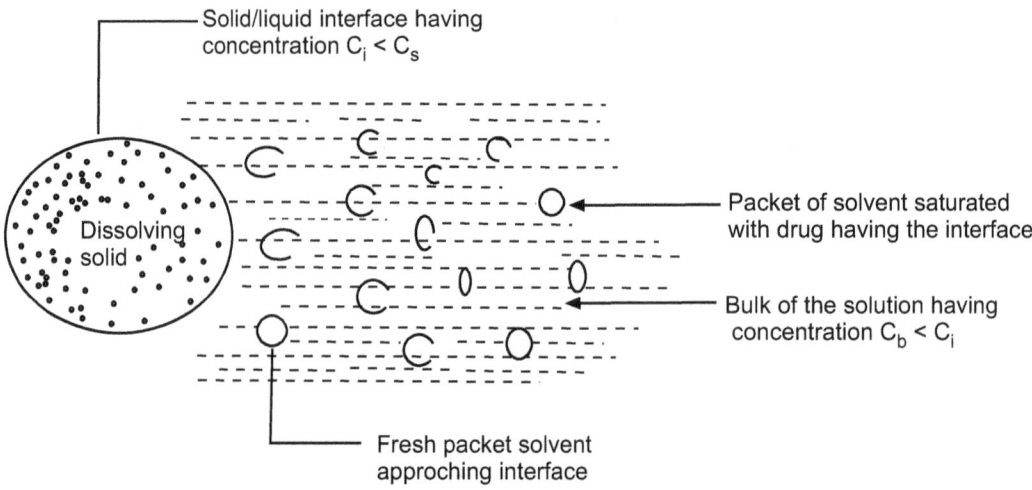

Fig. 3.4: Surface renewal model

Surface renewal model is based on solvation mechanism which is function of solubility rather than diffusion.

When considering the dissolution of the crystal we will have a different interfacial barrier given by following equation.

$$\alpha = K_i (C_s - C_b),$$

Where, α = dissolution per unit area

      k_i = effective interfacial transport constant.

The interfacial barrier model can be extended to both diffusion layer model and Danckwert model.

Fig. 3.5 shows diagrammatic representation of the free energy barrier to dissolution.

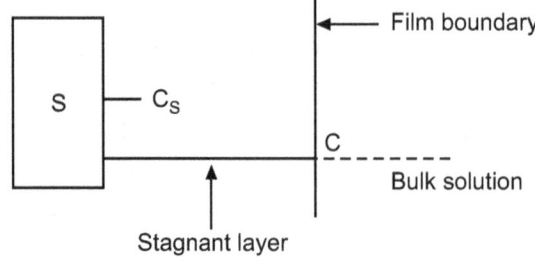

Fig. 3.5: Diagrammatic representation of the free energy barrier to dissolution

3.5 FACTORS AFFECTING DISSOLUTION

Following various factors are affected to dissolution.

Factors Related to Physicochemical Properties

- Polymorphism
- Amorphous state and solvation
- Free acid, free base or salt form
- Complexation
- Particle size
- Surfactants

Factors Related to Drug Product Formulation

- Excipients related factors
- Diluents
- Granulating agents and binder
- Disintegrating agents
- Lubricants
- Interfacial tension between drug and dissolution medium
- Surfactants

Factors Related to Dosage Form

- Manufacturing procedures
- Granule size
- Drug excipient interaction
- Compression force
- Deaggregation
- Storage of dosage form

Factors Related to Dissolution Testing Device

- Eccentricity of agitating element.
- Vibration
- Agitation intensity
- Stirring element alignment
- Sampling probes, position and filters
- Dosage form positions
- Type of device

Factors Related to Dissolution Test Parameters

- Temperature
- Dissolution medium
- Dissolved gases

- Dissolution media composition and pH
- Viscosity
- Other factors

Miscellaneous Factors

- Adsorption
- Sorption
- Humidity
- Detection errors

Factors Related to Physicochemical Properties

- **Polymorphism:**
  ✓ Crystalline forms are more stable than amorphous.
  ✓ Amorphous forms demonstrates faster dissolution.
  ✓ E.g. chlorpropamide- 4 metastable forms exhibit faster dissolution than stable form.
  ✓ Other e.g. include Erythromycin, ampicillin, chloramphenicol.

- **Complexation:**
  ✓ Complexation with PVP influence dissolution.
  ✓ Complexation enhances the dissolution of drug and mechanism may be due to:
    Formation of energetic amorphous form.
    Formation of coacervate.
  ✓ E.g. hydroflumethiazide-PVP compared with pure crystalline drug.

- **Particle size and surface area:**
  ✓ Dissolution rate is directly proportional to surface area.
    E.g. griseofulvin, chlormphenicol.
  ✓ If the drug is hydrophobic and dissolution medium has poor wetting properties, reduction in particle size may lead to decreased dissolution rate.
    E.g. phenacetin.

- **Drug solubility:**
  ✓ Solubility of drug plays a prime role in controlling its dissolution from dosage form. Aqueous solubility of drug is a major factor that determines its dissolution rate. Minimum aqueous solubility of 1% is required to avoid potential solubility limited absorption problems.
  ✓ Studies of different compounds of different chemical classes and a wide range of solubility revealed that initial dissolution rate of these substances is directly proportional to their respective solubility.

- **Salt formation:**
- ✓ It is one of the common approaches used to increase drug solubility and dissolution rate. It has always been assumed that sodium salts dissolve faster than their corresponding insoluble acids. Eg. sodium and potassium salts of Peniciilin G, sulfa drugs, phenytoin, barbiturates etc.
- ✓ While in case of Phenobarbital, dissolution of sodium salt was slower than that of weak acid. Same is the case for weak base drug, strong acid salts, such as hydrochlorides and sulphates of weak bases such as epinephrine, tetracycline which are commonly used due to high solubility. However, free bases of chlortetracycline, methacycline were more soluble than corresponding hydrochloride salt at gastric pH values, due to common ion suppression.

- **Particle size:**
- ✓ There is a direct relationship between surface area of drug and its dissolution rate. Since, surface area increases with decrease in particle size, higher dissolution rates may be achieved through reduction of particle size.
- ✓ Micronization of sparingly soluble drug to reduce particle size is always not sure of better dissolution and bioavailability.
- ✓ Micronization of hydrophobic powders can lead to aggregation and floatation when powder is dispersed into dissolution medium. So, increase in S.A. of drug does not sure an equivalent increase in dissolution rate. Rather, it is increase in the "effective" S.A., or area exposed to dissolution medium and not the absolute S.A. that is directly proportional to dissolution rate.
- ✓ Hydrophobic drugs like phenacetin, aspirin shows decrease in dissolution rate as they tend to adsorb air at the surface and inhibit their wettability. Problem is eliminated by evacuating surface from adsorbed air or by use of surfactants. So these drugs *in vivo* exhibit excellent wetting due to presence of natural surfactants such as bile salts.

- **Solid state characteristics:**
- ✓ Solid phase characteristics of drug, such as amorphicity, crystallinity, state of hydration and polymorphic structures have significant influence on dissolution rate.
- ✓ Anhydrous forms dissolve faster than hydrated form because they are thermodynamically more active than hydrates. For example; Ampicillin anhydrate has faster dissolution rate than trihydrate.
- ✓ Amorphous forms of drug tend to dissolve faster than crystalline materials. For example, Novobiocin suspension, Griseofulvin.
- ✓ In the dissolution rate of amorphous erythromycin estolate is markedly lower than the crystalline form of erythromycin estolate.

✓ Metastable (high activation energy) polymorphic forms have better dissolution than stable forms.

- **Co-precipitation:**

✓ Dissolution rate of sulfathiazole could be significantly increased by co-precipitating the drug with povidone.

Factors Related to Drug Product Formulation

Dissolution rate of pure drug can be altered significantly when mixed with various adjuncts during manufacturing process such as diluents, dyes, binders, granulating agents, disintegrants and lubricants.

- **Diluents:**

✓ Diluents in capsule and tablet influence the dissolution rate of drug.

✓ Studies of starch on dissolution rate of salicylic acid tablet by dry double compression process shows three times increase in dissolution rate when the starch content increases from 5 - 20 %.

✓ Here starch particles form a layer on the outer surface of hydrophobic drug particles resulting in imparting hydrophilic character to granules and thus increase in effective surface area and rate of dissolution.

✓ Different types of dissolution apparatus utilized, affect ranking of different varieties of starch. With stirring type of agitation, order was Potato starch > Corn starch > Arrowroot starch > Rice starch.

✓ The dissolution rate is not only affected by nature of the diluent but also affected by excipient dilution (drug/excipient ratio).

For example, in quinazoline compound dissolution rate increases as the excipient / drug ratio increases from 3:1 to 7:1 to 11:1.

✓ Commonly used lactose is starch.

For example, salicylic acid tablets. 3 fold increase in the dissolution rate was observed when starch content was increased from 5-20%.

✓ Mechanism in fine starch particles form a layer on the outer surface of hydrophobic drug, so imparts hydrophilic character to the drug and increase dissolution rate.

- **Granulating agents and binders:**

✓ The hydrophilic binder increases dissolution rate of poorly wettable drug.

✓ Large amount of binder increases hardness and decreases disintegration /dissolution rate of tablet.

✓ Non-aqueous binders such as ethyl cellulose also retard the drug dissolution.

✓ Phenobarbital tablet granulated with gelatin solution provides a faster dissolution rate in human gastric juice than those prepared using Na – carboxymethyl cellulose (CMC) or polyethylene glycol (PEG) 6000 as binder.

✓ Gelatin imparted hydrophilic character to hydrophobic drug surface whereas PEG 6000 formed a poorly soluble complex while Na-CMC was converted to its less soluble acid form at the low pH of gastric fluid.

✓ In Phenobarbital tablet, faster dissolution rate was observed with 10% gelatin whereas decrease in dissolution rate with 20% gelatin. This was due to higher concentration which formed a thick film around tablet.

✓ Water soluble granulating agent plasdone gives faster dissolution rate compared to gelatin.

✓ For example, phenobarbital granulated with gelatin (2%) provides faster dissolution than those prepared using sodium CMC or PEG 6000.

✓ This is because gelatin imparts hydrophilic character whereas PEG forms complex.

- **Disintegrating agents:**

✓ Disintegrating agent added before and after the granulation affects the dissolution rate.

✓ Studies of various disintegrating agents on phenobarbital tablet showed that when copagel (low viscosity grade of Na-CMC) is added before granulation decrease dissolution rate, but if added after granulation did not had any effect on dissolution rate.

✓ Microcrystalline cellulose is a very good disintegrating agent but at high compression force, it may retard drug dissolution.

✓ Starch is not only an excellent diluent but also superior disintegrant due to its hydrophilicity and swelling property.

✓ Disintegration and dissolution rate of disintegrants with moderate swelling capacity depend on a large extent of mixing time of drug/excipient preblende with lubricant.

✓ On the other hand, disintegrants with strong swelling capacity such as sodium starch glycolate were hardly affected by mixing time with lubricant.

✓ For example, nymcell, primogel and copagel.

- **Lubricants:**

✓ Hydrophobic in nature.

✓ They form a thin hydrophobic water repellent film and reduces the wettability of dosage form and thus dissolution rate.

  For example, salicylic acid tablet with magnesium stearate retards dissolution.

✓ Lubricants are hydrophobic in nature they prolong tablet disintegration time by forming water repellant coat around individual granules. This retarding effect is most important factor in influencing rate of dissolution of solid dosage forms.

✓ Both amount as well as method of addition affects the property of formulation. It should be added in small amount (1% or less) and should be tumbled or mixed gently for only very short time.

✓ However, if an enhancing effect in dissolution of hydrophobic granules is desired, water soluble lubricant such as SLS or CARBOWAXES may be used.

- **Surfactants:**

✓ They enhance the dissolution rate of poorly soluble drug. This is due to lowering of interfacial tension, increasing effective surface area, which in turn results in faster dissolution rate.

✓ For example, Non-ionic surfactant Polysorbate 80 increases dissolution rate of phenacetin granules. The increase was more pronounced when the surfactant was sprayed on granules as compared to, if it was dissolved in granulating agent.

- **Water-soluble dyes:**

✓ Dissolution rate of single crystal of sulphathiazole was found to decrease significantly in presence of FD&C Blue No.1. The inhibiting effect was related to preferential adsorption of dye molecules on primary dissolution sources of crystal surfaces. They inhibit the micellar solubilization effect of bile salts on drug.

✓ Cationic dyes are more reactive in lower concentration than anionic dyes.

- **Coating polymers:**

✓ Tablets with MC coating were found to exhibit lower dissolution profiles than those coated with HPMC at 37°C. The differences are attributed to thermal gelation of MC at temperature near 37°C, which creates a barrier to dissolution process and essentially changes the dissolution medium. This mechanism is substantiated by the fact that at temperature below the gel point and at increased agitation, the effect disappears.

- **Interfacial tension between drug and dissolution medium:**

✓ The properties of the interface between the drug and the dissolution medium can become a deciding factor as far as dissolution rate is concerned. The characteristics can be modified by the addition of surface active agent that act at the interface.

Factors Related to Dosage Form

- **Method of granulation:**

✓ The addition of hydrophillic diluents like CMC, spray dried lactose imparts hydrophillicity to the active drug.

✓ A newer technology called as APOC "Agglomerative Phase of Comminution" was found to produce mechanically stronger tablets with higher dissolution rates than those made by wet granulation. A possible mechanism is increased by internal surface area of granules produced by APOC method.

✓ For example, salicylic tablets made by direct compression and wet granulation showed that tablets prepared by direct compression shows rapid and complete dissolution.

- **Compression force:**
✓ Increased compression pressure of tableting may have varying effect on dissolution rate.

  First condition, higher compression force increases the density and hardness of tablet, decreases porosity and hence penetrability of solvent into the tablet retards the wettability by forming a firmer and more effective sealing layer by the lubricant and in many cases tighter bonding between the particles, so decrease in dissolution rate of tablet.

  Second condition, higher compression force cause deformation, crushing or fracture of drug particles into smaller ones or convert spherical granules into disc shaped particles with a large increase in the effective surface area so increase in dissolution rate.

  Combination of both conditions can occur

  In short, dissolution decreases at lower pressure (better bonding), and increases at higher pressure (crushing effect) but constant increase in pressure dissolution can decrease because of extra rebonding and formation of denser tablets with poorer dissolution characteristics.

- **Drug excipient interaction:**
✓ These interactions occur during any unit operation such as mixing, milling, blending, drying, and/or granulation. Due to these processes, produced dissolution rate get changed.

✓ The dissolution of prednisolone found to be dependant on the length of mixing time with magnesium stearate.

✓ Similarly, an increase in mixing time of formulation containing 97 to 99% microcrystalline cellulose or another slightly swelling disintegrant result in enhance dissolution rate.

✓ Polysorbate-80 used as excipient in capsules causes formation of formaldehyde by autoxidation which causes film formation by denaturing the inner surface of capsule. This causes decrease in dissolution rate of capsules.

- **Storage conditions:**
✓ Dissolution rate of hydrochlorthiazide tablets granulated with acacia, exhibit decrease in dissolution rate during 1 year of aging at room temperature. A similar decrease was observed in tablets stored for 14 days at 50-80°C or for 4 weeks at 37°C.

✓ For tablets granulated with PVP, there was no change at elevated temperature but slight decrease in dissolution rate at room temperature.

✓ Tablets with starch gave no change in dissolution rate either at room temperature or at elevated temperature.

Factors Related to the Dissolution Testing Device

- **Eccentricity of Agitating (Stirring) Element:**

✓ The current official compendium specifies that the stirring shaft must rotate smoothly without significant wobble. Ensure that such wobble does not significantly affect the dissolution rate.

✓ Additionally, USP XX/NF XV states that the axis of rotation of the stirring shaft must not deviate > 2 mm from the axis of the stirring vessel. This implies that, this specification permits eccentricity upto ±2 mm but note that such eccentricity must not significantly affect the dissolution rate.

- **Vibration:**

✓ The speed of the rotational device selected by official compendium is 100 rpm. Precise speed control is best obtained with a synchronous motor that locks into line frequency.

✓ Such motors are not only more rugged but are far from reliable. Periodic variations in rpm might result in possible disturbance in rotational acceleration. This phenomenon, present in almost all rotational devices, is commonly referred to as torsional vibration, such vibration indicates a variation in the velocity of rotation for short period of time. Average velocity was well within ±4% of the specified rate.

✓ Vibration is a common variable introduced into a dissolution system due to various causes. It can affect on the change in the flow patterns of the dissolution medium. Additionally, it can introduce unwanted energy to the dynamic system. Both effects may result in significant changes in dissolution rate.

- **Agitation intensity:**

✓ It can be stated with a significant amount of certainty that the degree of agitation, or the stirring conditions, is one of the most important variables to consider in dissolution. Given the background on the various theories of dissolution, it is apparent that agitation conditions can markedly affect diffusion-controlled dissolution, because the thickness of the diffusion layer is inversely proportional to agitation speed. Wurster and Taylor employed the empiritical relationship,

$$K = a(N)b$$

where N is the agitation rate, K the reaction (dissolution) rate, and a and b are constants.

For diffusion-controlled processes, b = 1.

For dissolution rate that is interfacial-reaction-rate-controlled will be independent of agitation intensity and thus b = 0.

- **Flow pattern disturbances:**
✓ For dissolution rate, the data should be reproducible and reliable, and the flow pattern should be consistent from test to test. The geometry and alignment of the stirring device, external vibration and rotational speed are some of the factors that can influence flow patterns.
✓ In 1978, DRTL conducted an extensive examination of these factors and their influence on dissolution testing. They concluded that the geometry of the rotating paddle and/or basket, the flask dimensions, and the sampling positions can all introduce various types of flow patterns that can alter the dissolution characteristics of the drug product.
✓ The influence on flow patterns of the vertical distance of the basket or paddle from the lowest point of the bottom of the round-bottomed flask should also be considered. The official compendium specifies this distance to be 2.5 cm (±2 mm).

- **Sampling probes, position and filters:**
✓ Large probes can affect the hydrodynamics of the system and therefore the dissolution rate of some dosage forms, causing results that differ from those obtained by manual sampling 30-35. USP/NF states that samples should be removed at approximately half the distance from the bottom of the basket or paddle to the surface of the dissolution medium and not closer than 1 cm to the side of the flask. The choice of a filter should be preceded by an investigation of the adsorption characteristics of the drug and the particular filter material.

Factors Related to Dissolution Test Parameters

- **Temperature:**
✓ USP/NF specifics that the dissolution medium must be held at 37°C. Although most commercial water baths can meet this standard of performance. It is often assumed that the water-bath temperature and the flask temperature are the same. Plastic flasks have a heat transfer coefficient approximately 3.5 times less than that of glass material.
✓ As the temperature difference between the bath and the flask's medium is lowered, the amount of heat transferred into the flask is reduced. It is vital to cover the flask at least during dissolution testing.
✓ Since the drug solubility is temperature dependent, its careful control during the dissolution process is crucial. The effect of temperature variations of the dissolution medium depends mainly on the temperature-solubility curves of the drug and excipients in the formulation. Stokes' equation explains the temperature dependency of a dissolved molecule and diffusion coefficient:

$$D = \frac{kT}{6\pi\,\eta\,r}$$

Where, k is the Boltzmann constant and the denominator expresses the Stokes force for a spherical molecule, η is the viscosity and r is the radius of the molecule.

- **Dissolution medium:**
  - ✓ The constituents, nature and overall characteristics of the dissolution medium have a significant bearing on the dissolution performance of a drug substance. Also, selection of the proper dissolution medium for dissolution testing depends on the solubility of the drug as well as on economics and practicality. Factors such as dissolved gases, media pH, and viscosity of the medium have been shown to be significantly influential as far as dissolution rate is concerned.
- **Viscosity:**
  - ✓ Dissolution rate decreases with increase in viscosity of the dissolution medium; especially in case of diffusion controlled dissolution process. Viscosity has very little effect on interfacial controlled dissolution process.

Miscellaneous Factors:

- **Sorption:**
  - ✓ The relative density of the tablets was found to decrease, resulting in increased disintegration time with increase in water sorption-rate constants.
- **Humidity:**
  - ✓ In relation to the dissolution rate of a drug substance, humidity is usually associated with storage effects. Moisture has been shown to influence the dissolution of many drugs from solid dosage forms. The environmental conditions to which the dosage forms are exposed, moisture content in particular, should be rigorously assessed if reproducible and reliable dissolution data are to be obtained. Additionally, humidity during the manufacture of the dosage form should be carefully controlled to maintain the quality of the product from batch to batch.
- **Detection errors:**
  - ✓ Analytical methods are checked carefully for each dissolution system. Extreme care must also be exercised when laboratory methods are introduced into quality control to ensure that no part of the equipment interferes with sensitive determination.

3.6 DISSOLUTION TESTING DEVICES

- Dissolution testing is conducted using a dissolution apparatus that conforms to the specifications outlined in the United States Pharmacopeia.
- There are seven types of dissolution apparatus; the apparatus chosen to perform dissolution testing depends primarily on the drug dosage form.

USP/NF Apparatus I (Rotating Basket Method):

- It consist of, a 1 m in diameter and 13/8 m high stainless steel, 40 mesh wire basket rotated at speed ranging between 25-150 rpm.
- It is immersed in the 900 ml of dissolution medium in a flask of 1000 ml capacity.

- The medium in the flask is maintained at a constant temperature of $37 \pm 0.5°C$ by means of a water bath.
- The stainless steel employed for the fabrication of basket is not totally resistant to corrosive media like dilute acid.
- Plating of gold upto 1×10^{-4} m thickness is permitted for use in the acid media.
- Certain analytical procedures such as flurometric determinations are sensitive to presence of nickel, chromium and 316 stainless steel.
- In such cases, basket as well as bottom part of the basket, drive shafts and warrants gold plating.
- This requires a 40 inch screen. 10, 20 and 30 inch screen can also be used.
- Usually 40 inch screen tends to clog and apparent rate of dissolution is lowered.
- This method is employed for dissolution testing of suppositories and microencapsulated particles.

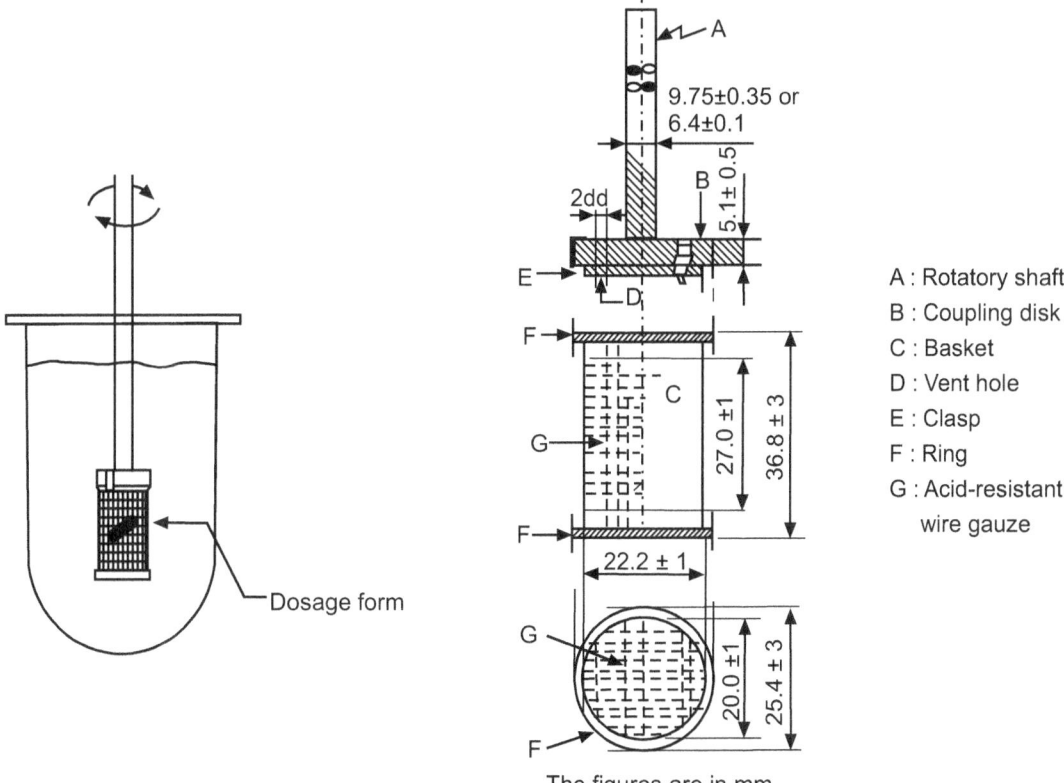

A : Rotatory shaft
B : Coupling disk
C : Basket
D : Vent hole
E : Clasp
F : Ring
G : Acid-resistant wire gauze

The figures are in mm.

Fig. 3.6: Dissolution apparatus -I

Uses:

- Capsules
- Beads

- Delayed release/enteric coated dosage forms
- Floating dosage form
- Surfactants in media

Advantage:

- pH change during the test can be easily automated which is important for routine investigations.

Disadvantages:

- Disintegration-dissolution interaction.
- Hydrodynamic "dead zone" under the basket.
- Degassing is particularly important.
- Limited volume, so sink conditions for poorly soluble drugs.

USP Apparatus II (Rotating Paddle):

- Paddle is substituted for the rotating basket.
- The contour of the paddle blade must not include any sharp edges at the tip which will not produce turbulent flow patterns.

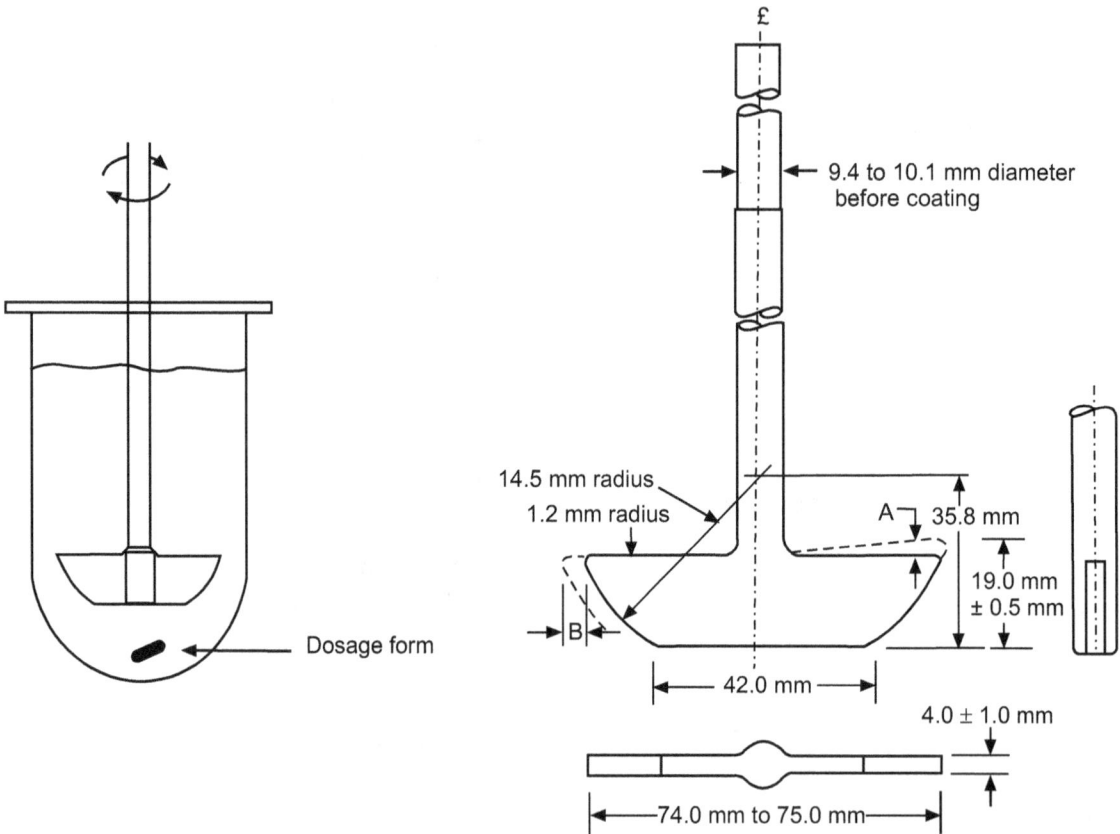

Fig. 3.7: Dissolution apparatus - II

- No significant wobble should be produced.
- The paddles should be coated with polyflurocarbon to prevent corrosion and entry of unwanted ions into the medium.

Note:

- Shaft and blade material : 303 (or equivalent) stainless steel.
- A and B dimensions should not vary more than 0.5 mm when part is rotated on £ axis.
- Tolerance is ± 1.0 mm, unless otherwise stated.
- The stirring paddle has been specified to be of stainless steel rather than glass with detachable blade.
- USP permits variations in the paddle method involving use of helix of non-reactive material as a "sinker" for floating dosage units.
- It is useful for solids, modified release tablets and transdermal patch.

Fig. 3.8: Sinkers for dissolution apparatus - II

Uses:

- Tablets
- Capsules
- Beads
- Delayed release / enteric coated dosage forms

Advantages:

- Easy to use.
- Robust.
- Can be easily adapted to apparatus.
- Long experience.
- pH change possible.
- Can be easily automated which is important for routine investigations.

Disadvantages:

- pH/media change is often difficult.
- Limited volume, so sink conditions for poorly soluble drugs.
- Hydrodynamics are complex, they vary with site of the dosage form in the vessel (sticking, floating) and therefore may significantly affect drug dissolution.
- Sinkers are required for floating dosage forms.

Table 3.1: Difference between USP-I and USP-II Apparatus

Parameter	USP-I (Rotating basket)	BP	USP-II (Rotating paddle)
Water bath temperature	36.5 - 37.5°C	37°C	36.5 - 37.5°C
Dissolution medium	900 ml	1000 ml	900 ml
Required samples	6 + 6 + 12	5 + 5	6 + 6 + 12
Shaft speed (rpm)	20 - 150	20 - 150	20 - 150
Shaft diameter (mm)	6 - 10.5 mm	6 mm	9.5 - 10.5 mm
Centering	2 mm	2 mm	2 mm
Eccentricity	No significant wobble.	No significant wobble.	No significant wobble.
Sampling point	Half way from top of the basket to top of fluid. Not closer than 1 cm to side of flask.	Half way between basket and side. At middle of basket.	Same as USP – I.
Flask	Cylindrical with spherical bottom	Cylindrical flat bottom	Same as USP – I.
Basket position (mm)	2.5 ± 0.2 mm	2 ± 0.2 mm	2.5 ± 0.2 mm

USP Apparatus - III (Reciprocating Cylinder):

Main features of USP Apparatus III are as given below :

- Cylinder with the mesh screen at top and bottom.
- It is useful for pH profile, sustained release dosage form.
- Standard volume : 200 - 250 ml per station.
- The assembly consists of a set of cylindrical, flat-bottomed glass vessels, a set of glass reciprocating cylinders, inert fitting and screens that are made of suitable non-sorbing and non-reactive material and fit the tops and bottoms of the reciprocating cylinders.

- Vessels are partially immersed in a suitable water both of any convenient size holding temperature at $37 \pm 0.5°C$.

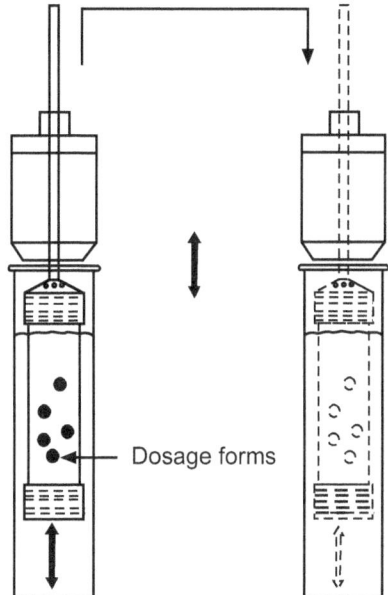

Fig. 3.9: Dissolution apparatus - III

Uses:

- Tablets
- Beads
- Controlled release formulations

Advantages:

- Easy to change the pH.
- pH-profiles.
- Hydrodynamics can be directly influenced by varying the dip rate.

Disadvantages:

- Small volume (Max. 250 ml).

USP Apparatus IV (Flow Through Cell) :

Main features of USP Apparatus IV are as given below :

- It is useful for low solubility drugs and drugs undergoing degradation.
- Large volume of dissolution medium is required for maintaining sink condition.
- To solve this problem, larger dissolution containers have been proposed, and another solution would be the continuous replacement of fluid.
- The flow through model effectively solves the problem of non-sink condition by supplying unlimited quantity of dissolution medium.

Principle:

- A sample is restrained in a small volume cell and subjected to a stream of dissolution media.
- Flow through model is characterized by a vertical cylindrical cell.
- The dissolution medium flows through the cell from bottom to top of the cell, achieved by means of an external pump.
- A filtration device at the top of the cell quantitatively retains all undissolved material and provide clear solution for subsequent assay.
- Depending on whether the effluent returns to the source or not, decides the nature of the system, open or closed.

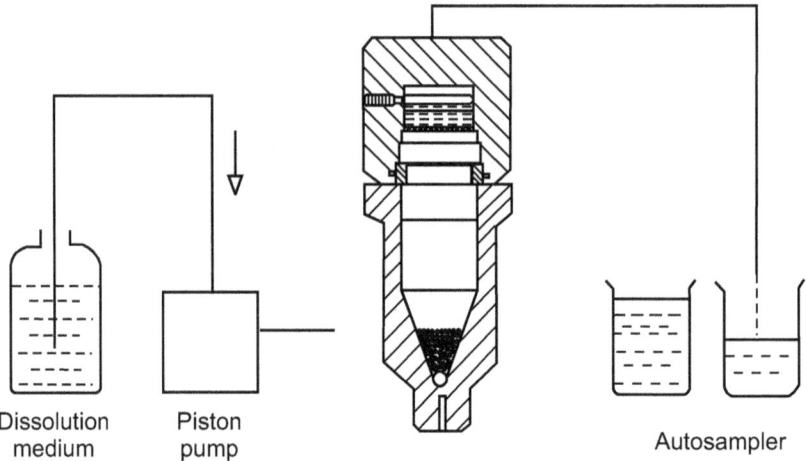

Dissolution   Piston
medium   pump   Autosampler

Fig. 3.10: Dissolution apparatus - IV

Uses:

- Low solubility drugs.
- Microparticulates.
- Implants.
- Suppositories.
- Controlled release formulations.

Variations:

- Open system.
- Closed system.

Advantages:

- Easy to change media pH.
- pH-profile possible.
- Sink conditions.

- Different modes:
    a) Open system
    b) Closed system

Disadvantages:
- Deaeration is necessary.
- High volumes of media.
- Labour intensive.

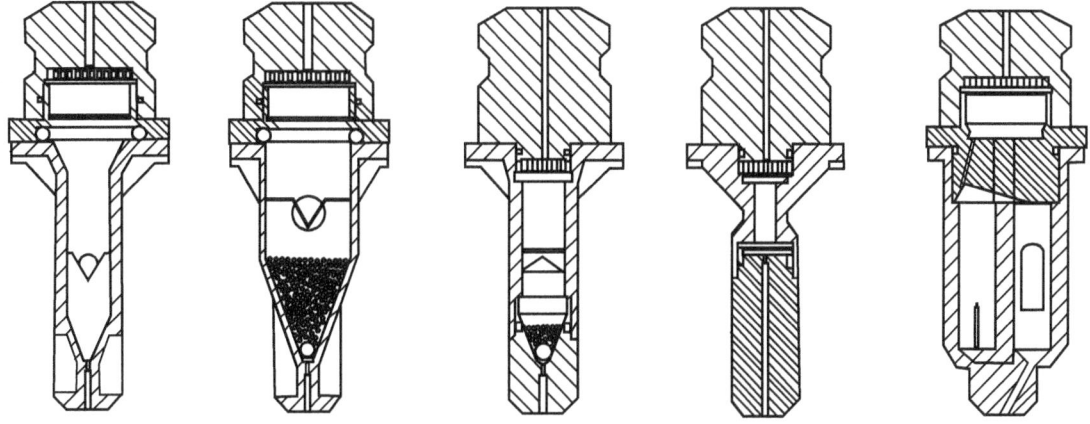

Fig. 3.11: Dissolution apparatus - IV (Cell types)

Advantages of Flow through over Basket and Paddle Method:
- The method permits the convenience of changing pH during dissolution testing.
- There are only a small number of apparatus parameters that affect the test and have to be standardized.
- The method has built-in filtration.
- The method eliminates most of the problems of sample position in the stream of dissolution media.
- The test can be run as either an open and closed system.

USP Apparatus V (Paddle Over Disc):
- In paddle over disc method, the paddle and vessel assembly from apparatus II with the addition of a stainless steel disc assembly is designed for holding the transdermal system at the bottom of the vessel.
- Apparatus is used to test transdermal patches, ointment, emulsions and floaters.
- Volume : 900 ml.

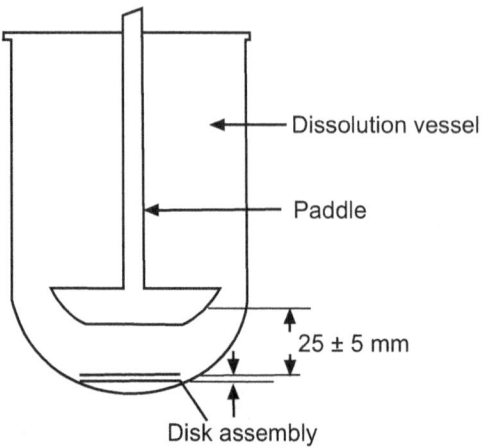

Fig. 3.12 : Dissolution apparatus – V

Advantages:

- Standard equipment (paddle) can be used, only add a stainless steel disk assembly.

Disadvantages:

- Disk assembly restricts patch size.

USP Apparatus - VI (Rotating Cylinder):

- This is a modification of basket apparatus. It uses the vessel assembly from apparatus I except to replace the basket and shaft with a stainless steel cylinder stirring element.
- Volume : 900 ml.
- Useful for transdermal patch.

USP Apparatus - VII (Reciprocating Disc):

- Originally introduced in the USP a small volume option per small transdermal patches, reciprocating disc apparatus was later renamed as the reciprocating holder with the four additional holders.
- Volume - 50 - 400 ml.
- Useful for transdermal patch, solid dosage form, pH profile.

3.6.1 Apparatus Used for Different Dosage Form

Immediate release dosage forms:

Apparatus I or II (preferably II).

Controlled release dosage forms:

Apparatus I or II using different media for QC.

Apparatus III or IV for R&D purposes.

3.7 AUTOMATION IN DISSOLUTION TESTING

Laboratories automate dissolution tests to increase capacity, improve accuracy and reduce costs per test. These factors lead one to consider automation as a method of choice for a quality-control laboratory as well as for a research laboratory. With the widespread acceptance of dissolution testing in pharmaceutical industry various automated procedures have been developed.

Fibre Optics Technology :

This development suggest that fiber optic technology is likely to emerge as a common analytical tool in future. One method reported is the development of a UV Fiber Optic Probe Dissolution System for the analysis of solid dosage forms. The system uses 12 dip-type fiber optic probes coupled to 12 separate PDA spectrophotometers to acquire continuous dissolution curves in real time. The system is applicable to the analysis of both immediate and controlled release formulations. The system is accurate, quicker and easier to set up when compared with conventional HPLC or UV-sipper systems.

Data Presentation and Interpretation

- The samples collected during the course of dissolution testing are assayed spectrophotometrically or by any other method like HPLC.
- The % of drug release by the dosage form is calcaluted and the data so obtained is presented as dissolution profile.
- The plot of % drug release Vs time is constructed.

Acceptance Criteria Accepted to IP :

S_1	6	All are not < Q + 5%
S_2	6 + 6	Average of 12 ≥ Q And no unit is < Q – 15%
S_3	6 + 6 + 12	Average of all 24 ≥ Q and not more than 2 units are < Q –15% and no unit is < Q – 25%

3.8 BCS CLASSIFICATION SYSTEM

The 'Biopharmaceutical Classification System' ('BCS') is a way to classify drugs into four categories according to their aqueous solubility and permeability:

Class I: High Solubility – High Permeability

Class II: Low Solubility – High Permeability

Class III: High Solubility – Low Permeability

Class IV: Low Solubility – Low Permeability

Purpose of the BCS Guidance:

Expands the regulatory application of the BCS and recommends methods for classifying drugs.

Explains when a waiver for *in vivo* bioavailability and bioequivalence studies may be requested based on the approach of BCS.

Goals of the BCS Guidance:

To improve the efficiency of drug development and the review process by recommending a strategy for identifying expendable clinical bioequivalence tests.

To recommend a class of immediate-release (IR) solid oral dosage forms for which bioequivalence may be assessed based on *in vitro* dissolution tests.

To recommend methods for classification according to dosage form dissolution, along with the solubility and permeability characteristics of the drug substance.

Absorption Number (A_n): Absorption number is defined as 'the ratio of the mean residence time to mean absorption time'. It denotes the dimensionless dose/solubility ratio for the particular drug formulation. The dose/solubility ratio indicates whether the capacity of the GI fluid is sufficient to dissolve the entire dose administered.

$$A_n = \frac{P_{eff} \times t_{res}}{R}$$

Dissolution Number (D_n): Dissolution number is defined as 'the ratio of mean residence time to mean dissolution time'.

$$D_n = \frac{t_{res}}{t_{Diss}}$$

Dose Number (D_o): Dose number is defined as 'the mass divided by the product of uptake volume (250 ml) and solubility of drug'.

$$D_o = \frac{M_o}{C_s V_o}$$

where M_o is the dose of drug administered, V_o is the initial gastric volume ($\approx$250 ml), C_s is the saturation solubility, t_{res} is the mean residence time ($\approx$180 min), t_{diss} is the time required for a drug particle to dissolve, P_{eff} is the effective permeability, and R is the radius of the intestinal segment.

3.8.1 Classification of Drugs According to BCS Classification System

Class I:

The drugs of this class exhibit high absorption number and high dissolution number. The rate-limiting step is drug dissolution, and if dissolution is very rapid, then the gastric-emptying rate becomes the rate-determining step. These compounds are well absorbed, and their absorption rate is usually higher than the excretion rate. Examples include metoprolol, diltiazem, verapamil and propranolol.

Class II:

The drugs of this class have a high absorption number but a low dissolution number. *In vivo* drug dissolution is then a rate-limiting step for absorption except at a very high dose number. The absorption for Class II drugs is usually slower than for Class I and occurs over a longer period of time. *In vitro–in vivo* correlation (IVIVC) is usually accepted for Class I and Class II drugs. The bioavailability of these products is limited by their solvation rates. Hence, a correlation between the *in vivo* bioavailability and the *in vitro* solvation can be found. Examples include glibenclamide, phenytoin, danazol, mefenamic acid, nifedinpine, ketoprofen, naproxen, carbamezapine and ketoconazole.

Class III:

Drug permeability is the rate-limiting step for drug absorption, but the drug is solvated very quickly. These drugs exhibit a high variation in the rate and extent of drug absorption. Since the dissolution is rapid, the variation is attributable to alteration of physiology and membrane permeability rather than the dosage form factors. If the formulation does not change the permeability or gastrointestinal duration time, then Class I criteria can be applied. Examples include cimetidine, ranitidine, acyclovir, neomycin B.

Class IV:

The drugs of this class are problematic for effective oral administration. These compounds have poor bioavailability. They are usually not well absorbed through the intestinal mucosa, and a high variability is expected. Class IV compounds are the exception rather than the rule and these are rarely developed and marketed. Examples include hydrochlorothiazide, taxol and furosemide.

3.8.2 Class Boundaries

- A drug substance is considered HIGHLY SOLUBLE when the highest dose strength is soluble in < 250 ml water over a pH range of 1 to 7.5 at 37°C.
- A drug substance is considered HIGHLY PERMEABLE when the extent of absorption in humans is determined to be > 90% of an administered dose, based on mass-balance or in comparison to an intravenous reference dose.
- A drug product is considered to be RAPIDLY DISSOLVING when > 85% of the labelled amount of drug substance dissolves within 30 minutes using USP apparatus I or II in a volume of < 900 ml buffer solutions.

3.8.3 Determination of Solubility

Solubility is the amount of a substance that has passed into solution when equilibrium is attained between the solution and excess (i.e., undissolved) substance at a given temperature and pressure.

A drug substance is considered highly soluble when the highest dose strength is soluble in 250 ml or less of aqueous medium over the pH range of 1 - 7.5.

Solubilities are determined by exposing an excess of solid (drug) to the liquid in buffer and water and assaying after equilibrium has been established. It usually takes 60 - 72 hrs. to establish equilibrium; however, sampling at earlier points is necessary. Solubilities cannot be determined by the precipitation method because of the so-called metastable (solubility) zone. The pH–solubility profile of the drug is determined at 37 ± 1°C in aqueous medium in the pH range of 1 - 7.5 (per FDA guidelines) or 1.2 - 6.8 (per WHO guidelines).

Solubility can be measured as either a kinetic or a thermodynamic value. Kinetic solubility measurements start from dissolved compound and represent the maximum (kinetic) solubility of the fastest precipitating species of a compound. Kinetic solubility values are strongly time-dependent. Due to the degree of super saturation that may occur, values are likely to over-predict the thermodynamic solubility and are not expected to be reproducible between different kinetic methods such as a turbidimetric–nephelometric method and UV absorption.

In thermodynamics, solubility can predict drug properties during lead optimization. These methods include a scaled-down shake-flask method and a solvent evaporation method.

3.8.4 Determination of Permeability

The permeability is based directly on the extent of intestinal absorption of a drug substance in humans or indirectly on the measurements of the rate of mass transfer across the human intestinal membrane.

The methods that are routinely used for the determination of permeability include :

- Human studies, mass balance pharmacokinetic studies, absolute bioavailability studies, intestinal perfusion methods.
- Intestinal permeability methods *in vivo,* intestinal perfusion studies in humans *in vivo* or *in situ,* intestinal perfusion studies in animals *in vitro,* permeation experiments with excised human or animal intestinal tissue.
- *In vitro* permeation experiments across epithelial cell monolayers (e.g., Caco-2 cells or TC7 cells).

3.8.5 Determination of Dissolution

Formulation composition and the manufacturing process generally influence *in vitro* drug dissolution. The BCS classifies a drug product as rapidly dissolving when no less than 85% of the labelled amount of the drug substance dissolves in 30 min using the following condition :

- USP Apparatus 1 (basket) at 100 rpm or USP Apparatus 2 (paddle) at 50 rpm.

- Dissolution medium volume of 900 ml or less is used in each of the following buffer conditions : (1) 0.1 N HCl or simulated gastric fluid (SGF) USP without enzymes. (2) A pH 4.5 buffer. (3) A pH 6.8 buffer or simulated intestinal fluid (SIF) USP without enzymes .

3.9 SELECTION OF DISSOLUTION MEDIA AND CONDITIONS

Choice of a dissolution medium is an important and critical variant for drug dissolution testing. The reported choices range from a simple solvent (water) to complex solutions, often drug and/or product dependent. However, making a choice is not so simple or straightforward, but confusing and often scientifically or logically not convincing or valid.

Required Common Characteristics of a Dissolution Medium

Since the objective of drug dissolution testing is to assess the expected drug dissolution in the GI tract, the medium should be representative of the liquid-phase present in the tract, which is aqueous. Therefore, to be physiologically or bio-relevant, the dissolution medium has to be water or water-based. However, one may not use media such as potassium or sodium hydroxide solutions which, although water-based, their use is restricted by their high pH values not found in the GI tract.

A general restriction imposed upon the choice of a dissolution medium by the physiological aspect is, therefore, that the medium be aqueous and have a pH in the range of 1 to 7. Furthermore, considering the physiological aspect with regard to dissolution testing, it is generally recognised that the most of time, absorption of drugs occurs in the intestinal part of the GI tract where the pH ranges from 5 - 7, and not in the gastric (stomach) section where the pH is usually 1 or sometimes 2 - 3.

Thus, since drug absorption depends on dissolution, and most absorption occurs in the intestine, physiological aspects dictate that a medium should be aqueous having pH in the range of 5 - 7. First choice for a dissolution medium would be water itself. Incidentally, the pH of purified water falls in the range of 5 - 7, thus it would fulfil the physiological relevancy of the pH aspect well. The following discussion will be built on this choice, with modifications as needed, for developing an appropriate dissolution medium to test a variety of products containing different types of APIs, having different release characteristics.

3.10 KEY OPERATING PARAMETERS

1. Volume:

The recommended volume of dissolution medium is 900 ml when using the basket or paddle apparatus.

The volume can be raised to between 2 and 4 lit, depending on the concentration and sink conditions of the drug solution.

2. Temperature:

The standard temperature for the dissolution medium is $37 \pm 0.5°C$ for oral dosage forms.

Slightly increased temperatures such as $38 \pm 0.5°C$ have been recommended for dosage forms such as suppositories.

Lower temperatures such as $32 \pm 0.5°C$ are utilized for topical dosage forms such as transdermal patches and topical ointments.

3. Deaeration:

Air bubbles can interfere with the test results.

Bubbles on the dosage unit may decrease the dissolution rate by decreasing the available surface area.

Some formulations will be sensitive to the presence of dissolved air in the dissolution.

Media containing surfactants are not usually deaerated after the surfactant has been added to the medium.

The USP deaeration method requires heating of the medium, followed by filtration and drawing of a vacuum for a short period of time. Other deaeration methods such as room temperature filtration, sonication and helium sparging are described in literature.

The deaeration method needs to be clearly characterized, since the method chosen might impact the dissolution release rate. It should be noted that dissolution tests using the flow through cell method could be particularly sensitive to the deaeration of the medium.

Media containing surfactants are not usually deaerated after the surfactant has been added to the medium because of excessive foaming.

-   Once the appropriate dissolution conditions have been established, the method should be validated for linearity, accuracy, precision, specificity and robustness/ruggedness.
-   All dissolution testing must be performed on a calibrated dissolution apparatus meeting the mechanical and system suitability standards specified in the appropriate compendia.
-   Therefore, the development and validation of a scientifically sound dissolution method requires the selection of key method parameters that provide accurate, reproducible data that are appropriate for the intended application of the methodology.

3.11 DISSOLUTION STUDIES OF VARIOUS DOSAGE FORMS

1. Immediate Release Tablet

Immediate release dosage forms are intended for rapid delivery of a drug into the blood circulation. However, drug absorption into systemic circulation may be limited by the dissolution rate. Studies of dissolution in immediate release drugs are typically done with USP apparatus 1 - 4, those being the rotating basket, paddle, reciprocating cylinder and flow-through cell, respectively. Aspirin, brompheniramine maleate and ethambutol hydrochloride tablets are examples of using apparatus-I. Bethanecol chloride, betaxolol and cefadroxil tablets are examples of using apparatus-II for USP dissolution test. To evaluate the application of a dynamic dissolution, protocol can be used to simulate the *in vivo* dissolution of glyburide, Biopharmaceutical Classification System (BCS) class II drug. In this study, SIF and bio-relevant dissolution media were used in apparatus-II to investigate the dissolution of different immediate release glyburide tablets. The pH of the dissolution medium was changed from pH 6.5 glyburide to pH 7.5 and back to pH 5.0. These changes simulate the physiological pH change in the small and large intestine.

2. Dosage Forms for the Oral Cavity

Dosage forms for the oral cavity such as sublingual tablets, buccal tablets, chewing gums and chewable tablets are solid dosage forms that are placed in the mouth, allowing the active ingredient to dissolve in the saliva and then absorb either via the oral route or by the buccal/sublingual mucosa within the mouth. However, there are challenges regarding the extent of drug delivery in the mouth as opposed to the oral route, namely due to a short residence time in the mouth, and the small volume of liquid available to dissolve the medication. As a result, modification in the standard USP test apparatus (as well as the development of novel apparatuses) is required in order to mimic *in vivo* conditions for accurate analysis of these dosage forms.

3. Liquid Oral Dosage Forms

Suspensions

Pharmaceutical suspensions are liquid preparations consisting of solid particles dispersed throughout a liquid phase in which the particles are not soluble. The external phase is an aqueous, organic or oily liquid phase in which the insoluble internal phase is uniformly dispersed.

Rationale for drug release testing of suspensions

Several individual product-specific monographs for suspensions have been included in the USP with some monographs requiring drug release testing. From a biopharmaceutical perspective, drug release may be the rate-limiting step for the absorption of oral suspensions with a chance to *in vitro – in vivo* correlations (IVIVC). Also, drug release testing is required for market release, evaluation of the impact of manufacturing processes on product performance, or substantiation of label claims.

4. Chewable Tablets

Rapidly disintegrating chewable tablets are used primarily for the oral route of administration, and are designed to increase compliance among individuals who are unable to swallow traditional tablets. But the extent to which each tablet will be chewed may vary from individual to individual, ranging from being completely chewed to swallowing the tablet in chunks. The USP has stated the need to use apparatus-II for chewable tablets, the same as for traditional tablets. Furthermore, it has been recommended that, the use of USP apparatus-III, a reciprocating cylinder, along with glass beads is used to create a large amount of agitation within the dissolution medium.

5. Buccal / Sublingual Tablets

Rapid orally disintegrating tablets may be used to achieve a fast onset of action. Alternatively, the buccal/sublingual route is also suitable for medications that cannot or shall not be taken by the oral route due to instability of drug at the low pH of the stomach, or their susceptibility to the hepatic first pass effect. USP states the use of disintegration test for ergoloid mesylate and ergotamine tartarate sublingual tablets and apparatus-II with water as dissolution medium for isosorbide dinitrate sublingual tablet which has been introduced recently, comprises a single stirred continuous flow-through filtration cell with a dip tube to remove finely divided solid. An alternative method is used to study the release of nicotine from buccal tablets. They used modified Franz diffusion cell for this purpose. The dissolution medium was 22 ml phosphate buffer saline (PBS) (pH 7.4) at 37°C.

6. Chewing Gums

The USP has not yet created an apparatus test for the release of medication. Today drugs are more and more delivered by convenient dosage forms like gums or lately by strips. The European Pharmacopoeia has developed a 3-piston apparatus, which in essence "chews" the gum at a rate of 60 cycles/min in a test medium with pH of 6.0 at 37°C. The medicated gum for a specific period of time (i.e. 10, 20, 30 or 40 min); followed by analyzing the residual quantity for the amount of active ingredient remaining in the gum.

7. Suppositories

Similar to lipid-filled soft gelatine capsules, it is challenging to find a standard method to test *in vitro* drug release from lipophilic suppositories. This is due to the medium and deformation of the suppository in the dissolution medium of the UPS states apparatus-II for conducting dissolution tests of indomethacin suppositories. Lipophilic suppositories release the drug after melting in the rectal cavity. Therefore rectal temperature greatly affects drug release. In the rectum, the drug partitions between the lipophilic base and the present fluid. Distribution equilibrium between the base and fluid can occur rather than complete dissolution. For *in vitro* release testing, one requires knowledge of the melting point range of the suppository base, and testing temperature should be similar with physiological conditions.

8. Transdermal Patches

For transdermal delivery system, many variables may alter the release of the drug into the skin. Large changes in the rate and extent of drug delivery may occur caused by the slightest change of the formulation. The USP has published three different *in vitro* drug release tests for dissolution testing of patches. These include paddle over disk, cylinder method and reciprocating disk method, apparatuses V, VI, VII respectively (USP 29). The paddle over disk method is the most widely used method because it is simple and easy to reproduce. The testing conditions should be ideally adjusted to pH 5 - 6 reflecting physiological skin condition. The temperature may increase when it is covered by the transdermal delivery system. The agitation speed rate should be set at 100 rpm. Nicotine transdermal patch is an official monograph in the USP. They use phosphate buffered saline (PBS) pH 4.5 containing 20% PEG 400; water, PBG 400; water, PBS at pH 7.4 and PBS at 5.4 as the dissolution medium in the receiver chamber respectively.

Although several apparatus and procedures have been utilized to study *in vitro* release characteristics of transdermal patches, it is desirable to avoid unnecessary proliferation of dissolution/drug release test equipment. Current compendial apparatus include the paddle over disk/disk assembly method (*European Pharmacopeia* 2.9.4.1/USP apparatus V), the rotating cylinder (*European Pharmacopeia* 2.9.4.3/USP apparatus VI), the reciprocating disk, and a paddle over extraction cell method (*European Pharmacopeia* 2.9.4.2).

The paddle over disk procedure with a watch glass-patch-screen sandwich assembly could be a suitable method as it has been shown experimentally that this procedure results in almost the same release profile as other, more complicated apparatus for all US marketed transdermal patches. The configuration of this assembly ensures that the patch is prevented from floating during the entire testing period. Alternatively, the patch can be fixed to the supporting disk (e.g., by double-sided adhesive), superseding the use of a screen for fixation. Special attention needs to be given to the proper positioning of the patch so that the drug-loaded surface is exposed to the medium.

The pH of the medium ideally should be adjusted to pH 5 - 6, reflecting physiological skin conditions. For the same reason, the test temperature is typically set at 32°C (even though the temperature may be higher when the skin is covered). One hundred revolutions per minute is considered a typical agitation rate by *European Pharmacopeia*.

The experimental setup (dissolution medium, agitation speed etc.) and testing time should take into account the amount of drug administered to the body during the application time of the patch. In cases, where drug release cannot be achieved in an appropriate time by using standard aqueous dissolution media, aqueous–organic solvent mixtures can also be used.

9. Semisolid Dosage Forms

Semisolid dosage forms include creams, ointments and gels. Currently no monograph exists in the USP with used dissolution testing of semisolid bases. In research, the drug release test is normally performed using the Franz cell diffusion system. Critical components of the *in vitro* release test for semisolid products include selection of an assay method, diffusion cell volume, selection of an appropriate membrane, nature of receiving medium, equipment related parameters, stirring speed, temperature and validation of the method. The membrane must be an inert material that does not interact chemically or physically with the drug. The membrane should not contain leachable that may interfere with the assay. Common membranes are Tuffryn®, Supor®, Cellulosic, Acetate Plus®, Nylon, Teflon and polycarbonate. The receiving medium must be similar to physiological conditions of the skin.

3.12 COMPENDIAL DISSOLUTION MEDIA

The following media are given in the USP.

1. Simulated Gastric Fluid

The traditional medium to simulate gastric conditions in the fasted state has been simulated gastric fluid (SGF) of the USP. This medium contains hydrochloric acid, sodium chloride, pepsin and water, and has a pH of 1.2. Although the medium addresses many of the qualities of gastric juice, there are some aspects that could be optimized. For weak acids and neutral compounds, this small difference makes absolutely significant effect in the dissolution characteristics, but for very poorly soluble weak bases, the dissolution results in compendial SGF are likely to over estimate the *in vivo* dissolution rate. Further deviations from gastric physiology are the pepsin concentration, which is very high compared to that observed in gastric juice aspirated under fasted state conditions and the surface tension of about 70 mN/m that does not take into account the much lower average surface tension of human gastric fluid, which has been repeatedly measured as lying in the 35 - 50 mN/m range.

2. Water

Water is an attractive medium and because of its simplicity, has been widely used for quality control purposes. It could even be argued that it is physiologically relevant since many formulations are intended to be ingested with a glass of water. Furthermore, in those patients with hypochlorhydria (elevated gastric pH), due to aging and/or co-therapy with H_2 receptor antagonists and proton pump inhibitors, water may be a somewhat suitable medium as it roughly reflects the increased gastric pH and the low buffer capacity. However, the pH of water may vary with its source, and water has no buffer capacity. Thus, for the latter purpose, a better alternative, which would be more biorelevant in this context, is a diluted HCl/NaCl solution or a diluted acetate buffer with a final pH of around 5.

3. **Simulated Intestinal Fluid**

A frequently used medium for the simulation of small intestinal (SI) conditions in the fasted state is simulated intestinal fluid (SIF), a medium that was first described as standard test solution in the USP more than 50 years ago. The only parameter that has been changed is the pH of the medium. As it was assumed that the pH in the small intestine is very close to blood plasma, the pH of SIF was initially set at 7.5. However, subsequent examinations of the pH in the intestinal tract revealed that a pH gradient exists within the small intestine, that the pH becomes less acidic at more distal locations, and that pH values close to 7.5 can only be measured in the terminal ileum. The use of an *in vitro* medium with an unsuitably high pH in contrast would most probably lead to false positive results, especially for poorly soluble, weakly acidic drugs and enteric coated dosage forms.

3.13 BIORELEVENT MEDIA

*   Biorelevant is a shortform of 'biologically relevant'.
*   Biorelevant media are virtually the same as intestinal juices. They contain key natural surfactants (bile salts, phospholipids) present in intestinal juices. These are missing from ordinary dissolution media.
*   They are virtually the same as the fluids inside the body. It can provide a much more accurate picture of how drugs and their formulations are likely to dissolve in vivo.
*   The aims are to highlight potential bioavailibility issues and attempt to achieve IVIVC.
*   Biorelevant media include Fasting state and Fed state simulated Gastro Intestinal fluids.

These are described below:

1. **Fasted State Gastric Conditions (FaSSGF)**

*   Several attempts have been made to improve simulation of fasting conditions in the stomach. In most of these media, particular attention was given to the simulation of the surface tension measured in human gastric aspirates.
*   However, in these media, non-physiologically relevant surface active agents, lower than physiological pH values or by far too high concentrations of pepsin or bile salts, were utilized.
*   Recently, a fasted state simulated gastric fluid (FaSSGF) containing pepsin and low amounts of bile salt and lecithin was developed by Vertzoni .
*   In these experiments, they could clearly show that compared with data in other frequently used media, solubility data in FaSSGF provide a better basis for the assessment of intragastric solubility during a bioavailability study in the fasted state.
*   Thus, to better predict drug solubility and dissolution rate in the fasted stomach, the use of FaSSGF is strongly recommended for future *in vitro* experiments.

- Sodium taurocholate was chosen as a representative bile salt because cholic acid is one of the more prevalent bile salts in human bile.

- For this media, Standard paddle or basket apparatus is used.

2. Fasted State Small Intestinal Conditions (FaSSIF)

- Specifically fasted state simulating intestinal fluid (FaSSIF) was developed to simulate fasting conditions in the proximal small intestine.

- The addition of a stable phosphate buffer system that results in a pH representative to values measured from the mid-duodenum to the proximal ileum.

- This medium contains bile salts and phospholipids (lecithin).

- These compounds facilitate the wetting of solids and the solubilization of lipophilic drugs into mixed micelles.

- Thus, the dissolution of poorly soluble, lipophilic drugs may be enhanced.

- Sodium taurocholate was chosen as a representative bile salt because cholic acid is one of the more prevalent bile salts in human bile.

- From pharmacokinetic studies of drug absorption in the fasted state, ingesting 200 - 250 ml of water with the dosage form, a maximum total volume of about 300 - 500 ml will be available in the proximal SI. Therefore, for dissolution tests, a volume of $\leq$ 500 ml is recommended.

3. Fed State Gastric Conditions: Milk and Ensure® Plus

- In the fed state, the luminal composition in the stomach will be highly dependent on the composition of the meal ingested.

- The composition and the amount of the food is different for every individual so we can not get correlation.

- However, none of these media reflects all parameters that are important for determining food effects on drug release in the stomach.

- The ideal medium representing initial gastric conditions in the fed state should have similar nutritional and physicochemical properties to that of a meal. For example, the standard breakfast recommended by the US FDA to study the effects of food in bioavailability and bioequivalence studies.

- Milk was first investigated as a dissolution medium about 20 years ago, the use of Ensure® Plus has been established only a few years ago.

- Ensure® Plus have a similar composition to a breakfast meal with respect to the ratio of carbohydrate/fat/protein.

- The pH (6.5 - 6.6) and additional physicochemical properties are similar to those of homogenized and undigested standard breakfasts, whereas Ensure® Plus comes closer to the properties of the FDA breakfast.

- In addition, as the stability of fresh milk at 37°C is a problem, heat-treated milk must be used.

4. **Fed State Small Intestinal Conditions (FeSSIF)**

- As in the stomach, conditions for drug dissolution in the proximal part of the small intestine are highly dependent on whether the drug is taken in the fed or the fasted state.

- After ingesting a meal, there are changes in both the hydrodynamics and the intralumenal volume.

- The pH of the chime after a solid meal is lower than the intestinal fluid pH in the fasted state, while buffer capacity and osmolality show a sharp increase.

- With these factors, the sharp increase in bile output could also be a major influence on the bioavailability of a drug.

- In order to achieve the higher buffer capacity and osmolality, while maintaining the lower pH value, representative of fed state conditions in the proximal small intestine, FeSSIF contains an acetate buffer.

- Taurocholate and lecithinare are present in considerably higher concentrations than in the fasted state medium to reflect the biliary response to meal intake.

- For example, Danadrol. The dissolution rate is maximum with the FeSSIF, than FaSSIF, than the SIF.

RECOMMENED DISSOLUTION MEDIUM COMPOSITION AND VOLUME FOR ROTATING BASKET OR ROTATING PADDLE APPARATUS

Table 3.2: Recommended Dissolution Conditions

Guidance or compendial reference	Volume	pH	Additives
Federation International Pharmaceutique (FIP)	500 - 1,000 ml; 900 ml historical; 1,000 ml recommended for future development	pH 1 - 6.8; above pH 6.8 with justification — not to exceed pH 8.	Enzymes, salts, surfactants with justification

Contd...

United States Pharmacopeia (USP)	500 - 1,000 ml; up to 2,000 ml for drug with limited solubility	Buffered aqueous solution pH 4 - 8 or dilute acid solutions (0.001N HCl to 0.1N HCl)	Enzymes, salts, surfactants balanced against loss of discriminatory power; enzymes can be used for crosslinking of gelatin capsules or gelatin-coated tablet
World Health Organization (WHO), European Pharmacopoeia (Ph Eur), Japanese Pharmacopoeia (JP)	Determined per product	Adjust pH within ±0.05 units of the prescribed value.	Determined per product.
Food and Drug Administration (FDA)	500, 900 or 1,000 ml	pH 1.2 - 6.8; higher pH is justified case - by case — in general, not to exceed pH 8.	Surfactants are recommended for poorly soluble drug products — need and amount should be justified; enzymes use need case - by case justification; utilized for the cross-linking of gelatin capsules or gelatin-coated tablets.

3.14 COMPARISON OF DISSOLUTION PROFILES

3.14.1 Model Independent Method

Dissolution of test and reference products should be conducted in each of the following three media:

1. Acidic media such as 0.1 N HCl.

2. pH 4.5 Buffer.

3. pH 6.8 Buffer.

Two scenarios for comparing the profiles obtained from multipoint dissolution are operative.

1. If both the test and reference product show more than 85% dissolution within 15 minutes, the profiles are considered similar (no calculation required).

2. If not, then calculate the f_2 value. If $f_2 \geq 50$, the profiles are normally regarded similar such that further *in vivo* studies are not necessary. Only one measurement should be considered after 85% dissolution of both products has occurred and excluding point zero.

The similarity factor (f_2) is a logarithmic reciprocal square root transformation of the sum of squared errors, and is a measurement of the similarity in the percentage (%) dissolution between two curves.

$$f_2 = 50 \cdot \log \left\{ [1 + \left(\frac{1}{n}\right) \sum_{t=1}^{n} (R.t - T.t)^2] .100 \right\}$$

Where, n is the number of time points, R is the dissolution value of the reference batch at time t and T is the dissolution value of the test batch at time t.

A specific procedure to determine difference and similarity factor is as follows:

a. Determine the dissolution profile of two products, i.e. of the test and reference products (using 12 units each).

b. For f_2 calculations a minimum of three time points (excluding point zero) must be used, and only one measurement included after 85% dissolution of both products has occurred.

c. For curves to be considered similar, f_2 values should be close to 100. Generally, f_2 values greater than 50 (50 to 100) ensure similarity or equivalence of the two curves and, thus, of the performance of the test and reference products.

3.14.2 Model Dependent Method

The kinetic models used were a zero order equation, First order equation, Higuchi's model and Korsmeyers – Peppas model.

1. Zero order kinetics : A zero order release would be predicted by the following equation

$$A_t = A_0 - K_0 t$$

Where,

A_t = Drug release at time t

A_0 = Initial drug concentration

K_0 = Zero-order rate constant (mg/ml hr)

When data is plotted as cumulative per cent drug release versus time, if the plot is linear then the data obeys zero order release kinetics, with a slope equal to K_0.

2. First order kinetics : A First order release would be predicted by the following equation

$$Log\ C = Log\ C_o - \frac{K_t}{2.303}$$

Where,

C = Concentration of drug remaining at time t

C_o = Initial concentration of drug

K = First order rate constant (lit/hr)

When the data is plotted as log cumulative per cent drug remaining versus time, yields a straight line, indicate that the release follows first order kinetics. The constant 'K' can be obtained by multiplying 2.303 with the slope values.

3. Higuchi's model : Drug released from the matrix devices by diffusion has been described by following Higuchi's classical diffusion equation

$$Q = \left[\frac{D\varepsilon}{T}(2A - eC_s)\right]C_s.t^{1/2}$$

Where,

Q = Amount of the drug released at time t

D = Diffusion coefficient of the drug in the matrix

A = Total amount of drug in the volume of matrix

C_s = The solubility of the drug in the diffusion medium

ε = Porosity of the matrix

T = Tortuosity

t = Time (hrs) at which Q amount of the drug is released

Equation becomes:

$$Q = K$$

When the data is plotted according to the equation i.e., cumulative drug release versus square root of time, yields a straight line, indicating that the drug was released by diffusion mechanism. The slope is equal to K.

4. Korsmeyer and Peppas model : The release rates from controlled release polymeric matrix can be described by the equation proposed by Korsmeyers et al .

$$Q = K\ t^n$$

Where,

Q = The percentage of drug released at time t

K = A kinetic constant incorporating structural and geometric characteristics of the tablets

n = The diffusional exponent indicative of the release mechanism;

For fickian release, n = 0.45 while for anomalous (Non-fickian) transport, n ranges between 0.45 and 0.89 and for zero order release, n = 0.89.

Table 3.3: Various Kinetic Models

Model	Equation	Specification
Zero Order	$C = K_0 t$	K_0 is the zero-order rate constant expressed in units of concentration/time and t is the time in minutes.
First Order	$\text{Log } C = \dfrac{\log C_0 - k.t}{2.303}$	C_0 is the initial concentration of drug, K is the first order constant and t is the time.
Higuchi	$Q_t = Kt^{1/2}$	Q_t is the amount of drug released in time t, K is the kinetic constant and t is the time in minutes.
Korsmeyer-Peppas	$Kt^n = \dfrac{M_t}{M_\infty}$	M_t represents amount of the released drug at time t, M_∞ is the total amount of drug released after an infinite time, K is the diffusional characteristic of system constant and n is an exponent that characterizes the mechanism of drug release. If n < 0.5, the mechanism is quasi Fickian diffusion, if n = 0.5 - 1.0; then it is non-Fickian or anomalous diffusion, if n = 1.0; mechanism is non-Fickian case II diffusion and if n > 1.0; mechanism is non-Fickian super case II).

3.15 BCS AND BDDS

3.15.1 BCS

The purpose of BCS is to characterize drugs for which products of those drugs may be eligible for a biowaiver of *in vivo* bioequivalence studies. The purpose of BDDCS is to predict drug disposition and potential drug-drug interactions in the intestine and the liver, and potentially the kidney and brain. Both BCS and BDDCS use solubility as one of the two classification criteria.

3.15.2 BDDS

BDDCS is to predict drug disposition and potential drug-drug interactions in the intestine and the liver with an emphasis on defining which drugs would be amenable to enzymatic disposition transporter disposition and drug-drug interactions, as well as where transporter-enzyme interplay may be important.

3.15.2.1 Classification of BDDCS

Class 1

High Solubility.

Extensive Metabolism.

(Rapid Dissolution and ≥70% Metabolism for Biowaiver.)

Class 2

Low Solubility.

Extensive Metabolism.

Class 3

High Solubility.

Poor Metabolism.

Class 4

Low Solubility.

Poor Metabolism.

The recognition of the correlation between intestinal permeability rate and extent of metabolism allows prediction of BDDCS class for an new molecular entity to be based on passive membrane permeability.

3.15.2.2 Role of BDDCS

The recognition of the correlation between intestinal permeability rate and extent of metabolism and our finding that a nonviable membrane can serve as surrogate marker preceded an explanation for these findings.

3.15.2.3 Use of BDDS for Drug Already in Market

- Predict potential drug–drug interactions not tested in the drug approval process.
- Predict the potential relevance of transporter–enzyme interplay.
- Assist the prediction of when and when not transporter and/or enzyme pharmacogenetic variants may be clinically relevant.
- Predict when transporter inhibition by uremic toxins may change hepatic elimination.
- Predict the brain disposition.
- Increase the eligibility of drugs for BCS Class 1 biowaivers using measures of metabolism.

Transporter effects predicted by BDDCS following oral doses :

Class 1

High solubility /High permeability.

Metabolism transporter effects minimal in gut and liver.

Class 2

Low solubility/High permeability.

Efflux transporter effects predominate in gut, but both uptake and efflux transporters can affect liver.

Class 3

High solubility/Low permiability.

Absorptive transporter effects predominate (but can be modulated by efflux transporters).

Class 4

Low solubiliy/Low permiability.

Absorptive and efflux transporter effects could be important.

3.15.3 Major Difference between BDDCS and BCS

BDDCS	BCS
1. Predicting drug disposition and drug–drug interaction in intestine and liver.	1. Faciliate biocoaivers of *in vivo* bioequivalence studies.
2. Predictions are based on intestinal permiability rate.	2. Biocoaviers are based on extent of permiability, which in a number of cases does not correlate with permiability rate.

3.16 APPLICATIONS OF DISSOLUTION

1. Product Development

Important tool during development of dosage form. Aids in guiding the selection of prototype formulations and for determining optimum levels of ingredients to achieve drug release profiles, particularly for extended release formulations. Also guides in selection of a "market-image" product to be used in pivotal *in vivo* bioavailability or bioequivalence studies.

2. Quality Assurance

Dissolution test is performed on future production lots and is used to assess the lot-to-lot performance characteristics of drug product and provide continued assurance of product integrity/similarity.

3. Product Stability

In vitro dissolution is also used to assess drug product quality with respect to stability and shelflife, as product age, physicochemical changes to the dosage form may alter dissolution characteristics of drug product over time. In some products, polymorph transformations are more stable and hence less soluble crystalline forms may result in reduced dissolution rates.

4. Comparability Assessment

Also useful for assessing the impact of pre- or post- approval changes to drug product such as changes to formulation or manufacturing process. Thus, *in vitro* comparability assessment is critical to ensure continued performance equivalency and product similarity.

5. Waivers of *In vivo* Bioequivalence Requirements

In vitro dissolution testing or drug release testing may be used for seeking waiver of required product to conduct *in vivo* bioavailability or bioequivalence studies.

 ❖ ❖ ❖

Chapter 4

STABILITY STUDY

4.1 INTRODUCTION

The purpose of stability testing is to provide evidence on how the quality of an active pharmaceutical ingredient or medicinal product varies with time under influence of variety of environmental factor such as temperature, humidity, light, and to establish a re-test period for active pharmaceutical ingredient or shelf life for the medicinal product.

4.2 ESSENTIAL ICH DEFINITIONS

1. Stability:

Stability is defined as 'the capacity of a drug substance (API) or drug product (FPP) to remain within established Physical, Chemical, Microbiological, Therapeutic and Toxicological specifications to maintain its identity, strength, quality and purity throughout the re-test or expiration dating periods'.

2. Regulatory/formal stability testing:

Long term and accelerated (and intermediate) studies undertaken on primary and/or commitment batches according to a prescribed stability protocol to establish or confirm the re-test period of an API or the shelf life of a FPP (Finished pharmaceutical product).

3. Stress testing – forced degradation of API:

Stress testing of the active pharmaceutical ingredient can help to identify the likely degradation product which can in turn help to establish the degradation pathway and the instrinsic stability of the molecule and validate the stability indicating power of the analytical procedure used.

4. Stress testing – forced degradation of FPP:

Studies are undertaken to assess the effect of severe conditions on the FPP. Such studies include photostability testing (ICH Q1B) and compatibility testing on APIs with each other in FDCs and API(s) with excipients during formulation development.

5. Accelerated stability testing:

These are the studies designed to increase the rate of chemical degradation and physical change of a drug by using exaggerated storage conditions as part of the formal stability testing programme. The data thus obtained, in addition to those derived from real – time stability studies, may be used to assess long-term chemical effects under non-accelerated conditions and to evaluate the impact of short-term excursions outside the label storage conditions, as might occur during shipping. The results of accelerated testing studies are not always predictive of physical changes.

6. Short-term temperature excursion study:

To be designed by anticipating the extreme high and low temperature conditions that may occur during drug product shipment.

7. Thermal cycling excursion study:

To be designed by anticipating which fluctuating environmental conditions may occur during drug product distribution.

8. Mean kinetic temperature (MKT):

MKT, as defined by the USP, is "a single calculated temperature at which the total amount of degradation over a particular period is equal to the sum of the individual degradations that would occur at various temperatures".

9. Re-test period:

The period of time during which the API should be examined to ensure that the material is still in compliance with the specification and, thus suitable for use in the manufacture of a given FPP, when stored under the defined conditions.

10. Shelf life (Expiration dating period) :

The time period during which an API or a FPP is expected to remain within the approved shelf-life specification, if stored under recommended conditions.

11. Specification - Release :

The combination of physical, chemical, biological and microbiological tests, and acceptance criteria that determine the suitability of a drug product at the time of its release.

12. Specification - Shelf life :

The combination of physical, chemical, biological and microbiological tests, and acceptance criteria that determine the suitability of an API throughout its re-test period, or that an FPP should meet throughout its shelf life.

13. Mass balance :

The process of adding together the assay value and levels of degradation products to see how closely these add upto 100% of the initial value, with due consideration of the margin of analytical error.

14. Primary batch (also called exhibit batch)

A batch of an API or FPP used in a formal stability study, from which stability data are submitted in a registration application for the purpose of establishing a re-test period or shelf life, respectively.

15. Commitment batches :

Production batches of a drug substance or drug product for which the stability studies are initiated or completed, post approval through a commitment made is in the registration application.

16. Production (scale) batch :

A batch of an API or FPP manufactured at production scale by using production equipment in a production facility as specified in the application.

4.3 OBJECTIVES BEHIND STABILITY STUDIES

- To determine shelf-life, storage conditions and labelling specifications.
- To verify that no changes have been introduced in the formulation or manufacturing process that can adversely affect the stability of the product.
- To select a suitable formulation and container closure system from the view point of stability for a predicted period.
- To determine degradation product and degradation pathway.
- To provide evidence on how quality of drug substance or product varies with the time under the influence of various factors like temperature, humidity and light.
- To determine the intrinsic stability of a drug molecule.
- To prevent great loss which may occur by recalling the batch due to some type of instability.

4.4 STAGES OF STABILITY STUDIES

Stability testing is done in five different stages when an NDA is being contemplated.

1. Preformulation and compatibility.
2. Preclinical formulation.
3. Clinical and NDA formulation.
4. Commitment and product monitoring.
5. Post NDA change of formulation.

1. Preformulation and compatibility:

In the early stage of drug designing, studies are done to find out what sort of decomposition is possible, mechanism, sensitivity to moisture and oxygen interaction probabilities (compatibilities), optimum pH and polymorphic information.

2. Preclinical formulation:

More than one or two formulations being used in Phase-I studies are manufactured and started on stability studies.

3. Clinical and NDA formulation:

When a product pass from Phase-I, its dosage level, interactions and stability profile are known to some extent, and armed with this knowledge, the "Clinical manufacturing group" of the company manufactures several batches of the product and keeps some products from every batch for stability. The required stability aspects of clinical formulation are simply to ascertain that each batch is within specifications during the length of the trail.

4. Commitment and product monitoring:

The ICH stability guidelines require that three substantial batches, made in the same type production equipment intended for the final product, be made and should maintain at least 12 months stability at the time of NDA submission.

5. Post NDA change of formulation:

At the time the NDA is filed, if the large clinical and scate-up batches are only about a year old, and the stability data on them is not yet complete. So at this time, the company can ask for an expiry date based on extrapolation of the existing stability data. The FDI will take all facts into consideration and grant an expiry date based on a commitment from the company that the company will continue to do stability studies on different batches.

The storage requirements and the sampling times are very clearly specified by the ICH guidelines.

4.5 TYPES OF STABILITY STUDIES

1. Regulatory / Formal Stability Study
   A) Accelerated
   B) Intermediate
   C) Long Term (Real Time)
2. Stress Testing / Short Term /Forced Degradation Testing
3. Thermal Cycling Stability Study

4.5.1 Accelerated Stability Study

These are the studies designed to increase the rate of chemical degradation and physical change of a drug by using exaggerated storage conditions as a part of the formal stability testing programme.

4.5.1.1 Stability Programme

WHO guidelines divide the world into four zones and specify the temperature and relative humidity conditions to be maintained by each zone for stability studies.

Climatic Zones and Conditions:

Table 4.1: Climatic Zones

Zones	Areas	Temperature	Relative humidity
I	Temperate/Moderate	21°C	45 %
II	Subtropical	25°C	60 %
III	Hot/Dry	30°C	35 %
IV	Hot/Humid/Tropical	30°C	70 %

Few Countries of Various Zones:

Zone I : Britain, North Europe, Russia, Canada

Zone II : U. S. A, Japan, South Europe

Zone III : Iran, Iraq, Sudan

Zone IV : Brazil, Ghana, Indonesia, Phillipines

Important Considerations for Stability Study

1. Accelerated stability testing on two batches should be conducted, one of which must be either commercial batch or a pilot-scale batch.

   - If accelerated stability testing was carried out on one laboratory batch, which was produced by similar manufacturing process and has the same composition of active ingredient/s and excipient/s as for the commercial batch, accelerated stability test on single commercial or pilot-scale batch should be acceptable.

   - Accelerated stability testing should be done on 0, 3 and 6 months

2. Initially, real time stability testing should be conducted on two batches for the expected shelf life of the product, one of which should be commercial batch. One batch can be a pilot scale batch.

   - Real time stability testing should be done on 0, 3, 6, 9 and 12 months in first year, every six-month in second year and once every year afterwards.

3. One initial batch of the pharmaceutical product should be tested for antimicrobial preservative effectiveness (in addition to preservative content) at the proposed shelf-life for verification purposes.

4. If significant change occurs between 3 and 6 months' testing at the accelerated storage condition, the proposed shelf-life should be based on the real-time data available from the long-term storage condition.

   - In general, "significant change" for a pharmaceutical product is defined as:
     a. A 5% change in assay from its initial value.
     b. Any degradation product exceeding its acceptance criterion.

    c. Failure to meet the acceptance criteria for appearance and physical attributes (e.g. colour, phase separation, re-suspendibility, caking, hardness). However, some changes in physical attributes (e.g. softening of suppositories, melting of creams, partial loss of adhesion for transdermal products) may be expected under accelerated conditions.

    d. Failure to meet the acceptance criterion for pH (for liquid preparation).

    e. Failure to meet the acceptance criteria for dissolution for 12 dosage units (tablet and capsule).

5. Stability studies for products stored in impermeable containers can be conducted under any controlled or ambient humidity condition.

6. If no significant change occurs during six-month's accelerated and real time stability testing, the product will be allowed to place in the market with a provisional shelf-life of upto twenty-four months. However, real time stability testing should be continued upto the proposed shelf-life.

    • The manufacturer should have a system of recall in place so that, the sale of any batch which does not remain within the limit of approved product specification be stopped within twenty-four hours.

7. Once the pharmaceutical product has been registered, additional stability studies are required whenever variations that may affect the stability of the active pharmaceutical substance or pharmaceutical product are made, such as major variations like the following:

    a. Change in the manufacturing process.

    b. Change in the composition of the pharmaceutical product.

    c. Change of the immediate packaging.

8. The ongoing stability programme should be described in a written protocol, and results formalized as a report.

9. Conditions of climatic zone IV will be applicable for Nepal, though the WHO document mentions climatic zone II.

    • Condition for real time stability testing: 30°C ± 2°C and 65% RH ± 5% RH;

    • Condition for accelerated stability testing: 40°C ± 2°C and 75% RH ± 5% RH.

Minimum Requirement for Applying for the Marketing Approval of the Product

1. Accelerated stability test result for at least one commercial batch, or pilot-scale batch intended to be placed in the market and produced using the same equipment and process approved for commercial batch. Accelerated stability testing should be done in 0, 3 and 6 months.

2. Real time stability study reports for 0, 3 and 6 months for the same batch for which accelerated stability testing is carried out.

3. Real time and acclerated stability test report should be self-explanatory and conclusion should be mentioned on the report.

4. Report of analysis from National Medicines Laboratory for the same batch for which accelerated stability report is being submitted.

4.5.1.2 Methods of Accelerated Stability Testing of the Pharmaceuticals

This method can be used to determine the shelf life of pharmaceuticals which are based on the principle of chemical kinetics demonstrated by :

1. Garret and Carper method
2. Free and Blythe method

1. Shelf Life Determination Based on Arrhenius Plot (Garret and Carper Method)

1. Determine the drug content at all three storage points (40°C, 50°C and 60°C) by taking a number of samples and take the mean drug content.

2. At each temperature, plot a graph between time and log per cent drug remaining. If the decomposition is of first order this gives a straight line. If it is of zero order, per cent drug remaining versus time will give a straight line.

3. Next, take the log K or log of reaction constant on Y axis and $\dfrac{1}{T \times 10^{-3}}$ on X axis and draw a best fit line. This line is the Arrhenius Plot, extrapolate this line to get K at 25°C and from this plot, calculate the shelf life.

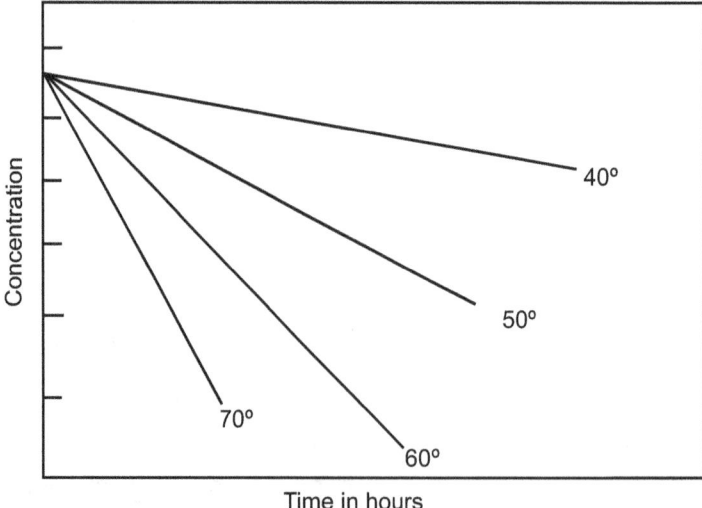

Fig. 4.1 : Arrhenius plot for predicting drug stability at room temperature

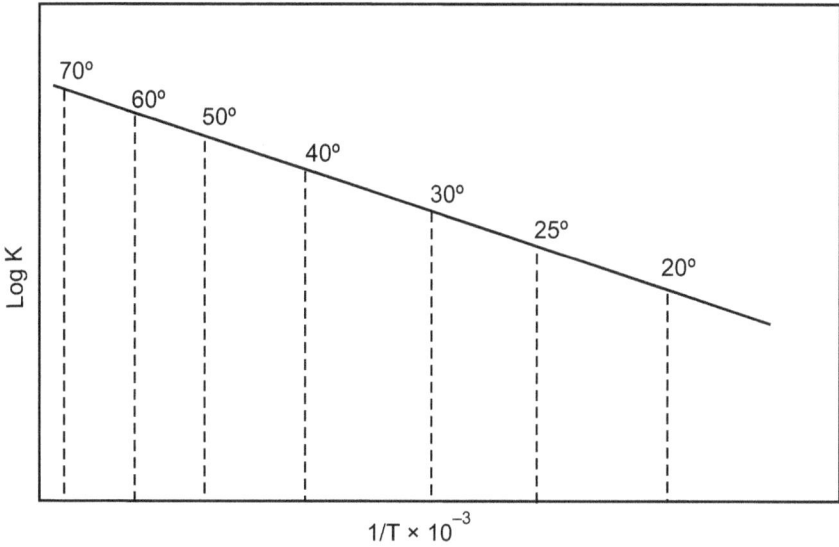

Fig. 4.2 : Arrhenius plot for predicting drug stability

If the reaction is following zero-order:

$$\text{Expiration date at } 25\,^{\circ}C\ (t_x) = \frac{\text{Initial potency} - \text{Minimum potency}}{\text{Reaction rate at } 25°C}$$

$$\therefore \qquad t_x = \frac{Y_o - Y_x}{K_o}$$

If the reaction is following first order:

$$\text{Expiration date at } 25\,^{\circ}C\ (t_x) = \frac{\text{Log initial potency} - \text{Log minimum potency}}{\text{Reaction rate at } 25\,°C}$$

$$t_x = \frac{\log Y_o - \log Y_x}{K_1}$$

Where Y_o = Initial potency

Y_x = Final potency

K_o = Zero order constant

K_1 = First order constant

2. Shelf Life Determination Based on T_{90} Values (Free and Blythe Method)

In this method, the fraction life period is plotted against a reciprocal temperature. And the time in days required for drug to decompose to some fraction of its original potency at room temperature. This approach is clearly illustrated in Fig. 4.3.

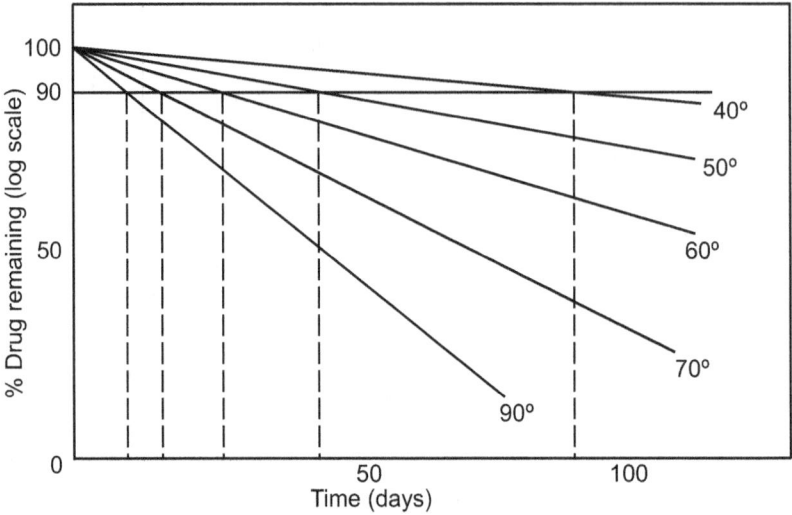

Fig. 4.3: Plotted against drug remaining and time

The log % of drug remaining is plotted against days and the time for the loss line at several temperatures to reach 90% of the theoretical potency is noted by the doted line.

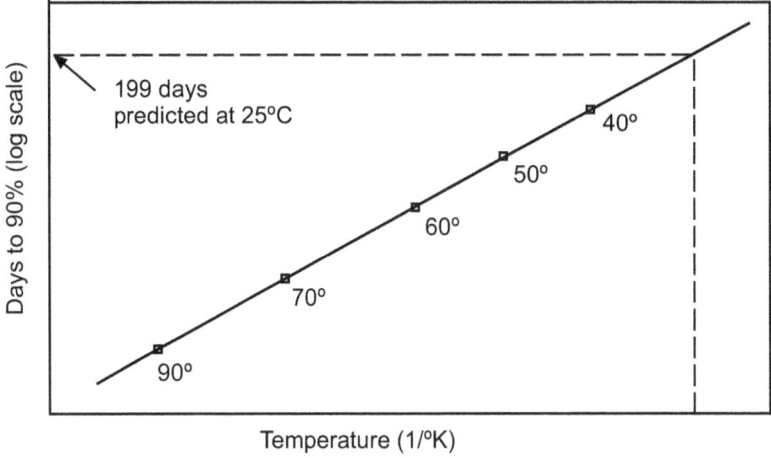

Fig. 4.4: Plotted against temperature and days to 90%

The log time to 90% is then plotted against 1/T and the time for 10% loss of potency at room temperature can be obtained from the resulting straight line by extrapolation to 25°C.

4.5.1.3 Limitations of Accelerated Stability Studies

• Accelerated stability studies are valid only when the breakdown depends on temperature.

• Accelerated stability studies are valid only when the energy of activation is about 10 to 30 kcal/mol. Solution have energy of activation in this range.

- Stability prediction at elevated temperature is of little use when degradation is due to diffusion, microbial contamination and photo-chemical reaction.

- Stability studies are meaningless when the product looses its physical integrity at higher temperature like coagulation of suspending agent, de-naturation of proteins.

- Prediction will become erroneous when the order changes at elevated temperatures, as in case of suspension (zero order) which at higher temperature get converted to solution which follow 1st order.

4.5.1.4 Shelf Life Determination Based on Real Time Testing

Real time stability testing is normally performed for longer duration of test period in order to allow significant product degradation under recommended storage condition.

Another method which involves real time testing and statistical analysis, is also followed for determinng shelf life.

Steps are given below:

1. Keep three batches for stability study at least for 1 year at one fixed temperature.

2. Test them at 0, 1, 3, 6, 9 and 12 months for drug content.

3. Plot the graph of % drug content on Y-axis and time on X-axis along with confidence intervals. Where the lower 95% confidence curve intersects minimum potency, there you fix the shelf life.

As an example, the data and figure are given in Tablets, Volume 3, page 355 by Hebet A Lieberman and Leon Lachman (Fig. 4.5).

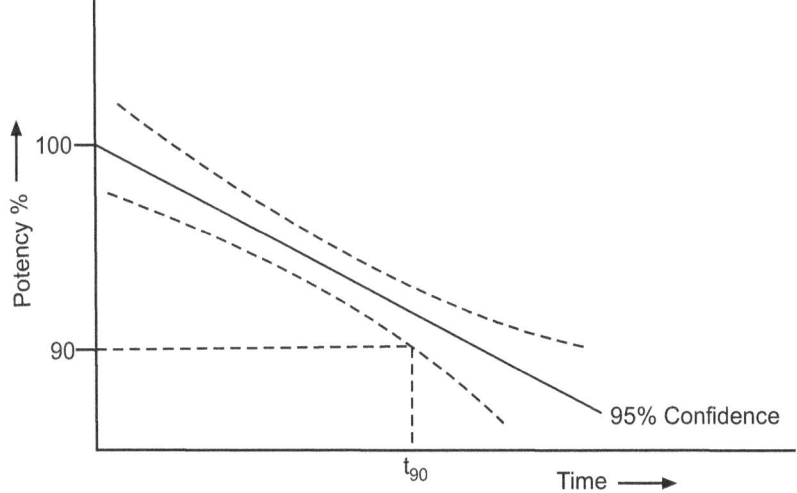

Fig. 4.5: Plot of inpotency against time showing 95% confidence limit line

Table 4.2 : Vitamin Tablets Stability Confidence Intervals at 40°C

Time (Months)	Results (mg/tablet)	Lower limit	Upper limit
0	100.0	95.2	104.9
1	91.2	88.7	93.8
3	83.1	79.3	87.3
6	75.8	69.8	82.5
9	69.1	61.2	78.2
12	63.0	53.6	74.0

Where estimate of the standard error of regression,

$$S = \sqrt{\frac{\Sigma (y_i - \hat{y}_i)^2}{n-2}}$$

y_i = Predicted value at t_i

For e.g.

y_1 = Predicted value at t_1

n = Sample size

S = Standard error of the line

α = 0.1 % two-sided

    = 0.05% one-sided

This method also helps in calculation of amount of overages in vitamin products.

4.5.1.5 Q_{10} Method for Shelf Life Estimation

Q_{10} approach is taken by Simonelli and Dresback.

Q_{10} is the factor by which the rate constant increases for a 10°C temperature increase.

It is the ratio of two different reaction rate constants.

Commonly used Q values of 2, 3 and 4 relate to the energy of activation of reaction for room temperature (25°C).

$$Q_{10} = \frac{K_{(T+10)}}{K_T}$$

$$\frac{K_2}{K_1} = \exp\left[\frac{-E_a}{R}\left(\frac{1}{T_2} - \frac{1}{T_1}\right)\right]$$

$$Q_{10} = \exp\left[\frac{-E_a}{R}\left(\frac{1}{(T+10)} - \frac{1}{T}\right)\right]$$

For different temperature change ΔT

$$Q_\Delta = \exp\left[\frac{-E_a}{R}\left(\frac{\Delta T}{(T + \Delta T)\,(T)}\right)\right]$$

$$Q_\Delta = \frac{K_{(T + 10)}}{K_T} = Q_{10}^{(\Delta T/10)}$$

As is evident from this relationship, an increase in T will decrease the shelf life and a decrease in T will increase shelf life.

$$Q_{10} = \exp\left[\frac{-E_a}{R}\left(\frac{1}{(T + 10)} - \frac{1}{T}\right)\right]$$

Activation energy (E_a) of all chemical decomposition reaction usually fall in the range 12 to 24 kcal/mol.

4.5.1.6 Importance of Q_{10} Method In Shelf Life Estimation

It solves many problems like, t_{90} (T_1) is the given shelf life at given temperature (T_1), to determine the shelf life at another temperature (T_2).

Some specific examples are:

- The expiration date is given for room temperature. What is the expected extension of the shelf life in a refrigerator?
- The expiration date is given for refrigeration condition. How long the product may be left at room temperature ?
- The expiration date is given for room temperature and it is desired to heat the product, what per cent decomposition can be expected at higher temperature ?
- The expiration date is given for refrigeration condition; the product is stored for a period of time at room temperature. And is then returned to the refrigerator. What will be the corrected expiration date?

4.6 TYPES OF REACTIONS

Homogenous reactions : Homogenous reaction occur in single phase, which proceed uniformly through whole of the system.

Heterogenous reactions : Heterogenous reactions involve more than one phase and are often confined to phase boundary, their rates being dependent on the supply of fresh reactants to that boundary. Examples are, decomposition of drugs in suspensions and enzyme-catalyzed reactions.

MOLECULARITY

Molecularity is the number of molecules involved in forming the product. For example, $N_2O_5 \rightarrow 2NO_2 + \frac{1}{2} O_2$ is a slow unimolecular reaction and $\frac{1}{2} O_2 + \frac{1}{2} O_2 \rightarrow O_2$ is a fast bimolecular reaction.

4.7 ORDER OF REACTION

The order of reaction with respect to a given substance (such as reactant, catalyst or product) is defined as 'the index, exponent to which its concentration term in the rate equation is raised'.

This is the number of concentration terms that determine the rate.

Consider the reaction:

$$A + B \longrightarrow C + D$$

The rate of the reaction is proportional to the concentration of A to the power of x; [A]x, and also the rate may be proportional to the concentration of B to the power of y; [B]y.

The overall equation is, Rate = k [A]x · [B]y

The overall order of reaction is **x + y.**

RATE CONSTANT

A rate constant is a proportionality constant that appears in a rate law. For example, k is the rate constant in the rate law $\frac{d[A]}{dt} = k[A]$.

Rate constants are independent of concentration but depend on other factors, most notably temperature.

4.7.1 Zero Order Reaction

When the reaction rate is independent of concentration of the reacting substance, it depends on the zero power of the reactant and therefore is zero order reaction.

In this type of reaction, the limiting factor is something other than concentration, for example, solubility or absorption of light in certain photochemical reactions.

The rate of decomposition can be described mathematically as:

$$\text{Rate of concentration decrease} = \frac{- dC_X}{dt} = K \qquad \text{... (4.1)}$$

Integrating the equation yields,

$$X = K_t + \text{constant} \qquad \text{... (4.2)}$$

A plot of X Vs time results in straight line with slope equal to K. The value of K indicate the amount of drug that is degraded per unit time, and intercept of line at time zero is equal to constant in equation (4.2).

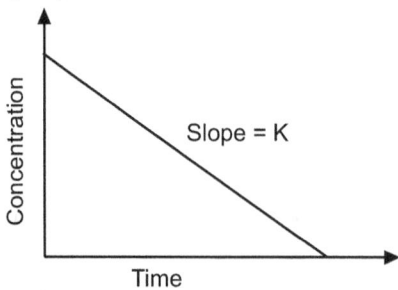

Fig. 4.6: Zero order reaction

The unit of K is conc. time^{-1}, with typical units of mole L^{-1} s^{-1}.

Half-life is given by equation $t_{1/2} = C_0/2K$

Examples: Vitamin A acetate to anhydrous vitamin A.

Photolysis of cefotaxime.

Loss in colour of multi-sulfa product.

4.7.2 First Order Reaction

When the reaction rate depends on the first power of concentration of a single reactant, it is considered to be **first order**. Examples are

- Absorption, distribution, elimination rates.

- Microbial death kinetics.

Thus, the rate of reaction is directly proportional to the concentration of reacting substance and can be expressed as follows:

$$\text{Rate of concentration} = \frac{-dC_X}{dt} = KC_X \qquad \qquad \text{... (4.3)}$$

If concentration of reactant X is 'a' at beginning of reaction when t = 0, and if amount that has reacted after time t is denoted by x then amount of X remaining at time t will be (a – x).

Therefore equation (4.3) can be rewritten as:

$$\frac{-dC_X}{dt} = K (a - x)$$

$$\frac{dC_X}{(a - x)} = -K\, dt \qquad \qquad \text{... (4.4)}$$

Integrating equation (4.4) between time limit 0 to t

$$\int_{a}^{a-x} dC_X = -K \int_{0}^{t} dt$$

$$\ln (a - x) - \ln a = -Kt$$

$$\log (a - x) - \log a = \frac{-Kt}{2.303}$$

$$\log (a - x) = \log a - \frac{Kt}{2.303} \qquad \qquad \text{... (4.5)}$$

Equation (4.5) is like y = mx + c (linear relationship)

If first order law is obeyed then a graph of log (a – x) Vs. time t will give straight line with slope of $\frac{-K}{2.303}$ and an intercept of log a at t = 0.

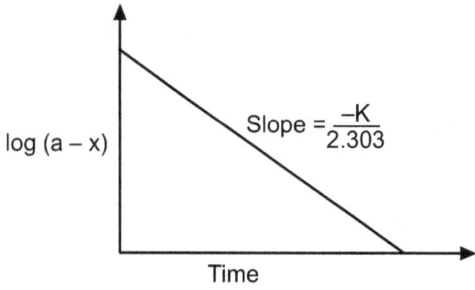

Fig. 4.7: First order reaction

Rearranging equation (4.5) we have,

$$K = \frac{2.303}{t} \log\left(\frac{a}{a-x}\right) \qquad \ldots (4.6)$$

Unit of K for first order is **time^{-1}** i.e. SI unit is (sec)$^{-1}$ because K is inversely proportional to t.

The half-life, $t_{1/2}$ of a drug is the time required for 50% of drug to degrade and can be calculated as follows:

$$t_{1/2} = \frac{2.303}{K} \log\left(\frac{C_0}{C}\right) = \frac{2.303}{K} \log\left(\frac{100}{50}\right)$$

$$= \frac{2.303}{K} \log(2) = \frac{0.693}{K}$$

$$\therefore \qquad t_{1/2} = \frac{0.693}{K} \qquad \ldots (4.7)$$

In pharmaceutical field, the time required for 10% of the drug to degrade is an important value to know, since it represents a reasonable limit of degradation of active ingredients. The $t_{10\%}$ value can be calculated as

$$t_{10\%} = \frac{2.303}{K} \log\left(\frac{100}{90}\right)$$

$$\therefore \qquad t_{10\%} = \frac{0.104}{K} \qquad \ldots (4.8)$$

or $\qquad t_{10\%} = 0.152\, t_{1/2}$

4.7.3 Second Order Reaction

Rate of change in concentration of product and reactant is dependent on second power of concentration of single reactant or to first powers of the concentrations of two reactants.

i.e. $$\frac{-dC_X}{dt} = K\,[X]\,[Y] \qquad \ldots (4.9)$$

Or $$\frac{-dC_X}{dt} = K\,[X]^2 \qquad \ldots (4.10)$$

$$\frac{-dC_X}{dt} = K\,[X]\,[Y]$$

Here decrease in concentration of Y is similar to X. If concentration of X and Y at time t = 0 are a and b respectively, and concentration of each substance that has reacted after time t is equal to x then concentration of X and Y remaining will be (a − x) and (b − x) respectively.

In case when (a ≠ b) :

$$\frac{-dx}{dt} = K(a-x)(b-x) \qquad \qquad \dots (4.11)$$

where, $\qquad -\dfrac{dx}{dt}$ = Rate of decrease in concentration of X or Y

Integrating equation (4.11) we get

$$Kt = \frac{2.303}{(a-b)} \log \frac{b(a-x)}{a(b-x)} \qquad \qquad \dots (4.12)$$

Rearranging equation (4.12) we get

$$\frac{\log(a-x)}{(b-x)} = \frac{(a-b)}{2.303} Kt + \log\left(\frac{a}{b}\right) \qquad \qquad \dots (4.13)$$

So, if second order reaction is observed then graph of $\log \dfrac{(a-x)}{(b-x)}$ Vs. t gives straight line with slope $\dfrac{(a-b)K}{2.303}$ and intercept $\log\left(\dfrac{a}{b}\right)$ at t = 0

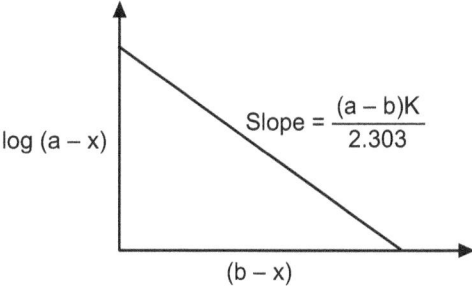

Fig. 4.8: Second order reaction time

In case when (a = b) :

$$\frac{-dC_X}{dt} = K[X]^2$$

Integration gives,

$$Kt = \frac{x}{a(a-x)} \qquad \qquad \dots (4.14)$$

Rearrangement of equation (4.14) gives us

$$Kt = \frac{1}{a-x} - \frac{1}{a} \qquad \qquad \dots (4.15)$$

If second order reaction is observed then graph of $\dfrac{1}{a-x}$ Vs. t gives straight line with slope K and intercept 1/a at t = 0.

Unit of second order reaction is concentration^{-1} time^{-1} and SI unit is mol^{-1} sec^{-1}.

Half-life in this case is $t_{1/2} = \dfrac{1}{aK}$.

4.7.4 Third Order and Higher Order Reaction

Rate of change in concentration is proportional to three concentration terms. However such reactions are rare and their analysis is complex. Reaction of even higher order is unlikely to occur.

Rate equation of third order reaction is as follows :

$$K = \frac{1}{2t}\left[\frac{1}{(a-x)^2} - \frac{1}{a^2}\right]$$

4.7.5 Pseudo Order Reactions

1. Pseudo-Zero Order Reaction

In solid state, sometimes drug decomposes by pseudo zero order i.e. reaction between drug and moisture in solid dosage form. The system behaves like suspensions and because of the presence of excess solid drug; the first order rate actually becomes pseudo zero order. Equation for it is similar to zero order except K is replaced by K′.

2. Pseudo-First Order Reaction

Here a second order or bimolecular reaction is made to behave like first order. This is found in the case in which one reacting material is present in great excess or is maintained at constant concentration as compared with other substance. Here reaction rate is determined by one reactant even though two are present.

Examples:

- Decomposition of ascorbic acid tablet.
- Aspirin hydrolysis.

4.7.6 Complex Reaction

Although most degradative reactions in pharmaceutical systems can be treated by simple zero order, first order and pseudo-first order kinetics, there are certain pharmaceutical formulations that exhibit more complicated reactions. These have opposing, consecutive and side reactions alongwith main reaction. They are as follows:

1. Opposing Reaction (Reversible)

The simplest case is in which both reactions are of first order

$$A \underset{K'}{\overset{K}{\rightleftharpoons}} B$$

A somewhat more complicated reaction is when forward is first order type and reverse reaction is second order type.

$$A \underset{K'}{\overset{K}{\rightleftharpoons}} B + C$$

Example: Epimerization of tetracycline.

2. Consecutive Reactions

$$A \xrightarrow{K_1} B \xrightarrow{K_2} C$$

Simplest is one where both the reactions are of first order.

If $K_2 > K_1$ then B can be considered as unstable intermediate and rate determining step for overall reaction would be conversion of A to C.

Examples:

Radioactive series/Isotopic decay follows first order, but it is a consecutive reaction.

Degradation of chlorbenzodiazepine by hydrolysis to lactum form and further to benzophenone.

3. Side Reactions (Parallel)

Here the reacting substance can be removed by two or more reactions occurring simultaneously, as depicted.

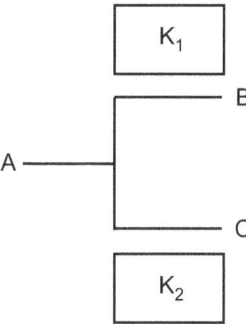

Examples: Purified insulin degrades by two mechanisms - deamidation and polymerization.

The relative rates of deamidation and polymerization are pH and temperature dependent.

4.7.7 Comparison of First, Second and Zero Order Reaction

A tablet decomposes after one year to 75% of its initial concentration.

In the following table the data of rate constant and half-life is given for particular order.

Table 4.3

Parameters	1st	2nd	Zero
K (per year)	1.38	0.03	75%
Half Life	0.50	0.33	0. 66

Initially speed of reaction is:

2nd order > 1st order > 0th order

- Because in 2nd order reaction, two molecules of reactants collide faster than one. Ideally, if every collision between molecules led to product, a second order reaction would be twice as fast as first order. But in our case this is not true as half-life of first order is not twice as that of second order. This indicates that not every collision between molecules lead to reaction. **After two years,**

Order of reaction	Zero	First	Second
Drug remaining	−50%	6.76%	20%

This shows that in 2nd year the speed of reaction reverses and 2nd order reaction becomes slowest as it is dependent upon the concentration of reactants and the concentration of reactants gets depleted as the reaction progresses. So the % of drug remaining is more in case of 2nd order reaction while in zero order all the drug got decomposed before two years.

4.7 METHODS TO DETERMINE ORDER OF REACTION

1. Substitution Method
2. Initial Rate Method
3. Data Plotting Method
4. Half-Life Determination Method

1. Substitution Method:

- The data accumulated in a kinetic study may be substituted in the integrated form of the equations which describes the various orders. When the equation is found in which the calculated K values remain constant, the reaction is considered to be of that order.

2. Initial Rate Method:

- Graphs of rate of reaction against concentration are plotted, and the initial rate is determined from the gradient at time = 0.
- If it is a straight line, the reaction is first order reaction.
- If a curve is obtained, then we can say it is second order reaction.
- A reaction which is independent on concentration is zero order reaction.

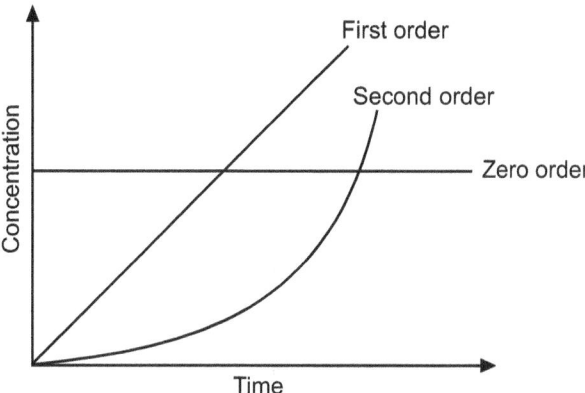

Fig. 4.9: Curves for different types of order

3. **Data Plotting Method:**

- If plot of concentration against time is linear, then it is zero order reaction.
- If plot of 1/c against time is linear then second order reaction.
- If plot of ln c against time is linear then first order reaction.

4. **Half-Life Determination Method:**

- The relationship, in general, between half-life of a reaction in which the concentrations of all reactants are identical, is

$$t_{1/2} \propto \frac{1}{a^{n-1}}$$

where n is the order of reaction.

- Thus, if two reactions are run at different initial concentrations, a_1 and a_2 with their respective half-lives and putting them in above equation in logarithmic form we finally get

$$n = \frac{\log\left[\dfrac{t_{1/2}\,(1)}{t_{1/2}\,(2)}\right]}{\log\left(\dfrac{a_2}{a_1}\right)} + 1$$

4.9 DETERMINATION OF $t_{10\%}$ BY ARRHENIUS EQUATION

Temperature influences rate and order of reaction. So shelf life of product can be obtained under exaggerated condition.

At every 10°C rise, rate of reaction increases by 2-3 times.

For this, **Arrhenius equation** is used i.e.

$$K = Ae^{-E_a/RT}$$

Where   A = frequency factor,

$$R = \text{gas constant,}$$
$$K = \text{rate constant,}$$
$$E_a = \text{energy of activation}$$

Therefore, $$\log K = \log A - \frac{E_a}{2.303\ RT}$$

Graph of log K Vs. 1/T gives straight line with slope $\frac{E_a}{2.303\ R}$ and intercept at $t = 0$.

ε_a represents energy required by molecule to react and undergo reaction. Higher is value of ε_a higher is dependency on temperature.

$$E_a = 2 - 3 \text{ kcal/mole} \qquad\qquad \text{.... Photolysis}$$
$$E_a = 10 - 30 \text{ kcal/mole} \qquad\qquad \text{.... Hydrolysis-Solvolysis}$$
$$E_a = \text{very high about } 50 - 70 \text{ kcal/mole} \qquad\qquad \text{.... Pyrolysis}$$

Rate constants at different temperatures can be obtained by

$$\log\left(\frac{K_2}{K_1}\right) = \frac{E_a\ (T_2 - T_1)}{1.303\ R\ (T_2 \times T_1)}$$

With the help of K at different temperatures we can predict $T_{10\%}$.

$$t_{10\%} = \frac{0.105}{K} \qquad\qquad \text{(For first order only)}$$

$$t_{10\%} = \frac{C_0}{10K} \qquad\qquad \text{(For zero order only)}$$

Disadvantages of Arrhenius Equation:

- At higher temperature evaporation of solvent takes place and thus changes in concentration.

- At higher temperature change in solubility and humidity (decreases) which cannot be correlated with room temperature.

- For disperse systems at higher temperature viscosity decreases which can change physical characteristics resulting in potentially large errors in prediction of stability.

- Different degradation mechanisms may predominate at different temperatures thus making stability prediction difficult.

4.10 METHOD TO DETERMINE OVERAGES

STEP I : Perform the experiment and find out concentration of drug remaining at different time intervals at different temperature including room temperature. Plot the graph of concentration Vs. time for different temperatures.

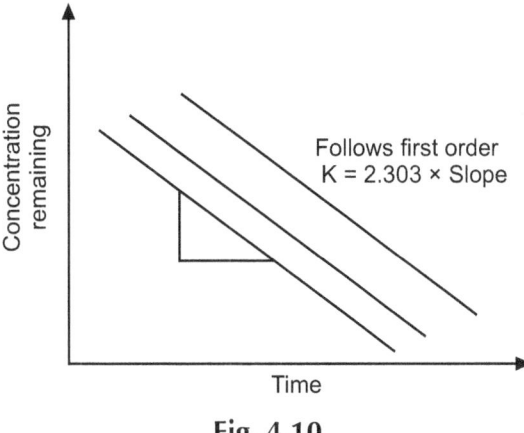

Fig. 4.10

As shown in the Fig. 4.10, measure the slope and from that get rate constant K.

STEP II : After measuring the K at different temperatures find value of K_{25} from the graph as shown in the Fig. 4.11.

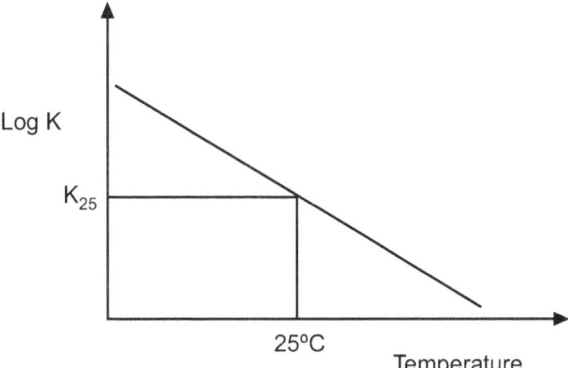

Fig. 4.11

STEP III : The value of K_{25} is substituted into the equation.

$$K = \frac{2.303}{t}\left[\log\frac{a}{(a-x)}\right]$$

And get the value of $t_{10\%}$, $t_{20\%}$ ..., $t_{90\%}$.

STEP IV : Calculation for overages

- Plot the graph of time (Days) Vs. concentration remaining.
- Extrapolate line from Y-axis at 90% to the X-axis. The intersect point will give shelf life.
- To maintain or increase the shelf life as per need (from a to b as shown in Fig. 4.12) draw a parallel line from Y to that of X, the intersect point at Y-axis will give the value of overages per 100 unit.

As shown in the Fig. 4.12 the value of overages is 20%. So need to add 20 unit drug to pre-existing formulation.

As per **European guidelines** the maximum amount of overages is **30%.**

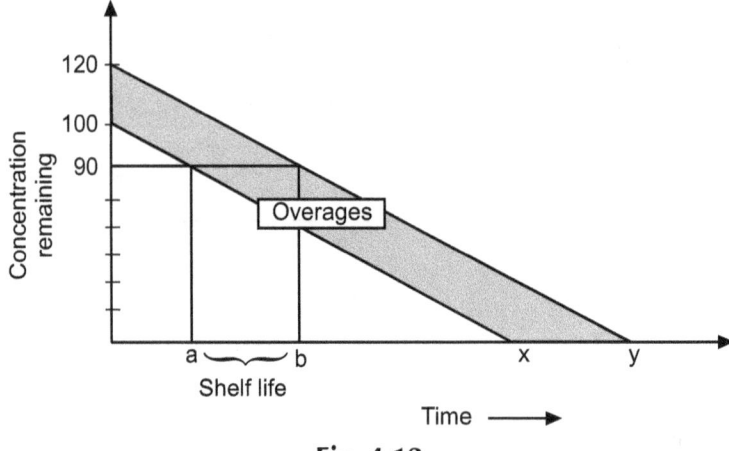

Fig. 4.12

STEP V : Expiration period

- Prime goal of stability testing is to establish an expiry date.
- **"The date placed on the immediate container label of a drug product that designates the date through which the product is expected to remain within specification".**
- If the expiration date includes only a month and year, it is expected that the product meet specification through the last day of the month.

4.11 MATRIXING AND BRACKETING

- Stability Study for any drug product can be done by two ways :
  (1) Full Design Stability Study
  (2) Reduced Design Stability Study

A Full Design Study is one in which samples for every combination of all design factors are tested at all time points. While a Reduced Design Study is one in which samples for every factor combination are not all tested at all time points.

Reduced design has ability to predict SHELF LIFE provided with certain justifications.

Reduced Design for stability studies can be prepared by two methods namely:
  (1) Bracketing
  (2) Matrixing

Objective of Guidelines :

- To provide guidance on application of Bracketing and Matrixing for stability studies of Drug product and Drug substance conducted in accordance with ICH guidelines.

Scope of the Guideline :

- This document provides guidance on bracketing and matrixing study designs.

- Specific principles are defined in this guideline for situations in which bracketing or matrixing can be applied.

4.11.1 Bracketing

- Bracketing is the design of stability schedule such that only samples of extremes of certain design factors (strength / container size and / or fill) are tested at all points as in full design.

- The design assumes that the stability of any immediate level is represented by the stability of extremes tested.

- The case of bracketing, design would be considered appropriate if design factors selected for testing are indeed the extremes.

Bracketing can be applied in :

(i) Capsules / tablets of different strengths, manufactured using the same granules/powder (linear formulation) varying in different quantity.

Examples :

Strength	Powder fill/Weight of tablet
10 mg	100 mg
20 mg	200 mg
50 mg	500 mg

Capsule of one size and similar composition is used.

(ii) Oral solutions of different strengths with formulations that differ only in minor excipients (e.g. Colour/Flavour).

Example : Paracetamol syrup 125 mg/5 ml:

with banana flavour

with vanilla flavour

Rest of the ingredients / process remains the same.

(iii) Applicable with justification to studies with multiple strengths where relative amounts of drug substance and excipients change in a formulation.

Bracketing is not applicable if different excipients are used among strengths.

(iv) Applicable without justification for same container closure system where either size or fill varies.

If both container size and fill vary, largest or smallest containers may not represent the extremes of all packaging configurations. Extremes should be selected comparing various characteristics:

- Container wall thickness,

- Closure geometry,

- Surface area to volume ratio,

- Headspace to volume ratio,

- Water vapour permeation rate per dosage unit.

Typical Design Example for Bracketing:

1. Full Design Study:

Samples for every combination for all design factors tested at all time points.

Strength		50 mg / 5 ml			75 mg / 5 ml			100 mg / 5 ml		
Batch No.		B_1	B_2	B_3	B_1	B_2	B_3	B_1	B_2	B_3
Container Size	50 ml	✓	✓	✓	✓	✓	✓	✓	✓	✓
	100 ml	✓	✓	✓	✓	✓	✓	✓	✓	✓
	500 ml	✓	✓	✓	✓	✓	✓	✓	✓	✓
✓ : Data required (test to be performed).										

2. Reduced Design Study:

Sample for every factor combination is not tested at all points (typical bracketing design).

Example 1 :

Strength		50 mg / 5 ml			75 mg / 5 ml			100 mg / 5 ml		
Batch No.		B_1	B_2	B_3	B_1	B_2	B_3	B_1	B_1	B_3
Container Size	50 ml	✓	✓	✓	✗	✗	✗	✓	✓	✓
	100 ml	✗	✗	✗	✗	✗	✗	✗	✗	✗
	500 ml	✓	✓	✓	✗	✗	✗	✓	✓	✓
✓ ✓ : Data required (test to be performed).										
✗ : Bracketing (test not necessary)										

Example 2 :

Different container sizes or different fills in the same container and closure system. It should not be assumed here that the largest and the smallest container represents the extremes of all packaging configurations.

Container wall thickness, Head space to volume ratio and Water vapour transmission rate are taken into consideration.

Type / Fill units	Size			
Polypropylene containers (ml)	30	50	100	500
Glass bottles/Vials.	30	100	200	500
Aluminium tubes (gm)	5	10	25	50

Stability data shown in shaded part can be deleted while bracketing, provided the factors such as wall thickness, head space, moisture permeation rate does not affect the stability study.

4.11.1.1 Design Consideration and Potential Risk

If the stability of the extremes is not satisfactory, the intermediate should be considered **NO** more stable than the extremes.

To reduce the risk applying bracketing, the number of strengths or container sizes should be balanced with the total number of strengths or container sizes.

This should be especially considered if bracketing is applied during the development stage of the drug product.

Therefore, the following general rules are fixed.

Table 4.3: General Rules for Reduced Design Study

Number of strength	Strength to be tested
1 - 2	All
3 - 4	Lowest and highest
$\geq$ 5+	Lowest, middle, highest

Number of Size	Size to be tested
1 - 2	Smallest
3 - 4	Smallest, biggest
$\geq$ 5+	Smallest, middle, biggest

Table 4.4: Comparison of Full Testing and Reduced Design

Full testing					Bracketing					
Strengths	Container sizes	Batches	Total batches	Total time points	Strengths	Container size	Batches	Total batches	Total time points	Savings
1	1	3	3	36	-	-	-	-	-	-
2	1	3	6	72	-	-	-	-	-	-
3	1	3	9	108	2	1	3	6	72	33%
3	2	3	18	207	2	1	3	6	72	65%
3	3	3	27	306	2	2	3	12	138	55%
4	1	3	12	144	2	1	3	6	72	50%
4	2	3	24	276	2	1	3	6	72	74%
4	3	3	36	408	2	2	3	12	138	66%

4.11.2 Matrixing

Matrixing is 'the design of a stability schedule such that a selected subset of the total number of possible samples for all factor combinations would be tested at a specified time point'. At a subsequent time point, another subset of samples for all factor combinations would be tested. The design assumes that the stability of each subset of samples tested represents the stability of all samples at a given time point. The differences in the samples for the same drug product should be identified as, for example, covering different batches, different strengths, different sizes of the same container closure system and possibly, in some cases, different container closure systems.

When a secondary packaging system contributes to the stability of the drug product, matrixing can be performed across the packaging systems. Each storage condition should be treated separately under its own matrixing design. Matrixing should not be performed across test attributes. However, alternative matrixing designs for different test attributes can be applied if justified.

4.7.2.1 Design Factors

Matrixing designs can be applied to strengths with identical or closely related formulations.

Examples are (1) capsules of different strengths made with different fill plug sizes from the same powder blend, (2) tablets of different strengths manufactured by compressing varying amounts of the same granulation, and (3) oral solutions of different strengths with formulations that differ only in minor excipients (e.g., colourants or flavourings). Other examples of design factors that can be matrixed include batches made by using the same process and equipment, and container sizes and/or fills in the same container closure system.

4.11.2.2 Design Considerations

A matrixing design should be balanced as far as possible so that each combination of factors is tested to the same extent over the intended duration of the study and through the last time point prior to submission.

In a design, where time points are matrixed, all selected factor combinations should be tested at the initial and final time points, while only certain fractions of the designated combinations should be tested at each intermediate time point. If full long-term data for the proposed shelf life will not be available for review before approval, all selected combinations of batch, strength, container size and fill, among other things, should also be tested at 12 months or at the last time point prior to submission. In addition, data from at least three time points, including initial, should be available for each selected combination through the first 12 months of the study. For matrixing at an accelerated or intermediate storage condition, care should be taken to ensure, testing occurs at a minimum of three time points, including initial and final, for each selected combination of factors.

When a matrix on design factors is applied, if one strength or container size and/or fill is no longer intended for marketing, stability testing of that strength or container size and/or fill can be continued to support the other strengths or container sizes and/or fills in the design.

4.11.2.3 Design Examples

Examples of matrixing designs on time points for a product in two strengths (S_1 and S_2) are shown in Table 4.5. The terms "one-half reduction" and "one-third reduction" refer to the reduction strategy initially applied to the full study design. For example, a "one half reduction" initially eliminates one in every two time points from the full study design and a "one-third reduction" initially removes one in every three. In the examples shown in Table 4.5 and 4.6, the reductions are less than one-half and one-third due to the inclusion of full testing of all factor combinations. These examples include full testing at the initial, final, and 12-month time points. The ultimate reduction is therefore less than one-half (24/48) or one-third (16/48), and is actually 15/48 or 10/48, respectively.

Table 4.5 : One half reduction for Matrixing Design
"One-Half Reduction"

Time Points (Months)			0	3	6	9	12	18	24	36
STRENGTH	S_1	BATCH 1	T	T		T	T		T	T
		BATCH 2	T	T		T	T	T		T
		BATCH 3	T		T		T	T		T
	S_2	BATCH 1	T		T		T		T	T
		BATCH 2	T	T		T	T	T		T
		BATCH 3	T		T		T		T	T

Key: T = Sample tested

Table 4.6: One half reduction for Matrixing Design
"One-Third Reduction"

Time Points (Months)			0	3	6	9	12	18	24	36
STRENGTH	S_1	BATCH 1	T	T		T	T		T	T
		BATCH 2	T	T	T		T	T		T
		BATCH 3	T		T	T	T	T	T	T
	S_2	BATCH 1	T		T	T	T	T	T	T
		BATCH 2	T	T		T	T		T	T
		BATCH 3	T	T	T		T	T		T

4.11.2.4 Applicability and Degree of Reduction

The following, although not an exhaustive list, should be considered when a matrixing design is contemplated:

- Knowledge of data variability,
- Expected stability of the product,
- Availability of supporting data,
- Stability differences in the product within a factor or among factors, and/or
- Number of factor combinations in the study.

In general, a matrixing design is applicable if the supporting data indicate predictable product stability. Matrixing is appropriate when the supporting data exhibit only small variability. However, where the supporting data exhibit moderate variability, a matrixing design should be statistically justified. If the supportive data show large variability, a matrixing design should not be applied.

A statistical justification could be based on an evaluation of the proposed matrixing design with respect to its power to detect differences among factors in the degradation rates or its precision in shelf life estimation.

4.11.2.5 Potential Risk

Due to the reduced amount of data collected, a matrixing design on factors other than time points generally has less precision in shelf life estimation and yields a shorter shelf life than the corresponding full design. In addition, such a matrixing design may have insufficient power to detect certain main or interaction effects, thus leading to incorrect pooling of data from different design factors during shelf life estimation. If there is an excessive reduction in the number of factor combinations tested and data from the tested factor combinations can not be pooled to establish a single shelf life, it may be impossible to estimate the shelf lives for the missing factor combinations.

A study design that matrixes on time points only would often have similar ability to that of a full design to detect differences in rates of change among factors and to establish a reliable shelf life. This feature exists because linearity is assumed and because full testing of all factor combinations would still be performed at both the initial time point and the last time point prior to submission.

4.11.2.6 Data Evaluation

Stability data from studies in a reduced design should be treated in the same manner as data from full design studies.

4.11.3 Application of Bracketing or Matrixing During the Whole Development

Bracketing and Matrixing is compliment to each other. Both the techniques helps to reduce the design of various combination factors based on strength, containers/ closures, fills and point of testing time. Both Matrixing and Bracketing is a reduced design on different principles. The use of Bracketing and Matrixing is generally applied together. The design should be scientifically justified. Bracketing is applicable to Drug product based on different strengths, containers, closures and fill volumes.

Table 4.7: Various Stages at Reducing Design

Stage of development	Preferable procedure
Predevelopment	Bracketing
Clinical phases I - III	Bracketing
Accelerated and long term testing with registration batches	Bracketing/Matrixing
On-going stability testing	Matrixing
Follow-up stability testing	Matrixing

Bracketing and Matrixing is a stability schedule and a reduced design. The number of tests to be performed on a different size, pack and strength should be logically justified to reduce the analytical load. Bracketing and Matrixing is more applicable for drug product.

Climatic Zone:

Special consideration must be made to the effect on products of the extremely adverse climatic conditions in certain countries to which the products may be exported. So for that ICH Q(1) F guidelines provides definitions of climatic zones.

Table 4.8: Definition and Storage/Test Conditions for Four Climatic Zones

Climatic zones	Definition	Storage/Test conditions	Examples
I	Temperate climate	21°C ± 2°C and 45% RH ± 5% RH	Northern Europe, Canada
II	Mediterranean and Subtropical climate	25°C ± 2°C and 60% RH ± 5% RH	Southern Europe, Japan, US.
III	Hot dry climate	30°C ± 2°C and 35% RH ± 5% RH	Egypt, Sudan
IV	Hot humid climate	30°C ± 2°C and 75% RH ± 5% RH	Central Africa, South Pacific.

4.12 PHOTOSTABILITY TESTING

General:

- Photostability testing (light testing) is an integral and important part of stress testing which is mentioned in ICH guideline.

Preamble:

- The intrinsic photostability characteristics of new drug substances and products should be evaluated to demonstrate that, as appropriate, light exposure does not result in unacceptable change.
- The guideline does not cover the photostability of drugs after administration.
- Normally, photostability testing is carried out on a single batch of material selected as described under Selection of Batches in the Parent Guideline. Under some circumstances these studies should be repeated if certain variations and changes are made to the product (e.g., formulation, packaging).

- A systematic approach for photostability testing is recommended in following conditions:

  (1) Tests on the drug substance;

  (2) Tests on the exposed drug product outside of the immediate pack; and if necessary;

  (3) Tests on the drug product in the immediate pack; and if necessary ;

  (4) Tests on the drug product in the marketing pack.

4.12.1 Light Sources

- The light sources described below may be used for photostability testing. The applicant should either maintain an appropriate control of temperature to minimize the effect of localized temperature changes or include a dark control in the same environment unless otherwise justified.
- For both options (1) and (2) given in preamble, a pharmaceutical manufacturer/ applicant may rely on the spectral distribution specification of the light source manufacturer.

Option 1 :

- Any light source that is designed to produce an output similar to the D_{65}/ID_{65} emission standard such as an artificial daylight fluorescent lamp combining visible and ultraviolet (UV) outputs, xenon or metal halide lamp.
- D_{65} is the internationally recognized standard for outdoor daylight as defined in ISO 10977 (1993). ID_{65} is the equivalent indoor indirect daylight standard.
- For a light source emitting significant radiation below 320 nm, an appropriate filter(s) may be fitted to eliminate such radiation.

Option 2 :

- For option 2, the same sample should be exposed to both the cool white fluorescent and near ultraviolet lamp.

  (i) A cool white fluorescent lamp is designed to produce an output similar to that specified in ISO 10977 (1993); and

  (ii) A near UV fluorescent lamp having a spectral distribution from 320 nm to 400 nm with a maximum energy emission between 350 nm and 370 nm; a significant proportion of UV should be in both bands of 320 to 360 nm and 360 to 400 nm.

Procedure:

- For confirmatory studies, samples should be exposed to light providing an overall illumination of not less than 1.2 million lux hours and an integrated near ultraviolet energy of not less than 200 watt hours/square metre to allow direct comparisons to be made between the drug substance and drug product.
- Samples may be exposed side-by-side with a validated chemical actinometric system to ensure the specified light exposure is obtained, or for the appropriate duration of time when conditions have been monitored using calibrated radiometers/lux meters.

- If protected samples (e.g., wrapped in aluminum foil) are used as dark controls to evaluate the contribution of thermally induced change to the total observed change, these should be placed alongside the authentic sample.

Decision Flow chart for Photostability Testing of Drug Products:

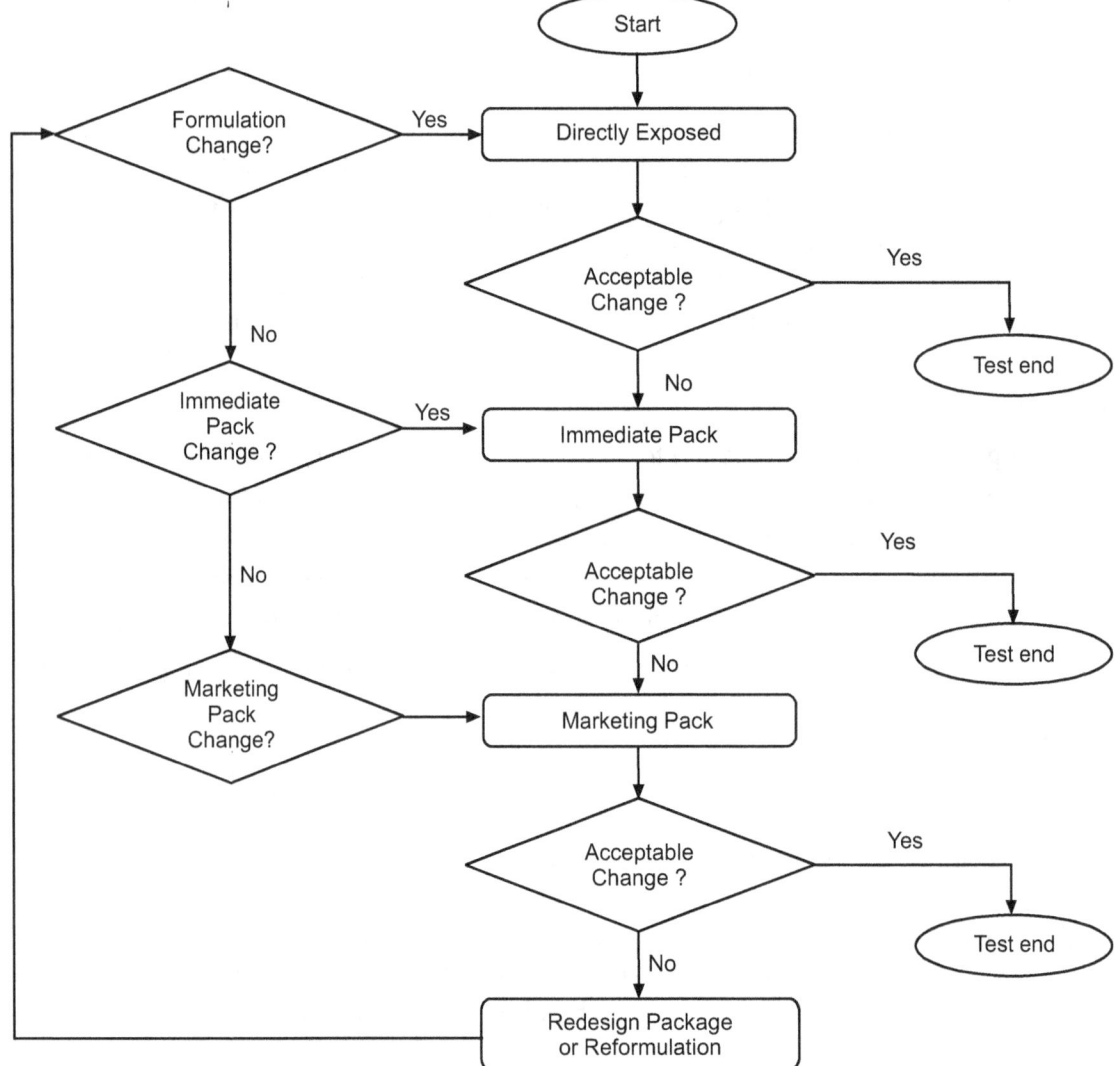

4.12.2 Drug Substances

- For drug substances, photostability testing should consist of two parts:

  (1) Forced degradation testing

  (2) Confirmatory testing.

- The purpose of forced degradation testing studies is to evaluate the overall photosensitivity of the material for method development purposes and/or degradation pathway elucidation.

- This testing may involve the drug substance alone and/or in simple solutions/ suspensions to validate the analytical procedures.

- In these studies, the samples should be kept in chemically inert and transparent containers.

- In these forced degradation studies, a variety of exposure conditions may be used, depending on the photosensitivity of the drug substance involved and the intensity of the light sources used.

- Under forcing conditions, decomposition products may be observed that are unlikely to be formed under the conditions used for confirmatory studies.

- Confirmatory studies should then be undertaken to provide the information necessary for handling, packaging and labelling.

Presentation of Samples

- Care should be taken to ensure that the physical characteristics of the samples under test are taken into account and efforts should be made, such as cooling and/or placing the samples in sealed containers, to ensure that the effects of the changes in physical states such as sublimation, evaporation or melting are minimized.

- All such precautions should be chosen to provide minimal interference with the exposure of samples under test. Possible interactions between the samples and any material used for containers or for general protection of the sample, should also be considered and eliminated wherever not relevant to the test being carried out.

- As a direct challenge for samples of solid drug substances, an appropriate amount of sample should be taken and placed in a suitable glass or plastic dish and protected with a suitable transparent cover if considered necessary.

- Solid drug substances should be spread across the container to give a thickness of typically not more than 3 mm.

- Drug substances that are liquids should be exposed in chemically inert and transparent containers.

Analysis of Samples

- At the end of the exposure period, the samples should be examined for any changes in physical properties (e.g., appearance, clarity or colour of solution) and for assay and degradants by a method suitably validated for products likely to arise from photochemical degradation processes.

- Where solid drug substance samples are involved, sampling should ensure that a representative portion is used in individual tests. Similar sampling considerations, such as homogenization of the entire sample, apply to other materials that may not be homogeneous after exposure.

- The analysis of the exposed sample should be performed concomitantly with that of any protected samples used as dark controls if these are used in the test.

Judgement of Results

- The forced degradation studies should be designed to provide suitable information to develop and validate test methods for the confirmatory studies.

- These test methods should be capable of resolving and detecting photolytic degradants that appear during the confirmatory studies.

- When evaluating the results of these studies, it is important to recognize that they form part of the stress testing and are not therefore designed to establish qualitative or quantitative limits for change.

- The confirmatory studies should identify precautionary measures needed in manufacturing or in formulation of the drug product, and if light resistant packaging is needed. When evaluating the results of confirmatory studies to determine whether change due to exposure to light is acceptable, it is important to consider the results from other formal stability studies in order to assure that the drug will be within justified limits at time of use (see the relevant ICH Q_1 stability and Q_3 impurity guidelines.

4.12.3 Drug Product

(It is same as that described in drug substances)

ANNEX

A. Quinine Chemical Actinometry

- The following provides details of an actinometric procedure for monitoring exposure to a near UV fluorescent lamp (based on FDA/National Institute of Standards and Technology study). For other light sources/actinometric systems, the same approach may be used, but each actinometric system should be calibrated for the light source used.

- Prepare a sufficient quantity of a 2 % weight/volume aqueous solution of quinine monohydrochloride dihydrate (if necessary, dissolve by heating).

  Option 1 : Use 20 ml colourless ampoules (seal hermetically).

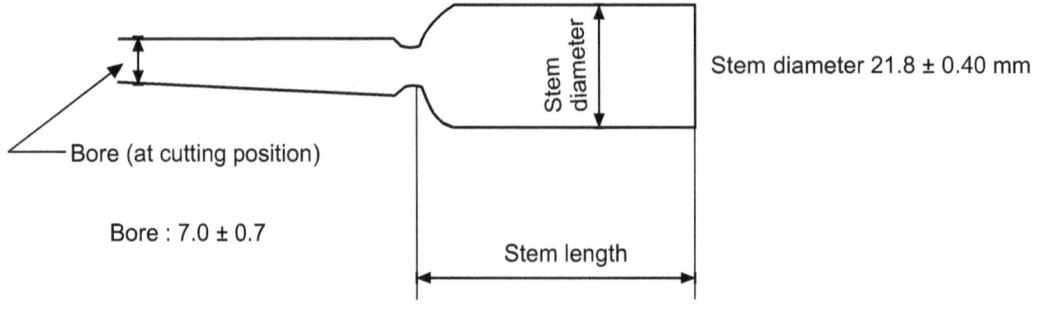

Fig. 4.13: Shape and dimensions for ampoule specifications

Option 2 : Use 1 cm quartz cell.

- For both the options, prepare sample and control wrap in aluminum foil to protect completely from light, and measure their absorbance A_t and A_o respectively at 400 nm using 1cm path length. Measure the change in absorbance.

- The length of exposure should be sufficient to ensure a change in absorbance of at least 0.9.

4.13 FACTORS AFFECTING STABILITY

The stability of the product is its ability to resist deterioration. It is always expressed in terms of shelf life.

As per USP there are five types of stability studies:

- Chemical
- Physical
- Environmental factor
- Microbiological
- Processing factors
- Toxicological

[I] EFFECT OF CHEMICAL FACTORS

Various ways of chemical degradation includes:

- Hydrolysis
- Dehydration
- Isomerization and Racemization
- Decarboxylation and Elimination
- Oxidation
- Photo degradation
- Drug–excipients and drug–drug interactions

These ways are described below:

1. HYDROLYSIS:

It is major cause of deterioration of drugs, especially for those in aqueous solution.

For example,

1) Procaine $\xrightarrow{\text{OH}}$ PABA + Diethyl amine ethanol

2) Chloramphenicol $\xrightarrow[\text{CH}_3\text{COOH}]{\text{H}^+}$ 2-Amino-p-nitro phenyl -1,3 propandiol

$$+$$

Dichloro acetiacid

Remedies:

- Removal of water, storage in dry form.
- Using an insoluble derivative in suspension form.
- Replacement of water by substantial quantity of some other solvent such as alcohol or polyhydroxy solvent mixtures.
- By Micellar formation using anionic and cationic surfectants.

2. DEHYDRATION:

There are two types of dehydration process:

(1) Covalent dehydration

(2) Physical dehydration

For example: Sugars such as glucose and lactose are known to undergo dehydration to form 5-(hydroxymethyl) furural.

Erythromycin is susceptible to acid catalyzed dehydration.

Batanopride undergoes an intramolecular ring-closure reaction in the acidic pH range due to dehydration.

3. ISOMERIZATION AND RACEMERIZATION

Isomerization : Conversion of active drug into less active or inactive drug.

For example: Vitamin A susceptible to isomerization in presence of light. Conversion of optically active drug into its enantiomer.

Racemerization : Conversion of optically active drug into its enantiomer.

The best known racemerization reaction of drugs are epinapherine, pilocarpine, ergotamine and tetracycline.

4. DECARBOXYLATION

Drug substances having a carboxylic acid group are sometimes susceptible to decarboxylation. 4-aminosalicylic acid is a good example.

Foscarnet also undergoes decarboxylation under strongly acidic conditions, whereas etodolac is susceptible to decarboxylation by acid catalysis.

Remedies:

- This action is minimised by passing carbon dioxide into the solution for one minute and sealing the container so as to make it gas-tight prior to autoclaving.

5. IONIC STRENGTH

For drug degradation involving reactions with or between ionic species, the rate is affected by the presence of other ionic species such as salts like sodium chloride.

Ionic strength affects the observed degradation rate constant, K. Its effect on the activity; n, coefficients; f, Ionic strength; μ, is described by

$$\mu = \frac{1}{2} \sum_{n} C_i Z_i^2$$

where C_i is the concentration of ionic species i and Z_i is its electric charge.

6. OXIDATION

Drugs can be affected by the availability of oxygen.

Some photo degradation reactions involve photo oxidative mechanisms that are dependent on concentration of oxygen.

Oxygen participates as reactant and also alters the degradation rate.

Oxygen exists in various states such as ground state, triplate oxygen etc.

The following excipients may have low level residues from manufacture that can lead to oxidative degradation in susceptible compounds.

Polyethylene glycol, Polysorbate 80, PVP, Talc.

Remedies:

- Minimum oxygen level is used which may be achieved by boiling the water and allowing cooling in an atmosphere free from oxygen.
- Hydrogenation of product.
- Incorporation of inert gas in containers.
- Use of anti-oxidant.
- Buffering the solution at favourable pH, Use of metal free solvents.

7. PHOTOLYSIS

- Reactions such as oxidation-reduction, ring alteration and polymerisation can be catalysed or accelerated by exposure to sun or artificial light.
- Photolytic degradation can be very complex, the products of such degradation being numerous and difficult to identify.
- Exposure to light can cause discolouration of both drugs and excipients even when degradation is modest and not even detectable analytically. This can lead to "off colour" product, perceived by the patient as a quality deficiency.

8. CATALYSIS

In parentrals, great care is taken to exclude metals, because only slight decomposition caused by trace metals may cause sufficient discolouration to the product unsatisfactory.

Example of metal catalysed oxidation in pharmaceutical system are cynocobalamine and erythromycin.

(II) PHYSICAL FACTORS

- Temperature.
- pH and pH rate profiles.
- Buffer.
- Light.
- Crystalline state and polymorphism in solid drugs.
- Moisture and humidity.
- Excipients.
- Miscellaneous factors.

1. TEMPERATURE

- The rate constant/temperature relationship has traditionally been described by the Arhenius equation,

$$K = Ae^{-E_a/RT}$$

Where, E_a = Activation energy

A = Frequency factor

Remedies:

- Pharmaceutical product should be stored within the temperature range in which they are stable.
- They should not be exposed to extremes of temperature.
- Usually they should be stored at low temperature if they lack sufficient stability at room temperature.

2. pH AND pH RATE PROFILE

The effect of pH on degradation rate can be explained by the catalytic effects that hydronium or hydroxide ions can have on various chemical reactions.

If critical path in a reaction involves a proton transfer or abstraction step, other acids and bases present in solution can affect the rate of reaction.

A reaction in which hydronium ion, hydroxide ion and water catalysis are observed can be described by

$$K_{obs} = (K_{H^+} \cdot a_{H^+}) + K_{H_2O} + (K_{OH^-} \cdot a_{OH^-})$$

Where, K_{obs} = Sum of specific rate constants

a_{H^+} = Activities of hydronium ion

a_{OH^-} = Activities of hydroxide ion

3. **BUFFER**

   - These buffer species, like H^+ and OH^-, participates in formation of break down of activated complexes of various reactions and determine their reaction rate.

   - These catalytic species are referred to as general acid-base catalysts.

   - Studies with phosphate buffer indicates that it enhance the degradation of various drug structures such as carbenicillin.

4. **LIGHT**

   - The number and wavelength of incident photons affect the photo degradation rate of drugs.

   - It is not easy to study the effect of light quantitatively as the wavelength dependence of degradation varies among drug substances and because light sources have different spectral distributions.

   - Photo degradation for drug strongly depend on the spectral properties of the drug substances and the spectral distribution of the light source.

5. **CRYSTALLINE STATE**

   - The stability of drugs in their amorphous form is generally lower than that of drugs in their crystalline form due to higher free energy level of amorphous form. Decreased chemical stability of solid drugs brought about by mechanical stresses such as grinding is said to be due to change in crystalline state.

   - For example; grinding of aspirin increase degradation rate in suspension form.

6. **MOISTURE AND HUMIDITY**

   - Drug degradation in heterogeneous system such as solid and semisolid states is affected by moisture.

   - Moisture plays important role in catalyzing chemical degradation.

   - Water participates in the drug degradation process itself as a reactant, leading to hydrolysis; hydration etc. Here degradation rate is directly affected by the concentration of water, hydronium ion, hydroxide ion. Water absorbs onto the drug surface and forms a moisture-sorbed layer in which the drug is dissolved and degraded.

   - For example; Sodium ampicillin, potassium propicillin

   Remedies:
   - Maintenance of controlled humidity condition.
   - Moisture proof packaging.

7. **EFFECT OF SOLUBILITY**

   - Applicable to drugs in solution form.

For example; Penicillins are very unstable in aqueous solution because of hydrolysis of β-lactam ring.

Remedies:

- Stabilized by using insoluble salts of API.
- Formulate the drug in suspension dosage form.

8. EXCIPIENTS

The role that excipients play in drug stability has been extensively reported. For example; accelerating the effect of talc on hydrolysis of thiamine hydrochloride, the accelerating effect of magnesium stearate on tablet containing amines and lactose etc.

9. VAPOURIZATION

Some drugs and pharmaceutical adjuvants possess sufficiently high vapour pressures at room temperature that their volatization constitutes a major route of drug loss.

Flavours may be lost from the formulation in this manner.

For example; Nitroglycerine = 0.00026 mm at 20°C = 0.31 mm at 93°C

10. AGING

This is a process through which changes in the disintegration and/or dissolution characteristics of the dosage form are caused by alteration in the physico chemical properties of the inert ingredient or the active drug in the dosage form.

For example; Melting point of aminophylline suppository increased from about 20 mins to over an hour after 24 weeks of storage at 22°C.

11. RADIATION

Radiation is generally used during gaseous sterilization of thermolabile drugs.

The exposure also produce deterious changes in the product since the procedures also cause ionization in the irradiated material.

Irradiation of a drug in aqueous solution produces greater changes than the irradiation of the pure material because irradiation of water produces H_2O_2, free oxidative action in drug.

Drugs affected by radiation are:

(1) Alkaloids

(2) Atropine

(3) Steroids

(4) Sulphonamides

(5) Biological products - Insulin, Heparin.

All the above examples are irradiated at low level of 2.5 µ rad.

[III] EFFECT OF PACKAGING COMPONENTS
CONTAINERS :
1. GLASS

Problems:

(a) Release of alkali.

(b) Release of insoluble flake.

Remedy for Preventation of Release of Alkali:
- By decreasing soda content.
- Siliconization of surface.
- By replacing sodium oxide with other oxides.
- Surface treatment by sulphur-di-oxide in presence of water vapour and heat.

Remedy for Preventation of Release of Insolutle Flake:
- Flake formation can be prevented by using borosilicate glass.
- Pretreatment of the container with dilute acid.

2. PLASTIC
- High molecular weight polymers like polyethylene, polypropylene, polystyrene, pvc etc.

Problems:

(a) Permeation of moisture.

(b) Leaching.

(c) Adsorption or Absorption.

(d) Chemical/Physical reaction of contents of containers with product.

Remedy:
- Lining of the container with an epoxy resin eliminates this problem but has to be evaluated separately for each product. (Epoxy lining does not prevent sorption of phenyl mercuric nitrate).

3. METALS
- Metals commonly used are tin, plastic coated tin, tin-coated lead, aluminum and coated aluminum.

Problems:

Reactivity :

For e.g. Aluminum + Fatty alcohol $\rightarrow$ White line on metals

Tin + Chloride $\rightarrow$ Errosion

Remedy:
- Application of an epoxy lining to internal surfaces of aluminum tubes was found to make them more resistant to attack.

CLOSURES :

1. RUBBER

Problems:

(a) Sorption of API into rubber.

(b) Extraction of one or more components of rubber into vial solution.

Remedies:

Epoxy lining applied to rubber stoppers :

(1) Reduction results in amount of extractive leached from stopper but no effect on sorption of preservative from solution.

(2) However use of Teflon coated rubber stoppers essentially prevents sorption and leaching of the rubber stopper.

[IV] ENVIRONMENTAL FACTORS

Environmental factors can be divided into two parts – the one being the environmental factors prevailing outside the dosage form and the second one is environmental factors inside the formulation itself both affecting the stability of the products.

1. Outside the Dosage Form

Temperature:

Temperature is one of the primary factors affecting the drug stability.

As temperature increases, a greater available free energy leads to a more rapid reaction and typically a 10° C increase in temperature produces a two to five fold increase in decay.

It catalyses hydrolysis, oxidation and thermal reaction followed just after initiation of photolytic reaction.

The most satisfactory method for expressing the influence of temperature on reaction velocity or rate is the quantitative relation proposed by Arrhenius:

$$K = A \times e^{-E_a/RT}$$

Where, K = Specific rate of degradation

         A = Frequency factor

         E_a = Arrhenius activation energy

         R = Gas constant

         T = Absolute température

Logarithmically it can be expressed as:

$$\text{Log } K = \log A - \frac{E_a}{2.303 \ RT}$$

From the graph of $K \rightarrow 1/T$ one can determine E_a from slope and A from intercept.

Ways for Stabilization:

- Pharmaceutical product should be stored within the temperature range in which they are stable.
- They should not be exposed to extremes of temperature.
- Usually they should be stored at low temperature if they lack sufficient stability at room temperature.
- There are few drugs on which freezing has an adverse effect, so freezing should be avoided unless until it is stable at such temperatures.

Light:

Light is not classified **as a catalyst**, and its effect on chemical reactions is treated as a separate topic.

Light energy, like heat, may provide the activation necessary for a reaction to occur.

Light induce degradation of drug.

Photolysis (i.e. decomposition of product resulting from the absorption of radiant energy) has now become an important degradative pathway because of the complex chemical structure of many new drugs.

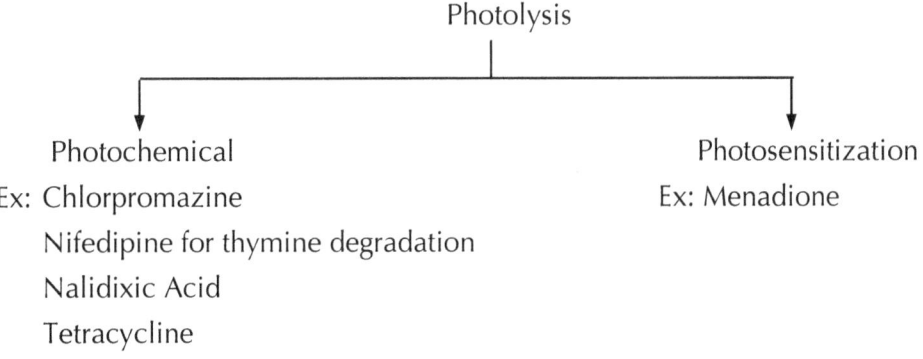

Photolysis

Photochemical
Ex: Chlorpromazine
   Nifedipine for thymine degradation
   Nalidixic Acid
   Tetracycline

Photosensitization
Ex: Menadione

Photostabilization of Molsidomine Tablet:

Molsidomine $\xrightarrow{\text{Sun light}}$ Morpholine derivative (potential carcinogenic)

It was stabilized by,

Incorporation of light absorbing excipients:

(a) colourants – Curcumine (E 100) and Azorubine (E 122).

(b) UV absorber – UV absorber A and B.

Incorporation of pigments: e.g. TiO_2 and ZnO

By coating:

(a) White coating (4.8% TiO_2).

(b) coloured coating (yellow and red iron oxide added to standard coating containing 4.8% TiO_2).

Also, protection of drug from light during manufacture or formulation of pharmaceutical product. For example, nifedipine, amlodipine are manufactured under sodium light to prevent photodegradation.

Humidity:

Higher humidity may lead to moisture adsorption.

It can affect the stability of pharmaceuticals by,

- Hydrolytic degradation
- Isomerization
- Crystallization
- Affecting flow and compaction properties etc.

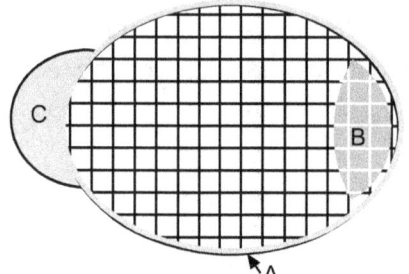

Three different ways in which water can be located within a solid.

(A) Monolayer adsorbed layer
(B) Adsorbed layer
(C) Condensed water

Fig. 4.14: Water vapour adsorption and deliquescence of a water soluble solid particle

Ways of Stabilization:

- Maintenance of controlled humidity condition.
- Moisture proof packaging.

Effects of RH on the Photocatalytic Activity of TiO_2 and Photostabilizing of Famotidine:

- TiO_2 is also known to be a strong photo catalyst.
- The photocatalytic activity of anatase form of TiO_2, as measured by four probe method, is approximately 1.5 times higher than that of the rutile form.

2. Inside the Dosage Form

- Oxidation
- pH
- Ionic strength
- General acid base catalysis/buffer

The effects of these factors have been discussed in preformulation study. Here it is not discussed.

Some research examples are discussed here.

The Kinetics of the Alkaline Degradation of Daptomycin:

The effect of buffer, pH, ionic strength, temperature have been studied on stability of daptomycin.

It was found that

- The observed degradation rate constant *did not change significantly* with increasing buffer concentration.
- In pH range of 2 - 9, the *degradation of daptomycin is proportional* to OH- concentration with hydrolytic cleavage.
- Daptomycin is *degraded* at 30°C in dilute NaOH solution in presence of varying concentration and type of natural salt.
- Degradation rate constant increases as temperature increases.

Effect of pH, Phosphate buffer and the Ionic Strength on the Stability of Cefotetan Disodium:

The stability of drug between the pH range of 2 - 8 has been studied by stability indicating HPLC method.

- The optimum pH range of stability appears to be 3.6 - 6.4.
- The phosphate buffer concentration and ionic strength did not affect the K_{obs} value of cefotetan.

[V] PACKAGING COMPONENTS

Packaging of pharmaceutical dosage is important parameter to evaluate the stability of product.

So, choice of container material should be made after thorough evaluation about its effect on stability of formulation.

Packaging of pharmaceutical product, protect the product during extended storage, under varying environmental conditions of temperature, humidity and light.

Most commonly materials employed are:

Glass, Plastic, Metal, Rubber.

Newer Techniques for Improving Stability

Supercritical Fluid

Supercritical fluids possess liquid like densities and gas like transport properties near the critical point.

CO_2 is choice for pharmaceutical applications.

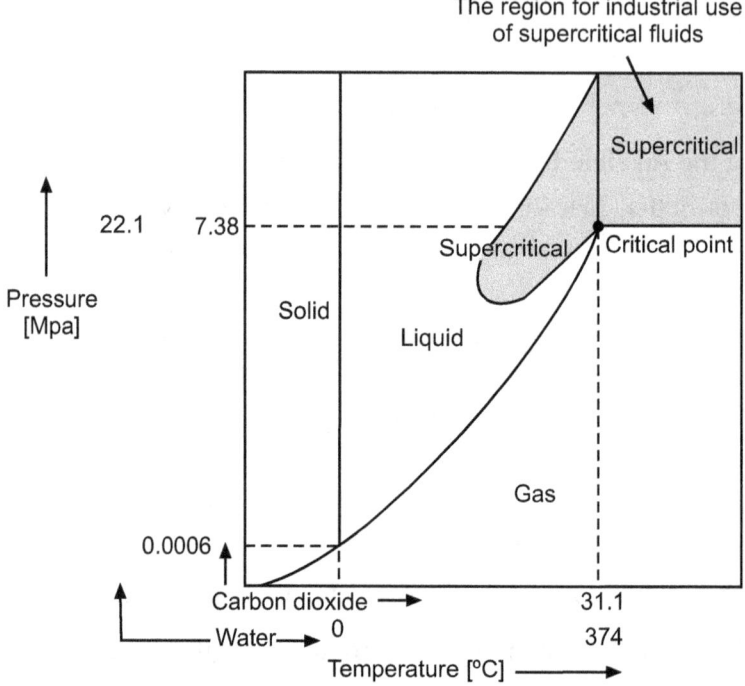

Fig. 4.17: Supercritical fluid technology

Dry powders of Stable Protein Formulations from aqueous solutions are prepared using supercritical carbon-di-oxide assisted Aerosolization.

Use of a new supercritical carbon dioxide-assisted aerosolization coupled with bubble drying technology :

- Two model proteins, lysozyme and lactate dehydrogenase (LDH).
- In the absence of excipients, lysozyme was observed to undergo perturbations of secondary structure observed by solid-state infrared spectroscopy. In the presence of sucrose, this unfolding was minimized.
- The more labile LDH suffered irrecoverable loss of activity on reconstituting in the absence of carbohydrate stabilizers.
- LDH could be stabilized thoroughly with the addition of sucrose, and almost complete preservation of activity was achieved with the further addition of a surface active agent, such as Tween 20.

Lyophilization:

- A method to produce physically stable formulation.
- Applicable for multivitamin preparation, antibiotics, hormones and proteins formulation etc.
- Cryoprotectant is added in formulation when product is lyophilized.

- To act successfully as a protectant, it should have,
  - A high glass transition temperature (T_g),
  - A poor hygroscopicity,
  - A low crystallization rate,
  - Contain no reducing groups.

[VI] PROCESSING FACTORS

- Blending
- Freeze-drying process
- Polymeric film coating process
- Milling
- Effect of compression
- Effect of local mobility
- Wet granulation

1. Blending

- It is **most important step** for manufacturing of solution dosage form. High speed of mixing may introduce air into the product and slow mixing may not form a satisfactory product.
- For mixing step, both **mixing time and speed should be evaluated** for API and Excipients.
- During mixing some other factors like type of agitator, temperature or vaccum etc. can affect the stability.

Remedies:

- Use of optimum time and rate of mixing.
- Use of optimum and controlled temperature.
- Application of vacuum.
- Use of closed system.

2. Freeze Drying Process

Freeze-drying process also affects the stability of product and there are various substances used for the process of freeze-drying which also leads to either increase or decrease in the stability.

Example : Freeze drying was found to have destructive effect on the ordered structure of starch and this effect is varied with respect to preparation condition.

3. Milling

The milling process results in a reduction in the particle size of a given material and can be conducted using the mildest conditions possible to render a homogeneous sample, or can use more rigorous milling to reduce the primary particle size.

These physical changes in the state of the drug substance can alter the stability, dissolution characteristics and possibly even the bioavailability of the drug.

Remedies:

- Use of moderate condition of milling.
- Use of optimum time of milling.

Example : The phase transformation of *chloramphenicol palmitate* associated with grinding and the effect of seed crystals.

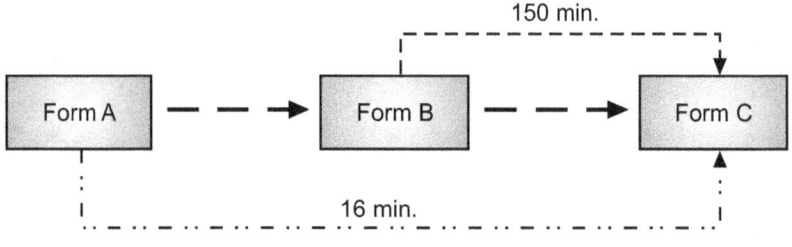

Fig. 4.18

4. Effect of Compression

- Overall amount of energy input into a formulation during compression is not sufficient to induce a phase transformation and for many substances this situation is certainly true. There are numerous examples, for which changes in phase composition do accompany a compression step.

  For example, **Carbamazepine** is a drug which shows differences in the dissolution rates that are associated with production of different polymorphs by tablet manufacturing process.

- It has 3 different crystalline form – α, β and Dihydrate form.

5. Effect of Local Mobility

- Local mobility in amorphous forms of pharmaceuticals can lead to changes in their glass transition temperature effect, of which is such that amorphous form converts to crystalline form.

6. Wet Granulation

- In wet granulation process, both the wetting phase solvent and drying phase conditions can cause a suitable environment for the transformation to alternate crystalline forms.

Polymorphic transformations during wet granulation can be divided to:

(1) Conversion of a metastable form to the stable form;

(2) Conversion of the stable form to a metastable form; or

(3) Conversion of an unsolvate form to a solvate form.

Remedies:

- Use of granulating liquid which will not produce polymorphic conversion. Moderate / Optimum condition for drying.

[VII] MICROBIOLOGICAL FACTORS

- Microbial growth in an oral liquid may cause foul odour and turbidity and adversely palatability and appearance. Byproducts of microbial metabolism may cause a change in the pH of the preparation and reduce the chemical stability or solubility of the drug.

Remedies:

- Microbial contamination during preparation must be minimised by using clean equipment, sterile water (Water for Irrigation BP) and avoiding contaminated raw materials and containers.

[VIII] TOXICOLOGICAL FACTORS

- Water, vitamins, minerals, enzymes and multitudes of functional groups are present in feed which can severely reduce the shelf life of a drug.

Stability testing is not the key procedural component in the pharmaceutical development program for a new drug as well as new formulation. Stability tests are carried out so that recommended storage condition and shelf life can be included on the lable to ensure that the medicine is safe and effective throughout its shelf life.

The stability test should be carried out following proper scientific principles and after understanding the current regulatory requirement and as per the climatic zone.

Chapter 5

ABSORPTION OF DRUGS

5.1 INTRODUCTION

Drug absorption is defined as "the process of movement of unchanged drug from the site of application to the systemic circulation".

• A drug injected intravascularly directly enters into the systemic circulation and exerts its pharmacological effects. However, the majority of the drugs are administered extravascularly.

• If intended to act systemically, such drugs can exert their pharmacological actions only when they come into blood circulation from their site of application, and for this, absorption is an pre-requisite step.

• The effectiveness of drug can only be assessed by its concentration at the site of action. However, it is difficult to measure the drug concentration at a site of action. Instead, the concentration can be measured more accurately in plasma.

• There always exist a co-relation between the plasma drug concentration and therapeutic response thus, absorption can be defined as, "the process of movement of unchanged drug from the site of administration to the site of measurement i.e. plasma".

5.2 STRUCTURE OF GASTRO INTESTINAL TRACT

The gastrointestinal tract consists of three major anatomical regions: stomach, small intestine and large intestine. The small intestine includes the duodenum, jejunum and ileum.

Gastro intestinal tract is a hollow structure.

It contains mainly 4 layers (Innermost to outer one) :

1. Mucosa
2. Submucosa
3. Muscularis externa
4. Serosa

Mucosa consist of :

1. Lining epithelium
2. Lamina propria
3. Muscularis mucosa

In stomach, this mucosal layer have several folds leading to increase in total surface area.

Table 5.1: Anatomical and Physiological Comparison of Different Regions of GIT

	Stomach	Small intestine	Large intestine
pH range	1 to 3	5 to 7.5	7.9 to 8.0
Length (cm)	20	285	110
Diameter (cm)	15	2.5	0.15
Surface area (sq.m.)	0.1 to 0.2	200	0.15
Blood flow (l/min)	0.15	1.0	0.02
Absorption	Lipophilic, acidic and neutral drugs	All types of drugs	Some drugs, water and electrolytes

5.3 STRUCTURE OF CELL MEMBRANE

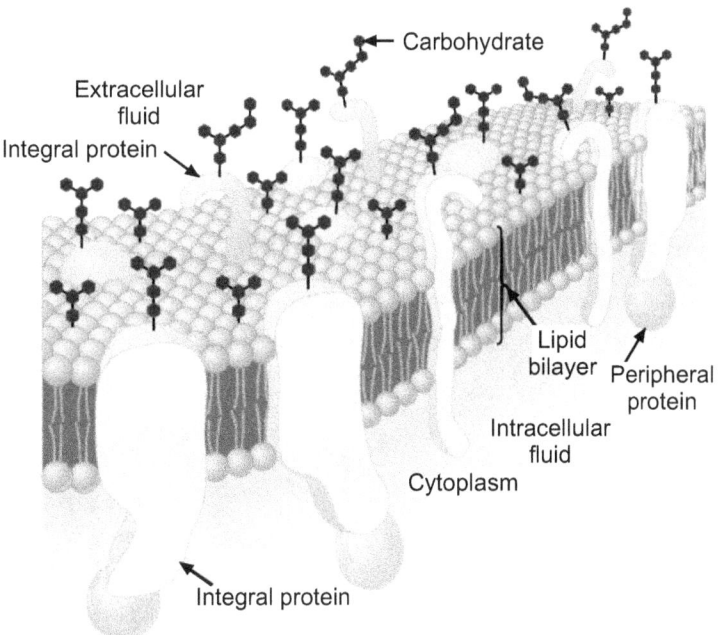

Fig. 5.1: Structure of cell membrane

- Cell membrane consist of double layer of amphiphilic phospholipid molecules arranged in such a pattern that their hydrocarbon chains are oriented inwards to form the hydrophobic or lipophillic phase and the polar ends are oriented to form the outer and inner hydrophilic boundaries of the cellular membrane that face the surrounding aqueous membrane. Globular proteins are also associated on the either side of these hydrophilic boundaries and also within the membrane structure.

- Various components of cell membrane such as :

- Phospholipids constitute the principle barrier influencing the entry and exit of the substance into and out of the cell. This capacity of cell membrane to control the passage of substance across its borders is called *selective permeability*. In general, lipid soluble molecules pass through this part of membrane with great ease, whereas water soluble molecules move through less easily.

5.3.1 Transport Mechanism Across the Cell Membrane

(1) Passive Transport

    (a) Diffusion

    (b) Facilitated Diffusion

    (c) Filtration (Pore Transport)

(2) Active Transport

(3) Ion-Pair Transport

(4) Ionic or Electrochemical Diffusion

(5) Endocytosis

(1) Passive Transport

(a) Diffusion

- Also called non-ionic diffusion.
- More than 90% of the drug is absorbed by this transport system.
- Driving force is the concentration gradient.
- Drug movement results from kinetic energy of molecules.
- No energy is required.

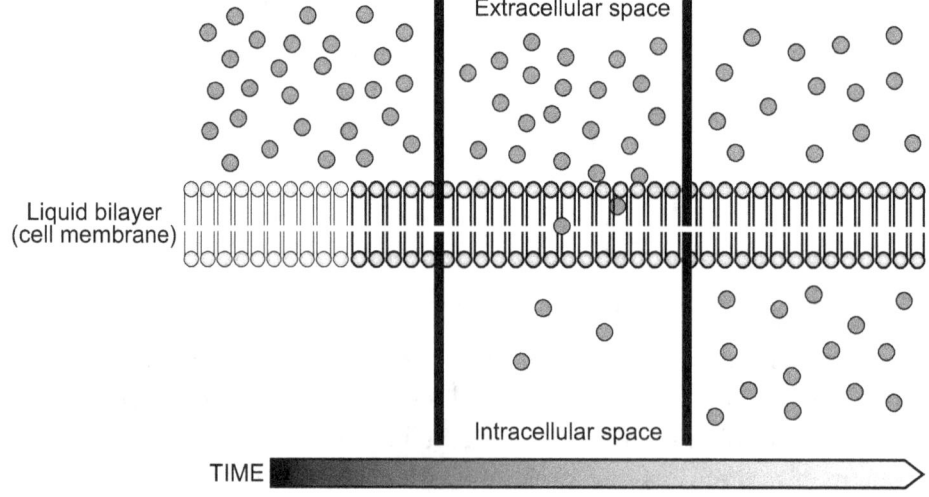

Fig. 5.2: Passive transport

- Best expressed by **Fick's First low of Diffusion**

$$\frac{dQ}{dt} = \frac{DAKm/w}{h} \times (C_{GIT} - C)$$

- If molecular weight of drug molecule increases, passive diffusion decreases and vice-versa.
- For example, Propronolol, Cimetidine, Atenolol, Naproxen.

(b) Facilitated Diffusion

- It is carrier-mediated transport system that operates through down concentration gradient (downhill transport).
- Much faster than simple passive diffusion.
- Driving force is concentration gradient (hence passive process).
- No energy expenditure. So the process is not inhibited by metabolic poisons that interfere with energy production.
- Examples are;
  - Entry of glucose into RBC.
  - Intestinal absorption of vitamin B_1 and B_2.
  - Gastro intestinal absorption of vitamin B_{12} and drugs like Cephalexin, Captopril, Bestatin, Levodopa.

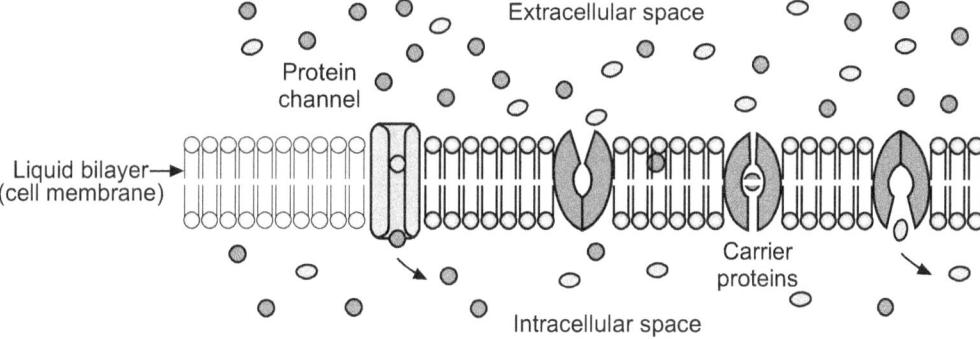

Fig. 5.3: Passive transport by facilitated diffusion

(c) Filtration (Pore Transport)

- Process is important in absorption of low molecular weight (less than 100 Dalton), low molecular size and generally water-soluble drugs through narrow, aqueous-filled channels or pores in the membrane.
- For example; urea, water and sugars.
- Driving force is constituted by the hydrostatic pressure.
- Drugs permeable through water-filled channels are of particular importance in;
  - Renal excretion,

- Removal of drugs from the cerebrospinal fluid, and
- Entry of drugs into the liver.

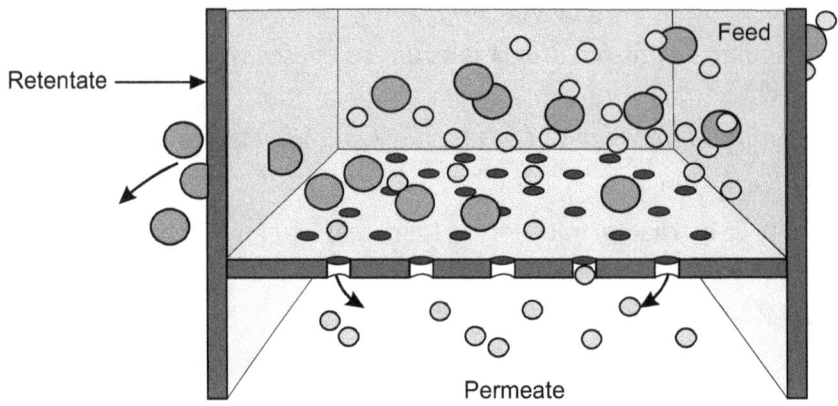

Fig. 5.3: Pore transport

(2) Active Transport

- The drug is transported from a region of lower to the higher concentration i.e. against the concentration gradient (uphill transport).
- It is carrier mediated transport system and require energy for work done by the carrier.
- It can be inhibited by metabolic poison like fluorides, cyanide, dinitrophenol and lack of oxygen etc.
- Endogenous substances that are transported actively include sodium, potassium, calcium, iron, glucose, certain amino acids and vitamins like niacin, pyridoxine, and ascorbic acid.

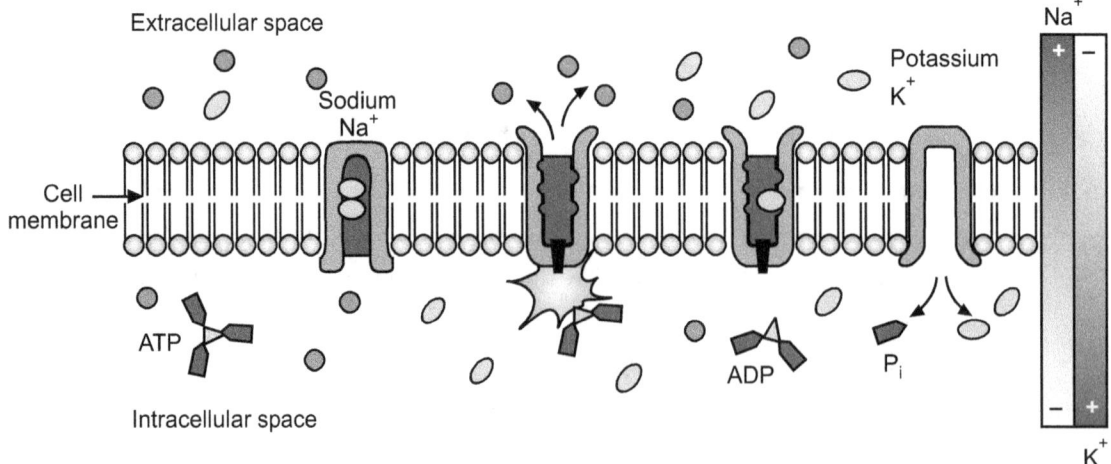

Fig. 5.4: Diffusion through active transport

(3) Ion-Pair Transport

- Like quaternary ammonium compounds and sulfonic acids, which ionize under all pH condition.
- Agents penetrate the membrane by forming reversible neutral complexes with endogenous ions.

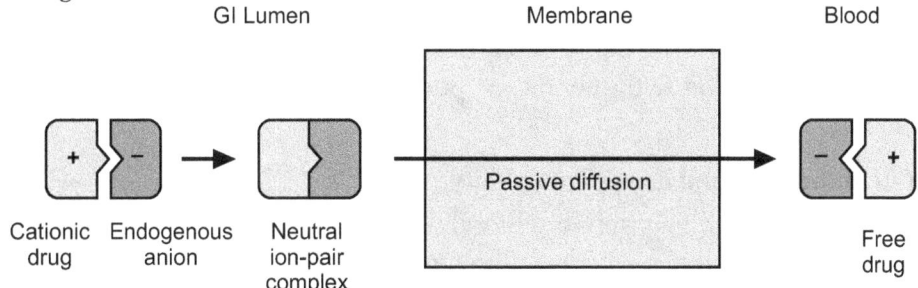

Fig. 5.5: Diffusion through ion pair transport

(4) Ionic or Electrochemical Diffusion

- The charge on the membrane influence permeation of drugs.
- Driving force is electrical gradient.
- Cationic drug is repelled due to positive charge on outside of the membrane.
- Like passive diffusion, continues until equilibrium is reached.

(5) Endocytosis

- Minor transport mechanism which involves engulfing extracellular materials within a segment of the cell membrane to form a vesicle.
- Cellular uptake of macromolecular nutrients like fat and lipid soluble vitamins like A, D, E and K and drug such as insulin.
  (a) Phagocytosis : (Cell eating) – adsorptive uptake of solid particulates
  (b) Pinocytosis : (Cell drinking) : Uptake of fluid solute.

Endocytosis

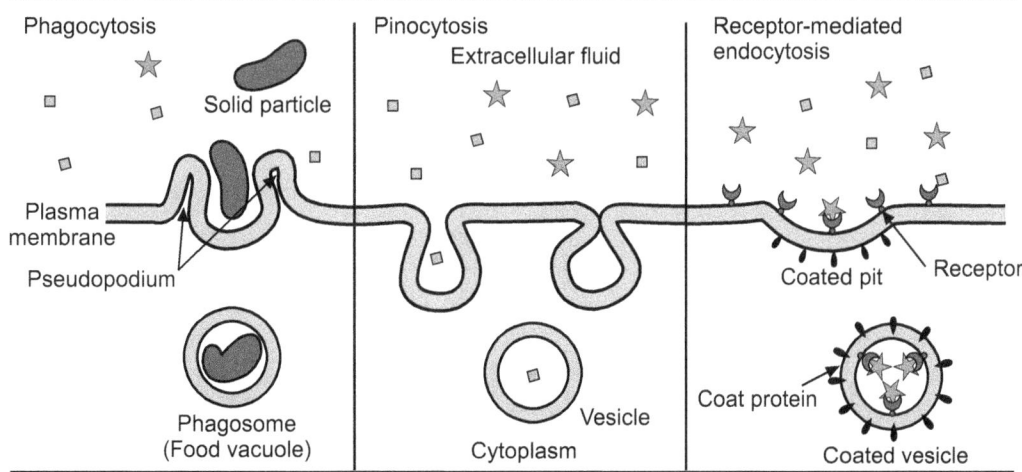

Fig. 5.6: Summary of endocytosis process

5.4 FACTORS AFFECTING DRUG ABSORPTION

5.4.1 Pharmaceutical Factors

[I] Physicochemical Properties of the Drug

(1) Drug solubility and dissolution rate:

There are mainly two rate limiting steps of orally administered drugs (i) rate of dissolution and (ii) rate of drug permeation, through the biomembrane. Rate of dissolution is rate limiting step for the hydrophobic or poorly aqueous soluble drugs like cromolyn sodium, Neomycin etc.

(2) Effect of blood flow and drug permeability :

The slowest or rate limiting steps are blood flow (perfusion rate - limited) or penetration through the membrene (diffusion rate - limited). By removing drug that passes through membrene, blood flow maintains a concentration gradient. Thus, assures continuous absorption process.

Absorption of ethanol and many lipophilic drugs is similarly perfusion rate limited.

For example; Urea is a compound with intermediate permeability characteristics. At low blood flow rates, absorption of urea is perfusion rate limited because the compound has sufficient time to diffuse across the membrane. At high blood flow rate membrane permeability becomes rate limiting and rate of urea absorption is unaffected to changes in blood flow.

For example; Neomycin relatively water soluble polar base, is absorbed rapidly from the intramuscular site where it has difficulty in penetrating gastro intestinal mucosa.

(3) Particle size and effective surface area :

- Inverse relationship is between the particle size and effective surface area. Particle size can play a major role in drug absorption. Particle size reduction has been used to increase the absorption of large number of drugs. For exmaple; griseofulvin, chloramphenicol and several salts of tetracycline.

- Improvement in drug dissolution rate can be achieved by reducing the particle size to a submicrone level. It is possible by :

1) Molecular dispersion/solid solution where the sparingly soluble drug is molecularly trapped in the lattice of a hydrophilic agent such as cyclodextrine.

2) Solid dispersion where such a drug is dispersed in a soluble carrier e.g. PVP, PEG, Urea.

(4) Hydrates or Solvates :

- The stoichiometric type of adducts where the solvent molecules are incorporated in the crystal lattice of the solid are called the *solvates*. The solvates can exist in different crystalline form called as *pseudopolymorphs* and this phenomenon is known as *pseudopolymorphism*.

- Generally, the anhydrous form of a drug has the greater water solubility than the hydrates since the hydrates are already in interaction with water and therefore have less energy for crystal break up compared to anhydrous form. On the other hand, the organic solvates have higher water solubility compared to anhydrates. For example; n-pentanol solvate of fludrocortisone and succinylsulfathaizole and chloroform solvates of griseofulvin.

(5) Salt form of drug :

- Most drugs are either weak acid or base so given as a salt form to enhance the solubility and dissolution. Generally, in weakly acidic drugs a strong base salt is formed.
- For example; Sodium and potassium base of barbiturates and sulfonamides.
- In case of weakly basic drugs strong acid salt is prepared like hydrochloride or sulphate salts of several alkaloidal drugs.
- At a given pH, the solubility of this salt form is constant, so this phenomenon is widely used to enhance the bioavailability of weakly acidic or basic drugs. But, the selection of proper salt form is very important factor.
- For example; The choline and the isopropanolamine salts of theophyline dissolves 3 to 4 times more rapidly than the ethylamine salt and it shows better bioavailability.

(6) pKa of drug and pH :

- The pH partition theory states that, the drug compounds of molecular weight greater than 100 dalton are primarily transported across the biomembrane by passive diffusion. This process is governed by the dissociation constant of a drug (pKa). pKa is determined by the Henderson-Hesselbach equations.

For weak acid:

$$pH = pKa + \log \frac{\text{(Ionized drug concentration)}}{\text{(Unionized drug concentration)}}$$

For weak bases:

$$pH = pKa + \log \frac{\text{(Unionized drug concentration)}}{\text{(Ionized drug concentration)}}$$

(7) Lipophilicity :

Lipophilicity also affects the absorption. E.g. Phenyl butazone and paracetamol have the same pKa value but due to difference in the lipophilicity thye show different absorption pattern.

(8) Nature and type of the dosage form :

The liquid dosage form is more readily absorbed than the solid one. In solid dosage form capsule is rapidly dissolved as compared to the tablet. Similarly, the sustained release tablet and enteric coated tablet have higher Dissolution time.

5.4.2 Patient Related Factors

1. Age :

In infants, the gastric pH is high and intestinal surface blood flow to the gastro intestinal tract is low, resulting in alteration of absorption pattern compared to adults. Similarly in elders, decrease in intestinal surface area and gastro intestinal blood flow, henc decreases the absorption.

2. Gastric Emptying Time :

The passage of the drug from the stomach to intestine is called as *gastric emptying*.

Rapid gastric emptying is advisable where –

1. Rapid onset of action, E.g. Sedative.
2. Dissolution required in intestine, E.g. Enteric coated dosage forms.
3. Drug unstable in gastric fluid, E.g. Penicillin.
4. Drug absorbed in from distal part of small intestine, E.g. Vitamin B_{12}.

3. Drug-drug Interaction :

- **Decreased GI transist:** Anticholinergics like propanthimide retard GI motility and promotes the absorption of drugs like Ranitidine and digoxin. While decrease absorption in case of paracetamol and sulfamethoxazole.
- **Increased GI emptying:** Metoclopramide promotes GI motility and enhances absorption of tetracycline, pivampicin and levodopa.
- **Altered GI Metabolism:** Antibiotics inhibit the bacterial metabolism of drugs, E.g. Erythromycin enhances efficacy of digoxin by this mechanism.

Drugs antacid Interaction :

Drug-antacids interaction have been reported for many drugs.

For example, Increase in absorption of drugs like aspirin, levo dopa etc., and decrease in absorption of drugs like iron, digitoxin, quinine etc.

5.5 ABSORPTION OF DRUG VIA DIFFERENT ROUTES OF ADMINISTRATION

[I] Buccal/Sublingual Administration

Various factors that must be considered for absorption via this routes are –

- **Lipophilicity of the drug:** Slightly higher lipophilicity is required compared to GIT.
- **Salivary secretion:** The drug should be soluble in buccal fluid.
- **pH of saliva:** Usually around pH 6 is favourable for drug which remain unionized at this pH.
- **Thickness of the epithelium:** Sublingual absorption is faster than buccal as the epithelium of former is thinner than buccal.
- For example; Nitrates and nitrites, antianginals, nifedipine, fenoterol oxytocin and steroids.

[II] Rectal Route

It is mainly beneficial for the children and old patients and in cases where patient is unable to swallow or unconscious.

The drugs are given either in suppository form or in solution form. Absorption from the solution is higher as compared to the suppositories.

For example; Aspirin, Paracetamol, Theophylline.

Various factors influencing the rectal drug absorption are :

- Co-administration of buffer can increase the rectal absorption by keeping it in unionized form, because rectal fluid has no buffer capacity.
- For rapid action, water soluble drugs should be formulated in fatty bases.
- The drug should have balanced portioning, first to diffuse from base into aqueous rectal fluid and second for partitioning into lipoidal rectal membrane.
- Insoluble drugs in micronised state cause less rectal irritation and has improved dissolution.

[III] Parentral Administration

(1) I.V. Administration

- It shows higher absorption as compared to another route.
- It can be used for the drugs which are not absorbed by mouth. E.g.; kanamycin.
- But main problem is drugs once injected cannot be recalled or controlled and embolism of foreign particles or air, hence sepsis or thrombosis is possible.

(2) I.M. Adminitration:

- Lipid solubility, ionization of drug. Volume of injection, drug concentration. pH composition and viscosity of injection vehicle affect the absorption of drug.

(3) S.C. Adminitration

The rate of absorption via subcutaneous route can be controlled by :

- Enhancing blood flow to the injection site, which incresases absorption.
- Increasing the drug tissue contact area, which increases absorption.
- Incorporation of vasoconstrictor which will retard absorption.
  E.g. Adrenaline, Insulin, Heparin.

(4) Pulmonary Administration

Drug absorption shows at pulmonary route due to the

- Large surface area of the alveoli. High permeability of the alveolar epithelium, rich perfusion.
- Bronchodilators like salbutamol, Anti-inflammatory steroids like beclomethasone and anti-allergic drugs are highly absorbed by this route.

(5) Intranasal Administration

- In case of lipophillic drugs, rapid absorption by diffusion is observed upto 400 dalton while satisfactory upto 1000 daltons.
- Even a drug having the molecular weight 6000 dalton show higher bioavailability, if permeability enhancers like surfactant are added.
- Polar compounds absorbed by pore transport upto 200 dalton.

Other factors that may influence nasal permeation are pH, viscosity of nasal secretion and pathologic conditions like common cold and rhinitis.

Disadvantages:

- Presence of several enzymes in the nasal mucosa affects the solubility of drugs. E.g. Proteins and peptides will be degraded by proteases and amino peptidases present in the nasal mucosa.
- Peptides may also form complexes with immunoglobulins in the nasal cavity leading to increase in the molecular weight and reduced absorption.
- Nasaly administered drugs in addition to loss by metabolism, can also be removed by mucous flow and cilliary movement.

(6) Intraocular Administration

Some important physical prameters should be considered for absorption of durg.

- **pH :** The pH of lacrimal fluid influences absorption of weak electrolytes such as pilocarpine.
- **Volume of fluid:** The volume of fluid instilled into eye also affect the bioavailability and effectiveness of the drug.
- **Viscosity of drug:** Viscosity of formulation imparts increased absorption and bioavailability by prolonging drug's contact time with the eye.

  E.g. Atropine, Pilocarpine, Adrenaline.

Table 5.1: Various Routes with Mechanism

Route	Absorption mechanism	Drug delivered
Buccal /Sublingual	Passive diffusion	Nitrates and Nitrites
	Carrier mediated transport	Antianginals, nifedipine, fenoterol
Rectal	Passive diffusion	Aspirin, Paracetamol, Theophylline
Transdermal	Passive diffusion	Nitroglycerine, Lidocaine, Scopolamine
Intramuscular	Passive diffusion, Endocytosis, Pore transport	Phenytoin, Digoxin, Several steroids

Contd...

Subcutaneous	Passive diffusion	Insulin, Heparin
Inhalation	Passive diffusion, Pore transport	Salbutamol, Cromolyn, Beclomethasone
Intranasal	Passive diffusion, Pore transport	Phenyl propanolamine, Antihistamines
Intraocular	Passive diffusion	Atropine, Pilocarpine, Adrenaline

5.6 METHODS TO DETERMINE ABSORPTION

There are three methods commonly used for determination of absorption:

(1) *In vitro* methods.

(2) *In vivo* methods.

(3) *In situ* methods.

(1) *In vitro* Methods :

In vitro methods are carried out outside of the body and used to determine the permeability of drug by using live animal tissues.

In vitro methods have introduced to assess the major factors involved in absorption process and predict the rate and extent of drug absorption.

Here, the intestine of animals such as rats, guinea pigs, rabbits are used for the study.

In vitro experiments are used to study the transport of drugs through different types of membranes or biological materials.

Different *in vitro* methods are as below:

(a) Diffusion cells.

(b) Segments of gastro intestinal tract of laboratory animals:

    (i) Everted small intestinal sac technique.

    (ii) Everted sac modification.

    (iii) Circulation techniques.

    (iv) Everted intestinal ring or slice techniques.

(c) Cell cultures of gut epithelium, E.g. Caco-2 cells.

(a) Diffusion Cell Method

Diffusion cells consist of two compartments –

1. *Donor compartment* which contains the drug solution and the lower end of which contains the synthetic or natural GI membrane that interfaces with the receptor compartment.

2. *Receptor compartment* which contains the buffer solution.

The procedure of uptake study using this technique involves measurement of rate of arrival of drug in the receptor compartment.

(b) Segments of Gastro Intestinal Tract of Laboratory Animals

(i) Everted Small Intestinal Sac Techniques

This method involves isolating a small segment of a laboratory animal such as rat, inverting the intestine and filling with small volume of drug free buffer solution.

Both the ends of the segment are tied off and immersed in an flask containing a large volume of buffer solution, containing the drug.

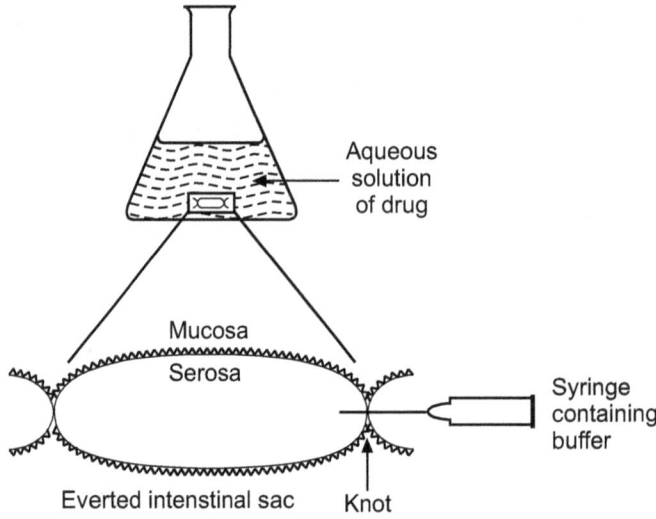

Fig. 5.7: Everted sac technique

Everted sac technique is used for studying drug transport uptake from gastro intestinal tract.

The flask and its content are oxygenated and agitated at 37°C for a specific period of time.

After incubation, the serosal fluid is assayed for drug content.

Advantages :

– The epithelial cell of the mucosal surface are exposed directly to the oxygenated mucosal surface.
– Prolongs the viability and integrity of the preparation after removal from the animal.
– Convenient and accurate.

Disadvantages :

– Difficulty in obtaining more than one sample per intestinal segment.

(ii) Everted Sac Modification

In this method, the test animal is fasted for a period of 20 – 24 hrs. The animal is killed and entire small intestine is everted. Segments of 5 - 15 cm in length are cut from a specific region of the intestine.

The distal end of the segment is tied and the proximal end is attached to the cannula.

The segment is suspended in mucosal solution which contain the drug. A drug free buffer solution is placed in the serosal compartments.

For determining the rate of drug transfer, the entire volume of serosal solution is removed from the sac at each time interval with the help of syringe and replaced with the same volume buffer solution.

The amount of drug that permeates the intestinal mucosa is plotted against time to describe profile of the drug at specific pH.

Advantages :
- A number of different solutions may be tested with a single segment of the intestine,
- Simple and reproducible. It distinguishes between active and passive absorption.
- It determines the region of the small intestine where absorption is optimal, in the case of active transport.
- Method is used to study about pH, surface active agents, complexation and enzymatic hydrolysis.

Disadvantages :
- The intestinal preparation is removed from the animal as well as from its normal blood supply. Under this condition, the permeability characteristics of the membrane are altered.
- The rate transport of drug as determined from the everted sac technique, is slower.

(iii) Circulation Techniques

In this method, small intestine may or may not be everted. This involves isolating either the entire small intestine or a segment and circulating oxygenated buffer containing the drug through the lumen.

Drug free buffer is circulated on the serosal side of the intestine membrane.

Absorption rates from the lumen to the outer solution are determined by sampling both the fluid circulating through the lumen and outside.

Advantages :
- Method is applicable to kinetic studies of the factors affecting drug absorption.

(iv) Everted Intestinal Ring or Slice Technique

In this technique, the entire small intestine is isolated from the fasted experimental animal and cut into ring like slices.

The slices are washed with a buffer and dried by blotting with filter paper. The dried rings are transferred to stoppered flasks containing the desired volume of buffer containing the drug. The contents are continuously agitated and aerate.

At selected time interval, the tissue slices are assayed for drug content.

Advantages :

– Simple and reproducible.

– Kinetic studies can be performed.

Disadvantages :

– Process of cutting the intestine into rings may expose highly permeable areas of cut or damage the tissue.

(2) *In vivo* **Methods :**

In vitro and *in situ* techniques gives us an idea about absorption, but *in vivo* method gives an idea about some important factor that influence absorption such as gastric emptying, intestinal motility, and the effects of drugs on the gastro intestinal tract can be determined.

The *in vivo* method can be classified into :

(a) Direct Method.

(b) Indirect Method.

(a) Direct Method

To determine the drug level in blood or urine: Sensitive reproducible analytical procedure should be developed to determine the drug in the biological fluid.

In this method, blank urine or blood sample is taken from the test animal before the experiment.

The test dosage form is administered to the animal, and at the appropriate interval of the time the blood or urine sample are collected and assayed for the drug content. From the data, determine the rate and extent of the drug absorption.

In this method, the experimental animal chosen should bear some resemble to man. Pigs most closely resemble to man but are not used due to the handling problems.

The other animals that can be used are rabbits and rats.

(b) Indirect Method

When the measurement of drug concentration in blood or urine is difficult or not possible, absorption studies can be done by indirect method.

In this method, pharmacological response of the drug is related to amount of a drug present in the body.

The response is determined after the administration of a test dosage form. LD_{50} appears to be dependent on the rate of the drug absorption.

(3) *In situ* **Methods :**

The term *in situ* refers to those methods in which the animal's blood supply remains intact, as a result of which the rate of absorption determined from this method may be realistic than those determined from *in vitro* techniques.

These *in situ* models are powerful tools to study the mechanistic aspects of these important processes. They act as bridge between the *in vitro* and *in vivo* methods.

The two perfusion methods used in laboratory animals are –

(a) Doluisio method

(b) Single pass perfusion.

(c) Cell culture technique

(a) Doluisio Method

In this method, the upper and lower parts of the small intestine of anaesthetised and dissected rat are connected by means of tubing to syringes of capacity 10 - 30 ml (see Fig. 5.8). After washing the intestinal segment with normal saline, the syringe is filled with a solution of radiolabelled drug and a non-absorbable marker which is used as an indicator of water flux during perfusion. Syringe containing drug is delivered to the intestinal segment which is then collected and analysed for drug content.

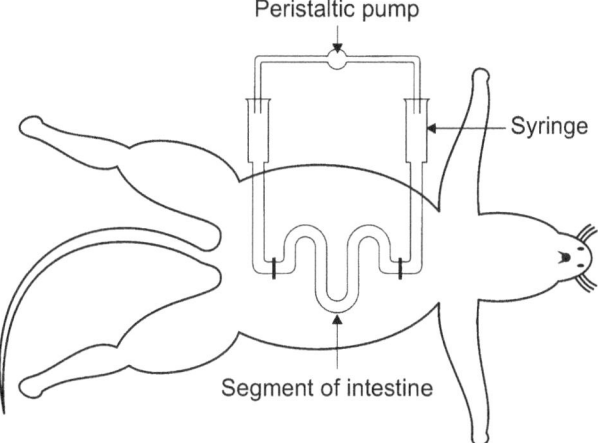

Fig. 5.8: Doluisio method

(b) Single-Pass Perfusion

In this technique, the drug solution passes through the intestinal segment.

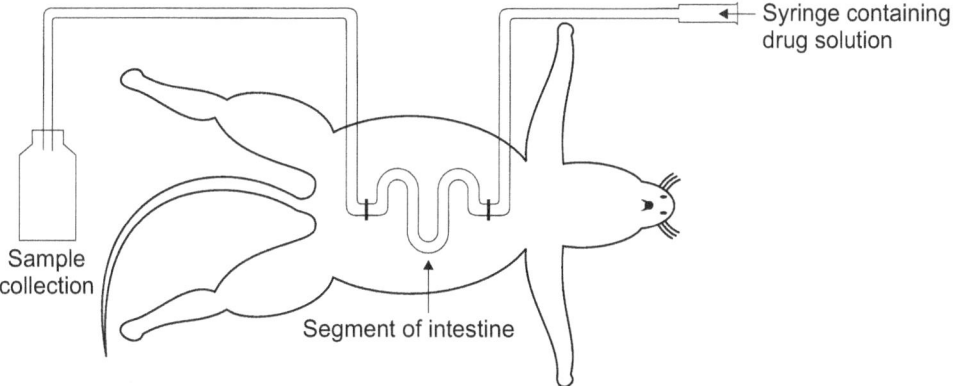

Fig. 5.9: Single-pass perfusion method

This technique is superior to Doluisio method. In this method, precise adjustment of hydrodynamic conditions that can influence blood circulation and puts stress on intestinal wall can be controlled.

(c) Cell Culture Technique

In this technique, differentiated cells of the intestine, originating from Caco-2 cells (cells of carcinoma of colon) are placed on synthetic polycarbonate membrane previously treated with an appropriate material such as collagen which on incubation aids reproduction of cells while not retarding drug permeation characteristics. Solution of drug is placed on this layer of cultured cells and the system is placed in a bath (receptor compartment) of buffer solution. The drug that reaches the latter compartment is sampled and analysed periodically.

5.7 ABSORPTION FROM SMALL INTESTINE

Absorption of drug from small intestine is described by two techniques.

(a) Perfusion technique

(b) Intestinal loop technique.

(a) Perfusion Technique

In this technique, adult male rats are fasted for about 16 to 24 hrs before the experiment. The animal is anaesthetised and a midline abdominal incision is made and the small intestine is isolated and cannulated at the duodenal.

The stomach and cecum are close off by ligature and the intestine is replaced in the rat's abdominal cavity. The incision is close and the duodenal cannula is attached to infusion pump.

The intestine is cleared off using drug free buffer solution for 30 min. Then, drug containing buffer solution is perfused for 30 min. Collect sample at 10 mins interval and assay for the drug content and calculate the relative rate of the absorption.

Many methods are used to demonstrate the validity of the pH partition hypothesis in the absorption of weakly acidic and basic drugs.

Among these, one method reported a simple and reproducible method for studying intestinal absorption of drugs in rats. Rat has been fasted overnight is anaesthetised, a midline abdominal incision is made, and the intestinal segment (jejunal) to be perfused is isolated.

A L shape glass inlet cannula is secured into the segment and the outlet cannula is placed 15 - 50 cm from the inlet cannula. These are secured with suture and the intestine is replaced in the abdominal cavity.

A hypodermic syringe containing perfusion solution, is attached to the duodenal cannula and the first intestinal lumen is cleared off by introducing the solution from the syringe.

The syringe is filled with drug solution and 10 ml volume is introduced into the intestine. At appropriate time interval, the solution in the intestine is pumped into other syringe, 0.1 ml sample is removed and assayed for drug content. The effective permeability (P) is calculated by the equation :

$$C_{out} = exp\left(\frac{-p(2\pi r l)}{Q}\right) C$$

where, r = radius of the gut lumen, l = length of the gut lumen, Q = perfusate flow rate, p = permeability of the compound.

(b) Intestinal Loop Technique

Single or multiple intestinal loops are used for studying the absorption. Adult male rats are fasted before the experiment under the anesthesia and abdominal midline incision is made and the small intestine is exposed. A proximal ligature is placed around the intestine from the pylorus and a distal ligature is squared at the distance of 4 inches to the proximal ligature.

The drug solution is introduced into the lumen of loop by means of syringe which is secured by the proximal ligature. After the injection, the needle is removed, the loop is replaced into the abdominal cavity and the incision is closed.

After a specific period of time the animal is sacrificed, the intestinal loop is excised, homogenised and the amount of unabsorbed drug is determined.

Advantage :

• Simple and reproducible.

Disadvantage :

• Only one sample can be obtained from the experimental animal.

5.8 ABSORPTION FROM THE STOMACH

Fasted adult male rats are anaesthetised and stomach is exposed. An incision is made in the pylorus, in which a cannula is introduced and ligated.

The lumen is washed several times with saline and 0.1 N HCl solution containing 0.15 M NaCl. Drug solution of a known concentration is introduced into stomach.

After 1 hour, the solution is removed from the gastric pouch and analysed for the drug content.

The percentage of drug absorbed in one hour may be calculated. The gastric pouch may also be homogenised and analysed for a drug.

In order to obtain the number of sample as a function of time, the following modification is done.

Drug solution is introduced into the gastric lumen through the cardiac cannula. A polyethyline tubing connected to 2 ml syringe is attached to the duodenal L shape cannula. At a specific interval, the stomach contents are sampled by withdrawing the solution in syringe.

Advantages :

• Simple and reproducible.

Disadvantages :

• Drug is accumulated or metabolized in the gut wall, so one may get an overestimate of the amount of drug absorbed.

Chapter 6

DISTRIBUTION OF DRUGS

6.1 INTRODUCTION

Drug distribution is defined as "the reversible transfer of drug between one compartment (blood) and another (extra vascular tissue)".

Drug goes into the systemic circulation after absorption. Then the drugs are distributed throughout the body and go to the site of action.

Distribution of drug means how the drug travels in the bloodstream and how it goes into and comes out of other areas of the body.

During this, drugs cross different membranes to reach other compartments of the body and cells of the tissues.

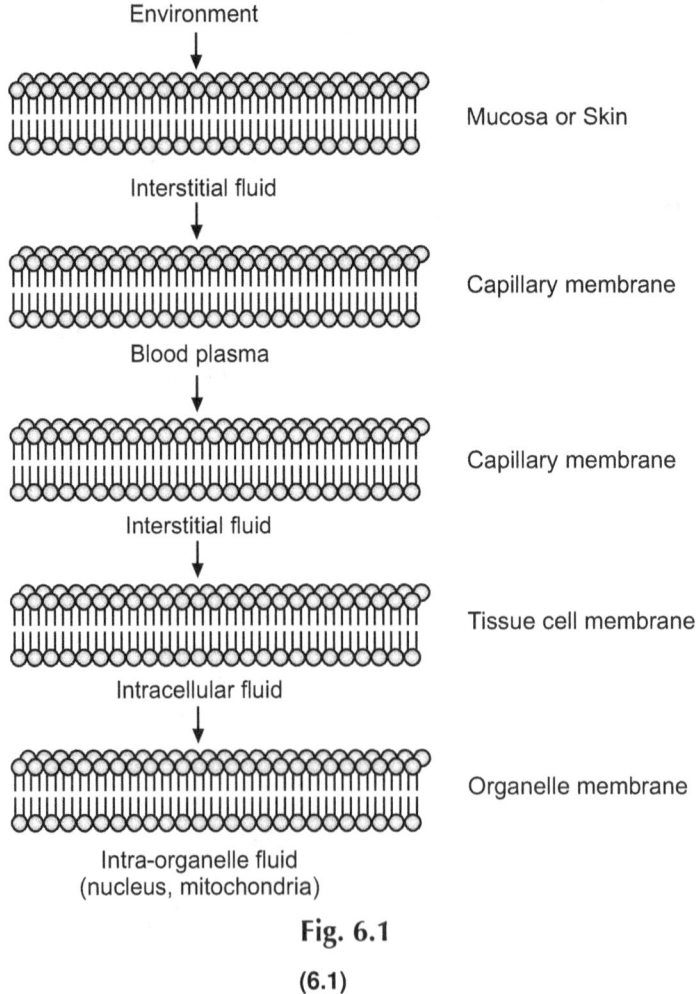

Fig. 6.1

Some drugs remain in plasma only (cannot cross the capillary membrane).

Some drugs remain in the ECF (plasma and interstitial fluid) as they can cross the capillary membrane but can not cross the cell membrane.

Some drugs can be distributed in the whole body fluid (both ECF and ICF) as they can cross the all membranes of the body. From plasma, drugs have to cross the capillary membrane to come to intestital space and then need to cross the cell membrane to enter into the intracellular fluid (Fig. 6.1).

6.2 REASONS FOR UNEQUAL DISTRIBUTION OF DRUGS

Distribution of drugs throughout the body fluid is not equal.

The reasons for unequal distribution of drugs are:

(1) Drug factors

(2) pH of the media

(3) Regional blood flow

(4) Drug binding to protein or tissue

(5) Membranes

(1) Drug Factors

- Lipid solubility of the drugs.
- Molecular weight of the drugs.

(i) Lipid solubility

- Lipid soluble drugs (non-ionized) can cross easily the membranes.
- Water soluble drugs (ionized) can not cross the cell membrane, and so remains mostly in extra cellular fluid.

(ii) Molecular weight

- Low molecular weight drugs can cross cell membrane easily.
- High molecular weight drugs (albumin) can not cross the capillary membrane and remains in plasma.

(2) pKa of Drug and pH of Media

- Acidic low pKa drugs will be more ionized and hence cross the membranes less.
- Basic low pKa drugs will be less ionized and hence cross the membranes more.

(3) Regional Blood Flow

- More blood flow shows more distribution.
- Drugs are distributed to tissues most rapidly with a high blood flow (heart, lungs, brain) as compared to the moderate blood flow (muscle) and poor blood flow (fat, tendons, cartilage).

6.3 STEPS IN DRUG DISTRIBUTION

- Distribution of drug preset in systemic circulation to extravascular tissues involves two steps.

  1) Permeation of free or unbound drug through capillary wall and enter into the Interstitial and ECF.

  2) Permeation of drugs from ECF (Extra Cellular Fluid) to ICF (Intra Cellular Fluid) through membrane of tissue cell.

  This step is rate limiting and depend upon :

  - Rate of perfusion to the ECF.

  - Membrane permeability of the drug.

Apparent Volume of Distribution (V_d)

- "A hypothetical volume of fluid into which a drug disseminates" is called apparent volume of fluid.
- Although the V_d has no physiologic or physical basis, it is sometimes useful to compare the distribution of a drug with the volumes of the water compartments in the body.

  Formula for V_d:

  - It is calculated as the total amount of drug in the body divided by the concentration of the drug in plasma.

  $$V_d = \frac{\text{Total dose administered}}{\text{Plasma concentration}} = \frac{D}{C}$$

Plasma Compartment

- If a drug has a very large molecular weight or binds extensively to plasma proteins, it is too large to move out through the endothelial slit junctions of capillaries, thus restricted within the vascular compartment e.g. Warfarin.

Extracellular Fluid

- If a drug has a low molecular weight but is hydrophilic (lipid insoluble), it can move through the endothelial slit junctions of capillaries into the interstitial fluid but cannot enter into the cells (E.g Mannitol).

Total Body Water

- If a drug has a low molecular weight and is hydrophobic (lipid soluble), it can move into the interstitial fluid as well as can enter cells.

  Thus, it distributes into total body water.

  E.g. Alcohol.

6.4 FACTORS AFFECTING DISTRIBUTION OF DRUGS

1. Tissue permeability of drugs.

2. Organ tissue size and perfusion rate.

3. Binding of drug to tissue component.

4. Miscellaneous.

These factors are described below in detail :

1. Tissue permeability of drugs

(a) Physicochemical properties of the drug :

(i) Molecular size: Molecular weight less than 500 - 600 daltons can easily cross capillary membrane of extra cellular fluid. Water soluble molecules and molecules having size less than 50 dalton particle pass through aqueous filled channels.

Large molecular size is restricted or require specialized transport system.

(ii) pKa: pH of blood plasma and ECF (7.4) play a major role in degree of ionization. A weak acid becomes unionized in a strong acidic environment and ionized in a neutral or basic environment.

All the drugs ionized at plasma pH cannot penetrate the lipoidal cell membrane.

(iii) O/w partition coefficient:

- Polar and hydrophillic drugs are less likely to cross the cell membrane.

- Non-polar and hydrophobic drugs are more likely to cross the cell membrane.

- Effective $k_{o/w}$ = Fraction unionized at pH 7.4 $\times$ $k_{o/w}$ of unionized drug.

- Lipoidal drugs penetrate the tissue rapidly. Among these drugs with same $k_{o/w}$ but difference in ionization of blood pH, if drug shows less ionization shows better distribution.

Physiological Barrier to the Diffusion:

(i) **Simple capillary endothelial barrier:** All drugs with molecular size less than 600 daltons easily diffuse through capillary endothelium to intestitial fluid.

(ii) **The simple cell membrane barrier :** It is similar to the lipoidal barrier in the GI absorption of the drugs. Once the drug diffuse through capillary to extracellular fluid, its further entry into cells of most tissues is limited. Lipophilic drugs with molecular size 50 – 600 dalton and hydrophilic polar drugs with molecular size < 50 dalton will pass this membrane.

(iii) Blood Brain Barrier :

- Highly specialized and less permeable to water soluble drugs.

- Brain capillary consist of endothelial cells which are joined one another by continuous tight intercellular junctions.

- Pericytes and astrocytes form a solid envelop around brain capillary and block intercellular passage.

  A solute may enter to brain via:

  1. Passive diffusion through the lipoidal barrier.
  2. Active transport of essential nutrients.

  Blood brain barrier crossing can be promoted by:

  1. Use of permeation enhancer like DMSO.
  2. Osmotic disruption of the blood brain barrier by infusing internal carotid artery with mannitol.
  3. Use of dihydropyridine redox system as a drug carriers to the brain. E.g. steroidal drug.

(iv) Blood Cerebrospinal Fluid Barrier:

- Formed by the choroid plexus of the lateral, third and fourth ventricles.
- It is similar to ECF of brain.
- The capillary endothelium, that line choroid plexus have open junctions or gaps, and drugs can flow freely between capillary wall and choroidal cells.
- The choroid cells are joined to each other by tight junctions forming the blood – CSF barrier which has permeability characteristic similar to blood brain barrier.
- Highly lipid soluble drugs can easily cross the blood-CSF barrier but moderately soluble and ionized drugs permeate slowly.
- Mechanism of drug transport is similar to CNS and CSF but degree of uptake may vary significantly.

(v) Blood Placental Barrier:

- It is the barrier between maternal and fetal blood vessels, separated by a number of tissue layers made of fetal trophoblast basement membrane and endothelium which together constitute the placental barrier.
- Drugs having molecular size less than 1000 daltons and moderate lipid solubility cross the placental barrier by simple diffusion rapidly.

  For example; ethanol, sulphonamide, barbiturate, Narcotic analgesic, anticonvulsant etc.

  Essential nutrients for fetal growth transported by carrier mediated process immunoglobulin are transported by endocytosis.

(vi) Blood Testis Barrier:

- This barrier is located at the sertoli-sertoli cell junction.
- The barrier is tight junction between neighbouring sertoli cells that act as barrier.
- The barrier restrict the passage of drugs to spermatocyte and spermatids.

2. Organ/Tissue Size and Perfusion Rate

Perfusion rate is limited when,

1) Drug is highly lipophilic.

2) Membrane across which the drug is supposed to diffuse is highly permeable such as those of the capillaries and muscles.

In above both cases, greater the blood flow, faster the distribution.

Distribution is permeability related in following cases :

- When the drug is ionic/polar/water soluble, where the highly selective physiology barrier restrict the diffusion of such drugs to the inside of cell distribution will be perfusion rate limited.

- When the drug is highly lipohilic, distribution will be perfusion rate limited.

- When the membrane is highly permeable, distribution will be perfusion rate limited.

Perfusion rate: It is defined as "the volume of the blood that flows per unit time per unit volume of the tissue".

Unit: ml/min/ml

$$K_t = \text{Perfusion rate} / K_{t/b}$$

$$\text{Distribution half life} = 0.693/K_t$$

$$= 0.693K_{t/b}/\text{Perfusion rate}$$

$$K_{t/b} = \text{Tissue/blood partition coefficient}$$

3. Binding of Drug to Tissue Components

(a) Binding of drugs to blood components :

- o Blood cells
- o Plasma proteins

(i) Binding of drugs to blood cells :

- The major component of blood is RBC. (95% cells)
- The RBC comprises of 3 components, each of which can bind to drugs:
  - Hemoglobin
  - Carbonic anhydrase
  - Cell membrane

(ii) Binding of drugs to plasma proteins :

Plasma protein-drug binding:

- The binding of drug to plasma protein is reversible.
- The extent or order of binding of drugs to various plasma proteins is:

  Albumin >α_1-Acid Glycoprotein > Lipoproteins > Globulins

(iii) Binding of drugs to human serum albumin :

- Most abundant plasma protein with large drug binding capacity.
- Both endogenous compounds and drugs bind to human serum albumin.
- Four different sites on human serum albumin :

    Site I: Warfarin and azapropazone binding site

    Site II: Diazepam binding site

    Site III: Digitoxin binding site

    Site IV: Tamoxifen binding site

(iv) Binding of drugs to α_1-acid glycoprotein :

- It binds to basic drugs like imipramine, amitryptyline, lidocaine.

(v) Binding of drugs to lipoproteins :

- A drug that binds to lipoproteins by dissolving in the lipid core of the protein and thus its capacity to bind depends upon its lipid content.

    Binding of drugs to lipoproteins is non-competitive.

(b) Binding of drug to extra vascular tissues:

40% of total body weight comprise of vascular tissues. Tissue drug binding result in localization of drug at specific site in body and act as a reservoir. As binding increase, it also increase biological half life.

Irreversible binding leads to drug toxicity.

4. Miscellaneous Factors

- Age:
    (a) Total body water
    (b) Fat content
    (c) Skeletal muscles
    (d) Organ composition
    (e) Plasma protein content
- Pregnancy
- Obesity
- Diet
- Disease state

The above miscellaneous factors are described in detail below:

1) **Age:** Difference in distribution pattern is mainly due to,

    Total body water – It is greater in infants.

    Fat content – It is higher in infant and elderly.

    Skeletal muscle – It is lesser in infant and elderly.

Organ composition – Blood Brain Barrier is poorly developed in infants, mylein content is low and cerebral blood flow is high, hence greater penetration of drug in brain.

Plasma protein contnet – Low albumin in both infants and elderly.

2) **Pregnancy :** During pregnancy due to the growth of uterus, placenta etc. there is increase in the volume available for distribution of drug.

Foetus have seperate compartment for distribution of drug. In foetus, plasma level and ECF volume are high but albumin content is low.

3) **Obesity :** In obese person there is high adipose, so high distribution of lipophilic drug.

4) **Diet :** A diet, high in fats, will increase free fatty acid level in circulation, thereby affecting binding of acidic drug.

5) **Disease state :** A number of mechanisms are involved in alteration of drug distribution in disease state:

(i)   Altered albumin and other drug binding protein concentration.

(ii) Alteration or reduced perfusion to organ tissue.

(iii) Altered tissue pH.

(iv) Alteration of permeability of physiological barrier.

Patient affect CCF, perfusion rate to entire body decrease, it affect distribution.

6.5 PLASMA PROTEIN BINDING (PPB)

Binding of drug to plasma protein is a major determinant of drug distribution.

When the drugs appear in the circulation,

- A fraction of drug molecules bind with plasma protein and another fraction remain free.
- In general, binding is reversible and obeys the law of mass action.
- There is always an equilibrium between bound and free drug concentration.

The proteins commonly involved in binding with drugs are albumin, lipoprotein and α_1-acid glycoprotein.

- Generally acidic drugs bind with albumin.
- Acidic drugs have high affinity and low capacity.
- Basic drugs have low affinity and high capacity.
- Basic drugs bind with α_1-acid, glycoprotein and LP.

The bound drug is kept in the blood stream while the unbound component may be metabolized or excreted.

- If a drug is 95% bound to a binding protein, 5% is free. Means that, 5% is active in the system and cause pharmacological effect.

Drug–protein binding may be reversible or an irreversible process.

- Irreversible drug-protein binding is usually a result of chemical activation of drug, attaches strongly to the protein by covalent chemical bond. Irreversible drug binding accounts certain types of drug toxicity over a long period of time.

- Reversible drug-protein binding implies that, the drug binds the protein with weak chemical bond like hydrogen bond.

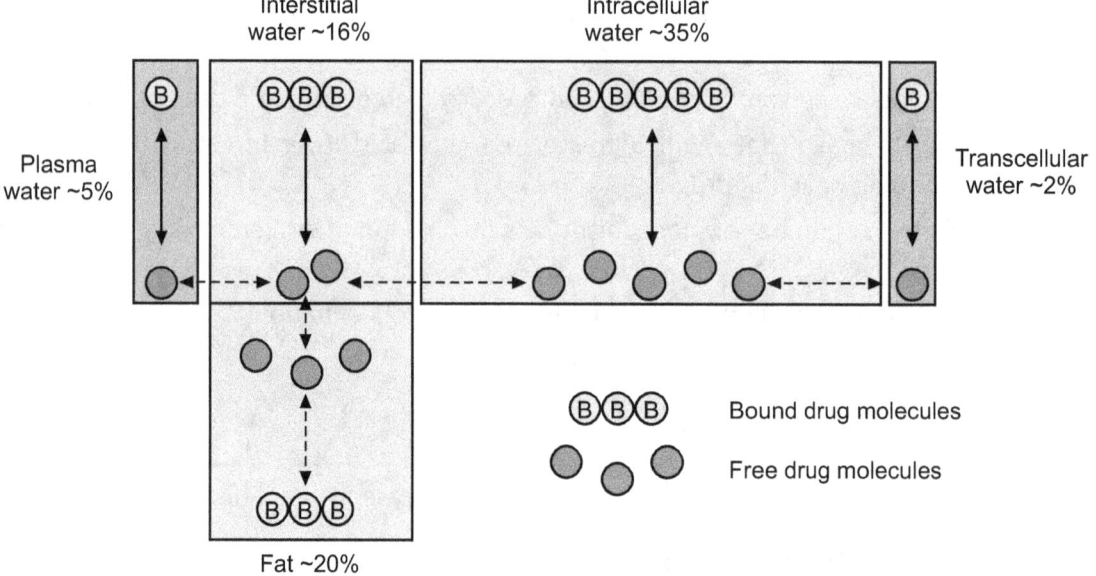

Fig. 6.3

6.6 TISSUE BINDING

- Some drugs have special affinity to some tissues.

  For example; Brain, adipose tissue, kidneys, cornea, bone etc.

- Some drugs get readily distributed in specific tissues and remain accumulated in those tissues.

  For example;

  Tetracycline to bone.

  Phenobarbitone to brain.

  Chlorpromazine to eye.

  Chloroquine to kidneys etc.

6.7 BLOOD BRAIN BARRIER

- The brain requires a protected environment in which it can function normally.

- A specialized structural barrier, the blood brain barrier, plays a key role in this protection and maintaining this environment.

- It is a tight junction. There is no fenestrations or slit inbetween the endothelial cells of capillaries. Layer of astrocyte foot processes makes this more impermeable. (Fig. 6.7)
- Only lipid soluble substances can cross the blood-brain barrier.
- The blood-brain barrier is the brain's most formidable gatekeeper.

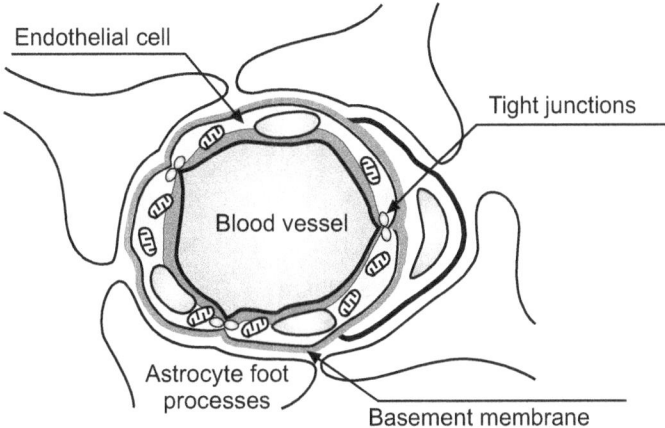

Fig. 6.7 : Blood-brain barrier

6.8 BLOOD-PLACENTAL BARRIER

- This barrier prevents the toxic substances to enter into fetal circulation.
- This is a tight junction like blood brain barrier.
- It is surrounded by chorionic villi.
- There is a tight layer of trophoblastic cells around capillary membrane.
- Only small molecular weight substances and lipid soluble drugs are permitted to cross the blood placental barrier.

6.9 VOLUME OF DISTRIBUTION

A drug in circulation distributes to various organs and tissues. When the process of distribution is complete, different organs contain varying concentration of drug which can be determined by the volume of drug in tissue.

The volume of distribution (V_d), also known as the apparent volume of distribution, is a calculated theoretical value. Apparent volume of distribution is a proportionality constant relating the plasma concentration to the total amount of drug in the body.

$$x \propto c \qquad \therefore \qquad x = V_d.c$$

$$\therefore \quad V_d = \frac{x}{c}$$

where, x = Amount of drug in body

c = Plasma drug concentration

It is used clinically, to determine the **loading dose** of a drug, and is also used for estimating a blood concentration in the treatment of overdose.

Objectives:

- Understand the physiological determinants of volume of distribution.
- Realize the limited relevance of plasma protein binding.
- Able to describe the time course of drug concentration for one and two compartment pharmacokinetic models.

Volume of distribution of drugs (V_d):

Volume of distribution is "the volume of plasma that would be necessary to account for the total amount of drug in the patient's body, if that drug was present throughout the body at the same concentration as found in the plasma". This value is usually further divided by the patient's body weight, and the result is expressed in terms of litres per kilogram.

For e.g.   If Dose given = 100 mg

Plasma concentration = 1 mg/l

Then $V_l = \dfrac{\text{Dose}}{\text{Plasma concentration } (C_p)}$

$= \dfrac{100}{1} = 100$ lit

Accordingly, a drug that accumulates in tissues as e.g. fat tissue, will have a relatively low plasma concentration with regard to the administered dose, and consequently, the calculated V_d will be high.

Typical liquid volumes are in % or in lit. for a man of average weight 70 kg :

Total water:	60% (50-80%)	42 lit.
Intracellular volume:	40%	28 lit.
Extracellular volume:	20%	14 lit.
Plasma volume:	4%	4 lit.
Blood volume:	8%	5.5 lit.

Plasma Compartment

- The plasma volume can be determined by using very high molecular weight drugs, or drugs that highly bind to existing plasma proteins. For example; heparin 4 lit. (3 - 5).

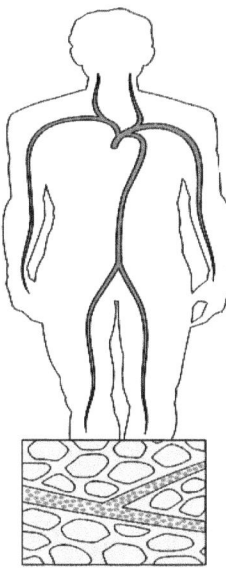

Fig. 6.8

Extracellular Fluid

- Volume of the extracellular fluid volume can be determined by substance that have a low molecular weight and which is hydrophilic but do not cross the cell membrane.

  For Example :

  Atracuronium 11 lit. (8 - 15)

  V_d : between 4 and 14 lit.

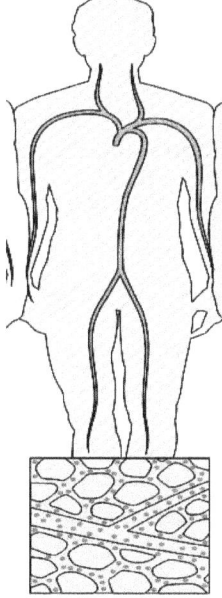

Fig. 6.9

Total body water:

- Total body water volume can be determined by using substances that distribute equally in all water compartments of the body e.g. tritiated water.

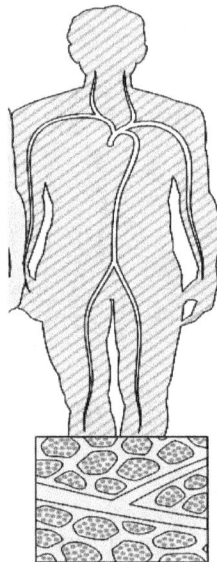

Fig. 6.10

Interpretation of Volumes of Distribution

A) If V_d approximates blood volume

- The drugs are mainly limited to vascular compartment.
- Maximum amount cannot cross the capillary membrane.
- They are highly protein bound.
- For example; Warfarin, Heparin.

B) If V_d approximates extracellular fluid volume

- They occupy the whole extracellular space.
- Can cross the capillary membrane.
- But cannot easily cross cell membranes to enter the intracellular fluid.
- For example; Aspirin, Gentamicin.

C) If V_d is close to total body water

- They occupy the whole extra and intracellular space.
- The drugs are highly lipid soluble.
- These drugs are able to cross cell membranes to enter the intracellular fluid from extracellular space.
- For example; Phenytoin, Ethanol

D) If V_d is greater than total body water (> 45 lit.)

- Drugs are highly lipid soluble.
- They enter into all cells easily.
- Also bind extensively to tissue proteins.
- Accumulation in certain organs.
- For example; Digoxin, Chloroquine.

Drugs with a very small V_d (<10 lit.) are mainly confined to the intravascular fluid, thus the blood, correspond to roughly twice the plasma volume. This may occur for two reasons :

1. The molecule is too large to leave this compartment.
2. The molecule binds preferably to plasma proteins (e.g. to albumin) and much less to tissue proteins. Competition for plasma protein binding sites can occur between such drugs or with endogenous substances.

Some drugs cannot enter cells because of their low lipid solubility. These drugs are distributed throughout the body water in the extracellular compartment and have a relatively small V_d (12-20 lit.).

Drugs that accumulate in organs either by active transport or by specific binding to tissue molecules have a high volume of distribution, which can exceed several times the anatomical body volume. Therefore, V_d should not be identified too closely with a particular anatomical compartment. Lipid-soluble drugs are stored in fat. Bone is a reservoir for drugs such as tetracycline and heavy metals.

Volume of distribution (V_d) of drugs are not real.

From plasma, drugs have to cross the capillary membrane to come to interstitial space, and then need crossing the cell-membrane to enter into the intracellular fluid.

But at the time of crossing the cell membrane,

- Some drugs remain in plasma only.
- Some drugs remain in the ECF.
- Some drugs can be distributed in the whole body fluid (both ECF and ICF).
- Some drugs have great affinity to some tissues. Hence, remain concentrated in that tissue. Thus, gives a low plasma concentration.

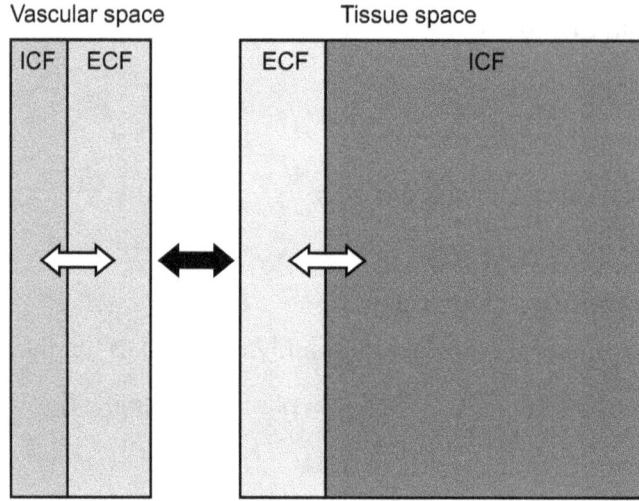

Fig. 6.11

Clinical Importance of V_d :

Determines the relationship between dose and plasma concentration.

It provides a reference,

- For the expected plasma concentration for a given dose, and
- For the dose required to produce a given concentration.

Relation between V_d and Plasma Concentration of Drug :

Less plasma concentration of a drug;

- means more distribution and hence greater V_d.

Greater plasma concentration of a drug;

- means less distribution and hence smaller V_d.

Difference of V_d for Acidic and Basic Drugs :

(i) V_d for acidic drugs :

- Many acidic drugs are highly protein-bound and thus have a small volume of distribution.

  For example; Warfarin, Salicylic acid.

(ii) V_d for basic drugs :

- Many basic drugs are taken up by tissues and thus have larger volume of distribution.

  For example; Amphetamine, Chloroquine.

BIOTRANSFORMATION OF DRUGS

7.1 INTRODUCTION

Biotransformation is "a process by which organic compounds are transformed from one form to another, aided by organisms such as bacteria, fungi and enzymes". Biotransformations are used as a valuable strategy to build molecules, similar to parent drug in the drug discovery programme. Biotransformations can also be used to synthesize compounds or materials, if synthetic approaches are challenging. Microbial biotransformations or microbial biotechnology are extensively used to generate metabolites in bulk amounts.

The biochemical alteration of drug or xenobiotic, in the presence of various enzymes that acts as a catalyst which themselves not consumed in the reaction and thereby may activate or deactivate the drug is called *biotransformation*.

Biotransformation of drugs is defined as "an irreversible conversion of drugs from one chemical form to another, by the enzymes present in the body".

Biotransformation is a chemical conversion by the aid of enzymes. Chemical modification may be needed because the drugs are xenobiotics, such substances need to be eliminated from the body. Drug may be excreted in urine if it is water soluble. If drug is lipophilic it is metabolized and eliminated by renal excretion.

The term biotransformation is used synonymously for metabolism. Biotransformations largely result in the elimination of drug from the body. Thus, removal of drug from the body is largely responsible for the termination of drug action.

In the body, chemical conversion or chemical instability may occur in two ways :

(i) When a drug transformation takes place by enzymes, it is known as drug metabolism. Eg. Penicillin is converted to penicilloic acid by bacterial penicilliases.

(ii) When a drug transformation takes place due to adverse conditions, it is known as metabolism. E.g. Penicillin is converted into penicillenic acid in acidic condition of the stomach.

Biotransformation is also known as *detoxification*. Most of the drugs are toxic. The body has natural mechanism to eliminate these from the body, so as to avoid its toxic effects. Thus, biotransformation is a protective measure to preserve the body.

In general sense, biotransformation is often referred to as metabolism. Based on the rate of metabolism of the drug, several properties of the drug like its biological halflife, its therapeutic efficacy and toxicity are determined. Therefore, it is worth to get through the factors affecting the biotransformation of drug.

7.1.1 Necessity of Biotransformation

Biotransformation is necessary :

- to easily eliminate the drug,
- to terminate drug action.

Table 7.1 : Physicochemical properties : Active to Inactive and Vice Versa

Active /Inactive	Inactive /Active
Lipophilic	Hydrophilic
Unionised	Ionised
Non-polar	Polar
Plasma protein bound	Free

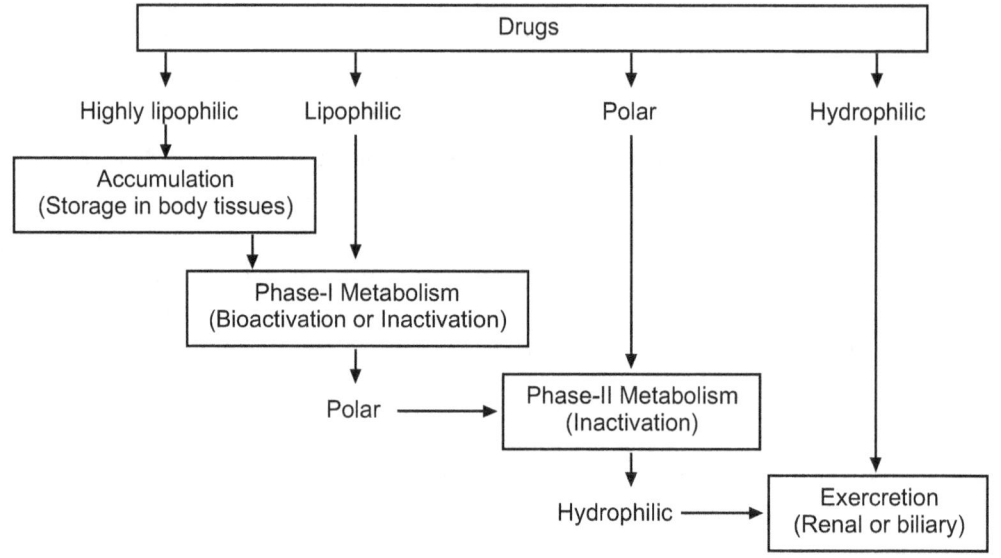

Classification of Drugs

7.1.2 Consequences of Biotransformation

- **Active to Inactive:**

    Phenobarbitone ⟶ Hydroxyphenobarbitone

- **Inactive (Prodrug) to Active :**

    L-Dopa ⟶ Dopamine

    Parathion ⟶ Paraoxon

    Talampicillin ⟶ Ampicillin

- **Active to Equally Active:**

    Diazepam ⟶ Oxazepam

Amitriptyline $\longrightarrow$ Nortriptyline

Imipramine $\longrightarrow$ Des-imipramine

Codeine $\longrightarrow$ Morphine

7.1.3 Sites of Biotransformation

- *In the body:* Liver, small and large intestines, lungs, skin, kidney, nasal mucosa and brain.

- Liver is considered "metabolite clearing house" for both endogenous substances and xenobiotics.

- Intestines are considered "initial site of drug metabolism".

7.2 FIRST PASS METABOLISM

- After oral administration, many drugs are absorbed from the small intestine - transported first via portal system to the liver, where they undergo extensive metabolism before reaching systemic circulation.

- First pass effect is carried out in :Liver - 90%, Gastro-Intestinal tract - 9% and Portal circulation - 1%.

Table 7.2 : Drugs which undergo First Pass Effect:

Liver	Intestinal mucosa	Bronchial mucosa
Isosorbide dinitrate	L-dopa	Nicotine
Glyceryl trinitrate	α–methyldopa	Isoprinaline
Morphine	Testosterone	
Pethidine	Progesterone	
Xylocaine	Chlorpromazine	
Imipramine	Clonazepam	
Amitriptyline	Midazolam	
Propranolol	Cyclosporine	

7.3 FACTORS AFFECTING BIOTRANSFORMATION OF DRUG

1. Physicochemical properties of the drug
2. Chemical factors
   (a) Induction of drug metabolising enzymes
   (b) Inhibition of drug metabolising enzymes
3. Biological factors
   (a) Age
   (b) Sex or Gender differences
   (c) Strain differences

   (d) Species differences

   (e) diet

   (f) Altered physiological factors

      (i) Pregnanacy

      (ii) Hormonal imbalance

      (iii) Disease states

   (g) Temporal factors

      (i) Circadian rhythm

      (ii) Circannual rhythm

   (h) Enviromental Factors

1. Physicochemical Properties of the Drug

- Molecular size and shape
- pKa
- Acidity/basicity
- Lipophilicity
- Steric and electronic characteristics

All physicochemical factors interact with the active site of enzyme and affect the metabolic process.

2. Chemical Factors

   (a) Enzyme Induction

   (b) Enzyme Inhibition

(a) Enzyme Induction

It is a process in which a drug induces or enhances the expression of an enzyme.

Examples

Rifampicin : If taken by female patients who are taking contraceptives, causes decreased therapeutic effect, leading to pregnancy.

Phenobarbitone : If administered to patients taking warfarin, may cause therapeutic failure, leading to increased bleeding tendency.

Auto induction: Auto induction is the type of enzyme induction. The phenomenon in which a drug induces metabolism of other drugs as well as its own. For example; carbamazepin antiepileptic.

(b) Enzyme Inhibition

Decrease in the drug metabolizing ability of enzymes. Competition for the active sites takes place between the inhibitor and the drugs. When enzyme inhibitor attaches, less metabolism occurs.

For example;

- **Sulfonamides** decrease the metabolism of **phenytoin** so that its blood levels become toxic.
- **Cimetidine** decreases the metabolism of **propanolol** leading to enhanced bradycardia.
- **Oral contraceptives** inhibit metabolism of **antipyrine**.

3. Biological Factors

(a) Age

In infants microsomal enzyme system is not fully developed. The rate of metabolism is very low.

For example,

(1) *Chloramphenicol* does not have great efficacy in infants. Toxic effects in the form of **grey baby syndrome** might occur. The baby may be cyanosed, hypothermic, flaccid and grey in colour. Shock and even death might occur if toxic levels get accumulated.

(2) **Diazepam** may result in **floppy baby syndrome** in which flaccidity of the baby is seen.

- In elderly patients, most processes slow down which leads to decreased metabolism. Shrinkage of organs occurs along with decreased liver functions and decreased blood flow through the liver. All these factors decrease the metabolism.
- The drug doses should be decreased in the elderly patients.

(b) Gender

Gender related differences in the rate of metabolism are attributed to sex hormones and are generally observed following puberty.

- Male have a higher BMR as compared to the females, thus can metabolize drugs more efficiently, e.g. **salicylates** and others might include **ethanol**, **propanolol**, **benzodiazepines**.
- Women who take an oral contraceptives metabolize drugs at a slower rate.

(c) Genetics

- Drugs behave differently in different individuals due to genetic variations.
- **Succinyl choline**, which is a skeletal muscle relaxant, is metabolized by *pseudocholine esterase*. Some people have lack of this enzyme, due to which lack of metabolism of succinyl choline might occur. When administered in those individuals, prolonged **Apnea** might occurs.
- Different groups of populations might be classified as fast metabolizers and poor metabolizers of drugs.

For drugs, like **Isoniazid**, fast acetylators as well as slow acetylators are present. Fast acetylators cause rapid acetylation, while poor metabolizers metabolize less. Slow acetylation might occur due to genetic malformation leading to decreased production.

(d) Race and Species

- Asians, orientals, blacks and whites might have different drug metabolizing capacity.

For example,

- Eskimos metabolize drugs faster than Asians.
- Laboratory animals can metabolize drugs faster than man e.g. barbiturates.

(e) Diet

The enzyme content and activity is altered by a number of dietary components.

- Low protein content in diet decreases and high protein content in diet increases the drug metabolizing ability.
- Dietary deficiency of vitamins and minerals retard the metabolic activity of enzymes.

(f) Altered Physiological Factors

(i) Pregnancy

During pregnancy, metabolism of some drugs is increased while that of others is decreased due to the presence of steroid hormones. For example;

- Phenytoin
- Phenobarbitone
- Pethidine

(ii) Hormonal Imbalance

Higher levels of one hormone may inhibit the activity of few enzymes while inducing that of others. For example;

- Hypothyroidism increases drug metabolizing capacity, For example; increased half life of antipyrine, digoxin, methimazole and practolol, while hyperthyroidism decreases it.

(iii) Diseased State

Liver disease such as hepatic carcinoma, cirrhosis, hepatitis, obstructive jaundice etc. reduce the hepatic drug metabolizing ability and thus increase the half lives of almost all drugs.

In **renal diseases** conjugation of salycylates, oxidation of vitamin D and hydrolysis of procaine are impaired.

Cardiovascular diseases, although have no direct effect, decrease the blood flow, which may slow down biotransformation of drugs like isoniazid, morphine and propanolol.

Pulmonary conditions may decrease biotransformation. Procaine and procainamide hydrolysis is impaired.

(g) Temporal Factors

Diurnal variations and variations in enzyme activity with light cycle is **circadian rhythm**.

Enzyme action is maximum during early morning and minimum in late afternoon which is probably due to high levels of *corticosterone*.

(h) Environmental Factors

- Aromatic hydrocarbon contained in Cigarette smokers act as enzyme inducers.
- Chronic alcoholism might lead to enzyme induction as well.
- Pesticides or Organophosphate insecticides may act as enzyme inducers.
- In hot and humid climate, biotransformation is decreased and vice versa.
- At high altitude, decreased biotransformation occurs due to decreased oxygen leading to decreased oxidation of drugs.

7.4 PHASES OF DRUG METABOLISM

- Enzymatic processes in liver and other tissues that modify the chemical structure of xenobiotics, render them more water-soluble, increase their elimination, decrease their half-life.
- Biotransformed metabolites are chemically different from the parent molecule.

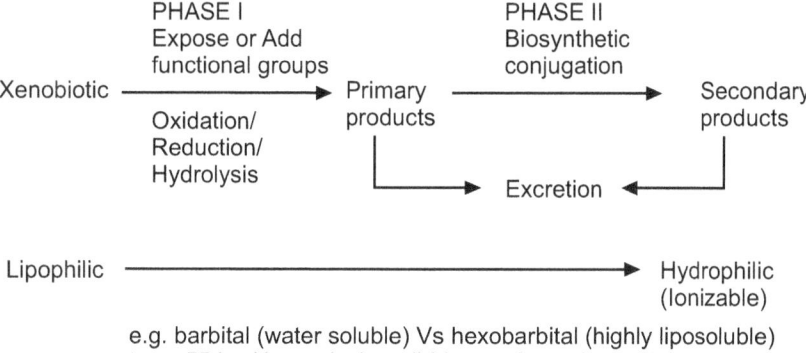

e.g. barbital (water soluble) Vs hexobarbital (highly liposoluble)
$t_{1/2}$ = 55 hr. (theoretical, real) Vs $t_{1/2}$ of months, real $t_{1/2}$ = 5 hr.

The Sites of Biotransformation:

Predominantly, the **liver** contributes to both the presystemic and the systemic elimination of many drugs.

Often **other tissues.** For example; in intestinal mucosa cells, presystemic elimination of several drugs in renal tubular cells etc.

In the colon, by bacteria – For example; azo reduction, hydrolytic reactions.

7.5 CLASSIFICATION OF BIOTRANSFORMATION

Phase I Reactions

    1. Oxidation

    2. Reduction

    3. Hydrolysis

Phase II Reactions (Conjugations)

    1. Glucuronidation

    2. Sulfation

    3. Conjugation with glycine (Gly)

    4. Conjugation with glutathione (GSH)

    5. Acetylation

    6. Methylation

The chemical role of Phase I and Phase II biotransformations:

PHASE–I: A *functional group* is added to the molecule or explored in the molecule at which conjugation can take place.

PHASE–II: An *organic acid (or acetyl or methyl group)* is conjugated to the molecule at a pre-existing functional group or at a functional group acquired in Phase I biotransformation

Phase I metabolites :

    Water-solubility: Increase (slightly faster excretion)

    Biological activity: In general, increase but often decrease.

Phase II metabolites (conjugates) :

    Water-solubility: For 1 – 4: (rapid excretion) For 5-6: (slower excretion)

    Biological activity: Almost always decrease, very seldom increase.

Table 7.3: Difference Between Phase I and Phase II Reactions

Phase I reaction	Phase II reaction
1. Degradative reaction.	1. Synthetic reaction.
2. Introduction of functional group ($-OH$, $-NH_2$, $-SH$, $-O-$, $-COOH$)	2. Conjugates phase I metabolite with glucuronic acid, sulfate, acetyl, methyl groups.
3. Mainly microsomal reaction.	3. Microsomal, Mitochondrial and Cytoplasmic reaction.
4. Metabolites formed may be smaller, polar/non-polar, active/inactive.	4. Metabolites formed are usually larger, polar, water soluble and inactive.

Table 7.4

Enzymes	Function
Phase I "Oxygenases"	
Cyp 450	C and o oxidation, dealkylation,
Fmo	N, s and p oxidation
Epoxide hydrolases	Hydrolysis of epoxides
Phase II "Transferases"	
Sulfotransferases (sult)	Addition of sulfate
Udp-glucuronosyltransferases (ugt)	Addition of glucuronic acid
Glutathione-s-transferases (gst)	Addition of glutathione
N-acetyl transferases (nat)	Addition of acetyl group
Methyltransferases (mt)	Addition of methyl group
Other Enzymes	
Alcohol dehydrogenases	Reduction of alcohols
Aldehyde dehydrogenases	Reduction of aldehydes
Nadph-quinone oxidoreductase (nqo)	Reduction of quinones

7.5.1 Oxidations Catalyzed by Cytochrome P-450 (CYP)

CYP is a heme-containing protein embedded in the membranes of the smooth endoplasmic reticulum (SER), the fragments of which in a tissue homogenate are sedimented after ultracentrifugation (at 100,000 g) in the microsomal fraction.

Origin of the name cytochrome P-450:

- **Cytochrome:** It is a coloured intracellular protein.
- **P:** It is pink.
- **450:** Its absorption spectrum is maximum at 450 nm.
- Its absorption spectrum is maximum at 450 nm.

CYP constitutes a superfamily of enzymes that are classified into families (numbered) and subfamilies (marked with capital letters), the latter of which contain the individual enzymes (numbered), e.g., CYP1A2, CYP2C9, CYP2D6, CYP3A4.

In the Oxido-reductase process, 2 microsomal enzymes play a key role :

- Flavo proteins, NADPH – CYT P-450.
- Haemoprotein, CYT P-450 serves as terminal oxidase.

7.5.2 Cytochrome P-450 (CYP) - Catalyzed Reactions - Mechanism

P-450 heme reduction is rate limiting step.

Microsomal drug oxidations require P-450, P-450 reductase, NADPH, O_2.

Very low substrate specificity. High lipid solubility is the only common structural feature of most of substrates.

P-450 isoforms in liver – CYT1A2, 2A6, 2B6, 2C8, 2C9, 2C18, 2C19, 2D6, 2E1, 3A4, 3A5.

Of these isoforms, 3A4 and 3A5 carry out biotransformation of about 50% of drugs.

P-450 enzymes are classified into families denoted by numbers – 1, 2, 3 and subfamilies by A, B, C and D on the basis of AA sequence and c-DNA. Another number indicates – specific isoenzymes.

Comparison between Phase I and Phase II

Enzyme	Phase I	Phase II
Type of reactions	Hydrolysis, oxidation, reduction.	Conjugations.
Increase in hydrophilicity	Small.	Large.
General mechanism	Exposes functional group.	Polar compound added to functional group.
Consequences	May result in metabolic activation.	Facilitates excretion.

7.5.3 Detail Classification of Biotransformation

[I] PHASE I – BIOTRANSFORMATIONS :

1. OXIDATION

A) Microsomal oxidation :

(a) CYP-catalyzed reactions

(i) Oxigenation

- Insertion of oxygen produces a stable oxigenated metabolite.
- C-hydroxylation: aliphatic hydroxylation, aromatic hydroxylation.
- N-hydroxylation
- Epoxidation
- Insertion of oxygen produces an unstable oxigenated metabolite which undergoes spontaneous cleavage into two molecules.
- Oxidative dealkylation (N- and O-dealkylation)
- Oxidative deamination

- Oxidative dehalogenation
- Oxidative desulfuration

(ii) Dehydrogenation

(iii) Reduction (reductive dehalogenation)

(b) FMO-catalyzed oxidations

B) **Non-microsomal oxidation :**

(i) MAO-catalyzed oxidations

(ii) Oxidations catalyzed by molybdenum-containing oxidases

Xanthine oxidase-catalyzed oxidations

Aldehyde oxidase-catalyzed oxidations

(iii) Alcohol dehydrogenase and aldehyde dehydrogenase-catalyzed oxidations

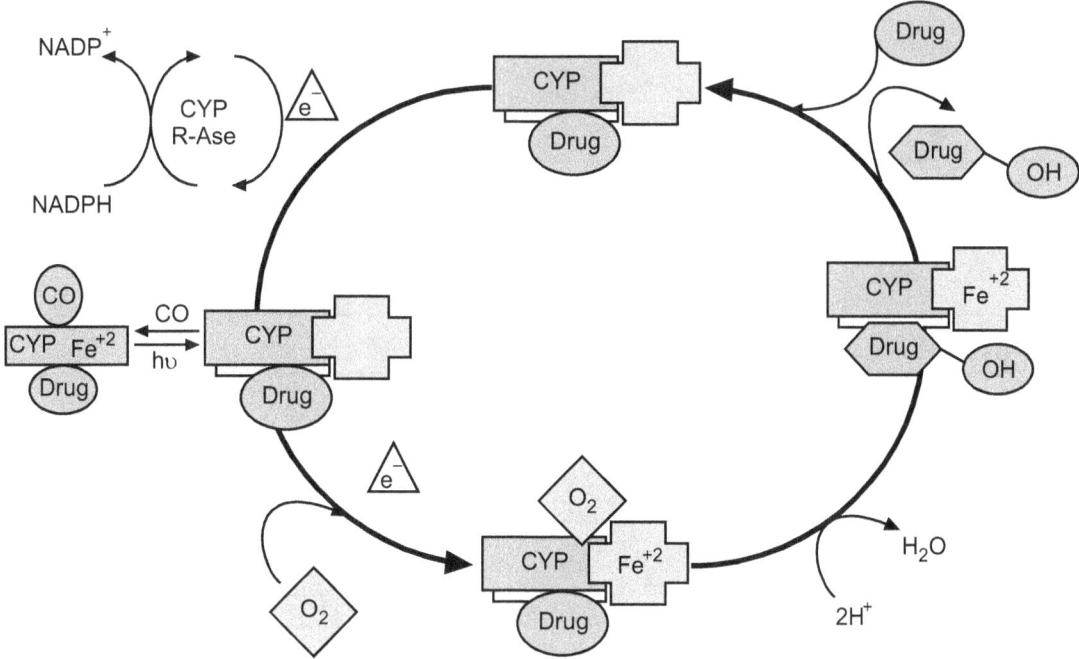

Fig. 7.1 : Electron flow in microsomal drug oxidizing system

2. **REDUCTION**

A) Azo-reduction

B) Nitro-reduction

C) Carbonyl-, aldehyde- and aldose-reduction (by aldo-keto reductases; AKR)

3. **HYDROLYSIS**

A) Hydrolysis by carboxylesterases

B) Hydrolysis by alkaline phosphatase

C) Hydrolysis by paraoxonases

D) Hydrolysis by epoxide hydrolase (illustrated under epoxidation)

E) Hydrolysis by microbial hydrolases in the colon

We, here in Table 7.5 explain the reaction mechanism with example for all reactions.

Table 7.5

Reaction	Structure	Examples
Microsomal (CYP 450 dependent):		
Oxidation :		
1. Aromatic hydroxylations	$R^- \longrightarrow R^- - OH$	Phenobarbitone, Phenytoin, Propranolol, Amphetamine, Warfarin, 17α-ethenyl estradiol
2. Aliphatic hydroxylations	$RCH_2CH_3 \longrightarrow RCHOHCH_3$	Digoxin, Ibuprofen, Secobarbital, Chlorpropamide
Oxidative Dealkylation :		
N-Dealkylation	$RN(CH_3)_2 \longrightarrow RNHCH_3 +$ CH_3CHO	Mephobarbitone, Amitriptyline, Morphine, Caffiene, Theophylline
O-Dealkylation	$R-O-CH_3 \longrightarrow R - OH + HCHO$	Phenacetin, Codiene, Paranitroanisole
S-Dealkylation	$R-SCH_3 \longrightarrow R-SH + HCHO$	6-methylthiopurine
N-Oxidation :		
Primary amines	$RNH_2 \longrightarrow RNHOH$	Aniline, Chlorpentermine
Secondary amines	$R_1-NH_2-R_2 \longrightarrow R_1-NOH-R_2$	2-acetyl aminofluorene, Acetaminophen
Tertiary amines	$NR_1R_2R_3 \longrightarrow R_1R_2R_3-N-O$	Nicotine, Methaqualone

Contd...

S-Oxidation :	$R_1-S-R_2 \longrightarrow R_1-SO-R_2$	Cimetidine, Chlorpromazine, Omeprazole, Thioridazine
Deamination	$R-CHNH_2-R \longrightarrow R-COR + NH_3$	Amphetamine, Diazepam
Desulfurisation	$R_1-PS-R_2 \longrightarrow R_1-PO-R_2$	Parathion, Thiopental
Dechlorination	$CCl_4 \longrightarrow [CCl_3^-] \longrightarrow CHCl_3$	Carbontetrachloride
Non-microsomal: **Oxidation :**		
Mitochondrial oxidation	$R-CH(OH)CH_2NH_2^- \longrightarrow$ $R-CH(OH)COOH^+NH_3$	Epinephrine
Cytoplasmic oxidation (dehydrogenation)	$C_2H_5OH^- \longrightarrow CH_3CHO^- \longrightarrow$ CH_3COOH	Alcohol
Plasma oxidative processes	Histamine $\longrightarrow$ Imidazole acetic acid Xanthine $\longrightarrow$ Uric acid	Allopurinol
Microsomal Reductions :		
Nitro reduction	$RNO_2 \longrightarrow RNH_2$	Chloramphenicol
Azo reduction	$RN = NR_1 \longrightarrow RNH_2 + R_1NH_2$	Prontosil, sulfasalazine
Keto reduction	$R-CO-R_1 \longrightarrow R-CHOH-R_1$	Cortisone, Methadone, Metyrapone
Non-microsomal Reductions:	$C(Cl)_3CH(OH)_2^- \longrightarrow C(Cl)_3CH_2OH$	Chloral hydrate
Microsomal Hydrolysis :		Pethidine, Lidocaine
Non-Microsomal Hydrolysis :		Procaine $\rightarrow$ PABA Atropine $\rightarrow$ Atropic acid Penicillin-G Procainamide

FLAVIN MONOOXYGENASES

- Also known as zeigler's enzyme. Neither inducible nor inhibited.
- FMO_3 is most abundant in liver.
- FMO_3 is able to metabolize nicotine, cimetidine, ranitidine, clozapine and itopride.
- A genetic deficiency in this enzyme causes the *fish-odour syndrome* due to a lack of metabolism of trimethylamine *N*-oxide (TMAO) to trimethylamine (TMA).

EPOXIDE HYDROLASE

- There are two types of epoxide hydrolase : soluble and microsomal
- Drug ⟶ Epoxide ⟶ Inactive metabolite.

Properties of Expoxide Hydrolase :
  (i) Highly reactive electrophile.
  (ii) Binds to DNA, RNA and Proteins.
  (iii) Produce less cell toxicity.

- For example;
  Carbamazepine ⟶ Carbamazepine-10-11-epoxide ⟶ Trans dihydrodiol
- Valnoctamide, Valproic acid inhibits mEH.

Non-Enzymatic Biotransformation

- Skeletal muscle relaxants like Atracurium are metabolised in the plasma spontaneously through molecular rearrangement without involvement of any enzyme action.

ENZYME INDUCTION

Xenobiotics can influence the extent of drug metabolism,
  1. By activating transcription.
  2. By inducing expression of genes.

Mechanism of Enzyme Induction:

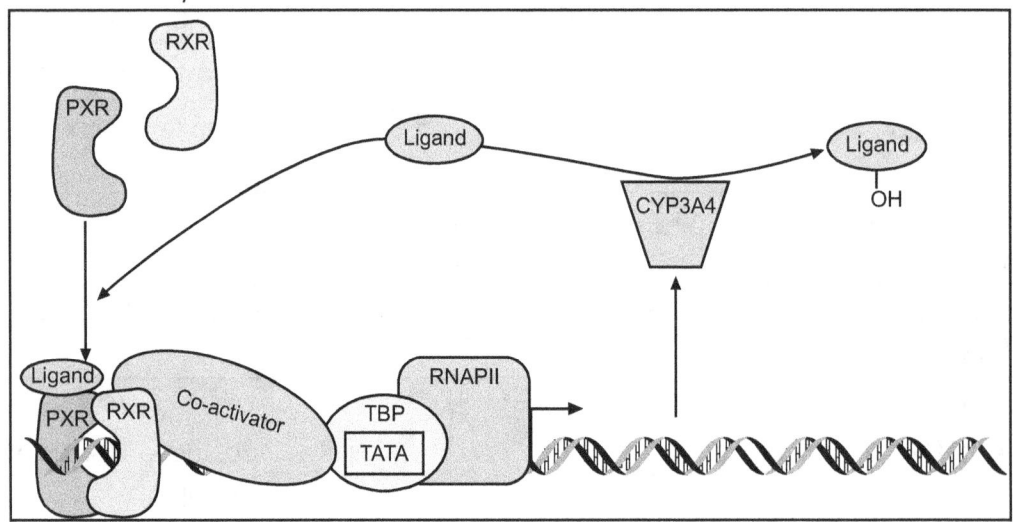

Fig. 7.2

Aryl Hydrocarbon Receptor (AHR):

- Induces CYP1A1,1A2,1B1——→ Activates procarcinogens
- Omeprazole is ligand.
- AHR is a member of superfamily of transcription factors.
- AHR has regulatory role in the development of mammalian CNS – modulating the response to chemical and oxidative stress.

Pregnane X Receptor:

- Structurally similar to steroid hormone receptors.
- Induces CYP3A4, Drug Transporters, SULT's, UGT's
- LIGANDS: Pregnanolone-16-carbonitrile, Rifampin, Troleandomycin, Nifidipine, Mevastatin, Troglitazone, Ritonavir, Paclitaxel, Hyperforin.
- Basis for contraceptive failure.

Constitutive Androstane Receptor (CAR):

- Can activate genes even in absence of their ligands.
- Ligands: Pesticide 1,4-bisbenzene, 5-pregnane-3,20-dione.
- Induces CYP2B6, 2C9, 3A4, GST, UGT, SULT, Drug and endobiotic transporters.
- Inverse agonists - androstanol, clotrimazole, meclizine.

Peroxisome Proliferator Activated Receptor-α (PPAR-α):

- Highly expressed in liver and kidney.
- Ligand:
  1. Fibrates (gemfibrozil, fenofibrate),
  2. Hypoglycemic drugs (rosiglitazone, pioglitazone)
- Induces
  1. Enzymes - fatty acids (Arachidonic acid)
  2. CYP4A - oxidation of FA and drugs with FA side chain (leukotiene analogues)
     PPAR α does not induce xenobiotic metabolism

Enzyme induction by decreased enzyme degradation (substrate S):

- Troleandomycin, clotrimazole induces CYP3A.
- Ethanol induces CYP2E1.
- Isosafrole induces CYP1A2.

ENZYME INHIBITION

It is basis for several drug interactions. It is a rapid process.

- **Microsomal:**
1. Reversible : Cimetidine and ketoconazole binds tightly to CYP-450 heme iron and inhibits metabolism of testosterone.

- Troleandomycin and Erythromycin $\longrightarrow$ CYP3A4 $\longrightarrow$ CYP3A4-metabolite complex.
- Proadifen (SKF-525-A) $\longrightarrow$ bind tightly to heme iron and partially irreversibly inhibits enzyme.

2. Irreversible (suicidal inhibitors) : Intermediate metabolite bind covalently with P450 apoprotien.
   - For example; spironolactone, ethinyl estradiol, ritonavir.
   - But Secobarbital inhibits CYP2B1 by binding to heme and protein moieties.

[II] PHASE-II REACTIONS

1. GLUCURODINATION (microsomal)

UDP-GA + Substrate (Phase-I metabolite)

ALCOHOL AND PHENOLIC HYDROXYL groups CARBOXYL, SULFURYL, CARBONYL moieties PRIMARY, SECONDARY AND TERTIARY AMINE linkages

Glucuronides (glucopyranosiduronic acids)

Decojugated substrate

For example; morphine, acetaminophen, diazepam, N-hydroxydapsone, digitoxin.

UGT are encoded by 19 genes (9 genes on UGT1 locus-chr.2 and 10 genes on UGT2 locus-chr.4)

- UGT1- Glucuronidation of Bilirubin-rate limiting step.

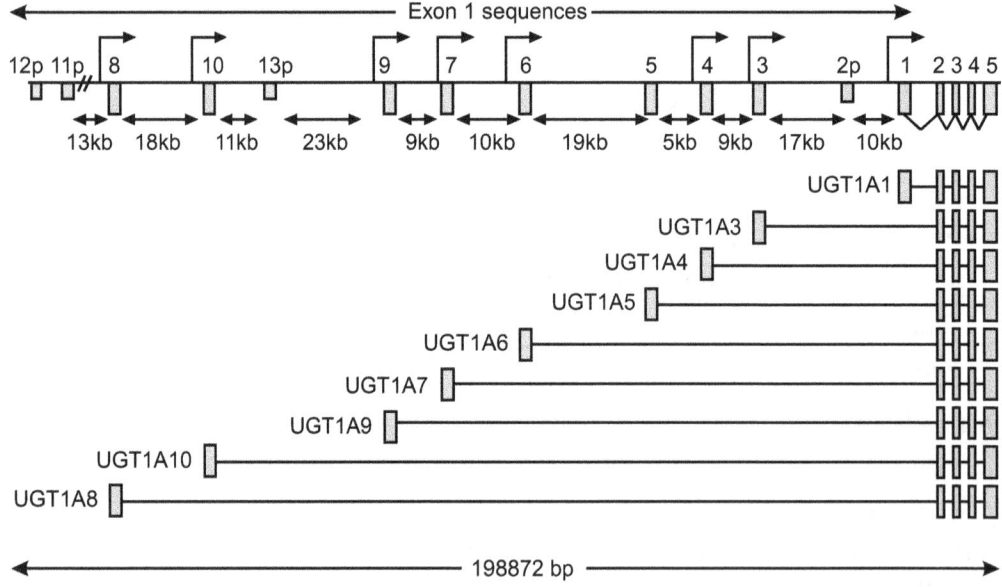

Fig. 7.3 : UGT1 Locus

UGT2 have greater specificity for endogenous substances (steroids) glucurodination.

2. SULFATION (cytosolic)

- Sulfotransferase (SULT) conjugates sulfate - PAPS to the hydroxyl groups and less frequently to aromatic and aliphatic amine groups (acetaminophen, hydroxyl coumarins).
- SULT has 13 isoforms.
- SULT play an important role in normal human homeostasis.
- SULT2B1b also act as a skin-cholesterol. Cholesterol sulfate regulates keratinocyte differentiation and skin development.
- SULT2A1refer as a fetal adrenal gland - de hydro epiandrosterone - DHEA sulfate - essential for placental Estrogen biosynthesis during 2nd half of pregnancy.
- SULT1A3 - Highly selective for catecholeamines.
- SULT1E1 - Sulfates endogenous and exogenous steroids. For example; Estrogen (17-estradiol)-estrogen sulfate.
- In humans significant fractions of circulating catecholamines, estrogens, iodothryronines, DHEA exist in sulfate form.

3. GLUTATHIONE CONJUGATION

- Glutathione (GSH) is a tripeptide of glycine - glutamic acid - cysteine.
- GSH exists in cell as oxidized form (GS-SH) and reduced form (GSH).
- GSH: GSSH ratio is critical in maintaining cellular environment to be in reduced state.
- GSH + Electrophilic compound

  $\downarrow$ Otherwise react with –O, –N, –S atoms leading to cell damage

  Electrophile-Glutathione

Glutathione-S-transferase (gst):

- Exists in 20 isoforms.
- Cytosolic GST isoforms : 7 classes - exogenous drugs and xenobiotics (acetaminophen, ethacrynic acid, bromobenzene)
- Microsomal GST isoforms : Endogenous leukotrienes and prostaglandins.
- GST play an important role in cellular detoxification.

  Its activity in cancerous tissue has been linked to development of resistance to chemotherapeutic agents.

  - Anticancer drug $\longrightarrow$ JNK, and P38 $\longrightarrow$ Apoptosis
  - Inhibition of GST activity sensitises tumour cells to anticancer drugs.
  - TLK199 (GSH analogue) activated by plasma esterase to TLK117 (GST inhibitor) which potentiates toxicity of anticancer drugs.

4. N-ACETYLATION (CYTOSOL)

Substrate : Aromatic amine groups and Hydrazine group such as sulfonamides, isoniazid, clonazepam, dapsone etc.

Co-substrate : Acetyl coenzyme A.

Enzyme : N-Acetyl Transferase.

- NAT1 and NAT2 : 25 Allelic variants are identified.
- NAT2 mutation : Slow and fast acetylation.
- Field of pharmacogenetics has established by the identification of "The characterization of an Acetylator phenotype".

5. METHYLATION (CYTOSOL)

Substrate: –N, –O, –S atoms containing compounds.

Co-substrate: S-Adenosyl Methionine.

Enzyme: Methyltransferase.

N-Methyltransferases : Histamine NMT – Histamine.

Nicotinamide NMT – Serotonin, Tryptophan, Nicotinamide.

Catechol-o-methyltransferase ⟶ Dopamine, Norepinephrine, Methyldopa, Ecstasy

Phenol-o-methyltransferase ⟶ Tyrosine metabolism

Thiopurine-s-methyltransferase ⟶ Azathioprine, Thioguanine, 6-MP

6. AMINO ACID CONJUGATION (MITOCHONDRIA):

Substrate: Aspirin, Benzoic acid, Nicotinic acid, Deoxycholic acid

Co-substrate: Glycine (or) Glutamine

Enzyme: Acyl coenzyme A-glycinetransferase

Riboside and Riboside Phosphates:

- Many purines and pyrimidines form their active metabolites by forming ribonucleosides and ribonucleotides.
- Purines and pyrimidines are used as antimetabolites in cancer chemotherapy.

Chapter 8

EXCRETION OF DRUGS

8.1 INTRODUCTION

Drugs and/or their metabolites are removed from the body by excretion.

Excretion is defined as 'the process where irreversible transfer of drug or drug metabolites from the plasma into the urine'.

Drug or drug metabolites must be hydrosoluble to be excreted in the urine. Factors that influence renal excretion include plasma drug concentration, plasma protein binding and renal function.

Drugs are transferred from the plasma into the urine by:

1. Glomerular filtration: Unbound drug molecules of less than 20,000 dalton are filtered through the glomerulus with the primary urine.

2. Active tubular secretion: This mechanism is predominant in the proximal tubule. Several transportors are responsible for the tubular secretion of drugs: P-glycoproteins (PGps), multidrug resistance-associated proteins (MRPs), organic anion transportors (OATs), oragnic cation transportors (OCTs) etc. These transporters are not highly specific and may become saturated at high drug concentrations.

Drugs may be reabsorbed from the tubular lumen by passive diffusion. The extent of reabsorption depends on the lipophilic properties of the drug, urine flow, urine pH and chelating agents. Concentrated urine favours reabsorption. Depending on the urine pH, a weak acid or base can be more or less ionised in the urine and therefore more or less reabsorbed (urine ion trapping). Active reabsorption occurs mainly for endogenous products such as vitamins, glucose, amino acids and similar substances.

8.2 CLINICAL IMPLICATIONS

Changes in renal function affect filtration, secretion and tubular reabsorption. Impairment of renal function and disease condition, leads to decrease in renal drug clearance. In such situations the dosage regimen must be adapted, specially for drugs with a low extrarenal fraction (Q_o). Reduced clearance can also result from competition between drugs or endogenous substances for the tubular secretion transporter sites (renal drug interactions).

Forced diuresis and urine pH control is useful to increase the renal excretion of certain drugs.

The major organ for the excretion of drugs is the kidney. The functional unit of the kidney is the nephron and components of the nephron include Bowman's capsule, Proximal tubule, Loop of henle, Distal tubule and the collecting duct (Fig. 8.1). Low molecular weight molecules are filtered in Bowman's capsule. Active secretion of weak electrolyte drugs (acids) and reabsorption of water occurs in the proximal tubules. Additional reabsorption of water occurs in the Loop of Henle. Passive reabsorption of water and lipid soluble drugs occurs in the distal tubule.

There are three major renal excretion processes to consider : 1) Glomerular filtration; 2) Tubular secretion; and 3) Tubular re-absorption.

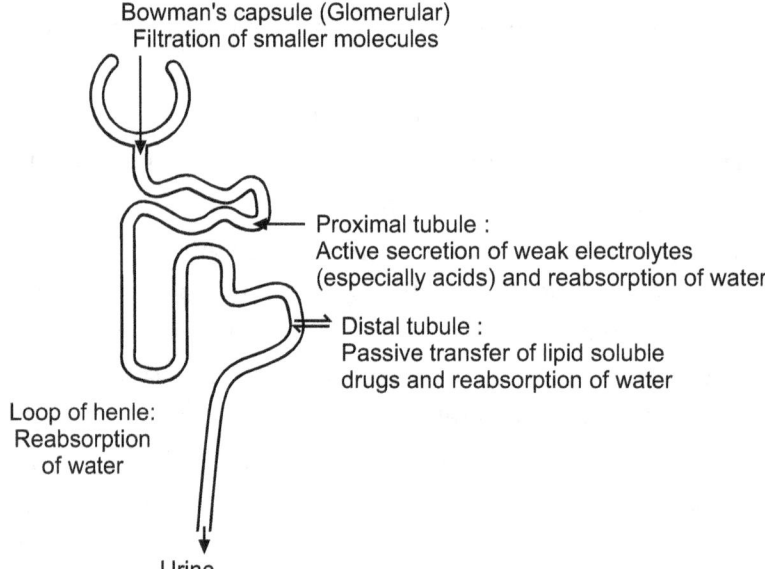

Fig. 8.1: Renal excretion process

8.3 GLOMERULAR FILTRATION

Glomerular filtration is passive filtration of the blood as blood flow through the glomeruli of the kidney. The extent to which a drug is filtered depends on the molecular size, protein binding, ionization, polarity and kidney function.

In the glomerular filtration, all low molecular weight molecules (< 60,000 Dalton) are filtered out of the blood. Most drugs are readily filtered from the blood unless they are tightly bound to large molecules such as plasma protein or have been incorporated into red blood cells. The glomerular filtration rate varies from individual to individual. But in healthy individuals the normal range is 110 to 130 ml/min (≈180 lit./day). About 10% of the blood which enters the glomerular is filtered. This filtration rate is often measured by determining the renal clearance of inulin. Inulin is readily filtered in the glomerular, and is not subject to tubular secretion or re-absorption. Thus, inulin clearance is equal to the glomerular filtration rate.

Most drugs are filtered from blood in the glomerular; however overall renal excretion controlled by condition occur in the tubules. More than 90% of the filtrate is reabsorbed. (120 ml/min i.e. 173 lit./day). Normal urine output is about 1 to 2 litre per day.

The ultrastructure of the glomerular capillary wall is such that, it permits a high degree of fluid filtration and restrict the passage of large molecular weight compounds. It prevents the filtration of plasma proteins (e.g., albumin) that are important for maintaining an osmotic gradient in the vasculature and thus plasma volume. Several factors affect glomerular filtration including molecular size, charge and shape.

- Compounds with 20 Å to 42Å may undergo glomerular filtration.
- Charged substances (e.g., sulfated dextrans) are usually filtered at slower rates than neutral compounds (e.g., neutral dextrans), even when their molecular sizes are comparable.
- The greater restriction to filtration of charged molecules, particularly anions, is probably due to an electrostatic interaction between the filtered molecule and the fixed negative charges within the glomerular capillary wall.

8.3.1 Factors that Affect the Glomerular Filtration Rate

(GFR) also can influence the rate of drug clearance.

- For instance, inflammation of the glomerular capillaries may increase GFR and hence drug filtration.
- Most drugs are at least partially bound to plasma proteins, and therefore their actual filtration rates are less than the theoretical GFR.
- Anything that alters drug–protein binding, however, will change the drug filtration rate.

The usual range of half-lives seen for most drugs that are cleared by glomerular filtration is 1 to 4 hours.

However, considerably longer half-lives will be seen if extensive protein binding occurs.

8.4 TUBULAR SECRETION

Tubular secretion can be increased by actively secreting the drug. The rate of secretion depends on the transporter. If the transporter is slow, the secretion will depend on flow of unbound fraction of drug.

In the proximal tubule there is re-absorption of water and active secretion of some weak electrolyte but especially weak acids. As this process is an active secretion it requires a carrier and a supply of energy. This may be a significant pathway for some compounds such as penicillins. Because tubular secretion is an active process. There may be competitive inhibition of the secretion of one compound by another. A common example of this phenomena is the inhibition of penicillin excretion by competition with probenecid.

Penicillin was expensive thus, probenecid was used, to reduce the excretion of the penicillin and thereby prolong penicillin plasma concentrations (PDR). Since then it has been shown that probenecid also alters the distribution of penicillins to various tissues causing more drug to distribute out of plasma, causing even less to be eliminated.

Actively transfered drugs from blood to luminal fluid, are independent of each other; one secretes organic anions, and the other secretes organic cations. The secretory capacity of both the organic anion and organic cation secretory systems can be saturated at high drug concentrations. Each drug will have its own characteristics like maximum rate of secretion (transport maximum, T_m). These active secretory systems are important in drug excretion because charged anions and cations are often strongly bound to plasma proteins and therefore are not readily available for excretion by filtration. Active secretory systems can rapidly and efficiently remove many protein-bound drugs from the blood and transport them into tubular fluid. Any drug known to be largely excreted by the kidney that has a half-life less than 2 hours is probably eliminated, by tubular secretion. These tubular transport mechanisms are not as well developed in the neonate as in the adult. Functional capacity may be diminished in the elderly people. Compounds that undergo active tubular secretion also are filtered at the glomerulus.

8.5 TUBULAR RE-ABSORPTION

In the distal tubule there is passive excretion and re-absorption of lipid soluble drugs. Drugs which are present in the glomerular filtrate can be reabsorbed in the tubules. The membrane is readily permeable to lipids. So filtered lipid soluble substances are extensively reabsorbed. If a drug is non-ionized or in the unionized form it may be readily reabsorbed.

Many drugs are either weak bases or acids and therefore the pH of the filtrate can greatly influence the extent of tubular re-absorption for many drugs. When urine is acidic weak acid drugs tend to be reabsorbed. Alternatively when urine is more alkaline, weak bases are more extensively reabsorbed. Making the urine more acidic can cause less reabsorption of weak bases or enhanced excretion. These changes can be quite significant as urine pH can vary from 4.5 to 8.0 depending on the diet (e.g. meat can cause a more acidic urine) or drugs (which can increase or decrease urine pH).

The effect of pH change on tubular re-absorption can be predicted by consideration of drug pKa according to the Henderson-Hesselbalch equation.

- Some substances filtered at the glomerulus are reabsorbed by active transport systems found primarily in the proximal tubules.

- Active reabsorption is particularly important for endogenous substances, such as ions, glucose, and amino acids, although a small number of drugs also may be actively reabsorbed.

- The probable location of the active transport system is on the luminal side of the proximal cell membrane.

- Bidirectional active transport across the proximal tubule also occurs for some compounds; that is, a drug may be both actively reabsorbed and secreted.

- The major portion of filtered urate is probably reabsorbed, whereas that eventually found in the urine is mostly derived from active tubular secretion.

- Most drugs act by reducing active transport rather than by enhancing it.

- Drugs that promote uric acid loss (uricosuric agents, such as probenecid and sulfinpyrazone) probably inhibit active urate reabsorption, while pyrazinamide, which reduces urate excretion, may block the active tubular secretion of uric acid.

- A complicating observation is that a drug may primarily inhibit active reabsorption at one dose and active secretion at another, frequently lower dose. For example, small amount of salicylate will decrease total urate excretion, while high doses have a uricosuric effect.

8.6 PASSIVE DIFFUSION

Urinary excretion of drugs (i.e., weak electrolytes) is the extent to which substances diffuse back across the tubular membranes and re-enter in the circulation. In general, the movement of drugs is favoured from the tubular lumen to blood, because of the reabsorption of water that occurs throughout most portions of the nephron, which results in an increased concentration of drug in the luminal fluid. The concentration gradient thus established will facilitate movement of the drug out of the tubular lumen, given that the lipid solubility and ionization of the drug are appropriate. The pH of the urine (usually between 4.5 and 8) can markedly affect the rate of passive back-diffusion. The back-diffusion occurs primarily in the distal tubules and collecting ducts (where most of the urine acidification takes place).

As the un-ionized form of the drug diffuses from the tubular fluid across the tubular cells into the blood, it follows that :

Acidification increases reabsorption (or decreases elimination) of weak acids, such as salicylates, and decreases reabsorption (or promotes elimination) of weak bases, such as amphetamines.

Effects of pH on urinary drug elimination may have important applications, especially in case of overdose. For example; It enhance the elimination of a barbiturate (a weak acid) by administering bicarbonate to the patient, hence alkalinizes the urine and thus promotes the excretion of more completely ionized drug.

Excretion of bases can be increased by making the urine more acidic through the use of an acidifying salt, such as ammonium chloride.

8.7 RENAL EXCRETION

8.7.1 Clinical Implications of Renal Excretion

The rate of urinary drug excretion will depend on the drug's volume of distribution, its degree of protein binding, and the following renal factors:

1. Glomerular filtration rate.
2. Tubular fluid pH.
3. Extent of back-diffusion of the unionized form.
4. Extent of active tubular secretion of the compound.
5. Possibly, extent of active tubular reabsorption.

Changes in any of these factors may result in clinically important alterations in drug action.

In the final analysis, the amount of drug that finally appears in the urine will represent a balance of filtered, reabsorbed (passively and actively), and secreted drug.

For many drugs, the duration and intensity of pharmacological effect will be influenced by the status of renal function, because of the major role played by the kidneys in drug and metabolite elimination.

8.7.2 Factors Affecting Renal Excretion

1) Urine pH and pKa.
2) Physicochemical properties of drug.
3) Distribution and Binding characteristics of drug.
4) Biological factors.
5) Blood flow to the kidneys.
6) Urine flow rate.
7) Drug interactions.
8) Disease states.

1. pH and pKa of the Urine

- It varies between 4.5 to 7.5.
- It depends upon diet, drug intake and pathophysiology of the patient. Acetazolamide and antacids produce alkaline urine, while ascorbic acid makes it acidic.
- IV infusion of sodium and ammonium chloride used in treatment of acid-base imbalance shows alteration in urine pH. Relative amount of ionized and unionized drug in the urine at particular pH and % drug ionized at this pH can be given by "HENDERSON-HESSELBACH" equation. The significance of pH-dependant excretion for any particular compound is greatly depends upon its pKa and lipid solubility.

- A characteristic of drugs, pKa value govern the degree of ionization at a particular pH. A polar and ionized drug will be poorly reabsorbed passively and excreted rapidly.
- Reabsorption is also affected by the lipid solubility of drug; an ionized but lipophilic drug will be reabsorbed while an unionized but polar one will be excreted.
- The toxicity due to overdose of the drug whose excretion is sensitive to pH change can be treated by acidification or alkalinisation of the urine.

2. **Physicochemical Properties of Drug**
   - Drugs with Molecular weight < 300 are excreted in kidney.
   - Molecular weight 300 to 500 dalton is excreted both through urine and bile.

   Drug Lipid Solubility
   - Urinary excretion is inversely related to lipophilicity, increase in lipid solubility increase the volume of distribution of drug and decrease renal excretion.

3. **Binding Characteristics of the Drugs**
   - Drugs that are bound to plasma proteins behave as macromolecules and cannot be filtered through glomerulus.
   - Only unbound or free drug appear in glomerular filtrate.

4. **Biological Factor**
   - Age, sex, species, strain difference etc. alter the excretion of the drug.
     Sex – Renal excretion is 10% lower in female than in males.
     Age – The renal excretion in newborn is 30 - 40 % less in comparison to adults.
     Old age – The GFR is reduced and tubular function is altered which results in slow excretion of drugs and prolonged half lives.

5. **Blood Flow to the Kidney**
   - Important in case of drug excreted by glomerular filteration and those are actively secreted only.
   - Increase in the perfusion, enhance the elimination.

6. **Urine Flow Rate**
   - Polar drugs are not affected by urine pH hence not get reabsorbed, so unaffected by urine flow rate.
   - Only those drugs whose reabsorption is pH sensitive, For example; Weak acids and bases, depend on urine flow rate. Urine flow rate can be incresed by forced diuresis by large fluid intake or other diuretics.

7. **Drug Interactions**

- Any drug interaction that result in alteration of binding characteristics, renal blood flow, active secretion, urine pH and forced diuresis would alter renal clearance of drug.

- Alkalinization of urine with citrates and bicarbonates promote excretion of acidic drugs.

8. **Disease State**

- **Renal Dysfunction:**

  o Greatly cause the elimination of drugs those are primarily excreted by kidney.

  o Some of the causes of renal failure are hypertention, diabetes and hypovolemiya (low blood supply to kidney).

- **Uremia:**

  o Characterized by impaired GF, accumulation of fluids and protein metabolites.

  o Increased half life results in drug accumulation and increased toxicity.

8.8 TYPES OF CLEARANCE

1. **Drug Clearance :**

Drug clearance is defined as "the hypothetical volume of body fluids containing drug, from which the drug is removed or cleared completely in a specific period of time".

$$\text{Clearance [CL]} = \frac{\text{Elimination rate}}{\text{Plasma drug concentration}}$$

The sum of individual clearance by all eliminating organs (kidney, liver, lungs, biliary systems) is called as 'Total body clearance'.

2. **Renal Clearance :**

Renal clearance is defined as, "The volume of plasma which completely clear the unchanged drug by the kidney per unit time".

One method of quantitatively describing the renal excretion of drugs is by means of the renal clearance value for the drug. Renal clearance relates the rate of excretion, and drug concentration. Unit is ml/min.

$$\text{Rate of Excretion} = \frac{\Delta U}{\Delta t} = CL_{renal} \cdot C_p$$

Renal clearance can be calculated as part of the total body clearance for a particular drug. Renal clearance can be used to investigate the mechanism of drug excretion. If the drug is filtered but not secreted or reabsorbed, the renal clearance will be about 120 ml/min in normal subjects. If the renal clearance is less than 120 ml/min then two processes are in operation, glomerular filtration and tubular re-absorption. If the renal clearance is greater than 120 ml/min then tubular secretion must be contributing to the elimination process. It is also possible that all three processes are occurring simultaneously. The drug renal clearance value can be compared with physiologically significant values, e.g. glomerular filtration rate (GFR) of approximately 120 ml/min or renal plasma flow of about 650 ml/min.

Renal clearance is then:

$$CL_{renal} = \frac{\text{Filtration rate} + \text{Secretion rate} - \text{Reabsorption rate}}{C_p}$$

Normal value for glucose is usually completely reabsorbed to a value equal to the renal plasma flow of about 650 ml/min for compounds like p-aminohippuric acid.

Calculate renal clearance using the pharmacokinetic parameters k_e and V. Thus, $CL_{renal} = k_e \cdot V$. Renal clearance can be determined as U^∞/AUC. Also calculate renal clearance by measuring the total amount of drug excreted over some time interval and dividing by the plasma concentration measured at the midpoint of the time interval.

$$\text{Renal Clearance} = \frac{\text{Rate of Excretion}}{\text{Plasma Concentration}}$$

$$\text{Renal Clearance} = CL_{renal} = \frac{\Delta U / \Delta t}{Cp_{midpoint}}$$

Renal clearance estimation from urine and plasma drug concentration:

$$CL_{renal} = \frac{\text{Urine flow} \times \text{Urine concentration}}{\text{Plasma concentration}}$$

Renal clearance estimation from the renal extraction ratio and renal perfusion:

$$CL_{renal} = Q \times E$$

$$f_e = \frac{CL_{renal}}{CL_{total}}$$

Where,

CL_{renal} = Renal clearance

CL_{total} = Total clearance

Q = Renal perfusion

E = Extraction ratio

f_e = The excreted fraction

Renal clearance tests are used to:

Determine the GFR.

Detect glomerular damage and diagnosed renal disease.

Effect of Exercise on Renal Clearance:

Exhaustive exercise reduce RBF (Renal Blood Flow) by 53.4% compared to the pre-exercise values, and returned to 82.5% and 78.9% of the pre-exercise values at 30 and 60 min into the recovery period, respectively. As the RBF decreases, CLR also decreases.

8.9 NON-RENAL ROUTE OF DRUG EXCRETION

Various routes are :

1) Biliary Excretion
2) Pulmonary Excretion
3) Salivary Excretion
4) Mammary Excretion
5) Skin/dermal Excretion
6) Gastrointestinal Excretion
7) Genital Excretion

1) **Biliary Excretion :**

- Bile juice is secreted by hepatic cells of the liver.
- It is important in the digestion and absorption of fats.
- 90% of bile acid is reabsorbed from intestine and transported back to the liver for resecretion.
- The metabolites are more excreted in bile than parent drugs due to increased polarity.

Several factors that influence secretion of drug in bile are;

1) Molecular weight.
2) Polarity.
3) Nature of biotransformation.
4) Other factors like sex, spices, disease state, drug interation.

Nature of Bio-transformation Process:

- Phase-II reactions, mainly glucuronidation and conjugation with glutathione result in metabolites with increased polarity and molecular weight for biliary excretion.
- Example of drugs excreted in the bile are chloromphenicol, morphine and indomethacin.
- For a drug to be excreted in bile must have polar groups like $-COOH$, $-SO_3H$.
- Conjugation with amino acids, acetylation, methylation do not result in metabolites with high molecular weight and polarity. Hence, little influence on biliary excretion.

- Efficacy of drug excretion by biliary system can be tested by an agent that is completely eliminated in bile, For example; sulfobromophthalein. This marker is excreted in half an hour in intestine when hepatic function is normal. Delay in its excretion indicates hepatic and biliary malfunction.

- Some drugs which are excreted as glucuronides or as glutathione conjugates are hydrolyzed by intestinal or bacterial enzymes to the parent drugs which are reabsorbed.

- The reabsorbed drugs are again carried to the liver for resecretion via bile into the intestine.

This phenomenon of drug cycling between the intestine and the liver is called 'Enterohepatic circulation'.

2) **Pulmonary Excretion:**
- Gaseous and volatile substances such as general anesthetics (Halothane) are absorbed through lungs by simple diffusion.

- Pulmonary blood flow, rate of respiration and solubility of substance affect the pulmonary excretion.

- Intact gaseous drugs are excreted but not metabolites.

- Alcohol which has high solubility in blood and tissues are excreted slowly by lungs.

3) **Salivary Excretion:**
- The pH of saliva varies from 5.8 to 8.4. Unionized lipid soluble drugs are excreted passively. Some basic drugs inhibit saliva secretion and are responsible for mouth dryness. Compounds excreted in saliva are Caffeine, Phenytoin and Theophylline.

4) **Mammary Excretion:**
- Milk consists of lactic secretion which is rich in fats and proteins. 0.5 to one litre of milk is secreted per day in lactating mothers.

- Excretion of drug in milk is important as it gains entry in breast feeding infants.

- pH of milk varies from 6.4 to 7.6. Free un-ionized and lipid soluble drugs diffuse passively.

- Highly plasma bound drug like Diazepam is less secreted in milk.

- Amount of drug excreted in milk is less than 1% and fraction consumed by infant is too less to produce toxic effects. Some potent drugs like barbiturates and morphine may induce toxicity.

5) **Skin Excretion:**
- Drugs excreted through skin via sweat follows pH partition hypothesis.

- Excretion of drugs through skin may lead to urticaria and dermatitis.
- Compounds like benzoic acid, salicylic acid, alcohol and heavy metals are excreted in sweat.

6) Gastrointestinal Excretion:

- Excretion of drugs through GIT usually occurs after parenteral administration.
- Water soluble and ionized form of weakly acidic and basic drugs are excreted in GIT.
- For example; nicotine and quinine are excreted in stomach.
- Drugs excreted in GIT are reabsorbed into systemic circulation.

8.10 TOTAL CLEARANCE

It is the volume of plasma completely cleared of drug per unit time by all routes and mechanisms. It is the sum of all the individual clearances by all the eliminating organs. i.e.

$$CLT = CLR + CLH + CLP + \ldots$$

Where, CLR = Renal clearance,

CLH = Hepatic clearance,

CLP = Pulmonary clearance.

Expressed in terms of ml/min

$$CLT = K_e \cdot V_d$$

Where, K_e = Elimination rate constant.

V_d = Volume of distribution.

If intrinsic capacity of an organ to clear drug is high and exceeds plasma flow to that organ, then the clearance equals plasma flow and is altered by changes in plasma flow.

The plasma half-life of a drug is inversely proportional to total clearance, and directly proportional to V. For a given V, the higher the total clearance, the shorter the half-life.

Extraction Ratio (E) :

Extraction ratio is defined as "the ratio of the clearance of a drug compared to the rate of blood flow through the clearing organ".

As such, it indicates what fraction of the drug in the blood is cleared (extracted) on each passage through the clearing organ.

Chapter 9...

PHARMACOKINETIC PARAMETERS

9.1 INTRODUCTION

Pharmacokinetic is "the science of the kinetics of drug absorption, distribution, Metabolism and elimination".

The term "Pharmacokinetics" is derived from Greek words Pharmakon (drug) and Kinesis (movement).

It includes

-   Mechanisms of absorption and distribution of an administered drug,
-   Rate at which the drug action begins and the duration of effect,
-   The chemical changes of the substance in the body,
-   Effect and routes of excretion of the drug metabolites.

In short, it is the information regarding how drugs move in the body, how quickly drugs come to, how long they stay in biophase and how quickly drugs leave the body.

The disposition of a drug includes the processes of **ADME**,

-   Absorption
-   Distribution
-   Metabolism
-   Excretion
-   Toxicity

It is the quantitative study of drug movement in, through and out of the body and their relationship with the pharmacological, therapeutic or toxicological response in human or animal.

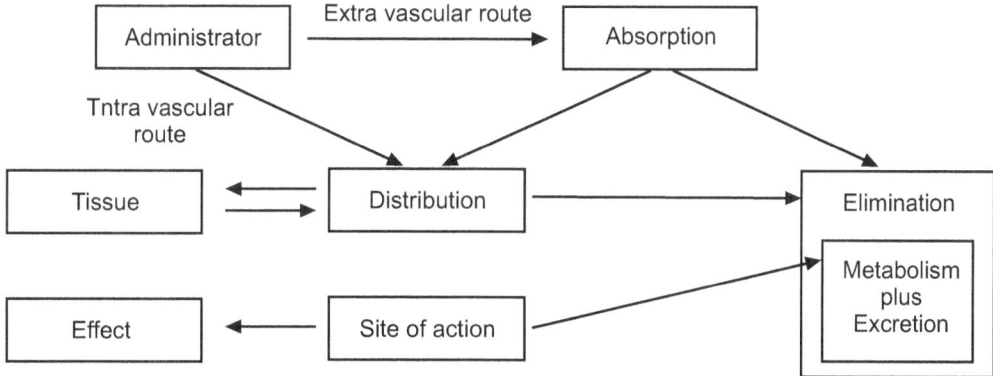

Fig. 9.1: General stage of drug after administration

(9.1)

9.2 IMPORTANCE OF PHARMACOKINETIC STUDY

Design of Dosage Regimens

- Optimal multiple dosage regimen is necessary in long duration illness.
- All pharmacokinetic parameters of the drug remain constant during the course of therapy.
- Parameter should be adjusted like dose size and dosing frequency.

In Clinical Pharmacokinetics

- Safe and effective management of illness in individual patient.
- Therapeutic index of drug and intersubject variability.
- Dosing of drugs in various population are measured based on pharmacokinetics parameters.

Measurement of Drug Concentrations

Drug concentration should be measured in tissues, urine, faeces and saliva.

In Therapeutic Drug Monitoring

- For very potent drug with a narrow therapeutic range, to optimize efficacy and to prevent adverse toxicity.
- It involves plasma drug concentration within a target concentration range.

Toxicokinetics and Clinical Toxicology

- To design, conduct and interpretation of drug safety evaluation studies, and in validating dose related exposure in animals and which is then extrapolated for human.
- Clinical toxicology is the study of adversed effect of drugs and toxic substances in body.

9.3 PHARMACOKINETICS OF DRUG ABSORPTION

In intravenous administration, the drug is injected directly into the plasma.

Extravascular delivery routes, particularly oral dosing, are important and popular for drug administration. Pharmacokinetic models after extravascular drug administration must consider systemic drug absorption from the site of administration, For example; the lung, the gut, etc., into the plasma.

The major advantage of intravenous administration is that the rate and extent of systemic drug input is carefully controlled.

The systemic drug absorption from the gastrointestinal (GI) tract or from any other extravascular site is dependent on

(1) The physicochemical properties of the drug,

(2) The dosage form used, and

(3) The anatomy and physiology of the absorption site.

For oral dosing, such factors as surface area of the GI tract, stomach-emptying rate, GI mobility, and blood flow to the absorption site all affect the rate and the extent of drug absorption.

In pharmacokinetics, the overall rate of drug absorption may be described as either a first-order or zero-order input process.

Most pharmacokinetic models assume first-order absorption unless an assumption of zero-order absorption improves the model significantly or has been verified experimentally.

The movement of drug molecules from the site of application to the systemic circulation, through various barriers, their conversion into another chemical form and exit out from the body is studied.

The velocity with which a reaction or a process occurs is called as its **rate**. The manner in which the concentration of drug (or reactants) influences the rate of reaction or process is called as the **order of reaction** or **order of process**.

Consider the following chemical reaction:

$$\text{Drug A} \longrightarrow \text{Drug B}$$

The rate of forward reaction is expressed as :

$$\frac{-dA}{dt}$$

Negative sign indicates that the concentration of drug A decreases with time t. As the reaction proceeds, the concentration of drug B increases and the rate of reaction can also be expressed as:

$$\frac{dB}{dt}$$

Experimentally, the rate of reaction is determined by measuring the decrease in concentration of drug A with time t.

$$\therefore \qquad\qquad\qquad \frac{dC}{dt} = -KC^n$$

If C is the concentration of drug A, the rate of decrease in C of drug A as it is changed to B can be described by a general expression as a function of time t.

Where, K = rate constant, n = order of reaction

If n = 0; it is a zero-order process, if n = 1; it is a first-order process and so on. The three commonly encountered rate processes in a physiological system are — Zero-order process, First-order process, Mixed-order process.

[I] Zero-Order Kinetics (Constant Rate Processes)

If n = 0

Equation becomes,
$$\frac{dC}{dt} = -K_0 C^0 = -K_0$$

Where, K_0 = zero-order rate constant (in mg/min).

The zero-order process can be defined as "the one whose rate is independent of the concentration of drug undergoing reaction i.e. the rate of reaction cannot be increased further by increasing the concentration of reactants".

Rearrangement of equation:
$$dC = -K_0 \, dt$$

Where, C_0 = Concentration of drug at t = 0, and

C = Concentration of drug yet to undergo reaction at time t.

A plot of C versus t yields such a straight line having slope $-K_0$ and y-intercept C_0.

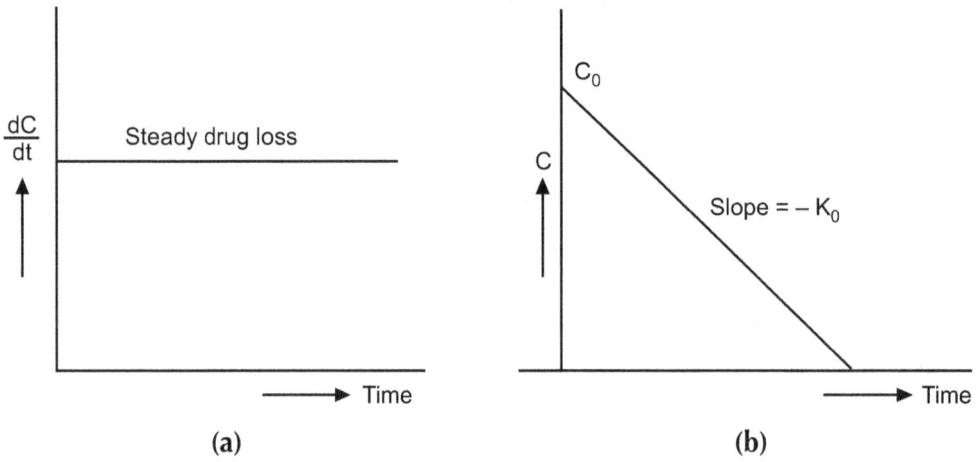

(a)   (b)

Fig. 9.2: Graphs of zero-order kinetics

Zero-Order Half-Life

$$t_{1/2} = \frac{C_0}{2K_0} = \frac{0.5\,C_0}{K_0}$$

Examples of zero-order processes are :

1. Metabolism/protein-drug binding/enzyme or carrier-mediated transport under saturated conditions. The rate of metabolism, binding or transport of drug remains constant as long as its concentration is in excess of saturating concentration.

2. Administration of a drug as a constant rate, i.v. infusion.

3. Controlled drug delivery such as that from, i.m. implants or osmotic pumps.

[II] First-Order Kinetics (Linear Kinetics)

If $n = 1$,

Equation becomes, $\dfrac{dC}{dt} = -KC$

Where, K = first-order rate constant (in time – 1 or per hour)

From above equation it is clear that a **first-order process** is the one whose rate is directly proportional to the concentration of drug undergoing reaction i.e. greater the concentration, faster the reaction. It is because of such proportionality between rate of reaction and the concentration of drug that a first-order process is said to follow **linear kinetics.**

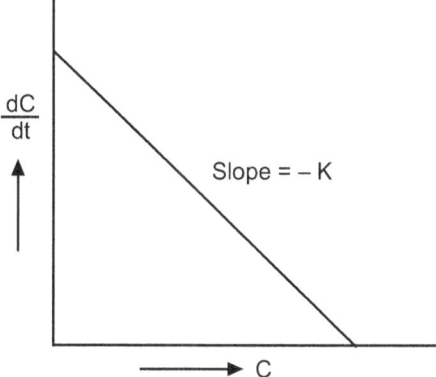

Fig. 9.3 : Graph of first-order kinetics showing linear relationship between rate of reaction and concentration of drug

$$C = C_0\, e^{-Kt}$$

The first-order process is also called as **monoexponential rate process**.

Thus, a first-order process is characterized by **logarithmic** or **exponential kinetics** i.e. a constant fraction of drug undergoes reaction per unit time.

Since $\ln = 2.303 \log$

$\log C = \log C_0 - 0.434\, Kt$

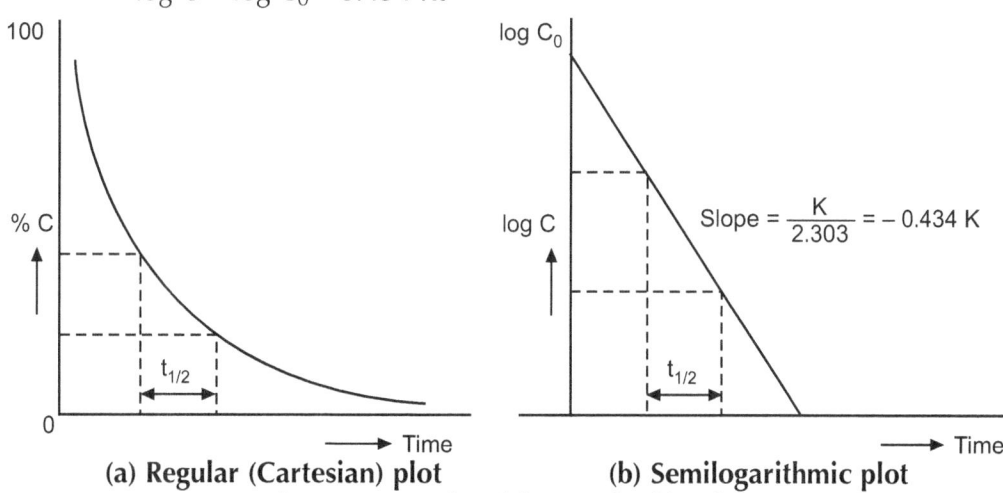

(a) **Regular (Cartesian) plot**   (b) **Semilogarithmic plot**

Fig. 9.4 : Graphs of first–order kinetics

First-Order Half-Life

The half-life of a first-order process is a constant, and independent of initial drug concentration i.e. irrespective of what the initial drug concentration is, the time required for the concentration to decrease by one-half remains the same.

The $t_{1/2}$ of a first-order process is an important pharmacokinetic parameter.

Most pharmacokinetic processes *viz.* absorption, distribution and elimination follow first-order kinetics.

[III] Mixed Order Kinetics

In some instances, the kinetics of a pharmacokinetic process changes from predominantly first-order to predominantly zero-order with increasing dose or chronic medication. A *mixture* of both first-order and zero-order kinetics is observed in such cases and therefore the process is said to follow **mixed-order kinetics**.

Since deviations from an originally linear pharmacokinetic profile are observed, the rate process of such a drug is called as **non-linear kinetics**.

Mixed order kinetics is also termed as **dose-dependent kinetics** as it is observed at increased or multiple doses of some drugs.

Non-linearities in pharmacokinetics have been observed in –

- Drug absorption (e.g. vitamin C),
- Drug distribution (e.g. naproxen), and
- Drug elimination (e.g. riboflavin).

The phenomena is seen when a particular pharmacokinetic process involves presence of carriers or enzymes which are substrate specific and have definite capacities and can get saturated at high drug concentrations (i.e. capacity-limited). The kinetics of such capacity-limited processes can be described by the **Michaelis-Menten kinetics**.

9.4 BASIC CONCEPTS IN DRUG DISPOSITION

The drug disposition is based on following assumptions –

1. The body is considered as a single, kinetically homogeneous unit that has no barriers to the movement of drug.
2. Final distribution equilibrium between the drug in plasma and other body fluids (i.e. mixing) is attained instantaneously and maintained at all times. This model thus applies only to those drugs that distribute rapidly throughout the body.
3. Drugs move dynamically, in (absorption) and out (elimination) of this compartment.
4. Elimination is a first-order (monoexponential) process with first-order rate constant.
5. Rate of input (absorption) > Rate of output (elimination).

6. The anatomical reference compartment is plasma and concentration of drug in plasma is representative of drug concentration in all body tissues i.e. any change in plasma drug concentration reflects a proportional change in drug concentration throughout the body.

The term open indicates that the input (absorption) and output (elimination) are unidirectional and that the drug can be eliminated from the body.

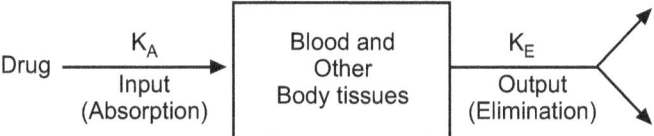

Intravenous Bolus Administration

When a drug that distributes rapidly in the body is given in the form of a rapid intravenous injection (i.e. i.v. bolus or slug), it takes about one to three minutes for complete circulation and therefore the rate of absorption is neglected in calculations. The model can be depicted as follows:

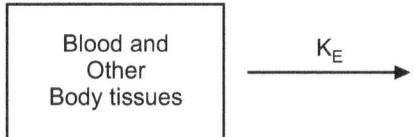

The general expression for rate of drug presentation to the body is:

$$\frac{dX}{dt} = \text{Rate in (Availability)} - \text{Rate out (Elimination)}$$

Since **rate in** or absorption is absent, the equation becomes

$$\frac{dX}{dt} = -\text{Rate out}$$

If the **rate out** or elimination follows first-order kinetics, then

$$\frac{dX}{dt} = -K_E X$$

Where, K_E = first-order elimination rate constant, and

X = amount of drug in the body at any time t remaining to be eliminated.

Negative sign indicates that the drug is being lost from the body.

9.5 ESTIMATION OF ELIMINATION RATE CONSTANTS

Elimination rate constant is the first order rate constant describing drug eliminaiton from the body.

$$\frac{dC_p}{dt} = -K_E \cdot C_p$$

$$\frac{dX}{dt} = -K_E \cdot X$$

Integrating the equation

$\ln X = \ln X_0 - K_E t$

Where, X_0 = amount of drug at time t = 0

i.e. the initial amount of drug injected, can also be written in the exponential form

$X = X_0 \, e^{-K_E t}$

Since it is difficult to determine directly the amount of drug in the body X, advantage is taken of the fact that a constant relationship exists between drug concentration in plasma C (easily measurable) and X; thus

$$X = V_d \, C$$

Where, V_d = proportionality constant popularly known as the apparent volume of distribution.

It is a pharmacokinetic parameter that permits the use of plasma drug concentration in place of amount of drug in the body. The equation therefore becomes:

$$\log C = \log C_0 - \frac{K_E \, t}{2.303}$$

Where, C_0 = plasma drug concentration immediately after i.v. injection.

Equation is that of a straight line and indicates that a semilogarithmic plot of log C versus t will be linear with Y-intercept log C_0.

The elimination rate constant is directly obtained from the slope of the line. It has unit min^{-1}.

Thus, a linear plot is easier to handle mathematically than a curve which in this case will be obtained from a plot of C versus t.

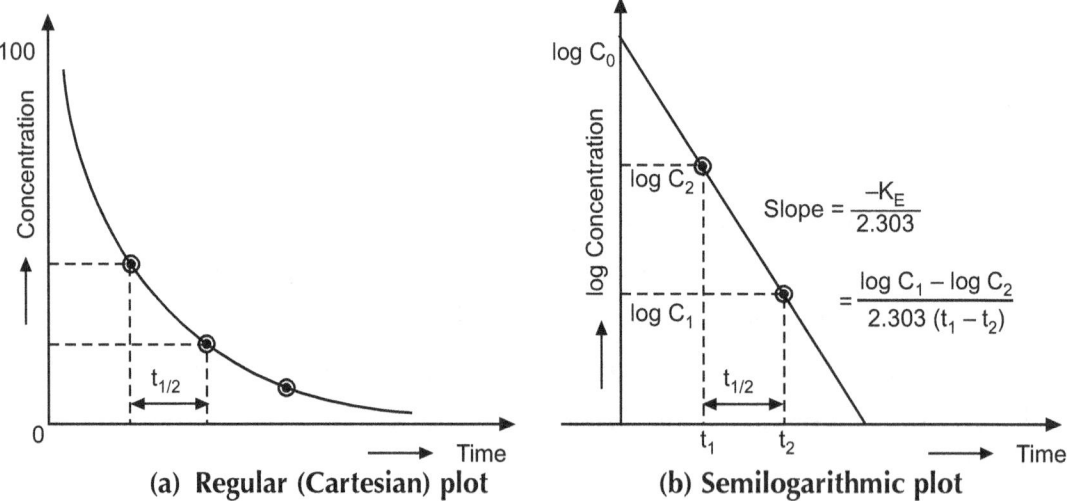

(a) Regular (Cartesian) plot   (b) Semilogarithmic plot

Fig. 9.5: (a) Shows cartesian plot of a drug that follows one-compartment kinetics and given by rapid i.v. injection, and (b) Shows semilogarithmic plot for the rate of elimination in a one-compartment model.

9.6 PHARMACOKINETIC AND PHARMACODYNAMIC PARAMETERS

9.6.1 Pharmacokinetic Parameters

Peak Plasma Concentration (C_{max}):

- Maximum drug concentration in plasma is known as peak plasma concentration.
- Expressed in mcg/ml.
- At C_{max}, Absorption rate = Elimination rate.
- Peak concentration of any drug is related to it's pharmacological response.

Time of Peak Concentration (t_{max}):

- Time taken by the drug to reach the maximum plasma concentration.
- Expressed in hours.
- Useful in estimating rate of absorption.
- Importance in assessing the efficacy of drugs used to treat acute conditions like pain and insomnia.

Area Under the Curve (AUC):

- It represent the total integrated area under the plasma level-time profile and expresses the total amount of drug that comes into the systemic circulation after its administration.
- Expressed in mcg/ml X hours.
- Important parameter in evaluating bioavailability of a drug from its dosage form.
- Bioavailability $= \dfrac{AUC_{Oral}}{AUC_{Injected}} \times 100$

9.6.2 Pharmacodynamic Parameters

Minimum Effective Concentration (MEC):

- It is defined as, "minimum concentration of drug in plasma required to produce therapeutic effect".
- Concentration of drug below MEC is said to be in the sub-therapeutic level.
- In case of antibiotics, minimum inhibitory concentration (MIC) is commonly used to determine therapeutic efficacy.

Maximum Safe Concentration (MSC):

- Concentration of drug in plasma, above which adverse or unwanted effects are precipitated.
- Also known as minimum toxic concentration (MTC).
- Concentration of drug above MSC is said to be in toxic level.

Onset of Action:
- Beginning of pharmacological response.
- Occurs as the plasma drug concentration just exceeds required MEC.

Onset Time:
- Time required for the drug to start producing pharmacological response.
- It is the time at which plasma drug concentration reach to MEC.

Duration of Action:
- Time period during which plasma drug concentration remains above the MEC.

Intensity of Action:
- Maximum pharmacological response produced by the peak plasma concentration of drug.
- Intensity of action depends on the height of peak plasma concentration.

Therapeutic Range:
- Concentration of drug between MEC and MSC represent therapeutic range.
- Also know as therapeutic window.

Therapeutic Index:
- Ratio of MSC to MEC.
- Also defined as, "the ratio of dose required to produce toxic or lethal effects to dose required to produce therapeutic effect".

Chapter 10

PHARMACOKINETIC MODELS

10.1 INTRODUCTION

The theoretical aspect of pharmacokinetics involves the development of pharmacokinetic models that predict the drug disposition after drug administration.

A model is a hypothesis that employs mathematical term to concisely describe quantitative relationship.

Pharmacokinetic models provide concise means of expressing mathematically or quantitatively, the time course of drug(s) throughout the body and compute meaningful pharmacokinetic parameters.

10.1.1 Importance of Pharmacokinetic Models

1. Characterizing the behaviour of drugs in patients.
2. Predicting the concentration of the drug in various body fluids with any dosage regimen.
3. Predicting the multiple-dose concentration curves from single dose experiments.
4. Calculating the optimum dosage regimen for individual patients.
5. Evaluating the risk of toxicity with certain dosage regimens.
6. Correlating plasma drug concentration with pharmacological response.
7. Evaluating the BA/BE between different formulations of same drug.
8. Estimating the possible drug and/or metabolite(s) accumulation in the body.
9. Determining the influence of altered physiology/disease state on drug ADME.
10. Explaining drug interactions.

It is ensured that the model fits the experimental data, otherwise, a new, more complex and suitable model may be proposed and tested.

10.1.2 Need of Pharmacokinetic Models

- Drug movement within the body is a complex process.
- To understand the movement of drug in biological system, pharmacokinetic model is required.
- For ease of understanding mathematical equation, pharmacokinetic model is required.

10.2 TYPES OF PHARMACOKINETIC MODELS

There are three types of pharmacokinetic models.

1. Compartmental model
2. Non-compartmental model
3. Physiologic model

10.2.1 Compartmental Models

- Here the body can be represented as series, or systems of compartments that communicate reversibly with each other. A compartment is not a real physiologic or anatomic region but is considered as a tissue or group of tissues that have similar blood flow and drug affinity. Within each compartment, the drug is considered to be uniformly distributed.

- Compartmental models are built on the same basic concepts as physiologic models, but with gross simplifications. The "one-compartment model" contains a single volume and a single clearance, as though built like buckets. For anesthetic drugs, resemble several buckets connected by pipes. These are usually modeled using two- or three-compartment models.

- Rate constants are used to represent the overall rate processes of drug entry into and exit from the compartment. The model is an open system since the drug can be eliminated from the system.

10.2.1.1 One-Compartment Model

One compartment open model consider body as one compartment. Body consist of blood and tissue. This compartment is open to the organ of drug input as well as to the organ of drug output.

One compartment model is known as 'rapid mixing and linear model'.

Example: One compartment open model assume that the drug loss from the body follow first order kinetics. Drug eliminated from the body can be mathematically represented by monoexponential equation.

$$D_C = D_{C(0)} \times e^{-K_{10}t}$$

D_C = Concentration of drug in the body

$D_{C(0)}$ = Concentration of drug in the body at zero time

K_{10} = Elimination rate constant

Derivation of Equation for One Compartment Open Model:

It is assumed that the drug loss from the body follow first order kinetics. As the time passes, the plasma drug concentration decreases.

As per the change in the amount of drug present in plasma:

$$\frac{-dc_1}{dt} = K_{10}c_1$$

$$\frac{dc_1}{c_1} = -K_{10}dt \qquad \qquad \text{... (10.1)}$$

Integrating equation (10.1).

$$\int_{c_0}^{c_1} \frac{dc_1}{c_1} = -K_{10} \int_0^t dt$$

$$\therefore \qquad [ln\ c_1]_{c_0}^{c_1} = -K_{10}\ [t]_0^t$$

$$ln\ c_1 - ln\ c_1\ (0) = -K_{10}\ (t-0) \qquad \qquad \text{... (10.2)}$$

Convert equation (10.2) to logarithm to the base 10,

$$\therefore\ 2.303\ [\log c_1 - \log c_1\ (0)] = -K_{10}t$$

$$\therefore \qquad \log c_1 - \log c_1\ (0) = \frac{-K_{10}t}{2.303}$$

$$\therefore \qquad \log c_1 = \log c_1\ (0) - \frac{K_{10}t}{2.303}$$

Depending upon whether the compartments are arranged parallel or in a series, compartmental models are divided in two categories :

1. Mammillary model.
2. Caternary model.

1. Mammillary Model:

It is the most common compartmental model used in pharmacokinetics. The model consists of one or more peripheral compartments connected to the central compartment in a manner similar to connection of satellites to a planet.

Central compartment (Compartment 1) :

- It comprises of plasma and highly perfused tissues such as lungs, liver, kidneys etc. which rapidly equilibrates with drug.
- The drug is directly absorbed into this compartment.
- Elimination too occurs from this compartment since the main organs involved in drug elimination are liver and kidneys, the highly perfused tissues and therefore presumed to be rapidly accessible to drug in the systemic circulation.

Peripheral compartments or Tissue compartment (Compartment 2, 3 etc.) :

- These are with low vascularity and poor perfusion.
- Distribution of drugs to these compartments is through blood.

- Elimination occur from central compartment.
- Movement of drug between compartments is defined by characteristic first order rate constant denoted by **"K".**
- $K_{12} \rightarrow$ Drug movement from compartment 1 to compartment 2.
- $K_{21} \rightarrow$ Reverse.
- Number of rate constants in a particular compartment model is given by R.
- For intravenous $\rightarrow$ R = 2n – 1
- For extravenous $\rightarrow$ R = 2n.

    Where n = number of compartments.

Model 1: One compartment open model, intravenous administration.

Model 2: One compartment open model, extravascular administration (oral, rectal etc.).

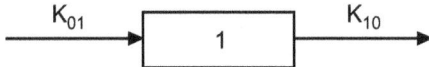

Model 3: Two compartment open model, intravenous administration.

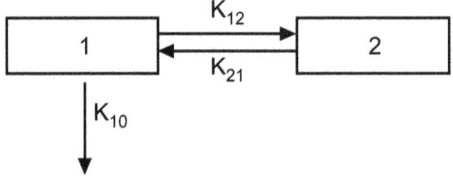

Model 4: Two compartment open model, extravascular administration.

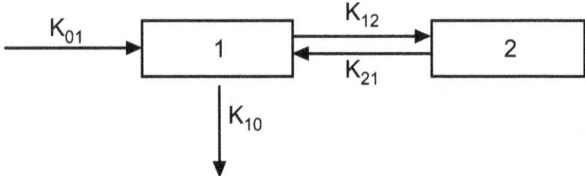

Model 5: Three compartment open model, intravenous administration.

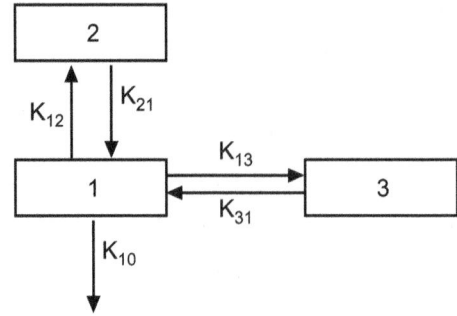

Model 6: Three compartment open model, extravascular administration.

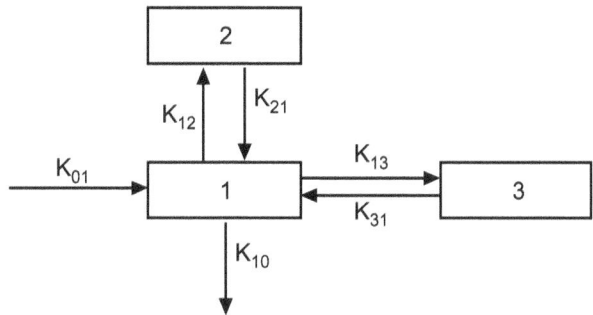

Fig. 10.1: Various mammillary compartment models

The rate constant K_{01} is basically K_a, the first order absorption rate constant and K_{10} is K_E the first order elimination rate constant.

2. Caternary Model:

In this model, the compartments are joined to one another in a series, like compartments of a train. This is not observable physiologically and anatomically as the various organs are directly linked to the blood compartment. Hence, this model is rarely used.

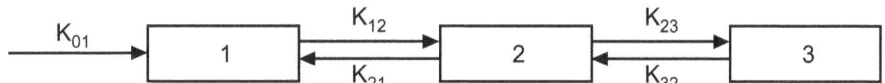

Fig. 10.2 : A caternary model

Advantages of Compartment Modelling:

- It is a simple and flexible approach.
- It gives visual representation of various rate processes involved in drug disposition.
- It shows how many rate constants are necessary to describe these processes.
- It is important in the development of dosage regimens.
- Used for comparison of multiple therepeutic agents.

Disadvantages of Compartment Model:

- The compartments and parameters bear no relationship with the physiologic functions or the anatomic structure of the species.
- The model is based on curve fitting of plasma concentration with complex multiexponential mathematical equations.
- The model may vary within population pharmacokinetics.
- This approach can be limited to a specific drug only.
- Difficulties generally arise when using model to interpret the differences between results from human and animal experiments.

10.2.2 Non-Compartmental Models

• This model is also called as *the model independent method*, based on the assumption that the drug or metabolite follow linear kinetics. It does not require assumption of specific compartmental model.

• Non–compartmental models describe the pharmacokinetics of drug disposition using time and concentration parameters.

• This method can however be applied to any compartmental model.

• The approach based on statistical moments theory, involves the collection of experimental data following a single dose of drug.

• Describe the pharmacokinetic of drug disposition using time and concentration parameters.

• If one considers the time course of drug concentration in plasma as a statistical distribution curve, then :

$$MRT = \frac{AUMC}{AUC}$$

where,   MRT = Mean residence time. (Average time spent by drug in the body before its elimination)

AUMC = Area under the *first moment* curve.

AUC = Area under the *zero moment* curve.

AUMC is obtained from a plot of product of plasma concentration and time (C × t) versus time t from zero to infinity. Mathematically, it is expressed by equation :

$$AUMC = \int_{0}^{\infty} Ct \, dt$$

AUC is obtained from a plot of plasma drug concentration versus time from zero to infinity. Mathematically, it is expressed by equation :

$$AUC = \int_{0}^{\infty} Cdt$$

Practically, the AUMC and AUC can be calculated from the respective graphs by trapezoidal rule.

• MRT is defined as "the average amount of time spent by the drug in the body before being eliminated".

• Non-compartmental model is widely used to estimate the important pharmacokinetic parameters like bioavailability, clearance and apparent volume of distribution. The method is also useful in determining half life, rate of absorption and first order absorption rate constant of drug.

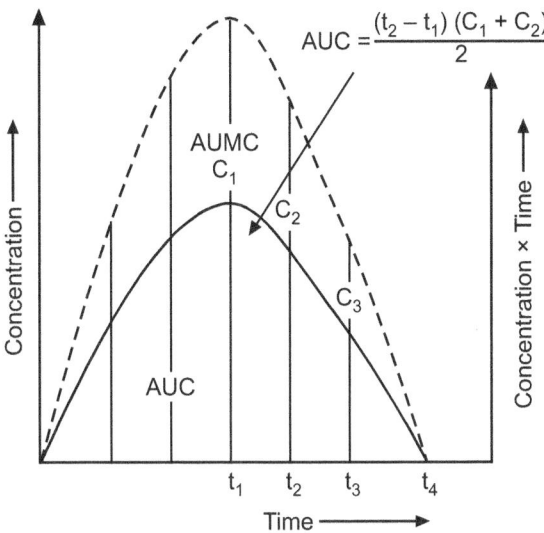

$$AUC = \frac{(t_2 - t_1)(C_1 + C_2)}{2}$$

Fig. 10.3 : AUC and AUMC plots

Advantages of Non-Compartmental Model :

- Pharmacokinetic parameters can be easily derived by simple algebraic equations.
- Applied for any drug or metabolite which follow first order kinetics.
- A detailed description of drug disposition characteristics is not required.

Disadvantages of Non-Compartmental Model :

- It provides limited information regarding the plasma drug concentration – time profile.
- This method does not adequately treat non-linear cases.

10.2.3 Physiologic Model

- Physiologic models are also called as *Blood flow rate–limited models* and *perfusion rate limited models*.
- Physiological models describe the drug disposition in terms of realistic physiological parameters such as blood flow and tissue partition co-efficient.
- The number of compartments to be included in the model depends upon the disposition characteristics of drug.
- Organs such as bone that have no drug penetration are excluded.
- RET (Rapidly Equilibrating Tissue) – lungs, liver, brain, kidney.
- SET (Slowly Equilibrating Tissue) – muscle and adipose tissue.
- Most physiologic models are based on the assumption that the drug movement within a body region is much more rapid than its rate of delivery to that region by the perfusion blood and, therefore the model is said to be perfusion rate limited. The assumption is however applicable to the highly membrane permeable drugs i.e. low molecular weight, poorly ionized and highly lipophilic drugs as lidocaine.

- For highly polar, ionized and charged drugs, the model is referred to as membrane permeation rate limited.
- The rate of drug carried to a tissue or tissue drug uptake is dependent upon two major factors –
  - Rate of blood flow to the organ.
  - Tissue / Blood partition co-efficient.
- This model is based on the assumption that the drug movement within a body region is more rapid than its ratio of delivery to that region by the perfusing blood.

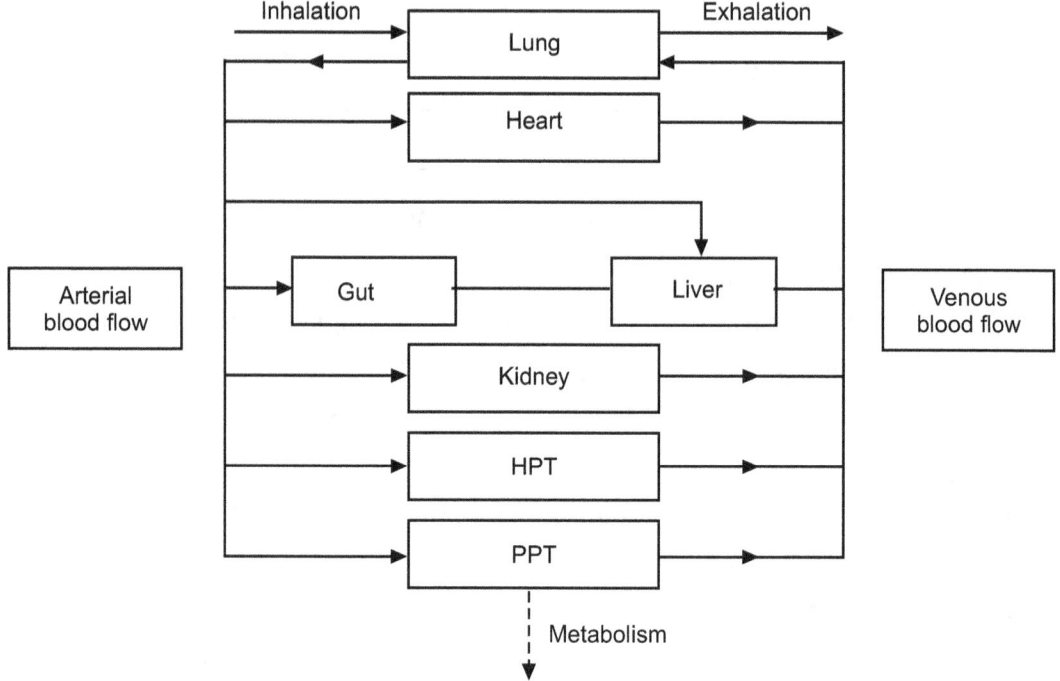

Fig. 10.4 : Physiologic models

Advantages of Physiologic Modelling:

- Mathematical treatment is straightforward.
- Data fitting is not required.
- Model is suitable where tissue drug concentration and binding are known.
- The influence of altered physiology or pathology on drug disposition can be easily predicted from changes in various pharmacokinetic parameters.
- Exact description of drug concentration – time profile in any organ can be obtained.

Disadvantages of Physiological Modelling :

- Obtaining experimental data is very exhaustive.
- Number of data point is less than the pharmacokinetic parameters to be assessed.
- Prediction of individualized dosing is difficult.

10.3 ONE COMPARTMENT OPEN MODELS

[I] ONE COMPARTMENT OPEN MODEL (Instantaneous Distribution Model)

- The one compartment open model is the simplest model which depicts the body as a single, kinetically homogeneous unit having no barriers to the movement of drug and final distribution equilibrium between drug in plasma and other body fluid is obtained instantaneously and maintained at all times.

- This model thus applies only to those drugs that distribute rapidly throughout the body.

- Drugs move dynamically in and out of this compartment.

- The anatomical reference compartment is the plasma, and concentration of drug in plasma is representative of drug concentration in all body tissues i.e. any change in plasma drug concentration reflects a proportional change in drug concentration throughout the body.

- The term **open** indicates that the input (absorption) and output (elimination) are unidirectional and that the drug can be eliminated from the body.

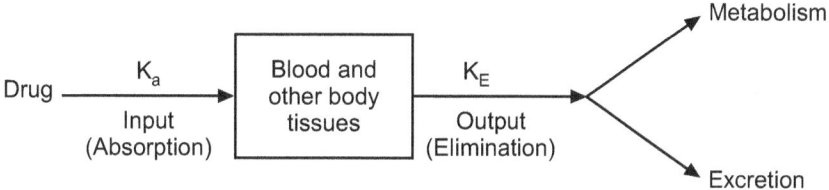

Fig. 10.5: One compartment open model showing input and output processes

- One compartment open model is generally used to describe plasma levels following administration of a single dose of a drug.

  Rate of input > Rate of output.

  Depending upon the rate of input, several one compartment open models can be defined :

  1. One compartment open model, intravenous bolus administration;

  2. One compartment open model, continuous intravenous infusion;

  3. One compartment open model, extravascular administration, zero order absorption; and

  4. One compartment open model, extravascular administration, first order absorption.

[II] ONE COMPARTMENT OPEN MODEL (Intravenous Bolus Administration)

- When a drug that distributes rapidly in the body is given in the form of a rapid intravenous injection (i.e. I.V. bolus or slug), it takes about one to three minutes for complete circulation and therefore the rate of absorption is neglected in calculations.

The model can be depicted as follows:

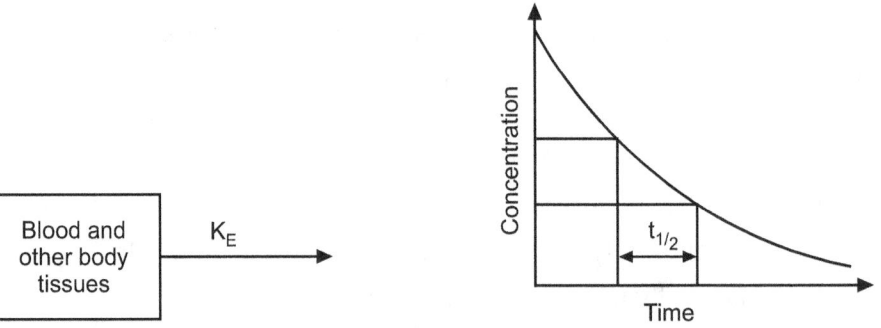

Fig. 10.6

$$\frac{dX}{dt} = \text{Rate in} - \text{Rate out} \qquad \qquad \dots (10.3)$$

Since rate in or absorption is absent, the equation (10.3) becomes

$$\frac{dX}{dt} = - \text{Rate out} \qquad \qquad \dots (10.4)$$

If the rate out or elimination follows first order kinetics then :

$$\frac{dX}{dt} = - K_E X \qquad \qquad \dots (10.5)$$

Where, K_E = First order elimination rate constant

     X = Amount of drug in body at any time t remaining to be eliminated.

Negative sign indicates that the drug is being lost from the body.

Estimation of Pharmacokinetic Parameters:

Elimination rate constant: $\frac{dX}{dt} = - K_E X$

Integrating above equation,

$$\ln(x) = \ln(x_0) - K_E t$$

Where x_0 = amount of drug at time t = 0.

Equation can be written as

$$x = x_0 e^{-K_E t}$$

Transforming into logarithm,

$$\log x = \log x_0 \frac{-K_E t}{2.303}$$

[III] ONE COMPARTMENT OPEN MODEL (Intravenous Infusion)

- Rapid IV injection is unsuitable when the drug has potential to precipitate toxicity or when maintenance of a stable concentration or amount of drug in the body is desired.

- In such a situation, the drug is administered at a constant rate (zero order) by IV infusion.

Advantages of such a Zero Order Infusion of Drugs:
- Ease of control of rate of infusion to fit individual patient needs.
- Prevents fluctuation between maxima and minima of plasma level, plasma level is desired especially when the drug has a narrow therapeutic index.
- Other drugs, electrolytes and nutrients can be conveniently administered simultaneously by the same infusion lie in critically ill patients.

The model can be presented as follows:

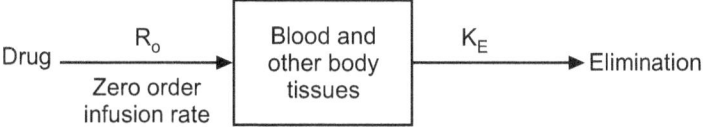

Fig. 10.7: One compartment open intravenous infusion model

- At any time during infusion, the rate of change in the amount of drug in the body, dX/dt is the difference between the zero order rate of drug infusion R_o and first order elimination, $-K_EX$.

$$\therefore \qquad \frac{dX}{dt} = R_o - K_EX \qquad \qquad ...(10.6)$$

Integration and rearrangement of above equation gives

$$X = \frac{R_o}{R_E}(1 - e^{-K_Et}) \qquad \qquad ...(10.7)$$

Since $X = V_d C$, the equation (10.7) can be transformed into concentration terms as follows :

$$C = \frac{R_o}{K_EV_d}(1 - e^{-K_Et}) = \frac{R_o}{CL_T} - (1 - e^{-K_Et}) \qquad \qquad ...(10.8)$$

- After infusion, as time passes, amount of drug rises gradually (elimination rate less than the rate of infusion) until a point after which the rate of elimination equals the rate of infusion i.e. the concentration of drug in plasma approaches a constant value called as steady state, plateau or infusion equilibrium.

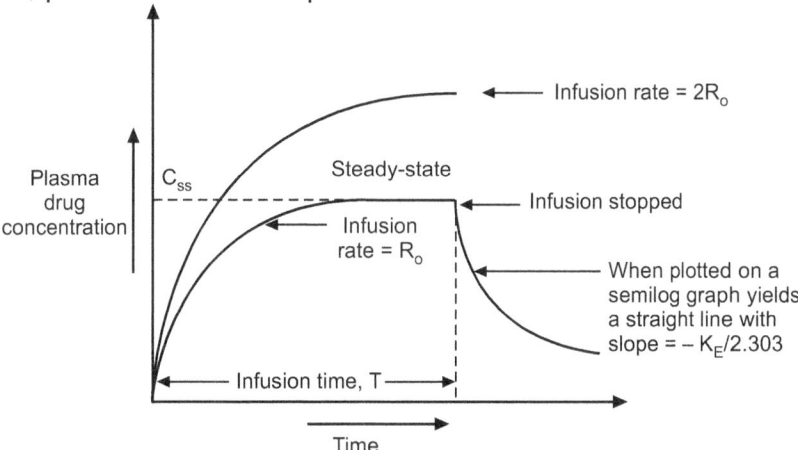

Fig. 10.8: Plasma concentration time profile for a drug given by constant rate IV infusion (the two curves indicate different infusion rates R_0 and $2R_0$ for the same drug).

- At steady-state, the rate of change of amount of drug in the body is zero hence the equation (10.6) becomes :

$$0 = R_o - K_E X_{SS}$$

Therefore, $\quad K_E X_{SS} = R_o \quad\quad\quad$ ... (10.9)

Transforming to concentration terms ($X_{SS} = V_d C_{SS}$) and rearranging the equation :

$$C_{SS} = \frac{R_o}{K_E V_d} = \frac{R_o}{CL_T} \text{ i.e. } \frac{\text{Infusion rate}}{\text{Clearance}} \quad\quad ...(10.10)$$

Where X_{SS} and C_{SS} are amount of drug in the body and concentration of drug in plasma at steady state respectively.

- The value of K_E (and hence $t_{1/2}$) can be obtained from the slope of straight line obtained after a semilogarithmic plot (log C versus T) of plasma concentration-time data gathered from the time when infusion is stopped.
- Alternatively K_E can be calculated from the data collected during infusion to steady state as follows :

Substituting $\dfrac{R_o}{CL_T} = C_{SS}$ from equation (10.10) in equation (10.8) we get :

$$C = C_{SS} (1 - e^{-K_E t}) \quad\quad ...(10.11)$$

- Rearrangement yields :

$$\left[\frac{C_{SS} - C}{C_{SS}}\right] = e^{-K_E t} \quad\quad ...(10.12)$$

- Transforming to log form the equation becomes,

$$\log\left[\frac{C_{SS} - C}{C_{SS}}\right] = \frac{-K_E T}{2.303} \quad\quad ...(10.13)$$

- Now, plot of $\log\left[\dfrac{C_{SS} - C}{C_{SS}}\right]$ versus Time gives straight line with slope $= \dfrac{-K_E}{2.303}$.

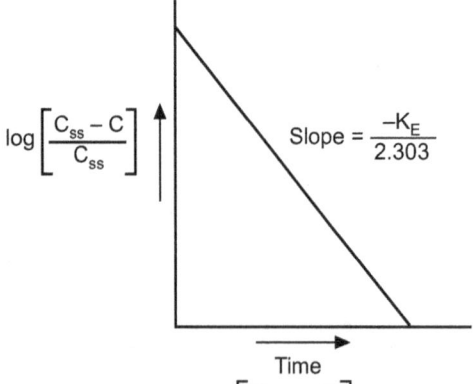

Fig. 10.9 : Plot of $\log\left[\dfrac{C_{SS} - C}{C_{SS}}\right]$ **versus Time**

- The time to reach steady state concentration is dependent upon the elimination half life and not infusion rate. An increase in infusion rate will merely increase the plasma concentration attained at steady state (Fig. 10.9). If n is the number of half-lives passed since the start of infusion $(t/t_{1/2})$, equation (10.11) can be written as :

$$C = C_{SS} \left[1 - \left(\frac{1}{2}\right)^n \right] \qquad \ldots (10.14)$$

- The per cent of C_{SS} achieved at the end of each $t_{1/2}$ is the sum of C_{SS} at previous $t_{1/2}$ and the concentration of drug remaining after a given $t_{1/2}$ (Table 10.1).

Table 10.1

Half life	% Remaining	% C_{SS} achieved
1	50	50
2	25	50 + 25 = 75
3	12.5	75 + 12.5 = 87.5
4	6.25	87.5 + 6.25 = 93.75
5	3.125	93.75 + 3.125 = 96.875
6	1.562	96.875 + 1.562 = 98.437
7	0.781	98.437 + 0.781 = 99.218

- For therapeutic purpose, more than 90% of the steady state drug concentration in the blood is desired which is reached in 3.3 half lives. It takes 6.6 half lives for the concentration to reach 99% of the steady state. Thus, the shorter the half life (e.g. Penicillin G, 30 minutes), sooner is the steady state reached.

[IV] INFUSION PLUS LOADING DOSE

- It takes a very long time for the drugs having longer half-lives before the steady state concentration is reached (e.g. Phenobarbital, 5 days).

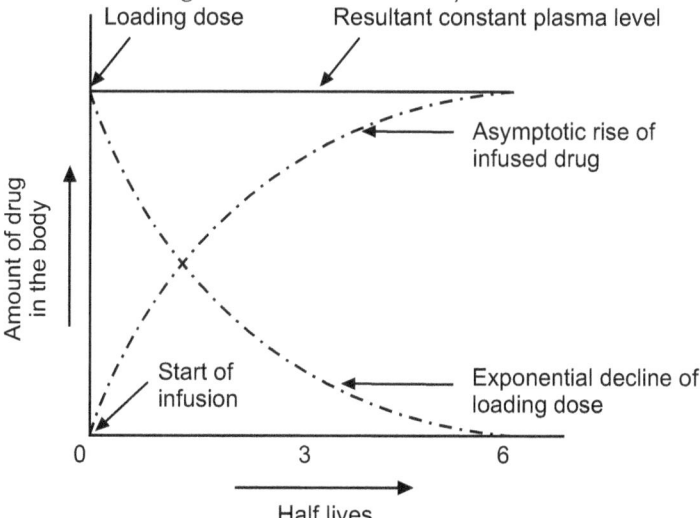

Fig. 10.10 : Intravenous infusion with loading dose

- An I.V. loading dose is given to yield the desired steady state immediately upon injection prior to starting the infusion. It should then be followed immediately by I.V. infusion at a rate enough to maintain this concentration.

  Note: As the amount of bolus dose remaining in the body falls, there is a complementary rise resulting from the infusion.

- Recalling once again the relationship $X = V_d C$, the equation for computing the loading dose X_{OL} can be given :

$$X_{OL} = C_{SS} V_d \qquad \qquad \text{... (10.15)}$$

- Substitution of $C_{SS} = R_o/K_E V_d$ from equation (10.10) in above equation yields another expression for loading dose in terms of infusion rate :

$$X_{OL} = \frac{R_o}{K_E} \qquad \qquad \text{... (10.16)}$$

- The equation describing the plasma concentration time profile following simultaneous IV loading dose (I.V. bolus) and constant rate IV infusion is the sum of following two equations ((10.17) and (10.18)) describing each process.

- Recall equation for IV bolus,

$$X = X_o e^{-K_E t}$$

And substituting $X = V_d C$ in above equation we get,

$$C = \frac{X_o e^{-K_E t}}{V_d} \qquad \qquad \text{... (10.17)}$$

And from equation (10.8) for constant rate IV infusion we know that

$$C = \frac{R_o}{K_E V_d} (1 - e^{-K_E t}) \qquad \qquad \text{... (10.18)}$$

$$C = \frac{X_{OL}}{V_d} e^{-K_E t} + \frac{R_o}{K_E V_d} (1 - e^{-K_E t}) \qquad \qquad \text{... (10.19)}$$

- It we substitute $\mathbf{C_{SS}\ V_d}$ **for** $\mathbf{X_{OL}}$ (from equation 10.15) and $\mathbf{C_{SS}\ K_E\ V_d}$ **for** $\mathbf{R_o}$ (from equation (10.10) in above equation and simplify, it reduces to $\mathbf{C = C_{SS}}$ indicating that concentration of drug in plasma remains constant (steady) throughout the infusion time.

[V] ONE COMPARTMENT OPEN MODEL (Extravascular Administration)

- When a drug is administered by extravascular route (e.g. oral, rectal etc.) absorption is a prerequisite for its therapeutic activity.

- The rate of absorption may be described mathematically as zero order or first order process.

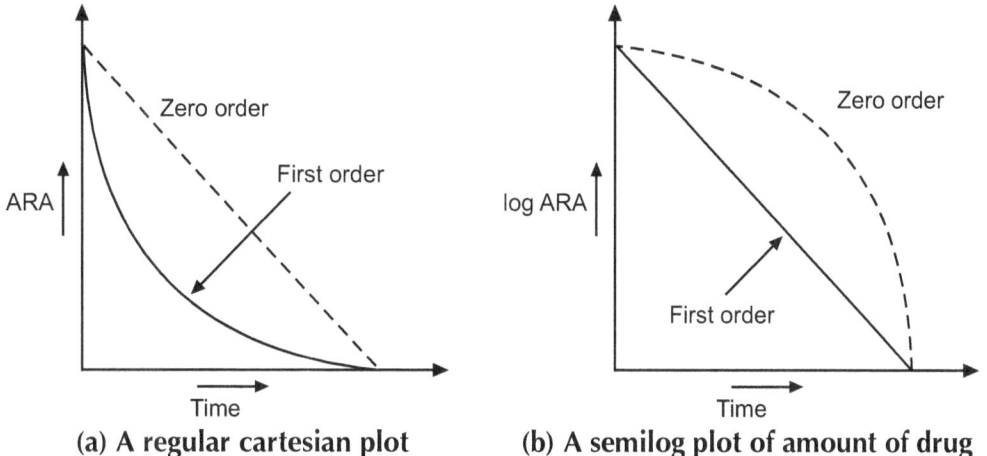

(a) **A regular cartesian plot** (b) **A semilog plot of amount of drug remaining to be absorbed (ARA) versus time**

Fig. 10.11 : Distinction between zero order and first order absorption processes

- After extravascular administration, the rate of change in the amount of drug in the body is given by

$$\frac{dX}{dt} = \text{Rate of absorption} - \text{Rate of elimination}$$

$$\frac{dX}{dt} = \frac{dX_{ev}}{dt} - \frac{dX_E}{dt} \qquad\qquad \dots (10.20)$$

Various phases of fate of drug in body has been shown in Fig. 10.12.

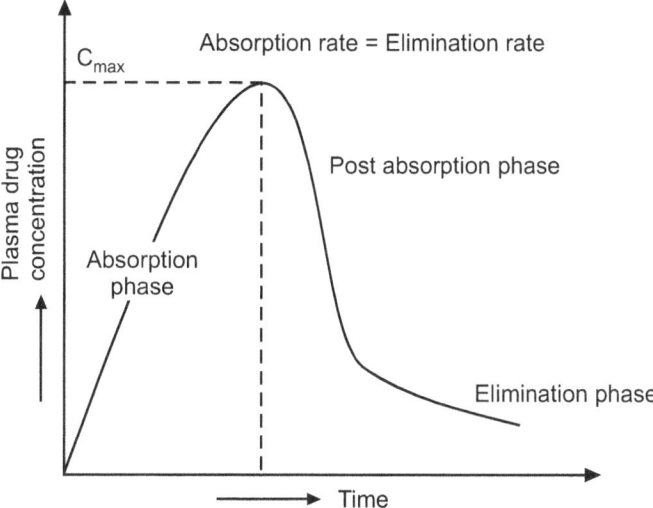

Fig. 10.12 : The absorption and elimination phase of the plasma concentration time profile obtained after extravascular administration of a single dose of a drug

During absorption phase, rate of absorption is greater than elimination phase.

$$\frac{dX_{ev}}{dt} > \frac{dX_E}{dt}$$

At peak plasma concentration

$$\frac{dX_{ev}}{dt} = \frac{dX_E}{dt}$$

During post absorption phase

$$\frac{dX_{ev}}{dt} < \frac{dX_E}{dt}$$

[VI] ZERO ORDER ABSORPTION MODEL

Drug at EV site
R_o
Zero order absorption
Blood and other body tissues
K_E
Elimination

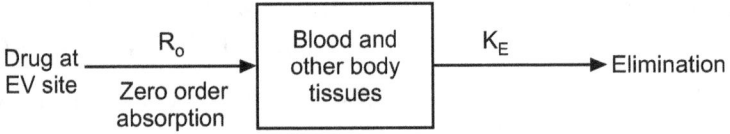

Fig. 10.13 : Zero order absorption model

- This model is similar to that of constant rate IV infusion.
- Example of zero order absorption, rate of drug absorption for controlled drug delivery systems.
- All equations that explain the plasma concentration-time profile for IV infusion are also applicable to this model.

[VII] FIRST ORDER ABSORPTION MODEL

Drug at EV site
K_a
First order absorption
Blood and other body tissues
K_E
Elimination

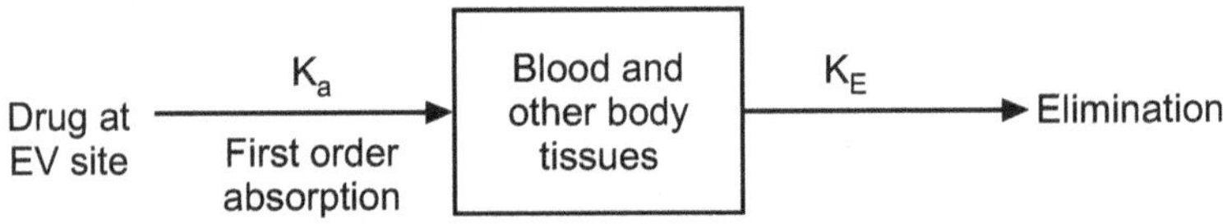

Fig. 10.14 : First order absorption model

Differential form of equation $\frac{dX}{dt} = \frac{dX_{ev}}{dt} - \frac{dX_E}{dt}$

$$\frac{dX}{dt} = K_a X_a - K_E X \qquad \dots (10.21)$$

Where, K_a = First order absorption rate constant

X_a = Amount of drug at the absorption site remaining to be absorbed

Integration of equation (10.21) gives

$$X = \frac{K_a FX_o}{(K_a - K_E)} [e^{-K_E t} - e^{-K_a t}] \qquad \dots (10.22)$$

Transforming into concentration terms, the equation becomes :

$$C = \frac{K_a FX_0}{V_d (K_a - K_E)} [e^{-K_E t} - e^{-K_a t}] \qquad \ldots (10.23)$$

Where F = Fraction of drug absorbed systemically after extravascular administration.

10.4 TWO COMPARTMENT OPEN MODEL

Definition : The two compartment open model treats the body as two compartments.

1. **Central compartment:** Comprising of blood and highly perfused tissues like liver, kidney, lungs etc. that equilibrate with the drug rapidly.

    Elimination usually occurs from this compartment.

2. **Peripheral or tissue compartment:** Comprising of poorly perfused and slow equilibrating tissues such as muscles, skin, adipose etc.

Classification of a particular tissue, for example; brain into central or peripheral compartment depends upon the physicochemical properties of the drug.

A highly lipophilic drug can cross the blood brain barrier and brain would then be included in the central compartment.

In contrast, a polar drug can not penetrate the blood brain barrier and brain in this case will be a part of peripheral compartment despite the fact that it is a highly perfused organ.

In two compartment model, all processes are of first order.

Input and output are from the "central" compartment.

Mixing is instantaneous within each compartment.

Mixing between the compartments is slow relative to mixing within the compartments.

- Three different type of models under this category are :

1. Two compartment model with elimination from central compartment.

2. Two compartment model with elimination from peripheral compartment.

3. Two compartment model with elimination from both compartments.

In the absence of information, elimination is assumed to occur exclusively from central compartment.

10.4.1 Bolus Administration

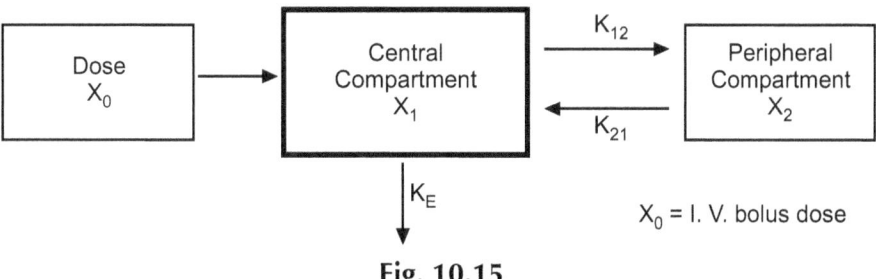

Fig. 10.15

After the I.V. bolus of a drug that follows two-compartment kinetics, the decline in plasma concentration is biexponential, indicating the presence of two processes viz. (see Fig. 10.15)

(A) Distribution i.e. (K_{12})

(B) Elimination i.e. (K_{21})

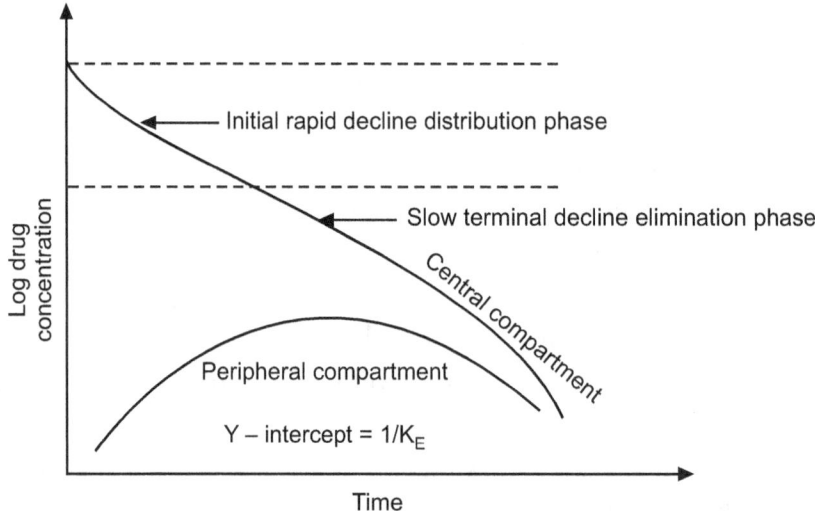

Fig. 10.16 : Changes in the drug concentration in the central and peripheral compartment after I.V. bolus of a drug that fits two compartment model

The rate of change in drug concentration in the central compartment is given by :

$$\frac{dC_c}{dt} = K_{21} C_p - K_{12} C_c - K_E C_c \qquad ...(10.24)$$

Extending the relationship $X = V_{dc}$ to the above equation, we have,

$$\frac{dC_c}{dt} = \frac{K_{21} X_p}{V_p} - \frac{K_{12} X_c}{V_c} - \frac{K_E X_c}{V_c} \qquad ... (10.25)$$

Where,

X_c = Amount of drug in the central compartment

X_p = Amount drug in the peripheral compartment

V_c = Apparent volume of the central compartment

V_p = Apparent volume of the peripheral compartment.

$$\frac{dC_p}{dt} = K_{12} C_c - K_{21} C_p \qquad ... (10.26)$$

$$\frac{dC_p}{dt} = \frac{K_{12} X_c}{V_c} - \frac{K_{21} X_p}{V_p} \qquad ... (10.27)$$

Integration of equations (10.26) and (10.27) yields equations that describe the concentration of drug in the central and peripheral compartments at any given time "t".

$$C_c = \frac{X_0}{V_c}\left(\frac{(K_{21} - \alpha)}{(\beta - \alpha)} e^{-\alpha t} + \frac{(K_{21} - \beta)}{(\alpha - \beta)} e^{-\beta t}\right) \qquad \text{... (10.28)}$$

$$C_p = \frac{X_0}{V_p}\left(\frac{K_{21}}{\beta - \alpha} e^{-\alpha t} + \frac{K_{21}}{\alpha - \beta} e^{-\beta t}\right) \qquad \text{... (10.29)}$$

Where X_0 = I.V. bolus dose, α and β are hybrid first-order constants for the rapid distribution phase and the slow elimination phase respectively.

The constants K_{12} and K_{21} that depict reversible transfer of drug between compartments are called as micro constants or transfer constants.

The mathematical relationships between hybrid and micro constants are given as :

$$\alpha + \beta = K_{12} + K_{21} + K_E \qquad \text{... (10.30)}$$

$$\alpha\beta = K_{21} K_E \qquad \text{... (10.31)}$$

Equation (10.28) can be written in simplified form

$$C_c = Ae^{-\alpha t} + Be^{-\beta t} \qquad \text{... (10.32)}$$

∴ $\qquad C_c$ = Distribution exponent + Elimination exponent

Where A and B are also hybrid constants for the two exponents and can be resolved graphically by the method of residuals.

i.e. $\qquad A = \dfrac{X_0}{V_c}\left(\dfrac{K_{21} - \alpha}{\beta - \alpha}\right) = C_0\left(\dfrac{K_{21} - \alpha}{\beta - \alpha}\right) \qquad \text{... (10.33)}$

and $\qquad B = \dfrac{X_0}{V_c}\left(\dfrac{K_{21} - \beta}{\alpha - \beta}\right) = C_0\left(\dfrac{K_{21} - \alpha}{\alpha - \beta}\right) \qquad \text{... (10.34)}$

where, $\qquad C_0$ = Plasma drug concentration immediately after i.v. injection

10.5 THREE COMPARTMENT MODEL

- In three compartment modelling, three compartments describe rate of a drug once administered : Central compartment, which represent the organ and tissue is highly and scarcely perfused by the blood (Fig. 10.17).

- Significant distribution of drug in deep tissues such as bone or fat, or strong binding to any tissues, may results in the appearance of a **TRIEXPONENTAL** blood level curve, indicating the presence of a third compartment.

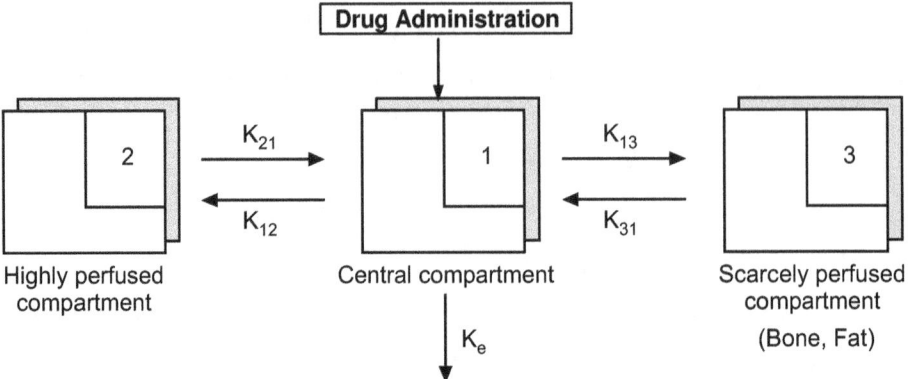

Fig. 10.17 : Three compartment open model

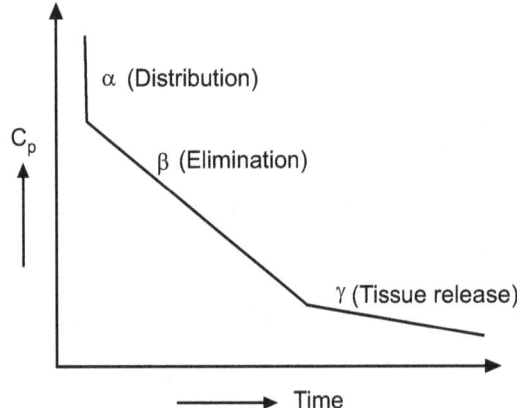

Fig. 10.18 : Semilog plot of C versus t of a drug with three compartment characteristics

$$C = A e^{-\alpha t} + B e^{-\beta t} + C e^{-\gamma t} \qquad \qquad ...(10.35)$$

Where, A, B, C are the intercept constant (m/lit.).

α, β, γ are the hybrid constant (T – 1).

The equation (10.35) is the same as the equation for two compartment model with an additional term (term 'C').

Three compartment model has been proposed for the several drugs like bihydroxycoumarin, turbocurarine etc.

10.6 MULTI-COMPARTMENTAL MODEL (Delayed distribution models)

The one compartment model adequately describes pharmacokinetics of many drugs.

Instantaneous distribution is assumed in such cases and decline in the amount of drug in the body with time is expressed by an equation with mono-exponential term. However, this is not possible in case of majority of drugs and also drug disposition is not always mono-exponential. It may be bi or multi-exponential.

This is because, the body is composed of a heterogeneous group of tissues each with different degree of blood flow and affinity for drug and therefore different rates of equilibration.

Ideally, a true pharmacokinetic model is one with a rate constant for each tissue undergoing equilibrium. However this approach is difficult mathematically.

The best approach is therefore to pool together the tissues on the basis of their distribution characteristics and group of tissues thus formed is called a *compartment*. So for particular drug there could be more than one compartment with difference in their distribution characteristics.

As in case of one compartment, drug distribution in multi-compartment model is also assumed to be of first order process. Multi-compartmental behaviour of drug can be well understood by giving drug as i.v. bolus and observing the manner in which its plasma concentration decrease with time.

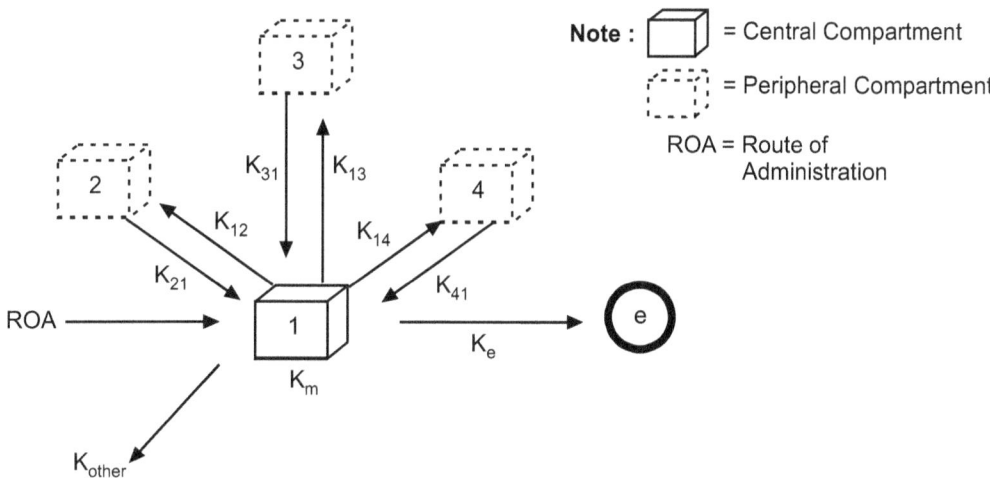

Fig. 10.19 : General multi-compartment pharmacokinetic model

10.7 METHOD OF RESIDUALS

The technique is also known as feathering, peeling and stripping.

For a drug that follows one-compartment kinetics and administered extra vascularlly, the time course of drug concentration in plasma is expressed by a bi-exponential equation (10.36).

$$C_p = \frac{K_a F X_0}{V_d (K_a - K_{el})} (e^{-K_{el} \cdot t} - e^{-K_a \cdot t}) \qquad \ldots (10.36)$$

Equation (10.36) can be written as

$$C_p = A \cdot e^{-K_{el} \cdot t} - A \cdot e^{-K_a \cdot t} \qquad \ldots (10.37)$$

where

$$A = \frac{K_a F X_0}{V_d (K_a - K_{el})}$$

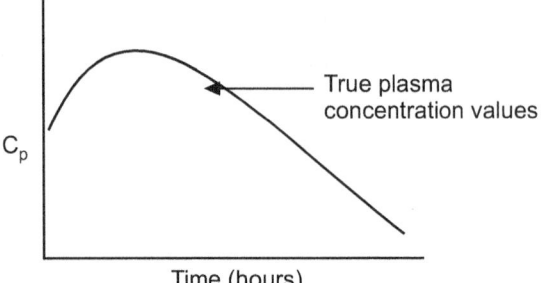

Fig. 10.20 : Semi-log plot C_p versus Time after oral administration

During the elimination phase, when absorption is almost over, ($K_a \gg K_{el}$) and the value of second exponential approaches zero ($e^{-K_a \cdot t}$) whereas the first exponentional ($e^{-k_{et}}$) retains some finite value.

At this time, the equation (10.37) reduced to

$$\overleftarrow{C_p} = A.e^{-K_{el}.t} \qquad \qquad ...(10.38)$$

where $\overleftarrow{C_p}$ represents the back extrapolated plasma concentration values.

A plot of log C_p versus t gives terminal linear phase having slope $= \dfrac{-K_{el}}{2.303}$.

Back extrapolation of this straight line to time zero yields y-intercept $=$ log A.

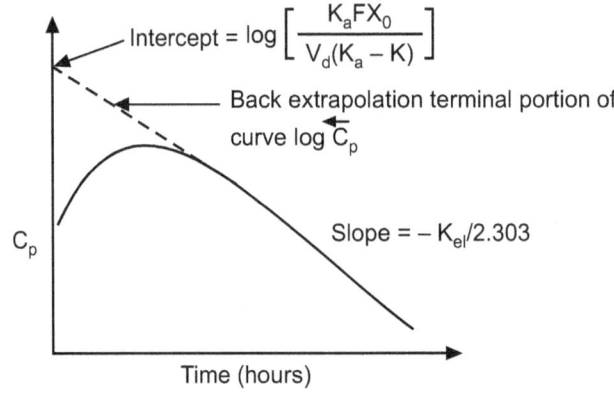

Fig. 10.21: Semi-log plot of C_p versus Time after oral administration of single dose

Subtracting true plasma concentration values i.e. equation (10.37) from extrapolated plasma concentration value i.e. equation (10.38) yields series of *residual concentration* values.

$$C_r = \overleftarrow{C_p} - C_p$$
$$C_r = A.e^{-K_a t} \qquad \qquad ...(10.39)$$

A plot of the C_r versus time should give another straight line graph with a slope equal to $-K_a/2.303$ and the same intercept as before, i.e. log A.

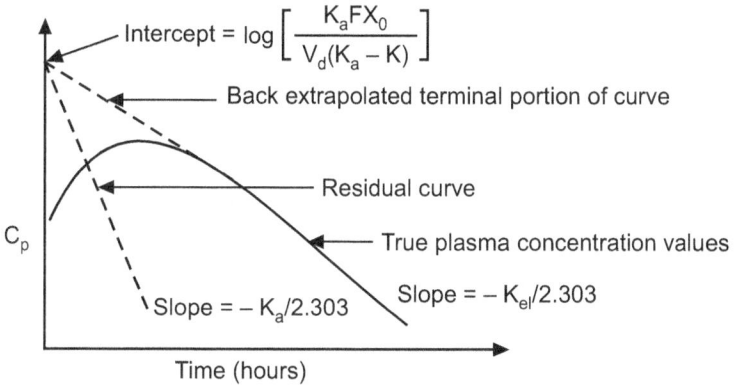

Fig. 10.22 : Semi-log plot of C_p versus time

From the slope, the absorption rate constant K_a can be estimated.

[I] Method of Residuals for Two Compartment Model

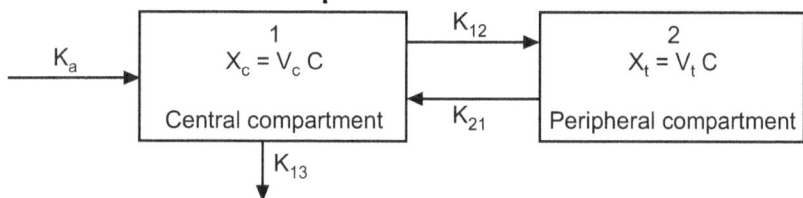

Fig. 10.23

There are three first order processes occurring simultaneously i.e. absorption, distribution and elimination.

Plasma concentration of the drug depends initially on three processes (three exponents), then on two processes of distribution and elimination (two exponentials) and finally on elimination process only (mono exponential).

$$C = C_0 \, e^{-k_a t} + A \, e^{-\alpha_t} + B \, e^{-\beta_t} \qquad \qquad \dots (10.40)$$

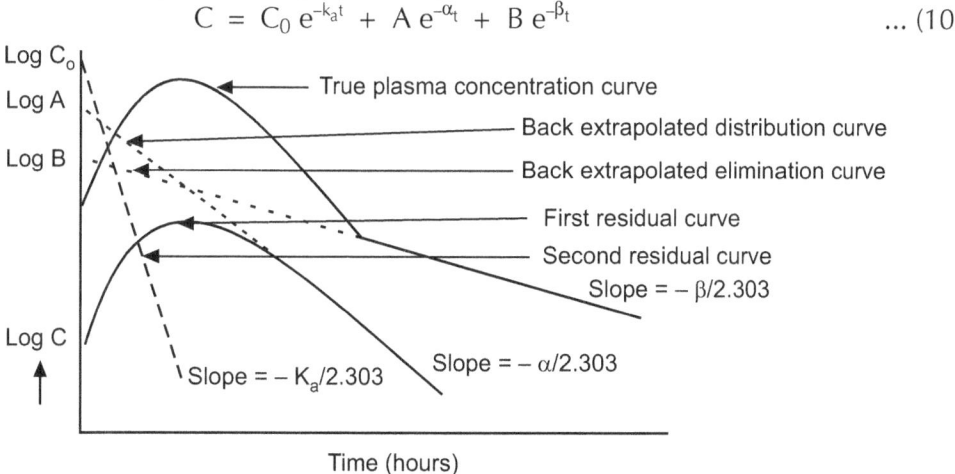

Fig. 10.24

$$A = \frac{X_o}{V_o} \frac{(\alpha - K_{12})}{(\alpha - \beta)} \qquad B = \frac{X_o}{V_o} \frac{(K_{12} - \beta)}{(\alpha - \beta)}$$

Applications:

To calculate absorption rate constant for a drug administered orally, absorbed by first order kinetics and confer the characteristics of one and two compartment open model.

Limitation:

The absorption is complex rather than a simple first order process.

Wanger-Nelson Method:

The Wanger-Nelson method of calculation does not require a model assumption concerning the absorption process.

The **assumptions** are :

(1) The body behaves as a single homogeneous compartment.

(2) Drug elimination obeys the first order kinetics.

For any extravascular administration,

The amount administered = The amount absorbed (A) + The Amount unabsorbed (U).

[The amount absorbed (A) to any time t] = [The amount of the drug in the body (X)]
     + [The amount of the drug eliminated from the body to any time, t (X_e)]

$$A = X + X_e \qquad \ldots (10.41)$$

Taking the derivative with respect to time

$$\frac{dA}{dt} = \frac{dX}{dt} + \frac{dX_e}{dt} \qquad \ldots (10.42)$$

But $X = V_d \cdot C$,

Hence
$$\frac{dX}{dt} = V_d \cdot \frac{dC}{dt}$$

and
$$\frac{dX_e}{dt} = KX$$

$$\therefore \qquad \frac{dX_e}{dt} = K.V_d.C$$

$$\therefore \qquad \frac{dA}{dt} = V_d \cdot \frac{dC}{dt} + K.V_d.C \qquad \ldots (10.43)$$

$$dA = V_d.dC + K.V_d.C.dt$$

Integrating equation (10.43) between limits t = 0 to t = t gives,

$$\int_0^t dA = V_d \int_0^t dC + K.V_d. \int_0^t C.dt$$

$$A_t - A_0 = V_d|C_t - C_o| + K.V_d \int_0^t C.dt$$

A_0 = amount of drug absorbed at t = 0 is zero, and C_0 = 0.

So, $$A_t = V_d.C_t + K.V_d \int_0^t C.dt$$

Rearranging the above equation

$$\frac{A_t}{V_d} = C_t + K.\int_0^t C.dt \qquad \qquad ... (10.44)$$

Where, $\frac{A_t}{V_d}$ = The amount of drug absorbed upto time t divided by the volume of distribution.

C_t = plasma concentration at time t

$$\int_0^t C.dt = AUC \text{ upto time t.}$$

Integrating equation (10.43) between the limits of t = 0 to t = ∞.
And rearranging the equation, gives

$$\int_0^\infty dA = V_d\int_0^\infty dC + K.V_d.\int_0^\infty C.dt$$

$$A_\infty = V_d.(C_\infty - C_0) + K.V_d. \int_0^\infty C.dt \qquad \qquad [\text{but } C_\infty = 0, C_0 = 0]$$

∴ $$\frac{A_\infty}{V_d} = K \int_0^\infty C.dt \qquad \qquad ... (10.45)$$

Where, $\frac{A_\infty}{V_d} = \dfrac{\text{The total amount of drug absorbed from the dosage form upto infinity time}}{\text{The volume of the distribution of the drug}}$

$$\int_0^\infty C.dt = AUC \text{ upto } \infty$$

The fraction of absorbed drug at any time is obtained when equation (10.44) is divided by equation 10.45.

$$\frac{A_t}{A_\infty} = \left(\frac{C_t + K\int_0^\infty C.dt}{K\int_0^\infty Cdt} \right) \qquad \qquad ... (10.46)$$

The fraction of unabsorbed drug at any time t is

$$1 - \frac{A_t}{A_\infty} = 1 - \left(\frac{C_t + K\int_0^t C.dt}{K\int_0^\infty C.dt} \right) \qquad \qquad ... (10.47)$$

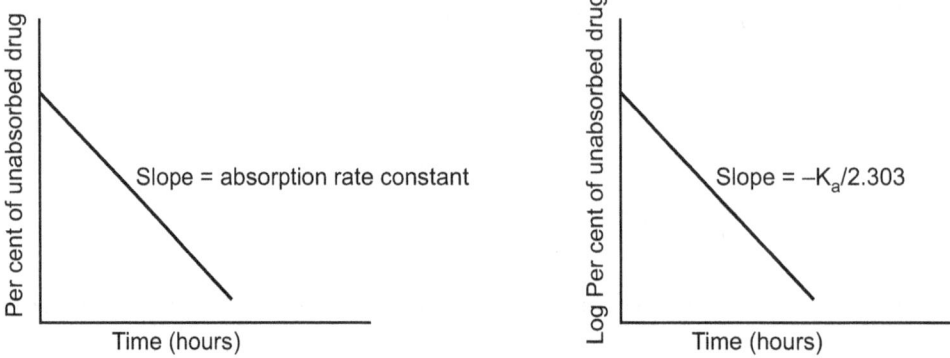

Fig. 10.25 : Per cent of unabsorbed drug versus time plot - Zero order

Fig. 10.26 : Logarithm per cent of unabsorbed drug versus time plot - First order

Application:

To understand the absorption kinetics without prior assumption.

Limitation:

It applies rigorously only to the drugs with one compartmental characteristics.

However, when concentration vs time curve after oral administration shows multi-compartmental characteristics and on I.V. administration shows one compartmental model, analysis by this method may gives incorrect result.

Loo-Riegelman Method

Loo-Riegelman method is useful in determining the absorption rate constant for a drug which follows a two compartment model.

It requires the plasma concentration time data after I.V. bolus and oral administration to obtain all necessary kinetic constants.

This method can be applied to drug that can be distributed by any number of compartments.

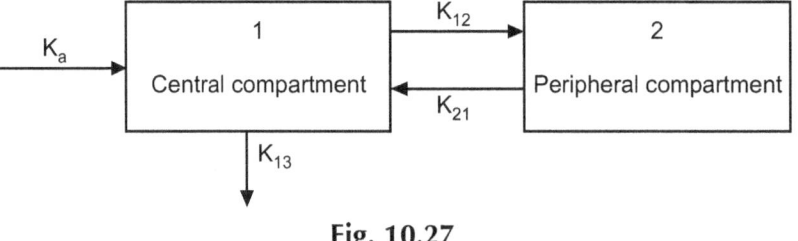

Fig. 10.27

$$A_b = X_c + X_t + X_3 \qquad \qquad \ldots (10.48)$$

where

$$X_c = V_c \cdot C_p$$

$$X_t = V_t \cdot Ct$$

$$X_3 = V_c \cdot K_{13} \int C.dt = V_c \cdot K_{13}.[AUC]_0^t$$

Substituting values of X_c and X_3 into equation (10.48)

$$Ab = V_c.C_p + Xt + V_c.K_{13}.[AUC]_0^t \qquad \text{... (10.49)}$$

Dividing the equation (10.49) by V_c, we get

$$\frac{Ab}{V_c} = C_p + \frac{X_t}{V_c} + K_{13}[AUC]_0^t \qquad \text{... (10.50)}$$

Setting the value of $t = \infty$, this equation becomes

$$\frac{Ab^\infty}{V_c} = 0 + 0 + K_{13}[AUC]_0^\infty$$

$$\frac{Ab^\infty}{V_c} = K_{13}[AUC]_0^\infty \qquad \text{... (10.51)}$$

Where, Ab^∞ is the amount of the drug that will be ultimately absorbed from the dosage form.

$$F = \frac{Ab^\infty}{X_0} \qquad \text{... (10.52)}$$

The fraction of the dose absorbed at any time in comparison with Ab^∞ can be obtained by dividing the equation (10.50) by equation (10.51).

$$\frac{Ab}{Ab^\infty} = \frac{C + \dfrac{X_t}{V_c} + K_{13}(AUC)_0^t}{K_{13}(AUC)_0^\infty} \qquad \text{... (10.53)}$$

where, $\dfrac{X_t}{V_c} = C_t =$ Tissue concentration

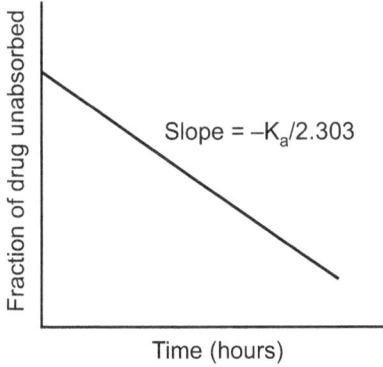

Fig. 10.28 : **Absorption rate constant by Loo-Riegelman method**

$$(C_t)_n = \frac{K_{12} \, \Delta C_p \, \Delta t}{2} + \frac{K_{12}}{K_{21}} (C_p)t_{n-1} \left(1 - e^{-K_{21}\Delta t}\right) + (C_t)t_{n-1} \, e^{-K_{21}\Delta t}$$

$$\text{... (10.54)}$$

Where

C_t =   Apparent tissue concentration

t_n =   Time of sampling for sample n

t_{n-1} =   Time of sampling for the sampling point preceding sample n

$(C_p)t_{n-1}$ =   Concentration of drug at in central compartment for sample n–1.

ΔC_p =   Concentration difference at central compartment between two sampling times.

Δt =   Time difference between two sampling times.

Applications:

- Loo Riegelman method is applicable for the drugs that confers multi-compartmental characteristics.

Limitations:

- It requires the concentration vs time data of both oral and IV administration of drug to same subject.

- An inherent limitation of this method is intra subject variability between oral and IV administration studies. The assumption can be made that kinetics of drug distribution and elimination remain unchanged in interval between doses.

10.8 NON-COMPARTMENTAL ANALYSIS

The **non-compartmental analysis**, also called as the **model-independent method**, does not require the assumption of specific compartment model. This method is, however, based on the assumption that the drugs or metabolites follow linear kinetics, and on this basis, this technique can be applied to any compartment model.

The non-compartmental approach, based on the **statistical moments theory**, involves collection of experimental data following a single dose of drug. If one considers the time course of drug concentration in plasma as a statistical distribution curve, then :

$$MRT = \frac{AUMC}{AUC}$$

$$AUMC = \int_{0}^{\infty} C_t \, dt$$

where,   MRT = Mean residence time

AUMC = Area under the *first-moment curve*

AUC = Area under the *zero-moment curve*

AUMC is obtained from a plot of product of plasma drug concentration and time (i.e. C.t) versus time t from zero to infinity.

AUC is obtained from a plot of plasma drug concentration versus time from zero to infinity. Mathematically, it is expressed by equation

$$AUC = \int_{0}^{\infty} C \, dt$$

Practically, the AUMC and AUC can be calculated from the respective graphs by the **trapezoidal rule**.

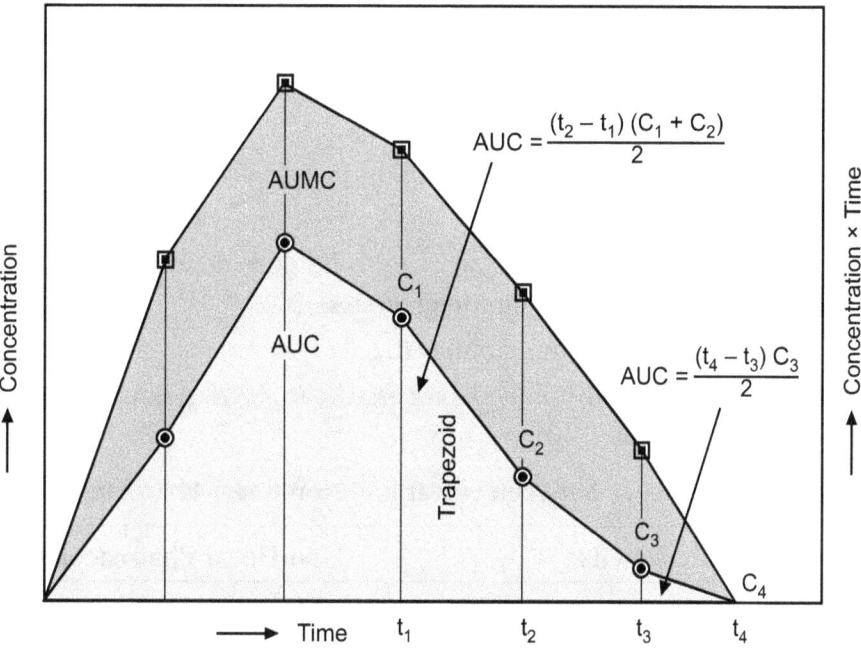

Fig. 10.29 : AUC and AUMC plots

Applications :

- It is widely used to estimate the important pharmacokinetic parameters like bioavailability, clearance and apparent volume of distribution.
- The method is also useful in determining half-life, rate of absorption and first-order absorption rate constant of the drug.

❖❖❖

Chapter 11

NON-LINEAR PHARMACOKINETICS

11.1 INTRODUCTION

Linear pharmacokinetic models were introduced to describe the drug disposition and action, and assumed that the pharmacokinetic parameters for a drug would not change when different doses or multiple doses of a drug were given. But in some drugs, if dose is increased can cause deviation from linear pharmacokinetics profile as compared to previously observed with single low dose of same drug.

In such cases essentially first order kinetic transforms into a mixture of first order and zero order rate processes.

The pharmacokinetics of such drugs are said to be **dose-dependent**. Other terms are **mixed-order**, **non-linear** and **capacity-limited kinetics**.

For example; vitamin C, naproxen, riboflavin.

The kinetics of such capacity limited processes can be described by the Michaelis-Menten kinetics.

Table 11.1: Difference between Linear and Non-linear Pharmacokinetics

Linear Pharmacokinetics	Non-Linear Pharmacokinetics
Pharmacokinetic parameters for a drug would not change with change in dose.	Pharmacokinetic parameters for a drug can change with change in dose.
Dose independent.	Dose dependent.
First order kinetics.	Also called as mixed order, saturated kinetics, capacity limited.
All semilog plots of C Vs. t for different doses are superimposable.	Not superimposable.

11.1.1 Detection of Non-linearity in Pharmacokinetics

Non-linear pharmacokinetic is detected by two ways :

1) **First:** Determination of steady state plasma concentration at different doses.

2) **Second:** Determination of some important pharmacokinetic parameters such as fraction bioavailability, elimination half life or total systemic clearance at different doses of drugs.

11.2 CAUSES OF NON-LINEARITY

➢ **Drug Absorption**

- Non-linearity in drug absorption can arise from 3 important sources :

  o *When absorption is solubility or dissolution rate-limited* e.g. griseofulvin. At higher doses, a saturated solution of the drug is formed in the GIT or at any other extravascular site and the rate of absorption attains a constant value.

  o *When absorption involves carrier-mediated transport systems* e.g. absorption of riboflavin, ascorbic acid, cyanocobalamin etc. Saturation of the transport system at higher doses of these vitamins results in non-linearity.

  o *When presystemic gut wall or hepatic metabolism attains saturation* e.g. propranolol, hydralazine and verapamil. Saturation of presystemic metabolism of these drugs at high doses leads to increased bioavailability.

➢ **Drug Distribution**

- Non-linearity in distribution of drugs administered at high doses may be due to :

  o *Saturation of binding sites on plasma proteins* e.g. phenylbutazone and naproxen. There is a finite number of binding sites for a particular drug on plasma proteins and theoretically as the concentration is raised, so more fractions are remain unbound.

  o *Saturation of tissue binding sites* e.g. Thiopental and fentanyl. With large single bolus doses or multiple dosing, saturation of tissue storage sites can occur.

➢ **Drug Metabolism**

- The non-linear kinetics of most clinical importance is capacity-limited metabolism since small changes in dose administered can produce large variations in plasma concentration at steady-state. It is a major source of large intersubject variability in pharmacological response.

  Two important causes of non-linearity in metabolism are :

  o *Capacity-limited metabolism due to enzyme or cofactor saturation.* Examples include phenytoin, alcohol, theophylline etc.

  o *Enzyme induction* e.g. carbamazepine, where a decrease in peak plasma concentration has been observed on repetitive administration over a period of time. Autoinduction characterized in this case is also dose-dependent. Thus, enzyme induction is a common cause of both dose and time-dependent kinetics.

➢ **Drug Excretion**

- Two active processes in renal excretion of a drug are :

  - *Active tubular secretion* e.g. penicillin G. After saturation of the carrier system, a decrease in renal clearance occurs.

- *Active tubular reabsorption* e.g. water soluble vitamins and glucose. After saturation of the carrier system, an increase in renal clearance occurs.

Table 11.2 : Examples of Drugs Showing Non-linear Kinetics

Non-linear Kinetics	Examples
GI Absorption:	
Absorption is carrier mediated.	Riboflavin, Gebapentin, L-dopa, Baclofen, ceftbuten.
Drugs with low solubility in GI but relatively high dose.	Chorothiazide, Griseofulvin, Danazol
Presystemic hepatic metabolism attains saturation.	Propranolol
Distribution :	
Saturable plasma protein binding	Phenylbutazone, Lidocaine, Salicylic acid, Ceftriaxone, Diazoxide, Phenytoin, Warfarin, Disopyramide
Cellular uptake	Methicillin (rabbit)
Tissue binding	Imiprimine (rat)
Saturable transport into or out of tissues	Methotrexate
Renal Elimination :	
Active secretion	Mezlocillin, Para-aminohippuric acid
Tubular reabsorption	Riboflavin, Ascorbic acid, Cephapirin
Change in urine pH	Salicylic acid, Dextroamphetamine
Metabolism :	
Saturable metabolism	Phenytoin, Salicyclic acid, Theophylline, Valproic acid
Cofactor or enzyme limitation	Acetaminophen, Alcohol
Enzyme induction	Carbamazepine
Altered hepatic blood flow	Propranolol, Verapamil
Metabolite inhibition	Diazepam

Biliary Excretion :	
Biliary secretion	Iodipamide, Sulfobromophthalein sodium
Enterohepatic recycling	Cimetidine, Isotretinoin

➤ **Drugs that demonstrate saturation kinetics usually show the following characteristics:**

1. Elimination of drug does not follow simple first-order kinetics — that is, elimination kinetics are non-linear.

2. The elimination half-life changes as dose is increased. Usually, the elimination half-life increases with increased dose due to saturation of an enzyme system. However, the elimination half-life might decrease due to "self induction" of liver biotransformation enzymes, as is observed for carbamazepine.

3. The area under the curve (AUC) is not proportional to the amount of bioavailable drug.

4. The saturation of capacity-limited processes may be affected by other drugs that require the same enzyme or carrier-mediated system (i.e. competition effects).

5. The composition or ratio of the metabolites of a drug may be affected by a change in the dose.

• **Large dose** curve is obtained with an initial slow elimination phase followed by a much more rapid elimination at lower blood concentrations (curve A).

• **Small dose** apparent first-order kinetics are observed, because no saturation kinetics occur (curve B).

• If the pharmacokinetic data were estimated only from the blood levels described by curve B, then a twofold increase in the dose would give the blood profile presented in curve C, which considerably underestimates the drug concentration as well as the duration of action.

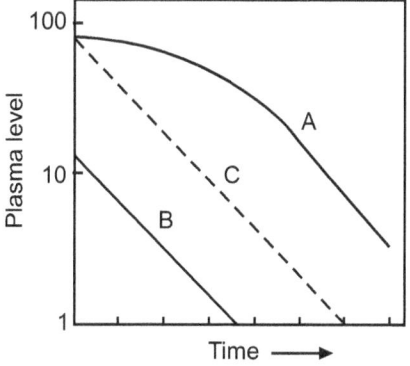

Curve A = Saturated kinetics
Curve B = No saturation
Curve C = Dose independent kinetics

Fig. 11.1

A plot of the areas under the plasma level–time curves at various doses should be linear.

11.3 MICHAELIS MENTEN EQUATION

The kinetics of capacity-limited or saturable processes is described by Michaelis-Menten equation :

$$-\frac{dC}{dt} = \frac{V_{max}\,C}{K_m + C} \qquad \qquad ...\,(11.1)$$

Where, $-dC/dt$ = Rate of decline of drug concentration with time,

$\qquad$ V_{max} = Theoretical maximum rate of the process, and

$\qquad$ K_m = Michaelis constant.

Three situations can now be considered depending upon the values of K_m and C:

1. **When $K_m = C$:**

   Under this situation, the equation (11.1) reduces to :

   $$-\frac{dC}{dt} = \frac{V_{max}}{2}$$

   The rate of process is equal to one half of its maximum rate (Fig. 11.2).

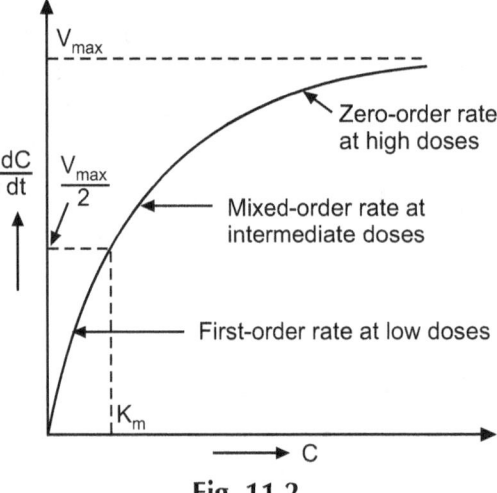

Fig. 11.2

2. **When $K_m \gg C$:**

   Here, $\qquad$ $K_m + C = K_m$ and the equation (11.1) reduces to :

   $$-\frac{dC}{dt} = \frac{V_{max}\,C}{K_m}$$

   The above equation describes first order elimination of a drug where $\dfrac{V_{max}}{K_m} = K_E$.

   e.g. Phenytoin, alcohol

3. **When $K_m \ll C$:**

Under this condition, $K_m + C_o\ C$ and the equation (11.1) will become

$$-\frac{dC}{dt} = V_{max}$$

Above equation is identical to equation of zero order process. Rate process occurs at a constant rate and is independent of drug concentration.

11.3.1 Estimation of K_m and V_{max} :

Parameters of capacity limited processes like metabolism, secretion and excretion can be easily defined by assuming one-compartment kinetics for drug.

After I.V. bolus administration of a drug with non-linear elimination, equation is as below:

$$\frac{-dC}{dt} = \frac{V_{max}\ C}{K_m + C}$$

Converting the above equation in logarithmic form, we get

$$\log C = \log C_o - \frac{V_{max}}{2.303\ K_m}$$

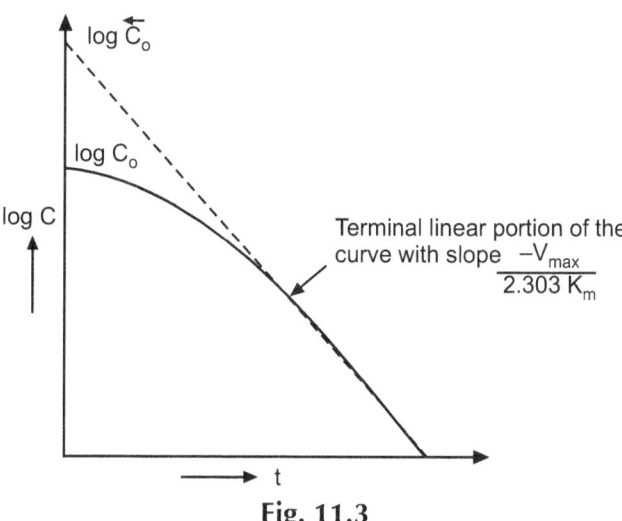

Fig. 11.3

Integration of Michaelis Menten Equation :

$$\log C = \log C_o + \frac{(C_o - C)}{2.303\ K_m} - \frac{V_{max}}{2.303\ K_m}$$

Semilog plot of C Vs. t yields a curve with terminal linear portion, which on back extrapolation to time zero give y-intercept $\log C_o$.

$$\log C = \log C_o - \frac{V_{max}}{2.303\ K_m}$$

At low plasma concentration

$$\frac{(C_o - C)}{2.303\ K_m} = \frac{\log C_o}{C_o}$$

So K_m can be obtained from this equation while V_{max} can be obtained from slope by putting value of K_m.

11.3.2 Estimation of K_m and V_{max} (Steady State)

In case of I.V. infusion a steady state concentration is maintained by a suitable dosing rate (DR).

$$DR = C_{SS}\ Cl_T$$

This DR at steady state equals rate of elimiantion.

So Michaclis Menten equation can be written as

$$DR = \frac{V_{max}\ (C_{SS})}{K_m + (C_{SS})}$$

Plot of C_{SS} versus DR yield a typical hockey stike shaped curve as shown in Fig. 11.4.

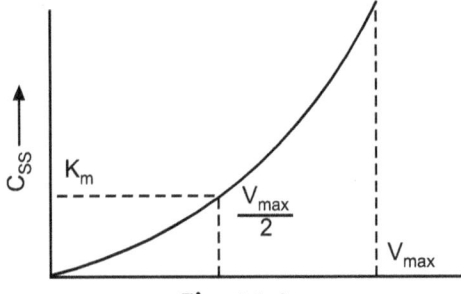

Fig. 11.4

Practically K_m and V_{max} are computed in different ways as given below:

(1) Lineweaver - Burke plot :

$$V = \frac{V_{max}\ C}{K_m + C}$$

$$\frac{1}{V} = \frac{K_m}{V_{max}}\frac{1}{C} + \frac{1}{V_{max}}$$

Plot of $\dfrac{1}{V}$ versus $\dfrac{1}{C}$ yield a straight line with y-intercept $= \dfrac{1}{V_{max}}$ and slope $= \dfrac{K_m}{V_{max}}$.

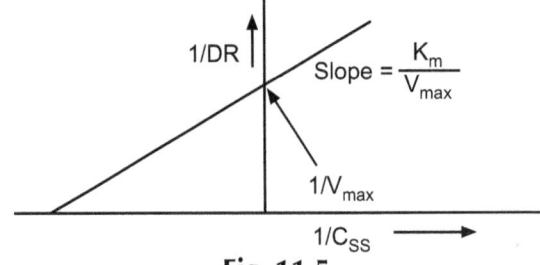

Fig. 11.5

Disadvantage:

The points are clustered.

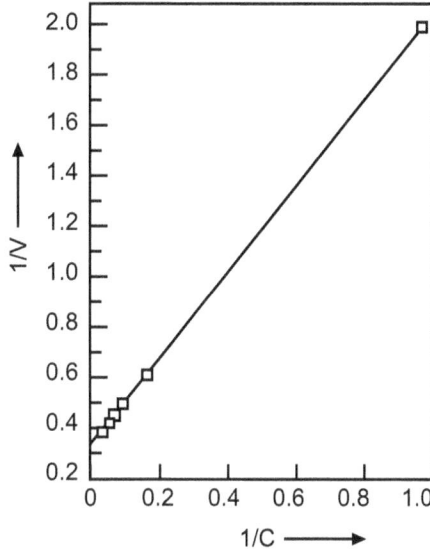

Fig. 11.6

(2) Plot of C/V versus C :

$$V = \frac{V_{max} C}{K_m + C}$$

$$\therefore \qquad \frac{C}{V} = \frac{1}{V_{max}} C + \frac{K_m}{V_{max}}$$

- Yield a straight line.
- Slope = $1/V_{max}$
- Intercept = K_m/V_{max}

(3) Plot of V Vs. V/C :

$$V = \frac{V_{max} C}{K_m + C}$$

$$\therefore \qquad V = -K_m + \frac{V}{C} + V_{max}$$

- Slope = $-K_m$
- Intercept = V_{max}

(4) From steady state plasma drug concentration :

$$R = \frac{V_{max} C_{ss}}{K_m + C_{ss}}$$

- At steady state:

  Rate of drug metabolism (v) = Rate of drug input R (dose/day).

- Inverting above equation :

$$\frac{1}{R} = \frac{K_m}{V_{max}} \frac{1}{C_{ss}} + \frac{1}{V_{max}}$$

A plot of R versus C_{ss} is plotted and following steps are followed :

1. Mark points for R of 300 mg/day and C_{ss} of 25.1 mg/l as shown. Connect with a straight line.

2. Mark points for R of 150 mg/day and C_{ss} of 8.6 mg/l as shown. Connect with a straight line.

3. Where lines from the first two steps cross, is called point A.

4. From point A, read V_{max} on the y-axis and K_m on the x-axis.

Typical example is shown in below Fig. 11.7.

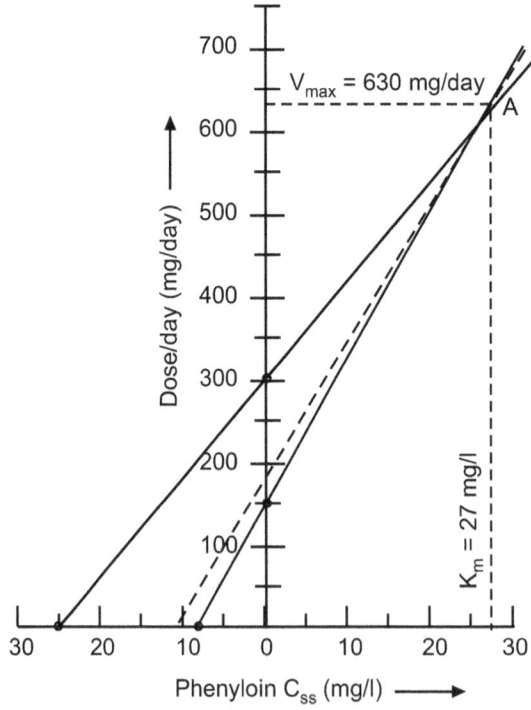

Fig. 11.7

(5) **Direct method :**

- This method is used when there are only two dose levels :

$$R_1 = \frac{V_{max} C_1}{K_m + C_1}$$

$$R_2 = \frac{V_{max} C_2}{K_m + C_2}$$

- Combining two equations :

$$K_m = \frac{R_2 - R_1}{(R_1/C_1) - (R_2/C_2)}$$

- C_1 is steady-state plasma drug concentration after dose 1,

- C_2 is steady-state plasma drug concentration after dose 2,

- R_1 is the first dosing rate,

- R_2 is the second dosing rate.

K_m and V_{max} are estimated by one compartment system and single capacity limited process. K_m and V_{max} will be large when following conditions occur:

1. The drug is estimated by more than one capacity limited process.

2. The drugs exhibit parallel capacity limited and first order elimination processes.

3. The drug follow multicompartment kinetics.

However K_m and V_{max} obtained under such circumstances have little practical application in dosage calculations.

Drugs that behave non-linearly within therapeutic range yield less predictable results in drug therapy and produce greater potential in precipitating toxic effects.

11.3.3 Interpretation of K_m and V_{max}

- An understanding of Michaelis–Menten kinetics provides insight into the non-linear kinetics and helps to avoid dosing a drug at a concentration near enzyme saturation.

    For example; Concentration = 8.6 mg/lit.

    $$K_m = 27.3 \text{ mg/lit.}$$

    $$\text{Dose} = 300 \text{ mg/day}$$
    $$V_{max} = 626 \text{ mg/day}$$

    50% V_{max}, i.e., 0.5×626 mg/day or 313 mg/day.

Subject is receiving 300 mg of phenytoin per day, the plasma drug concentration of phenytoin is 8.6 mg/lit, which is considerably below the K_m of 27.3 mg/lit.

- Fig. 11.8 shows the rate of metabolism.

  When V_{max} is constant (8 g/ml/hr) K_m is changed.

  $K_m = 2$ g/ml for top curve.

  $K_m = 4$ g/ml for bottom curve.

  The rate of metabolism is faster for the lower K_m, but saturation starts at lower concentration.

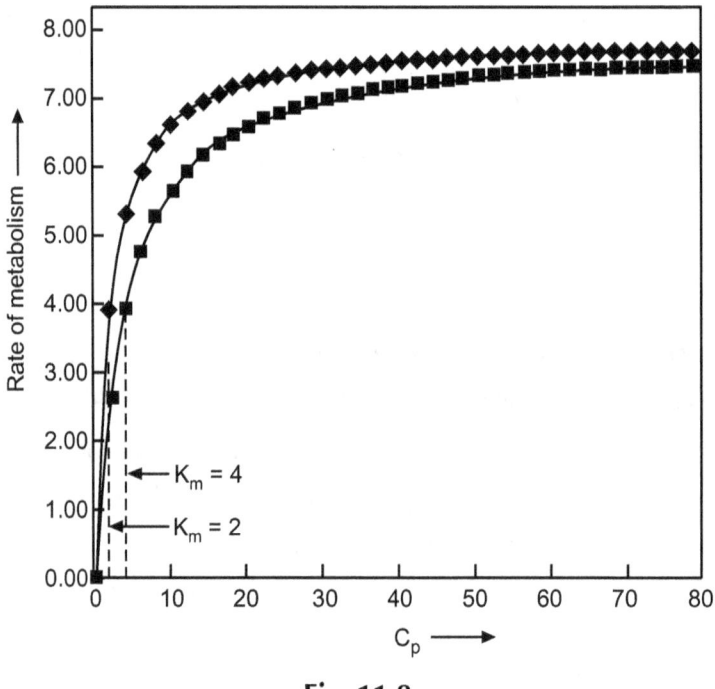

Fig. 11.8

Non-linear pharmakokinetics is dose dependent and does not occur significantly at lower dose of drug. Probable reasons to occur may be attributed to change in physiologic system, saturation, protein binding or enzyme induction.

Chapter 12

IN VIVO IN VITRO CORRELATION (IVIVC)

12.1 INTRODUCTION

According to USP : "Establishment of a rational relationship between a biological property or a parameter derived from a biological property produced by a dosage form and a physicochemical property of the same dosage form" is called *In vivo-In vitro* Correlation.

According to FDA : "A predictive mathematical model describing the relationship between an *in vitro* property of a dosage form and a relevant *in vivo* response" is called *In vivo In vitro* correlation.

Generally the *in vivo* property is the rate of extent of drug dissolution or release while the *in vivo* response is the plasma drug concentration or amount of drug absorbed.

IVIVC plays important role in product development :

1) Surrogate of *in vivo* and assists in supporting Biowaivers.
2) Supports or validates the use of dissolution method and specification.
3) Assists in quality control during manufacturing and selecting appropriate formulation.

12.2 CRITERIA FOR IVIVC

- Successful IVIVC can be developed when *in vitro dissolution is rate limiting step* in absorption and appearance of drug while in *in vivo* circulation following different routes of administration.
- These *studies are to be conducted during the early stages of drug product development* in order to select the most effective formulation and to establish appropriate dosage regimen.
- The release-controlling excipients in the formulations should either be identical or very similar.

12.3 OBJECTIVES OF IVIVC

- To reduce the number of human studies during the formulation development.
- To serve as a surrogate for *in vivo* bioavailability.
- To support biowaivers.
- To validate the use of dissolution methods and specification settings (IVIVC includes *in vivo* relevance to *in vitro* dissolution specifications).
- To assist quality control for certain scale-up and post-approval changes (SUPAC).
- Due to all above objectives, such IVIVC leads to

- o Shortens the drug development period,
- o Economizes the resources, and
- o Leads to improved product quality.

12.4 SOME COMMON TERMS

- **Mean Absorption Time:** The mean time required for drug to reach systemic circulation from the time of drug administration.

$$MAT = MRT_{oral} - MRT_{i.v.}$$

- **Mean *In Vivo* Dissolution Time:** It reflects the mean time for drug to dissolve *in vivo*, for solid dosage form.

$$MDT_{solid} = MRT_{solid} - MRT_{solution}$$

- **Mean Residence Time:** The mean time that the drug resides in the body. Also known as mean transit time.

$$MRT = \frac{AUMC}{AUC}$$

Where, AUMC = Area under first moment curve (Concentration × Time Vs. Time)

AUC = Area under curve (Concentration Vs. Time)

- **Per Cent Prediction Error:**

$$\% \ PE = \left(\frac{Observed \ value - Predicted \ value}{Observed \ value}\right) \times 100$$

12.5 LEVELS OF CORRELATION

- There are five levels of IVIVC, which include levels A, B, C, multiple C and D.

1. Level A Correlation

- This level of correlation is the highest category of correlation.
- Level A represents a point-to-point relationship between *in vitro* dissolution and *in vivo* dissolution (absorption rate).

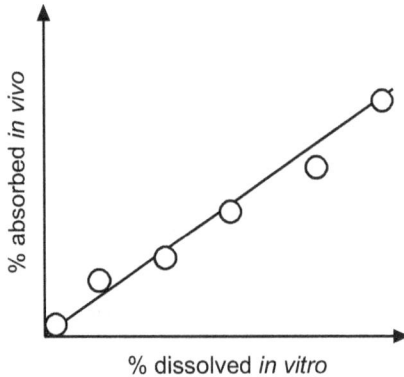

Fig. 12.1: Level A correlation

- Level A IVIVC is also viewed as a predictive model for the relationship between the entire *in vitro release time* and entire *in vivo response time*.
- This is also called as Wagner-Nelson method or Loo-Reigleman or Deconvolution method.
- Comparison of fraction of drug absorbed and fraction of drug dissolved *in vitro* is done to obtain a linear correlation. Since it allows biowaiving for changes in manufacturing site, raw material supplier and minor change in formulation. So, level A correlation is most preferred to achieve.

2. Level B Correlation

- It is a predictive mathematical model which compares the

  $$MDT_{vitro} \rightarrow MRT_{vivo},$$

  $$k_d \rightarrow k_a.$$

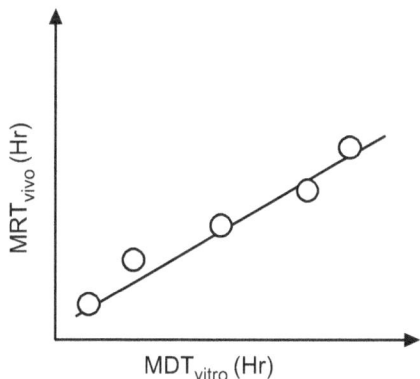

Fig. 12.2: Level B Correlation

- *In vitro* data can not be used for quality control standards.
- Hence, it is least useful for regulatory purpose.
- This type of correlation uses all of the *in vitro* and *in vivo* data; thus, it is not considered as a point-to-point correlation.
- This is of limited interest and use because more than one kind of plasma curve produces similar mean residence time.

3. Level C Correlation

- It is a predictive mathematical model of relationship between time required for *in vitro* dissolution of a fixed per cent of dose ($t_{50\%}$, $t_{90\%}$) and a mean pharmacokinetic parameter such as C_{max}, T_{max}, $t_{1/2}$ or AUC.
- This is the weakest level of correlation as partial relationship between absorption and dissolution is established since it does not reflect the complex shape of plasma drug concentration vs. time curve, which is the critical factor that defines the performance of a drug product.

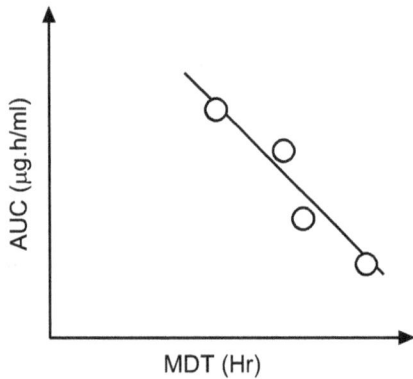

Fig. 12.3: Level C Correlation

Table 12.1: Overview of level A, B, C

Level	*In vitro*	*In vivo*
A	Dissolution curve	Absorption curves
B	Statistical Moments: MDT	Statistical Moments: MRT, MAT etc.
C	Disintegration time to have 10, 50, 90% drug dissolved, Dissolution rate, Dissolution efficiency are parameters taken in consideration.	C_{max}, T_{max}, K_a and AUC at 10, 50, 90 % drug absorbed. Parameter taken in consideration is AUC (total or cumulative).

Multiple Level C Correlations

- It relates one or more pharmacokinetic parameters (C_{max}, T_{max}, K_a) to the amount of drug dissolved at several time points of dissolution profile.
- If a multiple level C correlation exists, there is a possibility of Level A correlation.
- Justification of a biowaiver.

4. Level D Correlation

- Level D correlation is a qualitative analysis and is not considered useful for regulatory purposes.
- It is not a formal correlation but serves as an aid in the development of a formulation or processing procedure.

12.6 IMPORTANT CONSIDERATIONS IN DEVELOPING A CORRELATION

- When the dissolution is not influenced by factors such as *pH, surfactants, osmotic pressure, mixing intensity, enzyme, ionic strength*, a set of dissolution data obtained from one formulation is correlated with a deconvoluted plasma concentration-time data set.

- In a linear correlation, the *in vitro* dissolution and *in vivo* input curves may be directly superimposable or may be made to be superimposable by the use of appropriate *scaling factor* (time corrections). Time scaling factor should be the same for all formulations.

- If one or more formulations may not illustrate the same relationship between *in vitro* performance and *in vivo* profiles compared with the other formulations, the correlation is still valid within the range of release rate covered by remaining formulation.

- The *in vitro* dissolution methodology should be able to adequately discriminate between the study formulations.

- During the early stages of correlation development, dissolution conditions may be altered to attempt to develop a one-to-one correlation between the *in vitro* dissolution profile and the *in vivo* dissolution profile.

- An established correlation is valid only for a specific type of pharmaceutical dosage form (tablets, gelatin capsules etc.) with a particular release mechanism (matrix, osmotic system etc.) and particular additives.

- The release rates, as measured by per cent dissolved, for each formulation studied, should differ adequately (For exmaple; by 10%, 20% etc.).

12.7 BIO-PHARMACEUTICS CLASSIFICATION SYSTEM (BCS)

- Drug Development Tool allowing the estimation of contribution of three fundamental factors.

- Bio-pharmaceutics classification system govern the rate and extent of drug absorption from solid dosage form and also used to determine *in vitro* dissolution specification.
  1. Dissolution
  2. Solubility
  3. Intestinal Permeability

- BCS is a fundamental guideline for determining the condition under which *in vitro in vivo* correlations are expected.

- BCS deals with the dissolution and absorption model which considers the key parameters such as -
  1. Absorption Number (A_n)
  2. Dissolution Number (D_n)
  3. Dose Number (D_o)

Absorption Number (A_n)

- Ratio of Mean Residence Time (T_{res}) to Mean Absorption Time (T_{abs}).

$$A_n = \frac{T_{res}}{T_{abs}}$$

Dissolution Number (D_n)

- Ratio of Mean Residence Time (T_{res}) to Mean Dissolution Time (T_{diss}).

$$D_n = \frac{T_{res}}{T_{diss}}$$

Dose Number (D_o)

- Dose number is the mass divided by an uptake volume of 250 ml and the drug's solubility.

$$D_o = \frac{Dose}{V_o \times C_{Smin}}$$

V_o = Initial gastric volume = 250 ml

C_{Smin} = Aqueous solubility in physiological pH range.

Fraction of dose absorbed is estimated from above these three parametres.

Table 12.2 : BCS and IVIVC Expectations

Class	Solubility	Permeability	IVIVC expectation
I	High	High	If dissolution rate is slower than gastric emptying rate.
II	Low	High	If *in vitro* dissolution rate is similar to *in vivo* dissolution rate.
III	High	Low	Absorption/permeability is rate determining and limited or no correlation with dissolution rate.
IV	Low	Low	Limited or no IVIVC expected.

12.8 LEVELS IN METHODOLOGY

[I] Level A Methodology

- The purpose of this level is to define a direct relationship between *in vivo* and *in vitro* data so that the measurement of only *in vitro* dissolution rate is sufficient to give the biopharmaceutical fate of the dosage form.

Predictability of Level A Correlations

- IVIVC predicts the *in vivo* bioavailability results from the *in vitro* dissolution data.
- Error associated with this prediction must be known and it is evaluated using the two types of predictability :
  - Internal predictability
  - External predictability

- Internal predictability is based on Initial Data.
- External predictability is based on a New Set of Data (New Formulations).

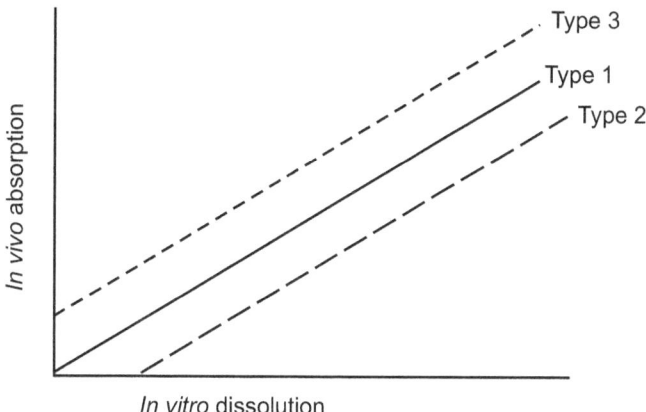

Fig. 12.4: Linear relationship in Level A Corelation

Internal Predictability

- Established for each formulation.
- Determination of prediction error.
- Acceptable when the Average per cent prediction error (Avg. % prediction error) is below 10% for C_{max} and AUC. None of the formulation shows more than 15% prediction error.
- Prediction Error (%PE)

$$= \frac{C_{max\,(observed)} - C_{max\,(predicted)}}{C_{max\,(observed)}} \times 100$$

$$= \frac{AUC_{observed} - AUC_{predicted}}{AUC_{observed}} \times 100$$

External Predictability

- Very Important.
- Demonstrates real predictive power of the IVIVC method.
- Validation process.
- Independent release requires only one formulation.
- Mandatory for drugs with narrow therapeutic index.
- Avg %PE < 10 for C_{max} and AUC.

[II] Level B/Level C Methodology

- Purpose of Level B : Establishment of relationship between *in vivo* and *in vitro* parameters such as MRT Vs. MDT.
- Purpose of level C : Establishment of relationship between C_{max} Vs. $T_{50\%}$.

Applications of IVIVC in Drug Delivery

- Early stages of drug delivery technology development.
- Formulation assessment.
- Dissolution specifications.
- Future biowaivers.

Limitations of IVIVC

- IVIVC mainly depends upon Physicochemical, Biological, Pharmacokinetic properties of drug substance, formulation design and methodology.
- Saturable absorption, absorption window, rate dependent absorption, pre-systemic metabolism are to be considered.
- Dissolution Rate limiting.
- Inter and Intra subject variability is ignored.
- Use of Wagner Nelson method.

IVIVC is a tool applied in various areas and stage of drug development to find a place in the regulatory bodies around the world. It can serve as surrogate for *in vivo* bioavailability and can support bio-waiver. It can also allow setting of the dissolution specification and method.

In the clinical trial, the use of IVIVC is most important feature. IVIVC can assist certain scale-up and post approval changes. Generally, IVIVC principles have been applied to oral products, others exists a need to develop methodologies and standards to develop more meaningful dissolution and permeation methods.

 ❖❖❖

REFERENCES

- Pharmaceutics: The Science of Dosage Form Design by M. E. Aulton; (2nd edition).
- The Theory & Practice of Industrial Pharmacy by Leon Lachman, Herbet A. Lieberman, Joseph L. Kaing; (3rd edition).
- The Science & Practice of Pharmacy by Remington; (19th edition).
- Modern Pharmaceutics by G. S. Banker and C. T. Rhodes; (4th edition).
- Pharmaceutical Dosage Forms by Leon Lachman, H. A. Lieberman; Vol.1.
- Pharmaceutical Dosage Forms & Delivery Systems by H. C. Ansel, L. V. Allen, N. G. Popvich; (7th edition).
- Text book of Biopharmaceutics and Pharmacokinetics, Concept and Apllications, CVS Subrahmanyam, Vallabh Prakashan.
- Biopharmaceutics and Pharmacokinetics, ATreatise, Sunil Brahmandkar, Sunil Jaiswal, Vallabh Prakashan.
- Pharmaceutical Preformulation and Formulation: A Practical Guide from Candidate Drug Selection to Commercial Dosage Form (Drugs and the Pharmaceutical Sciences, Mark gibsons, Informa Health Care, Second Edition.
- Essentials of Pharmaceutical Preformulation, Simon Gaisford, Mark Saunders, Wiley-Blackwell.
- Pharmaceutical Preformulation, Jens T. Carstensen, Taylor and Francis.
- Handbook of Preformulation: Chemical, Biological, and Botanical Drugs (Google ebook), Sarfaraz K. Niazi, CRC Press.
- Tarun Garg, Ajay Biland, A recent review on enhancement of solubilization and bioavailability of poorly soluble drugs by physical and chemical modifications, pharmatutor.
- Madhumita Bhowmick Ray, Photodegradation of the Volatile organic compounds in the Gas Phase: A Review, *Dev. Chem. Eng. Mineral Process., 8(5/6), pp.405-439, 2000.*
- JudytaCielecka-Piontek, Magdalena Paczkowska, Kornelia Lewandowska, Boleslaw Barszcz, Przemyslaw Zalewski, and Piotr Garbacki, Solid state stability study of meropenem solution based on spectrophotometric analysis, Chem Cent J. 2013; 7: 98.
- G. Sahitya, B. Krishnamoorthy, M. Muthukumaran, Importance of Preformulation Studies in Designing Formulations for Sustained Release Dosage Forms, IJPT, Jan-2013, Vol. 4, Issue no.4, 2311-2331.
- David Stepensky, Michael Chorny, Ziad Dabour, Ilana Schumachelong: Term Stability Study of L-Adrenaline Injections: Kinetics of Sulfonation and Racemization Pathways of Drug Degradation, Journal of Pharmaceutical Sciences, April 2004; 93(4): 969.
- Ming-Kung Yeh, Li-Chien Chang, and Andy Hong-Jey Chiou, Improving Tenoxicam Solubility and Bioavailability by Cosolvent System, Journal of Pharmaceutical Sciences, June 2004; 93(6): 1471.
- Joseph W. Lubach Dawei Xu[2]Brigitte E. Segmuller[2], Eric J. Munson, Investigation of the Effects of Pharmaceutical Processing upon Solid-State NMR Relaxation Times and Implications to Solid-State formulation Stability, Journal of Pharmaceutical Sciences, April 2007; 96(4): 777.
- Lingling Tian, Haibing He, Xing Tang, Stability and Degradation Kinetics of Etoposide-Loaded Parenteral Lipid Emulsion, Journal of Pharmaceutical Sciences, July 2007; 96(7): 1719.
- Gohil Kirtansinh N, Patel Piyushbhai M[1], Patel Natubhai M[2], Application of Analytical Techniques in Preformulation Study: A Review, International Journal of Pharmaceutical & Biological Archives, 2011; 2(5):1319-132.

- Adam I. Grzesiak, Meidong Lang, Kibum Kim, Adam J. Matzger, Comparison of the Four Anhydrous Polymorphs of Carbamazepine and the Crystal Structure of Form I Journal of Pharmaceutical Sciences, October 2003; 92(10): 2027.
- Micellar Solubilization of Some Poorly Soluble Antidiabetic Drugs: A Technical Note, Neelam Seedher and Mamta Kanojia, Journal of Pharmaceutical Sciences, April 2003; 92(4): 839.
- Encyclopedia of Pharmaceutical Technology, (Vol-19).
- Pharmaceutical Dosage forms By Leon Lachman and Liebermann.
- Hand book of Pharmaceutical Excipients.
- Hand book of Pharmaceutical Granulation Technology, Vol-81.
- Remington's Pharmaceutical Science, 21st edition, 2005.
- Ansel Pharmaceutical Dosages Form and Drug Delivery System, VIII edition.
- Modern Pharmaceutics by Banker & Rhodes, 4th edition, 2002.
- Theory and Practice of Industrial Pharmacy by Lachman and Lieberman.
- The Science of Dosage form Design, M. E. Aulton.
- Physical Pharmacy, Alfred Martin, 4th edition.
- The Science & Practice of Pharmacy, Remington, 20th Edition.
- Instrumental Methods of Analysis, Willard, 7th edition
- Journal of AOAC, Jan/Feb 2007, volume-90, Number-1.
- Encyclopedia of Pharmaceutical Technology, Swarbrick & Boylan, Vol-15.
- Encyclopedia of Pharmaceutical Technology, Swarbrick & Boylan, Vol-06.
- Encyclopedia of Pharmaceutical Technology, Swarbrick & Boylan, Vol-02.
- Encyclopedia of Pharmaceutical Technology, Swarbrick & Boylan, Vol-07.
- Practical Pharmaceutical chemistry, A. H. Beeckett & J. B. Stenlake, 3rd Edition, Vol-02.
- Biotechnology and Pharmacy by J. M. Pizzuto, H. R. Manasse, pg 118 – 124.
- Pharmaceutical Biotechnology by S. W. Zito, pg : 83-90.
- Biotechnology & Pharmacy by J M. Johnson & M. E. Johnson, pg : 116 – 137.
- Pharmaceutical Biotechnology by D. J. A. Crommelin and R. D. Sindelar.
- Biopharmaceuticals: Biochemistry and Biotechnology by G Walsch, pg 115 - 124,131.
- Peptide and Protein Drug Delivery by V. H. L. Lee, pg. 769 – 783.
- Biotechnology & Its Application in Pharmacy by G. T. Kulkarni, pg. 124 -126.
- In vitro-In vivo correlation, By J. M. Cardot, Erick Byssac, Encyclopedia of Pharmaceutical Technology, Informa Healthcare, USA, 2062-2075.
- In vitro-In vivo correlation, By Jaber Emami, Journal of Pharmaceutical Science, (www.capscanada.org), 169-189, 2006.

Web sites:
- Www.scci-inc.com/analytical
- Www.springerlink.com
- Www.ptli.com/test/opedia/tests
- Www.wikipedia.com
- Www.pubmed.com
- Www.ijpsonline.com/article.asp
- Www.ICH.org